DAMAGED

DAMAGED

Junctions Murder Mystery Series

Book Five:

DAMAGED

L. E. Fleury

The reader should be aware that the characters in the *Junctions Murder Mystery Series* are fictional. While most of the historical locations and events are accurate, the writer has taken artistic license on certain issues to enhance the plot or to paint a more beautiful mental picture. Enjoy the books!

First paperback edition June 2024.

Editing by Joyce M. Gilmour.

Cover design by Heylea, LLC.

Cover photo: Shutterstock credit: Anna North

Cover photo enhancements by
Kelly Rainbow Butterfly.

Published by Heylea, LLC.
cabininthewoods2021@gmail.com

ISBN: 979-8-9890236-3-9 (paperback)

I dedicate this book

…to the Father: Thank you for giving us eternal life.

…to the Son: Thank you for your Blood Covering that gets us back Home.

…to the Holy Spirit: Thank you for enriching our earthly sojourn.

"The effectual, fervent prayer of a righteous man availeth much."

James 5:16 (KJV)

CHAPTER ONE

4-H'ers

"Oh, my gawd, my gawd," Essex Junction Police Chief Rob Allen muttered. "This is a new one for me." He glanced over at Mr. Spofford's pale face. "You gonna be okay, Hank?"

The diminutive World War II veteran shook his manly shoulders. "I couldn't believe my eyes. I mean, I was in the thick of it in the war, and saw a whole lot of stuff, but this one takes the cake, Robbie. I almost lost my breakfast."

"Your family seen this yet?"

"Nope, and I don't want them to. The sooner this mess is gone, the better." He surveyed the slope of the side lawn, which ended at Indian Brook. "The wife just took off for the grocery store, and the girls are still in bed. We had a late night at the drive-in movie. It was our black lab, Suzie, who found the remains." His hands went to his hips. "So, what do you think? Is this going to take long? I'd prefer my family not having to see this."

The chief bent closer. "Looks like there was a hard blow to the skull. That was probably what killed him." He stood up. "Gee-awd. Why would the killer have to go so far? They didn't stop at a simple beheading. No, only a vicious, enraged person would have chopped up a body like this."

"Had to use a big knife or something like that, don't you think, Rob?"

"I would venture to guess it was an ax." He made a brief

visual sweep over the area. "Did you see anything like that?"

"Nope. Guess you'll have to do that search yourselves." Hank was referring to the officials who were, even now, on their way. "Anyway, I need to get back to the house. Don't want those young girls coming down here. I'm sure they were familiar with this poor guy." The five-foot-six submarine veteran paused halfway up to the small, neat home. "I... I'm assuming you will be letting his people know, Chief."

"Ay-yuh. I'm sure not looking forward to that."

***

Actually, the summer of 1956 had started out well in the village of Essex Junction. The high school graduation had been quite an event. More of the graduates were headed off to college in the fall than ever before, something the little community was rightly proud of. Most of these would-be scholars were scheduled to attend local business colleges in the nearby city of Burlington, Vermont, but several students, including Rob Allen's younger brother, were headed for the University of Vermont, in that same hub of commercial and social activities — the Queen City of the Green Mountain State. Scottie Allen had signed up for ROTC, while his little girlfriend, Penny, slipped into place with a music scholarship. On the other hand, Diana Bixby's absent-by-divorce daddy provided the finances for her to attend McGill University in Canada. Several of the young ladies in that class jumped into the nursing program with both feet. All in all, the future looked promising.

And for a few weeks longer, life continued as usual. While the class of 1956 transitioned into summer employment, folks in the village of Essex Junction began to prepare the Champlain Valley fairgrounds for another special event. The annual fair was the subject of conversation at the Maple Leaf Sewing Circle's Saturday meeting, held this time at Laura

Wilson's farmhouse. The ladies' cars filled the barnyard of the old Wilson Dairy Farm, while the women, themselves, parked in clusters inside the quaint clapboard house.

"My niece is entering a circle skirt into the 4-H display this year," said Lily White, the dispatcher for Essex Junction's Police Department. "I saw it last night, and it's a real beauty — yellow calico, with white Hamburg lace all around the hem. If she doesn't get at least Honorable Mention, I'll be surprised."

"I heard there's going to be a Doggy Dress-up Parade this year," Laura said as she bent her tall, willowy form to pour tea for Gracie Allen.

"I heard about that," the mother of Chief Rob and Scottie Allen replied. "It's also sponsored by the 4-H Clubs of Chittenden County." She took a long sip of the cool iced tea. "I think it should be lots of fun."

"I wonder how they'll manage to pull that off," Winnie Thompson murmured, as she glanced out the window at her home across the curve in Old Colchester Road. "I have all I can do to make Blow just stay on our own property."

Anna, secretary for Holy Family's Roman Catholic Church in the village laughed, recalling the errant behavior of the ugliest dog in Chittenden County. "I think you have your hands full, Win."

"That's for sure," Lily chimed in. "We couldn't get him to stop chasing traffic at the five-way intersection. It finally came to a halt when you and Ceese took in the poor, shaggy fellow." She held up a cracker topped with tuna fish. "I think that dog just likes to wander."

"Is that the big, black one with the yellow eyes and the white eyebrows?" Gracie's new neighbor turned her blonde head to ask.

"That's the one," Gracie assured Lenore, who, with her foster son, had recently moved to the village from South Burlington. "And, speaking of dogs, how does Joe like his new puppy?"

"That boy is in seventh heaven, I think. Not only has he left the scene of some bad memories, but he's discovered a whole new life, even having part-time work here on this farm. It's like he has a new identity, and yes, his puppy, Mop, is a big part of it."

"Mop! That's quite a name, Lenore." Anna looked up from her handiwork.

"Yes, well, he looks like a dust mop," the pretty foster mother replied.

"You know," Connie Collins, a Christian counselor and one of Essex Junction High School's teachers, spoke up, "it's amazing what a comforting and calming thing a pet can be to a person who's been through so much trauma." She smiled at the newest member of the sewing circle. "You've been a real blessing to that boy, Lenore."

"Oh, let's not forget the lawyer, John Courtney, and Father Tom, from right here at Holy Family Church. They have been keeping watch over the boy for some years now." She shook out her knitting. "Thank God for both of them."

Gracie got back to the subject at hand. "So, my son, the chief of police, told me how they intend to have access to the racetrack in front of the grandstand, and the dogs would be paraded across, all dressed in costumes of course, and it would be scheduled between the sulky races and the three o'clock stage show on Thursday, which will be Seniors Day and School Day." She hastened to add, "Ay-yuh, those are usually two different reduced-entry priced days, but they're changing it this year, and don't ask me why."

"Knowing the committee, it has something to do with increasing profits," Anna noted. The women hummed in agreement. "Of course, the 4-H club members are earning badges, but that's not enough to make it interesting, so the public is invited to join." She stretched back against the chair. "I think it was a really smart decision."

"Lowered gate prices usually results in more people attending," Lily explained to no one in particular. The women hummed again. Lily continued, "So, what's the prize in this canine contest?"

"Fifty dollars!" Gracie Allen announced. "And it's being judged on originality and its connection to Chittenden County history. There is a five-dollar entry fee for non-4-H'ers, by the way." She smiled. "A good investment in a worthy cause, though, wouldn't you agree?" Nobody objected, so she went on. "I guess it's all about just getting the right doggy costume to win the approval of the judges."

"That probably should include the history of 4-H in this county." Laura laughed. "Whoa! There's the winning ticket, my friends."

For a few minutes, it got very quiet in Laura Wilson's living room.

***

When twelve-year-old Joe Turner and his foster mother, Lenore Tanner Curtis, moved to the village, he did not get rid of the property inherited from his uncle. It remained a rental, managed by the law firm of Courtney and Courtney of Montpelier, Vermont. Although the boy had no direct contact with the renters, Lenore — ever the good neighbor — had quietly gotten acquainted with them... an older couple named Bernie and Della McBain. She found their history quite delightful. The trim, graying fellow and this pleasingly plump lady had met in a bar in Winooski, Vermont. Bernie, in his late fifties, had been employed as a woolen factory machine repairman in that busy, little mill town, while Della, also fifty-ish, had been employed in the Chace factory, just around the corner. Their marriage had taken place in that same bar, surrounded by a few friends, all of whom, after the rituals, threw peanuts instead of rice. Lenore quickly saw they were hard workers, keeping the property in shape far beyond the usual obligations of run-of-the-mill renters. Moreover, they were occasionally a source of great entertainment, both having numerous life stories resulting in conversations that lasted long into the afternoon, ending only when the McBains' bottles of Canadian stout were gone, or one of them fell asleep in the chair. These occasions took place only when the boy was in school or otherwise occupied, of course, but the insightful encounters sealed a friendship that was both fulfilling and private. The bond continued even after Lenore left the Tanner farm, although there were no more long afternoons. Still, she remembered the McBains, when she heard about the doggy parade.

It so happened that Bernie and Della had a chihuahua named Carmen, after the singer in the Chiquita Banana TV commercial, Carmen Miranda. Because this all seemed to be right up their alley, Lenore let them know about the contest. She made the call that evening. When Della hung up the phone, she scuffed her size nine slippers into the kitchen where her man was making a peanut butter and cheese sandwich.

"Don't be making a mess out here." She stiffened her pudgy body to a stop. "Dammit, Bernie, I just got it all cleaned up."

"Oh, yeh did, did yeh?" he replied with a Scottish brogue. Although he left Scotland for Canada as a teenager, served in the Canadian Forces, and lived over twenty years under the Maple Leaf, the accent had never disappeared. "Way-yell, I guess we'll half-ta get oot the old dishrag and clean 'er up, before the neighbors come fer tea." The wiry fellow twitched his little gray mustache as he slathered the gooey peanut mess across a thick slice of homemade bread.

"Hmph," she grunted, secretly enjoying how he took a healthy mouthful. "Just look at that. I only made bread yesterday — five loaves, mister — and you've already eaten half of the first one."

The stiff, frosted eyebrows wiggled above the sticky grin. "Ummm." He pushed the slice of cheese to a more central position on the bread. Then, swallowing the first mouthful, he answered, "Aye, but I mean, yeh got a real good batch this time, Del." He licked his lips before chomping down for the next bite; his home was his castle, after all, and he pretty much did what he wanted.

This time, she pushed a wayward strand of gray hair from her face with the flip of a flirtatious finger before issuing another indignant grunt. It was time to play the petulant princess. "I'm not making any more bread until you learn to make it last. It makes my hands hurt, in case you haven't noticed, you Scotch jackass." When he did not reply, she picked up the bread knife and cutting board to start the clean-up, something that gave her time to prepare her next move, for she had already decided to enter Carmen in the doggy parade. It turned out to be the Lord of McBain castle, who opened the door to that discussion.

"Who was that on the phone?" he muttered through the peanut butter.

"Oh," she replied nonchalantly, "just Lenore."

"What'd she want?"

"Says we have a chance to win fifty dollars at the fair this year."

He put the half-eaten slice down on the counter. "What?"

"Oh, for Pete's sake, mister, don't get crap all over the shelf like that." She picked it up and shoved it into his hand. "She said we might get fifty dollars, for entering Carmen in a 4-H dog show."

He stood there with the dripping slice, thinking about it. As she shoved a plate under the thick dribble, he was processing the concept. "Fifty dollars? Fer what?"

"Mostly just for her being her cute self."

"Naw. It can't be that simple." He put the plate down, his appetite now a secondary priority. "There's got t'be rules of some sort, lass. Don't be a fool."

"Well!" she spat back, "did you just call me a fool, you old goat?" There was a shake of her shoulders that rippled down over her expansive bosom. "Whatever happened to 'My mother was a Fart-quar,' which is Scottish for *a beloved man*, huh?"

"Farquhar," he corrected her.

"Humph." She sniffed it out with another voluptuous shrug of indignation which brought a mischievous gleam into the Scotchman's eye. She pretended to ignore it.

"Ah-hh, them words of endearment," he whispered.

She almost called him something even more unladylike, but decided against it, because she really wanted to enter Carmen in the canine contest. Instead, she huffed and shook her gray curls, then sashayed enticingly up the stairs. He blinked, then pushed the half-loaf into the breadbox before wiping the peanut butter off his smile, pulling up his sagging pants, and following his favorite medieval wench up to the royal chamber.

*****

The following Monday, Joe Turner's bike wobbled to a stop just outside the back door of the Wilson Dairy Farm's house.

In its front basket, a shaggy puppy jiggled in anticipation until the Abenaki youngster lifted him out and set him on the ground. "Now, don't go running off, Mop," he whispered, "I want you right where I can see you, understand?" The dog moved quickly over to Laura's flowerbed near the back step, took a short sniff, then lifted his leg. "Aw, heck. There you go again, you little turd. I hope she didn't see you."

But Laura had, indeed, seen him. She turned from the kitchen window to inform her son's girlfriend, "Well, Joe is here for work, and brought his dog again. It just watered my little lilac bush."

"Oh, gross," Diana Bixby murmured.

"Oh well, if it's not Mop, it's Blow, from across the road." She checked the pot where fresh beets were getting a thirty-second scalding to loosen their skins. "There are definitely some drawbacks to living on a farm."

"I guess that's true about any other place you might live,

Miz Dubya." The girl was carefully removing empty pint-sized canning jars from their cleansing bath. She lifted the tongs to make a point. "I guess it just depends on who you're living with, no matter *where* it might be. A family is a family, you know?"

The tall Miz Dubya made a mental note that this young girl lived in an apartment with her divorced mother. Little wonder that her perspective favored the notion of a loving family circle, on a farm, or anywhere else. "Right. Family is good." She glanced out the window again, noting Joe's waved greeting to Jack, who was coming from the dairy barn. The two moved toward each other, then disappeared in the flash of morning light glinting off the metal roof of the large barn. She turned back to the beets. "Joe really seems to have formed quite a bond with Jack, have you noticed?"

"Yee-ah. I guess that's probably a good thing. Poor kid's been through a lot of stuff." The girl placed the last steaming pint on the clean flour sack dish towel, and wiped her hands on the blue gingham apron. "What's next?"

Over the following two hours, the two of them put up eight pints of pickled beets. The small, juicy-red orbs glowed through the glass containers, and the country kitchen was filled with a sweet, spicy aroma. The two of them sat down at the table to take long dregs of cool lemonade. "Wow," Diana exclaimed, "I can't believe I just helped make pickles."

"Well, you certainly did," Laura laughed softly.

A rustling from the outside of the back door told them that farm boots were being removed. In a second, the tall boyfriend, a male version of his good-looking mother, stepped inside. He drew the pleasant, spiced air in deeply, before his gaze fell on Diana. "Smells really good in here."

"Pickled beets, Jack. Look." The girlfriend's blue eyes sparkled as she pointed to the ruby-colored double row.

"You did this, Di?"

"Um, have to admit, your mom held my hand all the way."

"Oh, not exactly," Miz Dubya smiled and shook her straight, flaxen hair. "Actually," she said to her son, "she's a natural. If we still have her here over the summer, I hope she'll show up and help me get lots more of the canning done." Even as she spoke, she felt a check in her spirit. The look on those two youngsters' faces exposed a hidden ache. Diana would leave for McGill University in just a few weeks. For a brief moment, their young eyes met. Then Jack shifted his weight.

"So, Mom, could I have a sandwich before Joe and I get started with the carriage house chores?"

"Sure, son." She rose to the task. "What about Joe? Is he hungry?"

"Nah. I asked him. Said his foster mom already fed him." He was washing his hands in the sink, but kept his attention on the blue-eyed girl in the blue apron. As he dried his knuckles, he leaned up against the sink shelf, still lost in her presence.

She brushed a spot off for him. "Come and sit down. You've been working hard all morning."

He slid his lanky form onto the wooden chair right next to her, leaning in to the comfort of the moment. "So, making pickles, huh?" She smiled and nodded. It was only natural that he move in a little bit closer. "That's my girl," he whispered.

The back door slid open again. Jessie Wilson stopped in his tracks at the sight of the pair bent head-to-head at the table. When they looked up, he softened his interruption with a snort. "Must be pickled beets." He looked to Laura for confirmation and got it. "My favorite." He saw the sandwich. "That for me?"

"Coming right up." The two adults exchanged knowing looks; the kids were moving into a deeper relationship. "I'll get washed upstairs," the father said.

He was halfway up when he turned to call out to his son: "Hey, Jack! See ya a minute? I'm a little concerned about Joe."

"Sure, Dad."

It wasn't about Joe, of course, and Jack knew that before his dad began to speak quietly, the words being muffled by the sound of running water at the sink. The man placed a fatherly hand on his boy's shoulder. "Looking pretty serious between you and Di." Jack nodded. "Right," Jessie replied to the confirmation. The hand slid slightly down behind to pat the younger man's shoulder blade. "Just want to remind you, son, that you're a guy of integrity. Your mom and I are very proud of you. So, just one more little reminder, if you would be good enough to allow me to repeat myself." Knowing what was coming, Jack's face took on a bit of color. "Us Wilson men try very hard to be up-standing gentlemen. We treat the ladies with respect, right?" The blush grew deeper. "Things are looking pretty intense between you two, and that has me concerned." Another pat. "We would never want to hurt that young lady, would we?"

"No, sir."

There was one final tap on the shoulder. "Thanks for letting your old man speak up. I appreciate it. And if you need to talk…"

"Sure, Dad."

He reached to give his son a man-hug. "Love you, Jack. Never forget that."

"I won't, Dad."

Jack stood politely outside the bathroom door, waiting his turn. By the time the two of them came down the stairs for lunch, the blush had completely disappeared.

Over at the counter, Laura kept her eyes to herself, but she knew her husband, and she knew all too well what had just happened upstairs, and suddenly, she felt an ache in her own heart, because now — regardless of how sweet or melancholy — things would be changing in the Wilson household.

She had no idea just what those changes would be.

CHAPTER TWO

Choices

The two Spofford girls, Bella May and Ina May, were both named after their mother, the spitfire brunette who married Hank just before the end of WWII. May was, like her husband, proud to be an eighth-generation Vermonter, but she wore that badge in a much more public way. While Hank settled down to teach school in Winooski, May was an active member of numerous organizations in Chittenden County, not the least of which, was the county's 4-H activities. Bella, aged ten, and Ina, eight, were members of Essex Junction's club, and May, when she wasn't out there decorating her house with bona-fide Vermont-style braided rugs and maple wood furniture, was the gung-ho leader of that group, known as The Village 4-H'ers.

The woman was outgoing, though raised in humble surroundings amongst just plain folks, but what she lacked in education and social graces, she made up for with her quick mind, a gift of gab, and arresting good looks. And everybody loved her dog, Suzie, the black lab who May called her "show dog." Suzie was registered under an official three-name title which nobody could remember without checking the paperwork. In fact, the paperwork was only important because May bred the dog and sold her puppies for a hefty price. It was a pretty good income for the lady, and she guarded her dog, day and night. But the chance to show Suzie off in a dog contest was a real temptation. Added to that, the contest financially and publicly supported 4-H clubs, county-wide. Nobody was surprised when May was the first to sign up for the Doggy Dress-up Parade.

On the other hand, folks in the village were somewhat taken aback to learn that the second one to pay the five-dollar entry fee was none other than the head priest at Holy Family Roman Catholic Church, right there in town. Father Joseph Levi was himself, an anomaly. Born a Jew, converted to Roman Catholicism as a teenager, and entering the priesthood right out of college, he had paid the price: When his family disowned him, he ended up working for room and board through high school and college. The way had been long, but, as he liked to say, "It was never lonely. God was there every single moment."

At the more worldly level, however, Father Joe found great comfort and companionship with his beloved long-haired dachshund, Abe. The shaggy fellow was named after Abraham, first of the Hebrew patriarchs in the Bible. The priest had enjoyed the idea that "Father Abraham" was a connection between Christianity and Judaism. Indeed, the little dog played a deeper role in this older man's life, than most people thought.

Young Joe Turner expressed his concern about the priest's dog. "It looks a lot like Mop," he told Jack Wilson.

Jack shook the hay off the pitchfork and leaned on it for a second. "Aw, I wouldn't worry about that. That dog has a pointed nose and a long plume of a tail. They're two different types." He picked up the fork again. "I wouldn't let that stop me from entering Mop in the contest."

This was good enough for the boy. That afternoon, he stood in line behind the McBains, who entered their chihuahua, Carmen, and Winnie Thompson, who registered Blow. The sign-up was conducted in the county extension office in Lincoln Hall, close to the five-way junction of the village. Connie Collins volunteered to help these pet owners get registered correctly. At six o'clock, the table was to close down for the night, but a last-minute customer hurried into the room. It was the Essex Junction High School music teacher, Mrs. Desmond.

"Wait! You have one more person!" she called out, as she hurried to the table.

Connie recognized her fellow-teacher's piercing stare, remembering the nickname the students had given her years ago: "Deadeye Desmond." She smiled and handed the lady a pen. Five minutes later, the woman's white poodle, Melody, was signed up, and the music teacher was out the door.

Connie tallied it up. "Twelve dogs, so far. Not bad."

When she got home to Winooski, she informed her bus driver/Christian counselor husband that the sign-up was looking really good. "And," she added, "it will probably be a lot of fun judging this canine dress-up contest, don't you think?"

Don Collins broke out his signature impish grin. "Hope so, babe, and speaking of that little task, have they found a third judge yet?"

"Sure have. It's the manager of the Lincoln Inn, Ira Whitcomb."

"Great. Hope he likes dogs."

***

Chief Rob Allen checked the doorknob of the county extension office to make sure it had been locked up for the day. He had spoken briefly with Connie before she left, and now it was time for him to head home for the night. Back in the Essex Junction Police Department office, just down the hall, he picked up his hat and headed for the door. The chief waved a goodbye to Ed, who was on the phone at the intake desk. The patrolman held up a halting hand as he hung up.

"Sorry, Chief, but that was a call from Hank Spofford over at the creamery train crossing. Some kid has been hurt on a bike." His mouth pinched tightly for a second. "Are you headed that way, by any chance?"

"In a roundabout manner, I suppose. Why do they want a law officer?"

"Spofford says it was some kind of wolf, or something. Came out of the shadows, just this side of the Indian Brook bridge... you know, the one near his house?"

He drove the squad car to the scene at the north end of the village, where the remains of the old creamery separated the train tracks from Vermont Route 2A's Colchester Road. The Spofford house sat a few hundred feet on the other side of those same tracks, right at the end of Grove Street. It was a pleasant-looking little cottage, considering the fact that it was built on several yards of clean soil that hid the old village dump. In typical fashion, May had gussied up the place, and Hank had a double garage put up at the top of the slope that led down to the brook.

He was standing in front of that structure when Chief Robbie drew up.

"He's down there, Chief." The head nodded toward the underside of the bridge. "Got spooked by a critter and slid down the slope. Got wedged under the bike." As the two men descended, he continued. "Not really hurt, I guess. Just mad as hell that he's stuck. I tried to move the damned bike, but it's in pretty tight."

"Okay, so maybe the two of us can get it loose." Rob spotted the boy. "Hey, son! You hurt?"

"Don't think so, mister. Just stuck. And wet."

The two men managed to release the trapped youngster in a few minutes, and the boy slogged out of the water. As they were climbing back to the road, Joe explained that he'd been surprised by a dog and swerved to miss it, ending all the way down under the cement curve of the bridge's underside. "It barked at me, and I just went flying." He swept a tan hand across that full head of hair. "Stupid dog."

"Okay, well, your bike looks no worse for the wear, so we

just need to make sure *you* have no injuries." The chief seemed to remember something. "So, what's your name, again?"

"Joe Turner."

The lawman addressed Hank. "We probably need to notify some parents, here."

"May just did that. Joe, here, is a foster kid. No foster father, just a really great foster mom, right, Joe? She should be here any minute."

Immediately, Robbie remembered that these two were his new neighbors. After all, he was the head of the police department, and it was his business to know these things. On the other hand, he wasn't a Welcome Wagon rep, either, so he had not met the woman, or the lad. He looked toward the train crossing. "Alright, we'll let her decide on any medical issues."

"Ay-yuh." The small man shoved his hands into his pockets. "Meanwhile, we need to address the wolf issue."

Robbie pushed his police hat to the back of his head. "What wolf issue is that?"

Mr. Spofford's intense stare moved across the tracks, past the creamery and Colchester Road, zeroing in on the newest cemetery for Essex Junction. "It's been spotted twice inside that fence, prowling around the graves, probably looking for rabbits." The eyes came back to Chief Allen. "We've seen it, and so have two other families in the area."

Rob cleared his throat. "Um, to the best of my knowledge, we no longer have wolves in the State of Vermont." The smaller man looked doubtful. "But we do have coyotes."

"This thing is bigger than a measly coyote, Rob."

"Actually, the eastern coyote is quite large, Hank. Its ancestors got ousted from their western hunting grounds, much like the Indians, by pioneer settlements. Those small western coyotes moved up into southern Canada, mostly into Quebec and Ontario. I got that from an educated uncle who loved to hunt, so trust me, he knew what he was talking about."

The Abenaki lad zoned in on the similarity between coyote and Indian displacements. "So how did they end up in Vermont?" he asked.

"Not exactly sure why, but the first one was spotted in this state around 1947 — not so long ago. And it was big. A lot bigger than the western breed. My uncle said the authorities figured it out: Those little coyotes bred with the wolves, and their offspring were larger than coyotes, and smarter than wolves." He shrugged. "Beats me why they're still called coyotes, though. After all, they're a mixed breed, wouldn't you say?"

"I guess so," the tan-faced boy replied, "but it doesn't matter, because what sent me flying into the brook wasn't a coyote. It was a dog. I know this, because it barked at me."

The squeal of brakes interrupted Robbie's reply. He turned to see a tangle of large, blonde curls around a pair of oversized black sunglasses leaning from the driver's window. She paused, then opened the door and slipped her sandaled feet to the ground. "Joe! For the love of Mike. Joe, what happened?" She approached the three of them, long legs moving swiftly beneath the ruffled shorts of her yellow-flowered sun suit. "My gosh, boy!" As her arms pulled his head to the blossomed bib in a frantic embrace, a whispery tenderness filled her voice. "Good grief!" She drew back and pushed the black hair straight back from his face. "Are you hurt? Huh? Are you okay?"

Joe tried to stand up straighter. "I'm good. Just some scratches."

She turned her attention toward the two men. "Okay." There was a moment to collect her thoughts. "Um, okay. Just what happened here? Why do we have the police here?" She removed the glasses to fix a green-eyed inquiry directly toward the officer, who, for some reason, began blinking rapidly. He was noticing the early evening sun glinting on the light moisture across her hairline.

"Do we have a problem, sir?" her melodious voice inquired.

"Uh, no. No, ma'am." The chief took a breath, but seemed to lose his tongue for a moment, so Hank started to fill her in.

"Lenore, this is our Chief of Police Rob Allen. I don't think you two have met. Am I correct?" She acknowledged this by extending her hand for a handshake.

"Thank you so much, Chief. I, uh, do have a couple of questions." As she pressed for details, her complexion went from peach to pink, whereupon, she put back on the dark glasses. At the end of the short conversation, it was obvious that no medical attention was needed.

May joined them just about then, having been watching from the window.

"Looks like everything is under control. No damages, right?" She was watching the lawman folding and unfolding his arms. "Thanks for coming right over, Chief. The kid could have been really hurt." She turned to the boy. "But you know what they say, Joe: Once burnt, twice shy." The woman not only had the gift of gab, but was renowned for her wide repertoire of quaint New England sayings. "From now on, you'll be watching for animals along the road, right?"

Robbie Allen nodded in agreement. "That's probably good advice for everybody, May." He nodded again, this time to the foster mom with the husky voice. "So," he said, as he tipped his hat, "it has been a long day. I need to get home."

He had taken only a couple of steps when Hank shouted: "We should get together and talk about this coyote, or whatever, is up to. We don't want this to happen again."

Rob suddenly remembered something important, turned, and called out to Lenore, who stopped the car. He went quickly to Joe's passenger seat window. "Just one thing you should know, Joe. You said you were spooked by a dog, right?"

"Yes, sir."

"Because it barked at you?"

"Yes, sir."

"Well, just so you know: Coyotes bark." The boy's mouth dropped open. "That's right. They yip and howl, but they also bark, much like a dog." He tapped the roof just above the open window. "Just thought you should know that." He bent down to once more tip his hat to Lenore. "Have a good evening, folks."

Chief Allen drove slowly home. When he turned off the engine, he sat still for a minute. "Wow," he whispered, "that was a real, honest-to-goodness blonde. No dark roots on that pretty head, for sure." He blinked slowly. "I mean, even her *eyebrows* are blonde."

***

Laura and Diana were in the kitchen again, but this time they were cooking up a fun costume for Mop. They stepped back and signaled Joe Turner to lead the fluffy mutt across in front of the sink shelf. The little dog responded to the gentle tug of the leash, brushing along the floor. On his back, a short mop handle wobbled ever-so-slightly. The ladies reveled in their success. "It's perfect!" Laura laughed.

"Yee-ah, we finally got it." Diana smiled. "What do you think, Joe?"

"Yup, perfect." He stopped his little pet and peered more closely. "You can hardly see the yarn strap." Reaching over to tap the construction-paper-on-wire handle, he grinned. "And the handle looks so real."

"And we got the right color yarn, for strapping," Jack's mom murmured. "Just be careful when you tie and untie, that you don't catch Mop's hair in the thing." It had been a long afternoon, but the look on that youngster's face made it all worth it. "So, Joe, we expect that you'll probably win some kind of award, what with a living, walking mop." She was surprised when he dropped the leash and came to give her a big hug. "Oh," she whispered, "that's okay, Joe. We enjoyed our time together."

Diana hid her face by glancing out the window toward the Thompson farm. "I wonder what Winnie is doing for Blow's get-up."

"Last I heard, all she can get him to put up with, is a red bandana," Laura answered. "Although she *is* kind of working on a straw hat for him."

Diana gave the boy a thumbs-up. "You've probably got this one, mister!" She looked at her watch. "Okay, perfect timing, Miz Dubya. I have a job interview for waitressing at the fair — you know, that restaurant that's under the grandstand." As soon as she had left, Miz Dubya slipped a couple of cookies into a napkin, then watched the happy guy lift his mop into the bike's basket, and peddle off toward the village.

Meanwhile, May Spofford was bent over her sewing machine, talking to her girls. "It's the perfect costume, for sure. What's better than a 4-H dog uniform to win a 4-H fundraiser?" She smiled as she cut the thread that attached a four-leaf clover badge to the back of a pale green jacket.

"It's a little crooked," Bella noted.

May shook it out. "Ay-yuh," she agreed, "but it'll never be seen on a galloping horse. So while you're leading her, keep her moving, in circles, if you need to. That should be fine."

***

The day of the contest finally arrived. It was hot, of course, and the racetrack was dusty, regardless of frequent wet-downs. That didn't deter the enthusiasm of fairgoers, nor the contest dignitaries who were to be seated beneath the elevated bleachers of the grandstand. Not only did their judges' table command a view of the racetrack's "runway" where the canine candidates would make their appearances, it provided a front row view of the wide stage set up just inside the racing oval, where the New York City Rockettes would strut their stuff at three o'clock. Right now, the dust was slowly settling after the sulkies had left the track, each cart tilting precariously on two large wheels as a single horse lunged forward, then left and right, to disappear somewhere behind the midway tents. Immediately, the pet owners lined up to the left of the crowd, waiting for the three judges to take seats behind their long folding table. Once the Collinses and Mr. Whitcomb were seated, the master of ceremonies walked out to the mike on the big stage, made some informative comments about the value of 4-H clubs all over the county, then turned to remind the judges and the dog handlers of the rules. Finally, he shook out a piece of paper, cleared his throat, and started calling each contestant, one at a time, to pass before the judges. The large crowd leaned forward in anticipation.

"First, we have a lovely French poodle, Melody, led by her owner, Mrs. A. Desmond." He looked down at the white pompoms undulating between a black French beret and four black netted stockings. "Oh, my," the man said, "could it be that this young lady dances in a Parisian cabaret?" Mrs. Desmond came to a stop and sang out in a perfect alto, "She certainly can... can-can!" The audience chuckled at the quoted song lyrics, as they clapped softly. The pom-poms waggled happily across to the end of the runway and out of sight.

"Our second contestant is a mixed-breed named Mop," the emcee announced. When he looked up from his paper's list, he added, "and we can certainly see why. If that doesn't look like a dust mop, I don't know what does!" A hum went through the crowd when the little fluffy thing plowed through the dust, led by a young boy. As the mop followed the leash in a couple of tight circles, the man quickly added, "And leading this cute little fellow, is Mister Joe Turner." The kid grinned nervously, then led Mop across the runway. The grandstand clapped enthusiastic approval.

There followed two more contestants — a collie in a clown outfit, and an Irish setter in something plaid, both of whom received polite applause. Then it was Bernie McBain's turn to bring out Carmen, the chihuahua. At center stage, Mr. McBain stopped and clapped his hand three times, then went into a shoulder wiggle as he sang loudly, "La Cucaracha! La Cucaracha!" sending billows through his bright, red silk shirt. Carmen, in her brilliantly colored ruffled belly band and little fake fruit hat, immediately rose to her hind legs and turned in tight circles for all of five seconds. Bernie turned to the audience and bowed deeply from the waist. The dog knew her cue, turned her tail toward the crowd and stretched her front paws out for her own version of thank-you-very-much. The laughter and applause accompanied the two all the way to the powdery exit.

More contestants paraded past the grandstand, all cute, but of little distinction, before it was time for Father Joe to lead Abe across the dry runway. The wily priest had stacked the deck, however, by registering his dog's name as something more than just "Abe." So when the announcer introduced the dog, the crowd took notice. "Our next entry is a longhaired dachshund by the name of Abraham Lincoln." The crowd roared as they checked out the outfit. The hound was sporting a long black jacket with the name, "ABE" on a placard along its side, while under the black top hat, his dyed whiskers had been pulled into a black beard. "Uh..." the emcee quickly added, "he is being led by Father Joseph Levi." At that point the two had reached the center mark, where the priest signaled his pet into a sudden, stiff pose. Quickly, the man stooped down to turn the jacket's sign over, revealing the national flag of the United States of America. Upon returning to a standing position, he clicked his heels and saluted the stars and stripes. Right on cue, Abe lifted his head for a long, reverberating howl, as Father Joe turned to salute the crowd, calling out over Abe's tremulous bay, "God bless America!" Instantly, Abraham Lincoln skittered a smoky circle around his owner, then broke out in a barking frenzy as the two of them charged forward — the happy cleric waving to the crowd, all the way to the exit. It was over the top, but the spectators loved it, some even standing as the applause reached a crescendo.

The announcer waited for a few moments before moving on. Again, there came a stream of half a dozen more dog outfits, none of which caused much of a response from the bleachers. Finally, the man at the mike prepared for the final showings. "Okay, we have the last two contenders for the fifty-dollar prize: First, won't you welcome the beautiful black lab, Suzie, led by Bella Spofford?" The young girl stepped forward, her 4-H'er costumed pet in tow, but then something went terribly wrong. A sharp, deep woofing came from just behind the two. Bella turned to see what was going on just as the lumbering form of a big, black dog in a red bandana suddenly leaped into view, charging toward the sleek female lab. Suzie turned to greet him, tail wagging. It was immediately apparent to the crowd, what with the nose-to-nose and nose-to-other parts, the two of them were already furry friends. The audience murmured in amusement as some woman down front screamed, "Don't let him near her, Bella! Kick that mutt in the slats!" But Bella was too small to control her dog, and before anybody could stop them, the two large friends went bounding toward the center stage, cavorting happily before disappearing somewhere behind it. The woman continued to scream, and Bella began to cry, while stage hands went running to retrieve the two pets. All eyes watched as the four men came to a sudden halt, staring at something around behind the big platform. The fellows waggled their heads and stood still, obviously unable to do anything. They finally shrugged at the emcee, big grins on their faces, and that was what tipped off the crowd. Adults tried to keep the snickering down, wives punching their husband's ribs while hiding lady-smirks behind the other hand. Unfortunately, things got even worse when May Spofford went shrieking onto the raceway in pursuit of her show dog, only to be stopped by two of the stage hands, which made her even more frantic. When one of the men spoke into her ear, it was too much, and she fell to her knees, pounding the ground in a purple fury. The two men picked her up and headed for the first-aid station under the grandstand.

Immediately, the master of ceremonies rose to the challenge, making small talk about the fundraising and thanking everyone for attending. Obviously, the last two dogs had been eliminated for being out of control. "That's one of the rules," he reminded everyone. "So, now it's time for the judges to make a decision, and while they deliberate, we have a special treat for you. We have a local trio from Essex Junction High School, the Velvetones, to serenade you."

Three young women took the platform to sing Blue Moon. While they were easy to look at, and pleasant to hear, the crowd's attention was on the activity in and out of the area behind the stage. At the end of the trio's performance, the judges announced that Abraham Lincoln had won the contest. No one seemed to be upset that one of the judges, Mr. Whitcomb, was proprietor of the Lincoln Inn. Folks just assumed all three were true patriots and following the lead of the audience. People clapped in approval, as Father Joseph received the check, but the real cheer went up when a stage hand led Suzie from behind the scene. Blow, however, was nowhere to be found.

***

Jack Wilson was amongst the crowd that afternoon, silently rooting for his friend, Joe, to win the contest. When it didn't happen, he was swift to meet with the boy and his foster mom in back of the grandstand, on the carnival edge of the fair.

"Hey, guy!" he shouted, as he approached the boy. "You were so good out there! Too bad the judges were swayed by that American flag thing." He slapped the youngster on the back and grinned at Lenore. "But there's always next year, right?"

"Thanks, Jack. We appreciate your support, for sure." She was stretching a protective arm around the crestfallen lad.

"And that's true. There is always next year, right, Joe?" The thick head of hair bowed in silence.

"So, are you two in a hurry to get home? Or could I interest you in a few carnival rides?" His offer was quickly refused, apparently because Joe wanted to get Mop out of the hubbub. "He's a little nervous," the boy said. And that was it. The two left, and Jack was on his own. He glanced at his watch.

"Might as well go back into the stand and take in the Rockettes, and whatever else is on the three o'clock program, 'cause Mom's volunteering at the Chittenden County Homemakers booth until nine o'clock, and Diana won't be off work at the restaurant until five." The time passed more quickly than he thought, and he was at the eatery, watching Diana hang up her apron near the side door.

She smiled. "How long do we have for this 'fair date'?"

"Mom gets off around nine."

"Three hours. Good." She squeezed his hand. "Let's find a place to sit for a few minutes. My feet are tired."

He bought a handful of tickets for the Ferris wheel, and they rode it for a half-hour, snuggling and talking as they took in the bird's-eye view of Essex Junction homes surrounding the Champlain Valley fairgrounds. He even managed to steal a kiss or two, up there on top of the world, when the wheel stopped to exchange passengers down below. After the Ferris wheel rides, they grabbed fair burgers, laden with greasy onions, munching as they passed the freak show and hoochie coochie tents. The barker for this girlie show was hunched over and murmuring thinly veiled enticements. "Cover your ears," he told her, as they passed that one. It was only seven-fifteen when they bumped into Diana's mom.

"You're early," the girl said.

"I know, but I have to get home. Another migraine. Sorry." The woman looked exhausted. "I was hoping you could drive the rest of the way. I can hardly see straight."

Jack spent the rest of the time going through exhibits and drinking sodas. When he and Laura got into his old truck, he was glad to be headed back to the farm. As they left the lights of the fairgrounds behind, he realized it was already dusk. Reaching over to pull the headlight knob on, he mumbled, "Oh-oh."

"What?" She glanced at her boy.

"Only got one headlight." He shook his head. "It's one thing after another with this tin can of a truck. The clutch is about to go out, I think."

"Well, just be careful, son." She pulled her nylon jacket closer against the cool of the evening, slipping only the top button into place.

They passed through the five-way circle at the center of the village and headed north toward the creamery crossing, where Grove Street ended and became Old Colchester Road. At the sharp curve, just a mile or so up that road, was a soft bed and a good night's sleep.

"Train's coming," she noted softly.

"Yup," he said as he checked out the northbound engine just leaving the station. "Got lots of time." He pulled around the curve to make the crossing before the locomotive got too close.

Since there was only one headlight, he didn't see the shadowy canine figure until it was right in front of him. His feet smashed both the brake pedal and the clutch to the floorboard. The old truck stalled in the middle of the train tracks. Quickly, he turned the key in the ignition and tried to shift into first gear. The stick shift wobbled and froze. He lifted his foot off the clutch, then stomped it to the floor as he tried to shift into first gear. The transmission screeched in distress. Jack lifted and stomped the clutch again, but the gear shift only squealed louder. "Damn!" he muttered.

"The train is coming." Her voice was trembling.

He peered past the woman at the oncoming danger. "Get out, Mom." He stomped the clutch once more. "Get out, Mom!"

The locomotive's wheels squealed under the brakes as the whistle screamed a dire warning. She looked at her boy. "You, too, Jack. Right now." Her hand was on the door handle. "Get out! Get out, Jack!!" She pushed the door open to slip to safety, but as she slid past the handle, it hooked tightly into the bottom buttonhole of her jacket. The boy saw what was happening. "Take off the coat!" he yelled.

She forgot she had buttoned it at the top, struggling to get loose, as the blinding headlight loomed closer. It was only a few feet away when she jumped back in, desperate to put something between her and the massive engine that was not stopping. He tried to pull her away from the door, but the coat held her in place, and it was suddenly, terrifyingly, too late.

It took two hours for the rescue team to get the two of them loose from the wreckage. They were taken by ambulance to Fanny Allen Hospital, just down the road from the fairgrounds. Jack was treated for shock and a broken right arm and released to go home.

Laura Wilson, however, was dead on arrival.

CHAPTER THREE

Revenge

"It was that damned coyote-wolf," Hank Spofford muttered to his wife. "Somebody better do something about that."

"More likely that ugly bastard from up the road," she shot back. "Somebody ought to do something about *that*." She poked her head around the bottom of the stairwell that led up to the bedrooms, making sure the girls were not listening. "I tell you what, that dog has spent more time trying to corner my Susie than I care to talk about."

"You're supposed to keep her inside when she's in heat. You know better, May."

"You make it sound so simple!" She put both hands on her hips. "Did you know that a bitch can be in heat for days, before you see the evidence? I'd have to be psychic, or something."

It was a sigh of resignation. "Okay, point taken." He turned to gaze out at the crossing where Laura had died. "Too bad the kid didn't take better care of his truck. Just a damned shame, you know?"

"Ay-yuh, it is, Hank."

"You bringing Jessie a pie or something?"

"Hamburger casserole. Just took it out of the oven."

It had only been a few days since the tragedy, days when Winnie and Lily had stepped up to start feeding the boy and his dad. They had made a list, of course, and May was scheduled to make the visit this time. She noticed with relief that Diana's car was there. That seemed to pave the way, somehow, as May approached the back door. Stepping gingerly up the worn steps, she noticed the large opening to what appeared to be a woodshed, just off the back of the house. "They must have a wood stove," she told herself, as she knocked softly.

It was Diana who answered. "Oh, Mrs. Spofford, how nice of you. Come on in."

The woman handed the dish to the girl before following her inside. "The guys are upstairs, resting," Diana spoke quietly. "It's been just horrible for them…" Her eyes began to glisten. "…as you can imagine."

"I can't. I really can't imagine the pain of such a loss, Diana." She glanced around, not sure what to do. "Is there anything else they need? I mean, anything else Hank and I can do?"

The young lady nodded slowly, wiping her eyes. "I don't think so. Jack's grandparents are coming tonight. Jessie's folks. That should be a help, I guess. Or maybe not. I don't know."

May's heart went out to the poor girl. "Here," she said, as she opened her arms, "I think you could use a hug, yourself."

As the two embraced, May whispered, "We only live once, but if we live right, once is enough." She drew back. "From what I hear, Laura did it right. You can all have that happy thought, anyway."

Moments later, she was driving slowly past the Thompson farm, the home of Blow, the roving menace. Suddenly, she wanted to dismiss her husband's remark. "Ay-yuh. Too bad about the truck not being properly cared for," she muttered, "but what about that dog wandering around half the night, and getting a good person crushed to death by a train?"

***

A week later, the Swift Street Pentecostal Church, just off Shelburne Road's Vermont State Route 7, was packed for the memorial service. Located near the southern limits of Burlington, this had been Laura's church for a few years, where she had gotten saved and where she had prayed for her husband and son so many times. A late August sun beat down upon the crowd as it filed into the sweltering sanctuary. Inside, the air was heavy with floral scents from a dozen or so bouquets which surrounded the closed, white casket. At precisely one o'clock, a lady in a pink dress sat down at the piano to start the program. Because the pastor and his family were on vacation, the head deacon, Don Collins, conducted the service. Mostly, he quoted Bible verses, lifting his head occasionally to give a touching word of his own, until it was time for the closing prayer, and then it was over.

The pallbearers gently moved the casket to the hearse, and a long line of cars followed it to the white-fenced cemetery plot at the far end of one of the Wilson Dairy Farm's cornfields. After a short ceremony, the gathering moved to the farm, itself. Food was served in the carriage barn, on long tables draped with patchwork quilts. Folks spilled out into the barnyard, talking and fellowshipping until late afternoon. Somewhere between the final farewells and clean-up, Don found himself alone in the living room with Jessie and Jack. He noted the strain on the father's face, but the man had held it together pretty well. Jack's countenance, on the other hand, was ashen, the eyes glazed over, the mouth a tight, thin line. Indeed, his whole body seemed tightly wired around the heavy plaster cast on his right arm. Don took a long, slow sip of his lemonade before he spoke. "So, gentlemen... a very nice tribute to her, wouldn't you say?"

"Ay-yuh. Can't thank you enough, Don." Jessie blinked a thank-you toward him, then turned to signal his son to follow through on that. The boy, however, just lowered his head. "Son? We have appreciated all that was done for your mother today, have we not?"

Don saw the explosion coming, and braced himself. Sure enough, the young man's face went livid, the wide eyes rimmed in red. "It should never have happened in the first place!!" He jumped to his feet. "That should not have happened to her... not to *her!*" He seemed to focus the fury toward the coffee table in front of him.

Jessie lifted a calming hand. "We know, son. It's not right. It's not fair. But it *did* happen, and there's nothing we can do about it. Nothing." He own lips trembled. "I'm so sorry... so sorry."

"Yeah? Well, that's not good enough, Dad. Not..." His foot drew back, then smashed forward, sending the table across the room. "...frickin' good enough!" There was a quick breath. "She's dead! She's really... really gone!" He bent his face close to his father's. "Can't you get that into your head, old man? She's gone, and she's never coming back!" He whirled around. "Never!!!" he yelled as he bolted from the room.

The father rose to follow his son.

"Wait, Jessie," Don called out gently to the man, "don't try to fix it. Not right now. You have your own grief to deal with, mister. Let the boy work it through." He motioned for the man to take his seat again. "Connie and I and a whole bunch of other people will be praying that God will keep him safe as he goes through this thing. And, I might add, we'll be praying for you, as well."

"Mmm," Jessie hummed, "I appreciate your well-meaning efforts, but I have to tell you, man, I don't believe in all that stuff."

"No?" The deacon tilted his head to the right. "Well, Laura sure did."

"Ay-yuh, and look where it got her. Where was the protection, or whatever, on that railroad track, huh?"

"Oh, I don't pretend to have all the answers, Jessie. All I know for sure, is when your wife died, she went immediately into the presence of her Savior, Jesus Christ."

"If there really *is* a Jesus Christ."

Don smiled just a little. "I promise you, Jesus Christ is alive and well, and He really did shed His blood to save sinners like you and me."

There was a little pause. "Must be nice." He looked at Don. "Believing all that."

"It's more than just nice, Jessie. It's the difference of going to Heaven or going to Hell." The impish smile appeared. "Sometime I'd like to tell you about it. Would you be agreeable to that?"

Another pause. "Uh, maybe. Some other time."

Don left it right there, knowing that Mr. Jessie Wilson was about to go through some pretty rough soul-searching over the next few weeks… maybe even months. No, he would wait for the phone call, because then, and only then, would the man be ready to listen.

***

LeRoy Dupree was the hired hand at the Wilson Dairy Farm who had stepped up immediately to cover for the grieving father and son. He had been there for a few years, at first as a room-and-boarder, then, when he remarried Doreen, living across the train tracks on the other side of Vermont Route 2A's Colchester Road. It was a short trek to work each day, and the man knew how to run a farm. After the loss of Laura, he had his hands full, putting in long hours and working mostly alone, but even so, he was also the one who was keeping a close watch on Jack. The young man was not doing well. There were some efforts to do chores, even with a broken arm, but it was difficult and awkward, and he dissolved into fits of frustration, which led to outbursts of anger.

"That fella's a walking time bomb," he told Doreen over supper, just three weeks after Laura's death. Jessie's folks had returned home to Hartford, Connecticut the day before; that left Diana to make frequent visits, keeping things up in the household. Roy shrugged. "I don't know what'll happen when that girl goes off to college." A worry moved across his face. "And I don't like what is happening with his young buddy, Joe."

"What do you mean?" Dory asked, as she picked up their fifth child, a little red-headed boy.

"The kid just seems to copy everything Jack is doing. If Jack gets mad, Joe gets mad. That seems to be going on a lot." He pushed his chair back. "I'm thinking maybe Joe should stay home for a while. At least 'til Jack gets it together."

"You're probably right," she said, as she took the one-year-old to his crib in the second bedroom Roy had built last spring. "Otherwise," she called out, "there could be trouble for both of them."

The trouble came only two days later.

Jessie had gone into the village to pick up supplies at the feed store. That left LeRoy in the dairy barn, alone. In the house, Joe Turner was watching his hero polish the barrel of a brand new Colt Python .357 magnum revolver. Jack smiled as he wiped a soft rag along the silvery metal. "My-my, ain't she purty," he purred.

"Is that your dad's, Jack?"

"Nope. Mine."

"Wow! How come you got a gun?"

"My grandfather works for the Colt factory in Hartford." He wiped the barrel again.

"Wow!" the almost-thirteen-year-old said, again. "And he gave it to you? How come?" He took a guess. "For your birthday, or something?"

Jack laughed. "Or something."

"You got any bullets?"

"'Course I got bullets. What good's a gun without bullets, pipsqueak?" He reached for a box, took the lid off, and held it out for the boy to inspect.

"Holy moley," Joe mimicked Superman, "real bullets." He

looked into Jack's face. "Can we go outside and shoot it?"

"Maybe after Roy goes home. He'd have a cow if he knew I had this." At that, he began to load the gun, making a big show of it, even though he was handicapped by the awkward cast on that right arm. When it was loaded, he laid the weapon upon the coffee table and sat back. "And that's how it's done."

"Can I try loading it? I watched you real close, Jack."

"Naw, you don't know how to handle a firear — "

The barking had been going on for a few seconds, but now it was getting louder. Jack sat up straight. "That damned dog."

"Sounds like Blow," the younger one said. "I think it's Blow, right?" The boy headed for the window. "Yup. He's barking at my dog, Mop. Guess he wants to play."

The look in Jack's eyes brought Joe's observations to a dead stop. His little body went stiff as Jack grabbed the gun and headed for the back door. "Uh, what's up, Jack?" The only answer he got was a resounding slam. In an instant he followed the angry gunman, tripping quickly across the barnyard to keep up. Suddenly, Jack stopped, pointing the gun toward the ugly mutt bounding into the driveway. "Get outta here, you frickin' killer!" Out of nowhere the clueless Mop bounced forward to meet his lumbering canine friend.

"Mop! Mop! Come here, boy!" the little Abenaki called to his dog. But Mop was all too intent upon a romp with his big, hairy buddy. "Mop! Get back here!"

Jack interrupted, screaming uncontrollably. "You gawdim, frickin' killer! Get outta here!" By then, the two dogs were nose-to-nose, oblivious to the shrieking, and the furious shooter let loose with one sharp crack after another. The bullets ricocheted off rocks and dirt until the gun chamber was empty, missing their mark only because the fellow could not get a straight aim with the left hand. But the dogs scattered — Mop toward the house, and Blow into the path of Diana's approaching car. It was a narrow miss.

"Jack! For goodness sake," she cried out, "what are you

doing?"

"Shooting that damned dog, that's what." As she drove into the driveway and exited the vehicle, he continued. "I'm shooting the dog that killed my mother, that's what I'm doing. If you don't like it, take a hike. I'm gonna kill that frickin' dog."

"Oh, Jack, you don't mean that. He's just a dog, a dumb animal..."

"...that killed my mother. Can't you understand that?" She opened her mouth to answer, but he cut her off. "I want that dog dead, you hear me? *Dead.*" He lifted the empty weapon, aiming at the retreating Blow, and repeatedly pulled the trigger — but it just made useless noises. The unbearable frustration drove him to raise the gun for a furious slam to the ground, but LeRoy grabbed his wrist before he could get leverage. In one swift move, the man pinned Jack's whole left arm behind.

"You either quit this tantrum right now, or you're gonna end up with another broken arm." Jack swore at him and stomped on the man's foot. LeRoy gritted his teeth and shoved.

"I give!" Jack howled through the pain. "I give up!"

"If you don't want to *really* get hurt, drop the gun — and if you stomp my foot again, I will finish the job. Got that?"

He moaned the answer. "Yeah-yeah-yeah, I got that." The gun dropped to the dirt.

Roy nodded for Diana to pick it up. "I need to hold onto that until Jessie gets home," he said to her. "You and Joe are my witnesses." Then he addressed his prisoner. "Okay, I'm gonna let you loose, but if you act out, I'm gonna have to deck ya. Got that?"

Jack whimpered his agreement, so the hired hand shoved the boss's son forward. Jack yelped in pain, but caught himself before actually falling. He turned to Diana, rubbing his arm.

"What the hell are *you* looking at, girl?" The shock on her face did not stop him. "What are you even *doing* here? You don't belong here anymore. You need to get on the bus and get up there to your fancy Canadian university, you know that? I'm done with you. I never want to see you again. *Get out of here.*"

"No, Jack. You don't mean that," she said quietly. But the look in his eyes told her differently. "You're just upset. It will be better, later on, you'll see."

"It's never gonna get better, girl. It's not gonna be the same, ever again. You just remind me of stuff that doesn't exist anymore. I don't want you around, doing that. I just want you *gone.*"

"Actually," she spoke through the tears, "I was going to tell you I have to leave by next weekend." There didn't seem to be anything else to say.

"Good," he said, turning toward the house. "Have a good life."

Little Joe Turner followed hesitantly, but stopped in his footsteps when Jack opened the back door and looked at the boy. "Damned frickin' dog," he muttered, and then he closed the door behind him.

Joe turned to watch Diana's car backing out of the driveway, then down the road.

"Damned frickin' dog," he whispered.

***

It had been a quiet week for Chief Rob Allen, with things settling down a bit after the accident. His rotating day off just happened to land on a Sunday, which meant he would attend church with his mother — a courtesy he honored faithfully. After all, the woman had to put up with the drama at all hours, day after day, that came with his job. She deserved a little normality in her life once in a while. Further, his younger brother, Scottie, was doing the weekend ROTC thing, leaving Gracie with a half-empty nest. And so, on this first Sunday in

September, Robbie sat quietly beside his mother in her usual pew at the village's First Congregational Church. It was while tugging at the collar of his white dress shirt, twisting his neck a bit to the right, that he noticed her coming down the aisle, to take a seat just two rows in front of him and his mom. "Mrs. Curtis," he whispered to his mother.

Gracie nodded. "Of course. Lenore's here every Sunday."

"Thought she was Roman Catholic, what with working alongside Father Tom — you know, taking care of Joe Turner."

"Umm," his mother replied, "I think there's a story there. She drops Joe off at Holy Family, then comes here." She shrugged. "She's probably got reasons for leaving the R.C. community. Maybe another wounded soldier, as they say. You know, sometimes a church shoots its own wounded."

He pondered this bit of information during the entire service, his eyes repeatedly going back to the blonde curls swaying above the back of her baby-blue dress.

The fellowship potluck was always held on the first Sunday of the month, and it was there that mother and son ended up seated with Lenore. She slid onto a chair across from them at the end of a long table, seeming to not find anywhere else to sit. After a brief greeting, Gracie motioned to her manly offspring. "Lenore, have you met my son, Robbie?"

He grinned like a schoolboy, then kept his eyes on Gracie. "We've met, Mom." Joe got tangled up in his bike a while back. Mrs. Curtis had to come and get him."

"I'm afraid I got a little theatrical, Chief." Joe's foster mother looked back down at her plate. "I apologize for that."

"No, not really." When she looked back up at him, he reassured her, "In fact, I thought you handled the situation very well." There was an awkward pause, and then he saw the soft color rising over her cheeks. When she concentrated on stabbing a piece of lettuce, he looked away. But he just had to check it out. *"Is she actually blushing?"* he thought, sneaking a quick peek.

Apparently, she was, for Gracie gave her son a knowing look, then changed the subject. "How are you enjoying your new house, neighbor?"

"I love it." She kept her attention on the mother. "I even enjoy mowing the lawn, if you can believe that."

"I think you really do," the older woman commented. "Out there pushing that hand mower around and around." She took a sip of her coffee. "Of course, when Old Man Winter comes around, you'll have some serious shoveling to do." She tilted her head toward Rob. "As it so happens, though, I have some live-in help, what with having two boys."

"Joe will help, I'm sure," Lenore said.

"Well, if it gets to be too much, I'm sure Rob can give you a hand. After all, you're just a few hundred feet away, right, son?"

"No problem." He shot a quick look at the blonde lady, who was focusing on her plate. "Just let us know," he said, as he stole another look. *"Whoa. She is. She's really blushing."*

He thought about that a lot over the next few days.

***

May Spofford was furious. "Our Suzie is pregnant, dammit, and I know who the culprit is: that ugly, good-for-nothing excuse for a dog."

"Well now, we can't be sure, May," her husband cautioned her. "The neighbors have spotted that coyote creature twice in the last week."

"I don't care what the neighbors say. It had to have happened at the fair. Count the days, Hank. The average gestation period for labs is sixty-three days. The bitch starts showing at a few weeks, and she is showing."

"But how can you be sure? You told me, yourself, it's hard to know when she's in heat."

"Oh, let me make it even more complicated for you, my

friend. The sperm of the stud can remain viable for up to eleven days after mating. Go figure that one out, if you can." She tapped the kitchen table with her coffee spoon. "I need to talk to the Thompsons."

"What for?" He threw his head back in disbelief. "You can't prove a thing."

"We'll see about that."

She waited until Winnie would be home from work. It would be a whole lot easier to confront her than Cecil. All she had to do was make sure the man was busy with the evening milking, so she knocked on the back door at six o'clock, ready to light into the poor, little Abenaki lady. She hadn't counted on Ceese coming into the house to use the bathroom. It was he who answered the door. "Everything all right, Mrs. Spofford?" he asked.

She gulped, but decided to go for it, anyway. "No, things are definitely *not* all right, Mr. Thompson.

Winnie heard the woman's voice and came quickly down the hallway from the kitchen. "Oh, May, what's going on?"

"I'll tell you what's going on, Winnie. My show dog is pregnant, and it's all because of what happened at that stupid dog parade at the fair." She addressed Ceese, again. "You weren't there, but your dog mounted my Suzie, out behind the grandstand stage, and nobody dared to interfere, and…" The tears started. "…and now we have these bastard puppies coming, and we can't breed her again, not this year, and you and your stupid mutt have cost me almost six hundred dollars, and I want to know what you're going to do about it," she bawled.

Winnie started to apologize, but her husband stepped in. "I can tell you exactly what we're going to do about it, Mrs. Spofford. *Nothing.*" He caught the baffled look, but kept going. "The fact is, *you* are responsible for keeping your show dog away from places like dog dress-up parades. Nobody made you do that. You are the one who was foolish, and we will not accept the blame for your problem." He pushed Winnie gently back inside before he shut the door, strode past the stunned accuser, and straight toward the milking parlor. For a few seconds, May Spofford could only stare. Then she took a big breath and let him have it: "You self-righteous ass! You will pay for this, and pay dearly." She headed for the car door. "I have friends, a *lot* of friends — as you are just about to find out!"

***

The call came at ten o'clock at night. "Is this Don Collins?"

"Yes, it is."

"This is Jessie Wilson. I need to talk to you."

"I'm listening."

"I hardly know where to start."

"Why don't you start with what's going on with Jack. I heard he's been having a rough time of it. Is that so?"

"That's putting it mildly. I don't even recognize my son, Don, and that's the truth." There was no reply, so he went on. "He's out of his head, I swear. He stole a gun right out of his grandfather's suitcase, and bullets."

"Mmmm," Don replied, "I heard about the shooting at the dogs. You're right. This is not the same son you and Laura were so proud of."

"He's snapped. That's it, pure and simple," the father moaned. "I need to get him some help. I need to do something." He paused, then corrected himself. "*We* need to do something, Don. Jack needs your help... and now, so do I."

"All right, Jessie. So, let's look at what's happening with you, because you can't help your boy until you get your own head on straight. Do you agree?"

"I... guess so." Don heard the choke in Jessie's voice, but let him go on. "Oh, my gawd, man, I don't know where to begin. It's like the whole world is going to Hell in a hand basket. My darling, my wife, is killed, and then my son goes off the deep end, and now, now this other thing. It's unbelievable, just too much, too much." The man was weeping. "How can it get any worse? I mean, isn't there any place *safe* anymore?"

"What else has happened, Jessie?"

There was a peculiar gurgle as he got the words out. "I just got a call from my neighbor across the road, Ceese Thompson. The chief of police came to notify him and Winnie that their dog, Blow, had been killed." He sobbed the rest of it out. Somebody bashed his head in, and, and…"

"And what, Jessie?"

"Oh gawd, Don, they cut off his head and all four paws."

CHAPTER FOUR

Rewards

"Oh, Cecil, I don't think this is a good idea," Chief Robbie cautioned. "It could cause a lot of trouble. You need to think of the people crawling all over your land, plus trampling around on other folks' property, all the way down to the underside of the bridge near the Spofford home." He shook his head. "And they could even destroy evidence, stomping all over the crime scene. I wish you wouldn't do this."

"Is it illegal, Chief?"

"Pretty close, my friend. If anything bad happens, you could be sued for inciting... whatever."

The farmer snorted. "They won't blame me for wanting justice, not for a despicable crime like that. And look at what has happened to Winnie, for gawd's sake. She's had so much trash in her life, already, and now this." He slid his rimless glasses off and started to wipe the lenses with his bandana. "No, sir, we need to get to the bottom of this. I'll take my chances."

"But a reward of five hundred dollars, Cecil?" The man's mouth pinched tightly. "You'll attract all kinds of weirdoes, man."

Ceese put his glasses back on, then blinked slowly. "Ay-yuh, that's probably a bit over the top. How about a reward of only one hundred dollars?" He tucked the bandana back into his pocket. "That might calm things down a bit, don't you think?"

The law officer sighed. "Um, okay, that might keep things within reasonable boundaries. But I still recommend that you back off and let the authorities work it out."

"The authorities," the weary dairy farmer replied, "have — in the past — left the Thompson household with some serious doubts as to their expertise." He folded his arms across his chest. "I think we'll just go for whatever we can get, right now."

The word got out the very next day: "Cecil Thompson is offering a one hundred dollar reward to anyone who can bring about the conviction of the person or persons who committed the horrendous killing of the family dog, Blow," Lenore Tanner Curtis told her friends, Bernie and Della. By the time he got the drift of the conversation, the man signaled his wife to share the phone.

"Hello, Lenore," he called across the room. "Can yeh hear me?"

"Oh yeah, I can hear you, Bernie. But it would be better if you could get closer."

He did. "So, what's up? We got some kinda contest goin' here?"

Lenore did her best to explain the situation before the McBains hung up. For a few minutes, it was quiet in this couple's kitchen out there on Hinesburg Road.

"So," Della finally ventured, "what are you thinking, mister?"

He shifted his weight on the wooden chair. "I need to think about this, Del."

"What's to think about?"

He shrugged. "About what I should tell yeh and what I shouldn't tell yeh."

She got up and pulled another Canadian stout from the refrigerator. Once she took a swig, she was ready to get into the details. "Is this something about your love life before we got married? If it is, I'm not interested. You Canucks did your thing, just like our American GIs, and I'm not going there, understand?"

It was hard to tell if it was a cough or a laugh. "Ah, no, Del, that's not what I'm talkin' about. Just cool it, lass... just cool it." He reached over to take the bottle from her, placing it dead center on the kitchen table. "Nah, Del, I need to tell yeh that I have a lot of experience, uh, in investigative matters. In the service. A lot of it, okay?" He watched her zero in.

"What're you telling me, Bernie? She laughed softly. "Were you some kind of spy, or what?"

"Not exactly." The room was quiet again. After a few seconds, she reached for the bottle, but he swiped it away to his side of the table.

She telegraphed her surprise. "What the heck is going on here?"

"Way-yell, when yer goin' on a mission, you don't smoke or drink, or spit in the sink. Got that, lass?"

She squirmed. "So, just who do you think is on a so-called mission, here, mister?"

"Somebody who wants to get a hundred dollars reward money, that's who."

"And just what makes you think we could do this?" she scoffed.

"Because I know exactly how to do this, me love." He grinned and took a big draught from the bottle of stout. "I just need to train you a little."

Then he burped.

***

Frustrated, Sheriff Max Duncan slapped his own forehead. "He's going to do what?!" He turned to address Chief Robbie Allen eye-to-eye. "In the history of the Chittenden County Sheriff's Department, I have never seen anything so damned dumb." He yanked at his gun belt. "Offering a reward like that is bound to complicate our investigation. What does that do for a good working relationship with the ASPCA, huh?

Think they're gonna like that bothersome detail, Chief?"

"As a matter of fact, Sheriff, the American Society for Prevention of Cruelty to Animals might look upon this move as beneficial, instead of a hindrance. And let me remind you, the only people who are applying for this independent investigation are an older couple, the McBains." He wet his lips. "I guess the old guy has some experience doing this stuff while in the Canadian Armed Forces."

"Like what?" Max was doubtful.

"He says it was top secret. That's all he'll tell me." Robbie drew a breath, then let it escape slowly. "I did manage to get him to back off and let the ASPCA do their job first. He said it wouldn't make any difference for him, because he works altogether differently from them. In fact, he was very accommodating on that issue."

"Ay-yuh? Well, I'd like it a lot better if he was accommodating enough to keep his nose out of the whole thing." He grunted. "It's just that the crime took place right on the border of our two jurisdictions, as if that's not involved enough. I mean, we already have my sheriff's department, your Essex Junction Police Department, and the ASPCA — that's three official agencies — working this case. We really don't need a private investigator adding to the chaos."

"Of course, Ceese Thompson has a say in all that, Sheriff, and knowing how that family, in the past, has come under scrutiny by the law, I certainly can understand why the man is looking elsewhere."

Max Duncan tipped his hat toward the back of his head. "I suppose you're referring to the Raymond René Smart case," he said, defensively. "Well, he was involved in that cheerleader's murder, and we all knew it. If he hadn't died while on the lam up there in Canada, we'd have solved that case a lot sooner." Robbie nodded in agreement; Max made a final point: "It was hard on them, sure, but it was hard on the whole community." He pulled the hat forward again. "At any rate, I do understand, but I still wish he would back off." There was a sudden thought. "What'd you say that McBain guy's full name is? I'll feel better if I run a background check on him."

***

Lenore Tanner Curtis was picking up a package at the village post office. She had decided to walk over to the building, located just off the five-way junction, to enjoy the golden afternoon glow bathing the village. The Indian summer stroll had been pleasant, so she wasn't too upset about the long line in front of the pick-up window. Even so, the wait was disturbed by the bustling entrance of two ladies, deep in conversation, who took their place in line, a couple of people back from her. A quick glance revealed that the talkative one was May Spofford. Lenore did not recognize the other lady.

"Ay-yuh," May's voice bounced off the hard surfaces of the room. "I heard about it, and mind you, I don't wish such a thing on anybody, but I am so blasted glad that ugly mutt is dead. I hated that thing, you know?" The other woman murmured something, to which May quickly replied, "Oh, you've hit the nail on the head, with that one. Good riddance to bad rubbish, right?" Her companion said something in a low voice. "Oh, I don't care who hears me. I didn't kill that old dog." She huffed. "But whoever did it, they did us all a favor, if you ask me."

The line moved forward, allowing Lenore to sneak a peek at whomever May's comments were directed. Instead, she met Mrs. Spofford's cocky, brown-eyed glare. There was nothing to do but give a friendly nod and turn back around. But the noisy conversation came to an abrupt end. It was when Lenore was carrying out her small bundle that May stepped out of line, just enough to block the exit.

"Aren't you one of those ladies in Winnie Thompson's sewing group?" When Lenore nodded, the warning came, loud and clear. "I don't care what any of you women think about me, or that damned dog. I never touched him. Got that?"

"Uh-huh, got that," the embarrassed blonde replied, as she hustled out the door.

She was almost all the way back home before she decided to be offended by the brash behavior of that loud woman. "Well, her reputation certainly precedes her. I heard about how abrasive and bossy she is, and now I have experienced it, for sure."

A car pulled into a driveway, crossing the sidewalk in front of her. When Gracie Allen stepped out and waved, Lenore realized she was passing that woman's house, already.

"You busy, neighbor?" Gracie called out.

"Uh, no, actually. Just coming back from the post office."

"Come in for some iced tea. It's all ready in the fridge."

A few minutes later, she was showing Gracie the sweater she had ordered from the Sears and Roebuck catalog.

"Oh, it's gorgeous," the older woman sang out. "Blue is really your color, what with your blonde hair and that peachy skin." She peered a bit closer. "Although, I must say, there are some extra roses on those cheeks right now. Have you been running or something?"

Lenore laughed lightly as she folded the sweater back into its box. "No, Gracie, I guess you're seeing a little indignation there."

"Really?" Mrs. Allen leaned forward.

"I just had a bit of a run-in with May Spofford in the post office." She took a sip of the golden iced tea before going into the short, but disturbing story. When she saw the serious look on her hostess's face, she stopped.

"I think," Gracie said quietly, "she's like that Shakespearian character. 'Methinks thou dost protest too much,' or something like that."

"I'm guessing that means she's probably guilty," Lenore ventured.

"Well, it is interesting that she is being quite loud about *not* being guilty. That gives me second thoughts, right there." Gracie stared at her own amber-filled glass. "You know," she mused, "I think Robbie needs to hear this. Not that it's hard evidence, but there's sure reason for taking note of such fierce denial, when in fact, there has been no accusation."

"Feel free to let him know, Gracie." She stood to leave.

"You know what, dear? I think he needs to hear it from you. Otherwise, he tends to categorize such talk as gossip. Nope, he definitely needs to hear it from you." She followed her guest to the back door. "May I ask him to get in touch with you, dear?"

**

"I thought I told you to stay away from this farm until Jack is doing better," LeRoy Dupree admonished thirteen-year-old Joe Turner.

The boy stood astride his bike, his head lowered. "N... nobody was telling me if he was getting better, so I just wanted to check for myself."

The hired hand had a moment of guilt. "Oh, I'm sorry, son. I thought maybe somebody was keeping you up-to-date on the situation." He noticed the lad's dog panting, drool dripping over the edge of the handlebars' basket. "Your dog looks thirsty."

"Yessir. My foster mom says it's an Indian summer, or somethin'." He looked up to make the appeal. "If I could just give Mop a little drink from the old pump."

"I don't see why not. Just don't be snooping around — things are not so good around here." He turned to go back to the barn. "Get on home, son. This is no place for you, right now."

The old pump was located about fifty feet from the back door of the house. The rusted thing had been used for watering horses back when milk was hauled through early morning fogs and snowstorms to the creamery at the north end of the village. Although the pump was no longer used regularly, it was still working. Joe had learned how to prime it with his hand over the spout, pumping until there was enough suction to pull the water up and out. He proceeded with this, removing his hand from the spout when it was ready, and water came gushing forth into the metal catcher below. Mop went eagerly into it, wetting his front paws in the process, but the boy's eyes were fixed on something else: the wide back entrance to the woodshed, from where he heard a rhythmic chopping. He knew that sound, for he had been in that shed many times before. After a quick visual check toward the barn, Joe shot forward into the woodshed. His feet dug to a sudden stop in the wood chips, and there was Jessie Wilson, Jack's father, in mid-swing. His eyes went up to the sudden visitor, as the heavy ax splintered a wedge of wood. "My gawd, boy! Don't be coming up on people like that. You'll get somebody hurt, for heaven's sake."

"Sorry. Mr. Dupree said I had to go back home and not bother anybody, but I just had to know how Jack is doing."

The dairyman placed the splintered logs on top of a full wagon, ready to bring the load inside for another chilly evening. "He's right. You need to go back home. This is no place for you right now." He picked up the handle and started to tow the wood toward the kitchen's back door. "Jack is not well. He's in a real tailspin. Right now, it looks like somebody from this family has butchered a dog, because it caused the train accident." His whole body shivered. "No, no, that can't be true. It can't be true." The weary face focused on the boy. "Just go home, son, and I will let you know when you can come back, okay?"

Jessie finished hauling the load to the wood stove that heated the house at night. He was passing back through the kitchen with the empty wagon when he heard the sobbing coming from Jack's room upstairs, the same sobbing he had been listening to for months now. Jessie stopped and sat down at the table, unable to take another weary step. It was like a stop sign in the middle of an unfamiliar highway. He was lost, really lost. Laura's death was a burden too great for him and his son to bear, and then there was the dissected body of an animal that Jack was trying to shoot. The boy needed help. "Oh, God," the father whispered in surrender, "*I need help!*" He went to Laura's kitchen bulletin board, and found the phone number for Don and Connie Collins. This time, he would make an appointment.

***

Cecil "Ceese" Thompson was a bit surprised that the ASPCA investigator was a real lawyer. He sat across the table from this volunteer legal beagle, sizing him up. The silver-haired fellow was in his sixties, ready to retire, probably the senior partner in the business. But the meeting was starting, with opening remarks from both Sheriff Duncan and Chief Rob Allen. These were followed with an introduction of the volunteer. Rob did the honors. "We want to welcome the ASPCA rep today, Mr. Douglas Courtney, of the Montpelier law firm, Courtney and Courtney." He bowed slightly toward the man. "Sir, if you would please give us a run-down on what it is you gentlemen do on animal cruelty cases, we can get off on the right foot in this whole thing." He glanced at Ceese, Max, and Bernie. "I don't think any of the rest of us has ever been involved in this particular type of proceedings."

Douglas Courtney gave a brief summary of his involvement in the investigation — overseeing the collection of forensic evidence and giving legal advice and support — then he took a few questions from the group.

"I'm Cecil Thompson. I just want to get the S.O.B. that did this to our dog. What can I do to get this thing started? What do you need from me, Mr. Courtney?"

"I, and these law officers will need a written statement from you, sir."

"No problem," Ceese replied. "What do you want to know?"

"Please, call me Doug. I like to keep things on a first-name basis. Makes it feel like we're all on the same team." He turned a pencil slowly in his hand. "So, one of the things we need to know is whether you have any suspects in mind."

"Hell, yes. Got a couple of 'em. May Spofford, for one. She threatened us with a lawsuit or something. Accused our dog of getting her show-off mutt pregnant. Like we planned it, or something." He watched the others all nod in agreement. "And then, I hate to say it, but my neighbor's son tried to shoot our poor, goofy old pet, because he thinks Blow actually caused the train accident that killed his mother."

"Oh yes. I heard about that," the barrister said. "So, anybody else?"

"Aw, I don't know. Ever since Laura, the mother, was killed, that whole Wilson Dairy Farm bunch has acted like... I don't know."

"Who else is over there?" Doug asked, leaning back in his chair.

"Oh, just a hired hand, and sometimes this young kid who used to hang out with the son, the one with the gun." His eyes focused on something not really up there on the ceiling. "But, the boy doesn't seem to be up there much, anymore. Guess maybe his foster mother is keeping him closer to home."

"I see. Well, Cecil, that is the sort of thing we need in your statement. There's more, of course, but our office would be happy to work with you on that. We'll definitely be in touch." He turned his attention to the wiry gentleman down at the end of the table. "Sir?"

"I'm Bernard McBain, but you can call me 'Bernie.'"

"Thank you. And why are *you* here, Bernie?"

His small, silver mustache twitched above the smirk.

"Money," he said.

CHAPTER FIVE

Flames

Even though Gracie had called to tell her Chief Robbie was coming at four-thirty to talk about the post office incident, Lenore wasn't ready for the sight of him coming up the front walk. She wasn't sure whether it was because he was a cop, or the uniform, or because he was so tall, or just exactly what, but that man made her feel very "...vulnerable," she concluded out loud. "And that has to stop. I'm a grown woman, for heaven's sake, and I haven't done anything wrong." She smoothed her hair. "Not that anyone has even suggested such a thing." She peeked out the window again. He had stopped to talk to Joe, who was making an attempt to mow the front lawn. After a couple of verbal exchanges, Robbie smiled and started back up the walk, where, seeing her at the window, he smiled and waved. "Oh darn, he saw me." She made an effort to save face by opening the door before he even hit the front step. "Hi, there! Thanks for coming over," she chirped. There was the scent of fresh aftershave as she stepped aside for him to come in. "I would have come over to your office, but Gracie said you'd rather keep this matter out of earshot — um, just whose earshot, I'm not sure." She coughed out a chuckle as she motioned for him to sit.

He chose the overstuffed chair next to the front door, looking around as he slid back into it. "Nice place."

"Oh, thank you. I like to decorate." She perched on the end

of the color-coordinated sofa, just across from him.

"Nice job." He slowly nodded, as if he were collecting his next words. "So..." He found himself looking directly into those green eyes. "My mom tells me you had a run-in with May Spofford."

She looked down at her hands. "I guess you could call it that." Her fingers entwined, then loosened "It was not pleasant."

"Yeah, I can imagine. I've known the Spoffords for quite a while, and she can be a handful." He kept eye contact. "Still, I would like to hear the actual details, Mrs. Curtis." He was surprised to see the color rise across her cheekbones, just before she looked back down at her hands. "Oh." He sat up straight, not sure what he had done. "Am I coming on too strong about this? Sorry."

She laughed softly and brushed the idea away with a flick of her fingers. "No-no, I just wasn't ready for the 'Mrs. Curtis' thing. Most people just call me 'Lenore.'"

"Oh, I see. Well, I can do that, if you don't mind. Or I could call you 'neighbor,' if you like." He smiled. "I'm certainly not going with the usual police-talk and call you 'Ma'am.' You're too young for that, in my opinion."

Her face was still a soft pink as she looked up. "Nope, nope, that's what Joe calls me: 'Ma'am.'" She glanced toward the window. "I've had him in my home for several years now, and he's never called me 'Mom.' Just 'Ma'am.'" This time she tossed her curls as she laughed. "Better than, 'Hey you,' right?"

"Right." He decided to pry a little. "So, he never knew your husband then?"

"Oh my goodness, no. My husband passed away back in forty-four. He was killed in action in Europe, just at the end of the war. We had only one week together before he was deployed." She touched her ring finger. I was only eighteen, so I just kept living at home with my mother. I went to secretarial school for a while. Then she passed on, and I was alone for a few years. So when old Joe Turner asked me to take the boy, I did. It was supposed to be only for a couple of weeks, but… well, it's a long story."

"I'm familiar with the old Joe Turner situation. Thank God you took that boy, young lady." He stood to sidle over to the window. "He's been through a lot."

"Ay-yuh, he has."

"What's that he's doing out there?" Robbie bent forward for a closer look.

"What?" She slipped over beside him to see for herself. The boy was jabbing at the rotary blades with a stick. "Oh," she said, "that's how he cleans out the debris." She turned to smile into the man's face, but he was still watching the boy.

"I see that now," he murmured. "You know, I'd be keeping an eye on him, if I were you. On top of all the crap he's already endured, he now has lost his job up at the Wilson farm, not to mention, contact with that whole group." He turned to look at her. "How's he doing, anyway?"

"Awfully quiet," she said, stepping closer to the glass. "I'm thinking he really needs another after-school job." She glanced quickly at Robbie and back to the window. "Making his own money seemed to keep him grounded."

They stood there together, for just a moment, until he pulled back, heading for the same chair. "I don't want to stick my nose into your business, Mrs.… uh, Lenore, but if there's anything Mom and I can do to help with the boy, let us know."

She returned to the end of the couch. "Thanks for the offer, but let's see how it goes." She needed to get back to the other subject. "So, let me see if I can remember what happened at the post office."

Ten minutes later, she watched him striding down the walk, waving at Joe, and sneaking a quick look back, to catch her at the window. He was smiling as he headed down the sidewalk toward his house.

She slipped into the chair where he'd been sitting, leaned back, and closed her eyes. It was barely there, but she could still get the aroma of his aftershave.

***

"I don't know about all this," Della said to her husband. "It seems like a whole lot of work for a measly one hundred dollars."

"Oh yeh think so, do yeh?" He hunched his shoulders in glee. "Way-yell, yeh'll just have to trust me, lass. I have a scheme." The stiff gray eyebrows moved mischievously.

Her eyes narrowed behind the plastic-rimmed glasses. "Oh, no you don't. Not another one of your wild-haired ideers." She twitched her fanny in the wooden rocking chair. "Last time we tried that, you nearly ended up in jail."

"Ha! But I didn't, now, did I?"

"Almost, mister."

"But 'almost' doesn't count, Del." Bernie McBain lifted the footrest of his beat-up recliner with a solid bang. "Besides, this time we don't need to use dynamite." He folded his hands across his flat chest. "We'll be goin' pure and simple."

"What does that mean?" she asked.

"Simple commando tactics, that's what."

"I still don't know what you're talking about. Don't be cute with me, you old goat."

He peered at the wristwatch on his left forearm. "So, we have nine o'clock in the mornin', Del. We've had breakfast and done our mornin' chores. We just need to take a little rest, and then we'll start our trainin' exercises."

She sat up straight, her feet planted on the floor to hold the rocker still. "Exercises? What exercises?"

An hour later, the two of them were down in the dimly lit cellar of their rented residence. "Now," he announced, "time to start." He turned to his wife, who was positioned in the only escape from this clandestine basic training site. The light from the doorway behind her silhouetted her stiff-legged, pigeon-toed warrior stance. The woman tugged at the waist of her gray sweatpants. "I feel fat," she declared.

"Aye. but never mind, that'll go away, soon as yeh drop to yer knees and crawl toward me."

"*Excuse me?*" You think I'm really going to do that?!" The fat lady suddenly had elbows protruding from each side.

"Nah, Del. Think about it: how many times have yeh dropped to yer knees in the garden to weed, and pick beans, or whatever?" His words were filled with confidence. "Yeh do it all the time." He squatted down in the dark. "Now, all yeh have to do, is drop down and crawl toward me, see? Just bring me the things I need to get the job done over here, on the other end of the field." He clapped his hands. "Just drop down. Yeh can do this, lass! Yeh can do this!"

She moaned. Then she took a breath and dropped down. "Ow!" She moved a bit before she repeated it: "Ow, dammit!"

"Del! Del, listen to me. Yeh need to get off yer knees. Yeh need to crawl on yer belly, that's all." He moved on his haunches. "Remember that. Yeh don't move on yer knees. That hurts. Yeh move on yer belly." He paused. "Okay. Try it again, only move like a mud turtle, on yer belly, pushin' with yer arms and legs." He waited for her to rethink the exercise. In a few seconds, he got his answer.

"Ouch... ouch... oh, dammit, Bernie, this isn't working."

"Why not? Just dig in yer toes and yer fingernails, and move."

"No, wait."

"What?"

"Maybe if we put a piece of cardboard under my belly, it might work."

"Naw, we can't carry a piece of cardboard on a mission. Try again. Just move along, toward me. Remember, I need the supplies yer carryin' to complete our mission, Del. This is crucial!"

There was more scuffling from the turtle warrior, accompanied by great grunts and groans until, suddenly, there came a high-pitched "Oh! Oh, ouch! Oh!" The sound of her head hitting the ground was followed by a muffled whimper, then silence.

"Della?" he called out.

She finally spit it through the dirt: "Damn you, you old fool! I can't move."

"Why not?"

There's something stuck in my belly button."

"What? How did *that* happen?"

"It happened because my sweatpants got dragged down, that's how. Now get over here and help me."

He rose from his squat to reach up and turn on the light. There, in its glow, was Della, flat on the dirt floor, her sweatpants halfway down her buttocks, and a dirt-smeared face glowering up at him. "How the hell...?" he muttered.

"Never mind how the hell, just get over here and get this splinter out, dammit!"

After he had removed the small sliver and doused the wound with red liniment, he concluded that this tactic wasn't going to work. "We'll have to change our plan just a bit," he told his seething patient.

"No kidding, buster," she snarled, "like maybe I don't go along with another of your dumb projects."

"Ah, but this is one yeh'll not want to miss, me lady," he grinned, as he wiped his hands. "This one is a sure thing. Trust me."

"Good luck with that one, you old goat."

***

Jessie Wilson was careful to arrive promptly for his first counseling session with Don and Connie Collins. He knew Don worked full time for Burlington Transit, and his wife was a teacher at Essex Junction High School, making scheduling often difficult. Nevertheless, the worried dad arrived, even though he was not sure it would all go well, but knowing he could trust Laura's good friends to respect his family's privacy. That was important. Although the small basement office was comfortable, he was nervous. "Never done this before," he commented, almost before Don had finished the opening prayer.

"Sure. Something new, but it gets easier after a few minutes." Don's impish smile telegraphed confidence across the desk. "Soon as folks see that we don't bite, they usually relax a little."

Connie laughed. "Trouble is, *we're* not always sure whether or not they're going to bite *us!*" She was glad to see the man grin.

Don leaned back in his squeaky desk chair, hands behind his head. "How's your day going?"

"It would be a lot better if my boy could get his head on straight."

"Well, don't get discouraged." Don's hands came down to fold over his belt buckle. "These things take time. You probably need to get some things in order, yourself."

"You got that right, man." Jessie looked at the floor. "I don't understand how this could happen to us. This stuff is supposed to only happen to *other* people." His head stayed bowed. "We were a good, happy family. We loved each other. We helped other people. We paid our taxes." The eyes were tear-filled when he looked up at Don. "What the hell happened, man?"

The imp's mouth drew back in a grimace. "Life," he answered, "life on planet earth." His fingers rippled across the buckle. "And life on earth is not fair. It's anything but." The dairy farmer waited, hoping for something more. "So, what happened, Jessie, is something called a 'fallen world.' Ever heard of it?"

"Maybe. Maybe Laura said something, but I don't really remember. She did talk about a real place called Hell, though."

"Okay, but did she mention anything about the fall of man — you know, in the Garden of Eden?" The fellow acknowledged it, but Don went into the story, pointing it out in the Bible which lay handy on his desk. At the end, he folded up the Book and put the final explanation out there: "So, it all comes down to free will, Jessie. God doesn't want robots; He wants children who choose to love Him. He wants kids who listen to His warnings and make the right, safe choices. Adam and Eve failed the test, and they paid the price. Unfortunately, the rest of us are still suffering those consequences. That's why the world is not fair. That's why we have pain and disasters, and we lose lovely people like Laura."

His eyes were focused on the floor again. "Don't know if I can really believe all that stuff, Don." Jessie bent forward, elbows on knees, still concentrating on the carpet. "All I know is that she's gone, and life will never be the same — not for me, and not for the boy who thinks he must have killed his mother."

"It was an accident, Jessie," Don reassured him.

"I know that, but Jack can't seem to deal with it. He's so mixed up. One minute he hates himself; the next minute he hates the dog." He glanced over at Connie. "I don't believe he killed Blow. No, Jack *has* to know that it could have been another dog, or even a coyote."

"You know what, Jessie?" she asked, "when the authorities find the killer, your son will get that part of it straight. In the meantime, we need to help him to forgive himself. That's it, don't you think, Don?"

Her husband nodded. "And we need to be patient; this could take a while." The brows drew together. "Right at the moment, though, we need to help you get your own feelings sorted out." He leaned back in the squeaky seat. "Let's talk about Laura for a few minutes."

"Yeah? Like what?" the man asked carefully.

"I'm thinking you two had a pretty good marriage," the counselor prompted.

"Oh yeah. We had a great marriage, for sure. We were a real team, you know? I don't think that woman ever threw a fit — gawd knows she put up with a lot from me, what with

59

my temper. But she was real patient. She was a good woman, beautiful inside and out, for sure."

"So, Jessie, what do you miss the most?"

The man seemed to check out the ceiling. "I guess it would be the way we just loved each other so much." There was a pause. "She… she called me 'Mr. Dairyman' and I called her 'Mrs. Dairyman,' and we would kind of flirt before we…" It was almost a small hiccup. The hands went up to cover his face, as the shoulders began to shake.

A soft wailing filled the small basement office.

***

When Father Thomas Ladue bumped into Chief Robbie Allen at the Lincoln Inn's coffee shop, he decided to take advantage of the encounter. "Got a few minutes, Chief?"

"Sure. Have a seat."

The priest slid into the booth, signaled the waitress for a black coffee, and turned his full attention toward the policeman. "Understand you've volunteered to help out with my young charge, Joe Turner." He smiled at the surprised look across the table. "Lenore told me you volunteered your mother, but I read between the lines."

The two men laughed together. "I see her pretty regularly, Chief, as you can imagine, and now that she's your neighbor, I just imagine you do, too."

"Well, I'm pretty busy," the fellow replied, "but yes, I did volunteer my mom to help out over there, if needed."

"I'll let it go at that," Tom said, with a twinkle in his eye. He sat back to let the cup of coffee slide in front of him. "I hope it's not too soon to take you up on that offer."

"What's up?" Robbie placed his hat on the seat beside him.

"You know the kid lost his job up at the farm when Laura was killed, right?"

"Ay-yuh, I'm aware of that. Matter of fact, Lenore brought

that up. Even suggested he get another after-school gig. She thinks he needs the encouragement. I agree."

"So do I. I tried to get him to join the Catholic Youth Club, but he said he didn't want anything to do with a god who allows a good mother to be killed, 'especially by a stupid dog,' as he put it." He wrapped his hand around the hot cup, then drew back. "So much for that effort." He rubbed the seared hand. "So, Lenore told me that you might be able to get him a paper route. Is that correct?"

"I do know a kid who could use some help. Says it's so big, there's not enough time to get it all done." He moved the hat a bit. "Think Joe could handle this?"

"He's plenty smart. More like, there's an attitude problem, right now."

"So, not a good idea?"

"Oh, it's probably do-able. But we need to get him into counseling, or we could be wasting our time."

"Got somebody in mind, Father Tom?"

"I do. Tell you what, you handle the paper route, and I'll set up the counseling, okay?"

"Okay. You know where to reach me, right?"

So it was, that the Collinses ended up counseling all three of them — Jack, Jessie, and Joe. Progress was going smoothly with Jessie, but Jack was sullen and uncooperative. If not for the insistence of his father, the boy would have not even shown up for the second session. But when Joe Turner showed up for his first appointment, the two Christian counselors had their hands full. The thirteen-year-old sat squarely in the counselee's chair, arms folded, a full-blown sulk on his face.

"Thanks for coming, Joe," Don said.

"Not welcome," the boy muttered.

"Don't want to be here?"

"'Course not." The look showed contempt for a stupid question.

The couple exchanged a look, and Don stood up. "What do you say, the three of us take a walk?"

They spent a good hour strolling on the green of St. Michael's College, out there behind their home. As they approached the back yard once again, Don motioned to the folding chairs in their sheltered patio. "That was a good chat, Joe. Let's have a seat before you leave us today." When all three were seated, he went for the closure, at least for this session. "So, you really think the Thompsons killed their own dog, because it was out of control?"

"Yup." The boy nodded emphatically.

He looked at his wife. "Babe, in all the years we've been counseling, have you ever heard of that?"

"No, can't say I have," she mused. "It's been just the opposite. Dog owners are the last folks in the world to kill their pets; those are like their own sweet little children. And in this case, the killing was horrible; I can't imagine the Thompsons chopping up their dear, old Blow."

The young man grunted and looked at his shoes.

"I can't, either, but mind you, we could be wrong." Don crossed his ankles, and slumped back into the wobbling chair. "But let's just suppose we are right about that. Let's assume the Thompsons didn't do it, Joe. Would you stop being mad?"

The boy's mouth went into a hard pout. "Nope."

"Why not?" Don uncrossed his feet, positioning them directly in front of the chair.

Joe shrugged. "Guess because Mrs. Wilson still got killed." He looked like he might cry.

"Of course," Connie conceded. "Of course we can understand that. You had grown pretty darned close to her — and the rest of them, for that matter."

Don leaned toward the boy. "Oh my goodness, Joe! Maybe that's it. Maybe this is the question you need to ask yourself."

"What question?" the kid asked warily.

"Are you mad at God because Mrs. Wilson was killed by a dog, or are you mad because you lost your new family?" Don waited for what seemed a long time before the boy simply shrugged, and then fixed his gaze on this own tennis shoes, which were tapping gently together.

"Joe?"

The answer was another noncommittal shrug, as though he had lost his tongue.

The session was over.

CHAPTER SIX

Motives

Chief Rob Allen looked around at the men assembled in his Essex Junction Police Department office. "I guess you got copies of the ASPCA report." He noted the nods from Sheriff Duncan, Cecil Thompson, and the lawyer, Douglas Courtney. Turning to Hank Spofford, he explained, "Only the actual investigation personnel received this written information, but I thought it was appropriate that you be here, Hank, since the body was found on your property."

"I appreciate it," Hank replied. "So, what did they say?"

"The dog died from the blow on the head. All the rest was a vicious attack, done after the poor animal was dead."

"Gee-awd," Ceese murmured, "I hope so."

"The weapon seems to have been a medium or small metal blade, but they can't be sure because the killing actually took place at another location, and they couldn't find any slash marks or blood splatters near the victim's body."

"Another location?" Hank asked.

"Right," the lawyer noted. "Only the body was there; no evidence of actual violence in the surrounding area." He shook his head. "Nobody could do all that damage without making a real mess, for sure."

There was a short pause before Hank inquired, "Any clues as to the actual killing site?"

Doug Courtney answered that one, also. "Well, they did find traces of raw beef in the dog's mouth, so he was probably lured into the whole thing." He folded the paper in half as he continued. "The question is still 'where?'"

Max Duncan tugged at his gun belt. "Probably not too far. That's a pretty big dog, even if the body was in pieces." He looked around the room. "Had to be moved in a wagon, or piecemeal in a smaller carrier, or — most likely — a strong plastic bag."

Hank wondered, "Why not in a car or a truck?"

The sheriff looked straight at the man. "I think somebody may have heard the engine from that kind of vehicle. Right? Anyways. I'm betting it wasn't too far to the crime scene."

"Why not?" Rob asked.

"The killer had to work pretty fast. Remember, this happened sometime early in the morning, and the Spofford's dog discovered it when she went out for her morning sniff and pee. Otherwise, she would have found it before the Spoffords turned in the night before, and remember, they had been to the drive-in movie, so they came home pretty late." He stopped to hear what Doug Courtney had to say.

"I think," the man said slowly, "we have a highly motivated, cold-blooded killer here, and he probably worked hard and fast" The others waited for him to finish. "That means he probably made a mistake, maybe two. We just need to be patient."

"I only want to see justice," Ceese muttered, "and I'd like to know when that's going to happen."

"Ay-yuh, it will," Doug assured him, "but first, we need to find the scene of the crime."

***

"Nah-nah-nah, yer not goin' to give up so easily, lass. There's still plenty o' ways yeh can help me on this mission." Bernie was leading his sweat-suited wife out to the small grove of birches, just behind the barn. He was ready to implement Plan B. "Yeh can be my lookout."

"Are you remembering I still have a band aid on my belly button, for gawd's sake?"

He drew to a stop in front of the fattest tree trunk in the bunch. "Nah, but I mean, this won't even bother yer belly button. No crawlin', Del. Just hiding behind the trees and bushes."

"What for?" She pulled the drooping drawers up. "Who's watching you, anyway?"

He placed both hands on his hips, bending forward. "Way-yell now, we don't know that, now, do we?" There was an attempt to look very wise. "Yeh just can't be too careful, can yeh?"

This time, *her* hands went to the hips. "Careful about what, Bernie? Just answer me that one!"

"I told yeh, Del, I have a plan."

"That's what I'm afraid of, you old fool." She turned to head back to the house.

"No, wait, Del! It'll make us rich. Never have to work again. All our bills paid, and more!"

She hesitated. "So what are you talking about? What's the plan *this* time?"

"Yeh just have to hide behind the trees, Del. Trust me. That's all yeh have to do."

"Why?"

"To watch for spies."

She laughed. "What the heck are you talking about? We don't have any secret stuff going on."

"Yeh'd be surprised, Della." It was an amused smile. "Yeh'd be very, very surprised." He moved in closer, whispering. "We're talking a steady income, here, lass. A check in the mail every month." The smile continued. "And all yeh have to do, is watch for spies."

The petulant pout came into play. "Hmph! I'm not doing anything until you tell me all the details."

"Nah-nah-nah! I won't be doin' that, lass. Yeh just have to trust me." Plan B took him another fifteen minutes, but his wife finally found herself scrunched up behind the thickest trunk in the grove, hiding from the enemy, a bird whistle hanging from her pursed lips.

"Alright, lass, just tuck yer body tight against the tree and watch for movement in the forest."

"This is not a forest," she objected between clenched teeth.

"Just pretend, woman!" came the weary reply. "Now, here I am, down in the bushes and yeh're up there, hidin' behind the tree." He stopped, went silent, then slid down onto the leafy ground. "Uhm," he finally called out to her, "could yeh maybe suck it in a little? I'm seein' a bosom bump and a belly bump protrudin' from the trunk of yer tree."

She stifled a laugh. "So, what do you want me to do?"

"Uhm, try droppin' yer shoulders and squeezing back a ways." He watched as the bosom bump drooped down to touch the belly bump. "Uhm, so maybe yeh could move backwards a little more, Del."

"Like this?" The two front bumps slipped behind the tree, whereupon — to Bernie's great dismay — a butt bump emerged from behind the other side of the trunk.

Bernie rolled his eyes, knowing she couldn't see him do it. "So," he finally said, "could yeh maybe flatten yerself against the middle of the tree trunk, lassie?" When the shoulder and hip bumps emerged on both sides of the white birch column, he knew it was time to move on to Plan C. He would have to watch his own backside during this clandestine operation.

"So, I can see yer not comfortable doin' this lookout thing, Del. That's okay. That's really okay, because what I really, really need for yeh to do, is drive the car that takes me to and from this mission." He led her slowly back to the house, explaining how important it was for her to be there at the drop-off and the pick-up points. "And I know that yeh can do this, and do it very well, Del." He sat her down at the kitchen table and served up a Canadian stout. "Now then, lass, there's only one last thing I need for yeh to do: Call our friend up there in the village."

In a few minutes, Della was on the phone with Lenore.

After the usual courtesies, she got to the point: "So, I guess you know Bernie wants to get the hundred-dollar reward from that Cecil Thompson guy."

"The owner of the dog that was killed?"

"Yeah, that's the one. So Bernie has a plan to do some investigating on his own."

"Oh, really?" Lenore was surprised.

"Yeah, that's right. Around the whole area between the Thompson farm and the Spofford place. He says it will probably take a couple of days, but if we could maybe stay with you, it would cut down on the travel time." She cleared her throat. "I told him it wasn't practical, what with us having to bring Carmen along. We sure can't leave her here alone for two days."

"Oh my goodness, Della, of course you can stay. As a matter of fact, Mop would probably enjoy the company."

"Well, thanks, Lenore. That's real nice of you."

"So, will you be helping Bernie with this investigation?"

"Well, we tried a couple of ways, but they didn't work out." She suddenly felt rather important. "So, instead, I'll be driving the get-away car."

***

"How's our young charge doing? I'm assuming you've been keeping a pretty close watch on the situation," noted Johnny Courtney, nephew and law partner of Douglas Courtney.

Father Tom Ladue shifted his weight in the chair, glanced around at the busy interior of the home-style eatery generally referred to by the locals as Muncy's Diner. He leaned in closer to his long-time friend, and gave a guarded answer. "Laura Wilson's death hit him pretty darned hard. Well, hit the whole family pretty hard, as you can imagine. But instead of drawing together for strength, that group has shattered in umpteen directions." He waggled his head, sadly. "The father and son are at each other's throats, the son has broken up with his girlfriend, the farm is being run pretty much by Roy Dupree, and our boy, Joe, not only lost his job up there, but the relative security of a family atmosphere. It's a mess, and the youngster is reeling from it."

"Have you talked with Lenore?" Johnny asked.

"Just this morning, as a matter of fact." He pushed his coffee cup aside. "She says he's pretty depressed, but that Chief Robbie is getting him started on a paper route this week. Figures it will settle him down, having his own money again." He folded his arms over his edge of the table. "Still, it'll take more than that. He needs to meet the real Jesus. No more pretending to be 'all good with God,' if you get my drift."

"Got it." The young lawyer wiped his mouth with the paper napkin. "So," he approached the subject carefully, "what about this dog-killing, Tom? Think he's involved in that? I mean, most folks figured this was the animal that caused the accident. Has Joe talked about it?"

"He's getting counseling from the Collinses, so I would imagine that has come up. But he's not said anything to me or to Lenore about it. I don't know what to think."

"I heard Jessie and Jack are also getting counseling from Collinses; is that right?"

"Ay-yuh. Hopefully, all three of them — the Wilsons and Joe — will get to the real source of their troubles. As sad as losing Laura is, this could be a golden opportunity to get some souls saved, Johnny." He rose, placing his lunch money on the table for the waitress. The lawyer did the same, then followed his friend out onto the sidewalk.

"Just the guys I want to see," Sheriff Max Duncan called from behind them. As they turned to greet him, he went right into the business at hand. "Got a couple of questions for you two." He motioned to a bench across the five-way traffic circle. "Let's take a seat over there in front of the library." Upon arriving, the lawman motioned for the other two to be seated. He was clearly going to be in charge of this conversation.

"The reason why I wanted to talk to you fellows is, if I remember correctly, when we found the body of Dicky Dupree on the Turner property, you two were in charge of young Joe Turner's affairs. I think you, sir, were in charge of his finances, is that correct?" John Courtney acknowledged this fact with a short hum. "And you, Father Tom, were in charge of the boy's spiritual and/or social welfare."

"Pretty much. Although, the youngster is being monitored by Social Services, as though being in a foster home. Mrs. Curtis is sort of like his caretaker, but those folks refer to her as a foster mother." He looked at his friend. "Johnny can explain it to you; I'm not the lawyer, here."

"Right." The sheriff decided not to get into the details. "Regardless, you both know this kid and his background, and that's what I need to talk about, here." He slipped his arms behind and locked knuckles. "So, the kid is full-blooded Abenaki, isn't that right?" Both men agreed. "Okay, and so that ties in with some other information I've been working with, for some time." He studied the grass near his feet for a few seconds. "This dog that was killed, he belonged to the Thompsons. Interesting people, the Thompsons. The wife's uncle disappeared, on the very same night that cheerleader from the high school was murdered in their barn. You guys remember this whole thing?" The two men nodded again. "Well, it so happens that both Winnie Thompson and her uncle, Raymond René Smart were, or are, full-blooded Abenakis also."

Father Tom moved uneasily on the bench. "Where are you going with this, Sheriff?"

"I'm simply pointing out that, back then, somebody stuck a pitchfork into a cheerleader after she was already dead, and now, somebody has butchered a dog, which also happened to be already dead." He waited for it to settle in. "Pretty similar behavior, wouldn't you say? And," his hands came forward to slip into the front pockets of his uniform's trousers, "pretty damned *savage* behavior, wouldn't you say?"

The lawyer began to bristle. "So, are you telling us that those three Indians are somehow in cahoots, Sheriff?"

"Oh, I don't know that they're working together, Mr. Courtney. I'm merely pointing out the similarity in such raw brutality." His eyes narrowed. "There's a reason why American Indians are called 'savages,' gentlemen."

The priest rose suddenly. "I think this conversation is finished, Sheriff."

"Not quite, Father." He leaned in to speak just inches from the man's face. "There's something unfinished in the Thompson household, sir, and I intend to get to the bottom of it. The dog-killing is no big deal to me; it only opens up new opportunities to find out what happened with that pitchfork, and what happened to Mister Raymond René Smart."

"He died in Canada, and you know that," the clergyman firmly reminded him.

"Do I? Do I really know that?" He snorted. "I know these people. They slip into the woods and you never find them. I'm not at all sure that this native is dead. I never saw the body. Never got any paperwork. Nothing." He drew back to address the lawyer. "This case is still open, as far as I'm concerned." He wiped his hand across his forehead, then pulled the visor back into place. "It wouldn't surprise me if this kid did kill that dog; it's exactly how they would do it!"

John Courtney took to his feet. "I think you will find, Sheriff Duncan, that vicious killers come in all sizes, shapes, and colors. They're *all* savages."

"Right," the priest followed up, "and, unless you have solid evidence that any one of those three people killed that dog, I suggest you keep your opinion to yourself."

The sheriff smiled. "Sure. You're right. But just keep this one question in mind: Does each one of them have an alibi for the night this dog was slain?" He touched the brim of his hat and strode away.

The two friends stood looking at each other. Finally, Father Tom ventured a comment. "I never thought to ask if Joe had an alibi." He shoved his hands into his jacket pockets. "I know the Thompsons were having a hard time keeping Blow at home, but that dog was always like that." He shrugged off the thought that Winnie had attacked the mutt with the same pitchfork, while she was sleepwalking.

"We'll just clear this up with a little talk with Joe," Johnny said as he steered his friend back toward the rectory.

Father Thomas Ladue had little to say on the way; his mind was filled with questions about certain folks' possible motives for getting rid of Blow, and about Raymond René Smart — who may or may not still be alive.

CHAPTER SEVEN

Accidents

In the cool of the mid-September evening, Chief Robbie Allen pulled the squad car into his driveway. Before he even got out, he spotted her raking leaves at the edge of their property line. She looked up at the slam of his car door, paused to wave, then went back to the rhythmic swish of the task. He pretended to inspect something around the front bumper as he decided whether or not to say a friendly hello. When the swishing stopped again, he glanced her way.

"Did you lose something?" she called out.

"No, no, I was just checking for, um, whatever was making that noise."

"What noise?"

"Oh, whatever it was." He poked at something inside the chrome structure. "Oh, there it is. Just a little, old pebble," he grinned as he flipped a nonexistent rock to the ground." He paused to assess her situation. "Looks like you have your hands full, neighbor. That's a lot of leaves."

"Yes it is, and I hate to bring it up, but they're mostly from your trees, mister."

He approached her, checking out the facts. When he reached her side, he looked around. "You know what?" he addressed the lady with the rosy countenance, "I think you might actually be right."

"Thank you," she replied with a shake of her flaxen curls.

"I would feel real guilty about that, if I didn't know you

have a healthy, thirteen-year-old to pitch in," he teased.

A cloud passed over her cherubic face. "Ay-yuh, if I knew where he was right now."

"Really?" He watched her unzip the light jacket. "Is this unusual, or what?" he asked.

She flipped the pale blue garment to allow air inside, then wiped the moisture from her throat with the tips of her fingers. "It isn't, I mean, it's not..." She was struggling. He waited.

"I don't think he means to worry me." She fluffed the jacket again. "He's just a kid, you know. And the paper route has gone well, for the first week." Her voice was hopeful. "I know it will probably be a while before he gets over Laura's death, but right now he's so depressed."

"Makes you wonder, doesn't it?" He needed to handle this carefully. "How does a youngster with all that history of rejection and disappointment, get a handle on life again?" He let her think about it before he went on. "At what point does even the most noble, innocent soul, finally break?"

"What are you saying?" She bit her bottom lip to stop the sudden quiver.

"I don't know, Lenore. I don't know."

Something moved inside her; he had called her by her given name. She blinked and replied in the same spirit of intimacy.

"Why are you even asking that, Robbie?"

He wasn't ready for the "Robbie," either. It took a moment before he answered. "I, uh, can't help but wonder where he was when that dog was killed." He took a deep breath. "After all, I am the chief of police in this village. I need to look at all possibilities." He grimaced. "Part of my job that I don't like, sorry." He stole a sideways look at the beautiful woman beside him. "Again, sorry, but do you know where Joe was on the night Blow was killed?"

"What?!" She couldn't believe the question. "I... never even thought to ask such a thing."

"No bloody clothes or anything, right? We need to make

sure he's not a suspect, right? Just think about it: No bloody clothes, no wandering at night."

"No! Of course not! This is a twelve, thirteen — " Her words were interrupted by the skidding stop of Joe's bike at their front sidewalk. Relief filled the green eyes, and she smiled at the man. "So, there he is. All that worry for nothing. He's a good kid. He really is."

Robbie grunted, folded his arms, and turned his attention to the boy. "Hey, Mr. Turner. Where've you been? Your mom is working up a sweat, here." The voice was casual, but the police uniform spoke volumes.

"I was letting Mop take a swim," the boy explained as he steered his bicycle toward the two adults. Sure enough, a dripping-wet Mop was panting from the front basket.

"Oh, for the love of Mike, Joe, that dog will catch pneumonia!" She handed the rake to Robbie, and picked up the sloppy-wet animal. "Let me have him."

The chief of police stepped up to the boy, handing him the rake. "Here you go, son. I'll take your bike, so you can rake up a few leaves before the sun goes down.

Joe Turner stood there as the two headed for Lenore's backyard patio. "What?" he murmured. Then, suspecting he was already in enough trouble, he slowly turned around and started raking.

Lenore tethered Mop before she pulled off the jacket, and fluffed the pink cotton t-shirt for just a little more air. Then she grabbed a hand towel off one of the chairs, engulfing the happy dog in warm, gentle rubs. "You poor thing," she said tenderly. "What was that boy thinking? That brook is cold now; it's not like it's the middle of summer."

"You talking about Indian Brook?" He was steadying the bike, not sure where to put it, but not particularly wanting to stop watching her cuddle the dog, either.

"That's what he told me." She sat back on her haunches to answer him. "Oh. The bike goes over there against the garage. She watched him move the bike, out of the corner of her eye, still patting the damp little fellow wiggling in front of her.

When Rob came back to take his leave, she lifted one of Mop's paws and peered closely. "What is this?" She brushed some sand from the folds of the pads. "Is that going to cause a problem? I mean, sand is very abrasive." She lifted her eyes to him for an answer. "What do you think?"

"Let's have a look," he said, squatting down beside her to get a closer view of the dog's toes. He took the paw from her and moved a gentle finger along the creases. "Hmm. You should probably swish all four feet in warm water."

In a few minutes, he was balancing a pan of warm water from the kitchen sink to the patio. "Be careful, don't soil your uniform," she cautioned.

"No problem. I change to a new set tomorrow." He placed the pan down in front of the waggling dog.

"Are you sure?" she asked, "because he's probably going to splash something fierce."

"Let 'er rip!" The words were hardly out of his mouth, before the rambunctious pet was scratch-dancing around in the pan of warm water. Then, in a move of great affection, Mop leapt into Lenore's arms. The lady squealed and put the dog back into the water, but Mop went for the hug once again, whereupon, the pan of water went flying across the cement patio, and the woman was thoroughly doused.

"Oh dear," she declared, shaking out her sagging shirt, "I'm soaked to the skin."

He saw that and quickly averted his eyes. "Uh, where's that towel?" he muttered.

"Behind you," she answered.

He grabbed it and held it out to her, still keeping his head politely turned. "There you go."

Suddenly, Joe Turner was standing there. "What happened?" he asked, looking at the mess.

"Uh, Mop got a little affectionate." She stood up, tucking the towel into her neckline like a big napkin. "Help me clean this up, would you?"

In a few minutes, all was in order, except for the wet

clothing on the two adults. "Guess I'd better get this uniform to the cleaners first thing in the morning," the chief said.

"I'm so sorry," she almost whispered.

"No problem. A dog is a dog." He turned to the boy, hoping to lighten the conversation. "Right, Joe?"

"Yeah," the youngster replied.

"So, I hear your paper route is going well." Joe nodded. "That's great. But pretty soon, it's going to turn into winter, and I've been thinking about that." He laid a hand on the boy's shoulder. "I know where I can get a container that will keep your papers clean and dry. If you like, I can get that to you this week." He raised his brows. "Would you be interested in having something like that?"

"Yes, sir."

With that, Robbie said his goodnight, and hurried back across the property line. Once there, he made a beeline for the safety of his own "nice guy" territory.

But it was too late; a boundary had already been broken, by accident or not. It was like every wet t-shirt joke he'd ever heard in the men's locker room was now flashing through his head, and Lenore Curtis did not deserve such disrespect. Nevertheless, some things, once seen, are difficult to un-see.

Robbie Allen had a restless night.

***

The bright orange canvas bag kept the newspapers dry in the soft rain, but it filled the front basket of his bike, so Joe Turner had to let Mop just trot alongside throughout the whole delivery process. The route had been specially designed for the youngster, who rose at five each morning to get twenty deliveries done, all between Main Street and the north end of town, the last one being at the Spofford home. It was there that the trouble began, and it was because of the orange bag.

Up until that time, Mop was kept under control, snuggled in amongst the rolled-up papers in that basket. But now he was free to wander, stopping to do doggy things along the way, while still keeping up a safe distance from his master on the bike, crossing roads together and moving pretty much as a team for the whole time. About the third morning, however, the dog caught on to the new routine: The Spofford house was the last stop, where Joe would turn the bike around, lift Mop into the basket and pedal back home like a race car on an empty track. He had ridden before in that basket during these raceway antics, but now there was a slippery canvas bag underneath and the poor little animal could not get a foothold. That was something he no longer wanted to do. So, on that third morning, he dodged away from the hefting hand and made wide, wild circles on the Spofford's lawn. When Joe called him, he replied with a loud yap and stood still, watching to see if Joe would try to catch him, or maybe just head for home, letting the faithful pet follow at full speed. Either way, Mop was *not* getting into that basket. It was all that noise that brought Hank to the front door. Seeing what was happening, he called out to the newspaper boy, "Just head on home! He'll follow you. He knows who feeds him."

On the fourth morning, there was a repeat show, this time, with May coming to the front door. "Get that damned dog off our lawn, mister!"

"I'm trying," the boy yelled back. He suddenly remembered to just head home. Calling out, "Mop! C'mon!" he lunged the bicycle forward. A quick glance back over his shoulder revealed the little, shaggy dog digging in for a fast run, right behind.

So, on the fifth rainy morning, Joe knew exactly what to do. Only, by this time, it had all become a big game to the dog, who ran a circle in the yard, barking full-time. Joe turned the bike around and called for Mop to follow. He'd pedaled half a block, before he realized that the little guy was not following. That was the same moment May Spofford slammed out through the front door, a kitchen broom in hand. He called the dog again, but Mop thought he had a new playmate and went into circling mode, his hairy body flopping rapidly as it skimmed the wet ground. When she couldn't catch him, May swore and aimed the broom at a spot just in front of the animal. Mop yelped as it caught him on the nose.

"Mop! Get over here!" the boy shouted as he turned the bike and took off. This time the errant pet got the message. They could hear May still screaming threats, two blocks away.

That night, the paper delivery supervisor called to tell Joe that the dog could no longer accompany him on the route. So, the next morning Mop was tethered on the back patio. Joe completed his deliveries, but there was a surprise at the Spofford house. Mop was there, dragging the broken chain. He yapped a happy greeting.

"Oh no," the boy muttered. Then he called out in a soft voice, "Mop! Here, boy! Come on!" Mop crouched down, ready to run his circles, and let out a couple of loud yaps. Joe started to pedal away, hoping his dog would follow, but something was wrong. "The chain," he whispered. "It must be caught on something." He turned around to rescue the yapping creature, and sure enough, May came slamming out the door, livid.

"I told you to keep that damned dog off our property. Are you stupid or what?" When the boy grabbed the chain, she got the picture. "Oh, so you can't even control him at home, either. Well, that's going to cost you your job, kid."

And it did. Joe was allowed to finish the week, and when he got back home that final morning, drenched to the bone, he came in through the back door from the patio. "Ma'am, is Mop in here?"

"No. He's tethered out there on the patio."

"No, Ma'am, he's not."

"Did somebody let him loose, Joe?"

He went out and checked. "Nope. But the chain is broken again."

She came out to see for herself. "I see. Well, we'll just have to wait until he comes back on his own, and he will." She put a comforting hand on his glistening raincoat. "Wow! You're a wet mess. You need to change and get ready for school."

***

"I absolutely did not kill that dog," Jack Wilson told his counselors. "I hated it, because it killed my mother, that's true, but I didn't kill it. I did *not* kill it."

"That's not what I was saying," his father objected from the other side of Don's desk. "I just said you're probably on their list of suspects. That's different."

Don leaned forward, elbows on the desktop. "Right. That's different. You know, we should probably address what or who is actually to blame for this accident. I think once we do that, we can get over the blame-shifting or whatever."

"Good idea," Connie commented from her seat in the corner of the small office. "Let's start with Blow, the dog," she suggested. "Are we even sure that's what you saw, Jack? Could it have been another animal, like the coyote Hank Spofford has been harping about?"

The young man shrugged. "We're not even sure there *is* a coyote. But we do know that Blow had a long history of being a wanderer. Heck, he even wandered when he belonged to that family at the greenhouse, remember?" He folded his arms. "Nope, I'm not backing down on this one."

"Mmm," Don hummed. "So, what about the failure of the truck's transmission, or whatever it was? The fact is, the vehicle could have come to a sudden stop to avoid the animal, then started right up again to get off the track before the engine hit it."

"I suppose that would be my fault," Jack admitted. "I should have taken better care of my truck." His voice cracked. "But I never wanted to hurt my mother."

"By the same token," Connie noted, "neither did the dog."

"It was an accident, which brings up another point: Let's not forget about the buttonhole that hooked onto the door handle," Don said.

"If she had buttoned her coat, or not have worn that coat, she may very well have escaped unscathed; and you, as well," Connie added.

"I guess I forgot all about that," Jack replied.

It was Connie who turned the blame tactic around to something more noble. "May I remind you that you stayed in the truck, to try to get your mom loose and pull her out through your door? You were trying to *save* your mother, not kill her." She tapped her pencil lightly against the spiral notebook on her lap. "And we could go on about this, but the bottom line is, this was a whole set of circumstances where, if even *one* of them had not happened, we would still have our Laura."

There was a prolonged silence as they each pondered the list: No animal, no sudden stop. No transmission failure, no being trapped on the tracks. No buttonhole, no being hooked to the door handle.

Don finally brought the session to an end for the day. "So, we need to stop pointing fingers. It was an accident, and it happened even though you tried to prevent it at the last minute. We will never forget this tragedy, but we need to deal with it for what it really is — the perfect storm, if you will." Before they prayed, he looked straight at the heartbroken son. "Got that straight, Jack?"

"Knowing what it is, doesn't fix it," the young man retorted.

"Right. The thing is, during these sessions, we'll learn how to deal with it," Don reassured him.

"Well, I can tell you, part of it has been dealt with," Jack quickly replied. "At least that damned, frickin' dog is dead."

CHAPTER EIGHT

Discoveries

Two days after Mop disappeared, Bernie and Della McBain arrived at Lenore's place, to commence their investigation. While Della unpacked, Bernie drove their '45 Ford sedan up to Cecil Thompsons's farm, for an information update.

"Anythin' new, Mr. Thompson?"

"I don't think so. They haven't found the crime scene yet. And, we still have the same suspects: Jack Wilson, May Spofford, and maybe a couple of folks who were involved in the dog contest at the fair." He pulled a red-and-white bandana from his overalls bib pocket, then pulled off his rimless glasses. Shaking out the bandana, he let the investigator know there were some folks who even suspected Winnie. "Of course," he said as he wiped the lenses carefully, "I don't believe that for one minute. We loved that old dufus."

"Aye, of course yeh did." Bernie took a quick look at his notepad. "So, if it's all the same with yeh, sir, I'd like to start checkin' out the surroundin' land, and if it's alright with yeh, I'd like to begin here at yer farm and work my way south to the creamery."

"That's fine. But I have to tell you, the ASPCA team has already covered that area."

"I understand that, sir, but I have my own methods." He rose to leave. "I'll be startin' in the mornin', sir."

Because Mop had not yet returned home, Della decided to

bring the chihuahua, Carmen, along for the early morning ride. It was still raining lightly when she dropped Bernie off at the Thompsons' front yard. "Stay dry. I don't want you dying on me, you old goat."

He grinned as he said it: "Ah, them words of endearment."

The first thing he did, was to make note of where the ASPCA team had left a trail. He would, of course, go where they had not — at least at first. The reconnaissance expert adjusted his backpack and stepped out. The first area was around the farm, itself. When he found no evidence, he moved on to the long, narrow pasture between the Old Colchester Road and the new one, moving through areas on both sides of the railroad tracks, all the while, keeping his head and body down in order to escape notice by drivers or neighbors who might pass by. After all, this was to be *his* reward money. He wasn't sharing.

He moved along quickly, sharp eyes keeping a lookout for something unusual, so much so, that he barely missed the cow pie, slipping a bit to his left before regaining his balance. "Damn. I should have watched for that," he muttered. Still, his attention was focused on every blade of grass, every mud puddle, as he moved slowly along. The second cow pie sent him to his right knee. "Damn!" he muttered, again. But he still sought that elusive clue, something unusual, probably just a few feet ahead. Before he knew it, he had reached the creamery, lightly splattered in mud and manure. Della was standing outside the car, holding Carmen's leash.

"Oh man… oh, man…" She was saying over and over.

He wanted to get cleaned off. "Yeh got a towel or somethin'?"

"Oh man," she said, again.

"What?" He wasn't listening, brushing off the clothing.

"Um, I let Carmen out to go potty. I thought you would be a little longer. So, I let her out, and she went over there behind the loading ramp for this — what is it? A creamery or something?" She looked around, to get her bearings. "Yeah, this is where I'm supposed to meet you, right?"

"Aye, lass. And so yeh have. But what's the matter with yeh?"

"Oh, my gawd, mister… you have to see for yourself."

"What?"

"What Carmen found." She motioned for him to follow her, down the eroded loading ramp, and around to the back of the building. There, she pointed to a messy area of tall grasses. "Carmen found this, Bernie. Carmen found this."

"Stop!" he cautioned her. "Have yeh touched anything?"

"N-no. Just saw it, and grabbed Carmen and went back to the car."

In the next five minutes, Bernie McBain concluded that Blow had been lured to a piece of meat that had been nailed onto a wooden platform, killed by a blow to the head, and sliced by a sharp instrument, before being removed to the Spofford residence. He noted the overhang that had prevented the dissolution of blood in the whole area, even during the several rain storms that had taken place since the killing. He also measured the distance of a mere six feet where the ASPCA team had walked by, and missed it. "How could they have missed it?" he wondered. Then he noticed the blood again. "Somebody had to be covered with splatters. Somebody had to hide or destroy their clothes, and maybe even shoes."

Bernie made two phone calls as soon as he'd changed his clothes: one to Cecil Thompson, and one to Chief Rob Allen.

"I'll go take a look, get some photos, then I'd like to come over and talk with you," the chief said. Before leaving home, he called Douglas Courtney, the lawyer who was advising the ASPCA, who said he could be at Lenore's in an hour. Rob ended up joining the four of them — Lenore, Joe, and the McBains — for pot pies and salad, even though it meant waiting a little longer for that private conversation. The upside of it was, he got to enjoy the presence of his blonde hostess for a little while. When Douglas Courtney arrived, he had his nephew, John, with him. The four men strolled out to the back patio, and got down to business.

When Bernie finished filling in the other three, he scratched his head. "I have a couple of questions for yeh."

"Sure. Go ahead." Douglas encouraged him.

"What d'yeh think a person would do, to hide blood-covered clothes? I mean, it's not likely *this* killer is trained in this sort of thing, yeh know?"

Rob answered first. "Probably wouldn't burn them; that would attract attention." Johnny shifted his small frame. "More likely, hid them in a trash heap somewhere, or maybe buried them."

The older man nodded. "So, my other question is, which group joined the ASPCA team for that part of the search?"

"The Chittenden County Sheriff's Department," came Rob's reply. "Hard to believe Sheriff Max Duncan missed all that evidence." Suddenly he had an additional thought. *"Unless it was intentional."*

The conversation was pretty much over, so the three of them wandered back into the house. Joe stood up from where he had been waiting purposefully. "So, Uncle Johnny, what do you think about Mop coming up missing?"

The handsome fellow put both hands on the boy's shoulders. "I think it's far too soon to be worrying about that, Joe. He's probably found somebody who is feeding him. Probably somebody who has kids, and the kids want to keep him." He gave a reassuring double squeeze. "Don't be jumping to conclusions, okay? Dogs run away all the time, but they usually come back... sooner or later." He looked up and winked at Lenore. "Am I right, Ma'am?"

Her head bowed in agreement. "You're probably right, Uncle Johnny."

It came out of his mouth before he realized it. "Listen, Joe, I'm the chief of police in this village, and if Mop isn't home by tomorrow night, I will organize a search team and find that little rascal, one way or another." He stopped there, pinching his lips together.

Uncle Johnny smiled his surprise, then turned back to the

boy. "So, there you are, son. We've gotcha covered, okay?"

The boy seemed to be satisfied with this answer, and turned down the hallway toward his room. The Courtney men shook the chief's and Bernie's hands, and headed down the sidewalk to their car. Lenore followed along, as though to send off a couple of family members. Della McBain sidled up to where Rob was watching from the front window. They both noticed how, in the muted moonlight, Douglas waved and went around to the driver's side of the car, while Johnny reached for a hug and a kiss on Lenore's cheek before he slipped into the passenger seat.

"Oo-oo, look at that," Della crooned. "Don't they make a cute couple?"

"Uh, well, maybe." Robbie observed. "But he's a little short for her."

She chuckled. "Maybe so, but I can tell you, my Bernie is no Charles Atlas, but that doesn't mean he can't rock *my* world!"

He covered his goodnight with a phony laugh, before striding down the front sidewalk to thank Lenore for the meal, and the meeting place. She stood silently for a moment, still at the edge of the street. Then her head tilted to one side. "I was happy to do all that, Chief."

He wasn't used to this sudden tightness in his throat. His hand covered the soft cough, then dropped down behind his back to join the other one. "Sure. Good. That's really good of you."

"Thank you," she whispered. "You're always welcome to meet with, um, committees... or whatever." The moonlight flickered off her hair as she slowly nodded for emphasis. "And... um... yeah. Any time, as long as it doesn't interfere with my raising Joe. I'm sure you understand that, Robbie."

"Of course, of course, Lenore. I respect that. I..." There didn't seem to be anything else, so he tipped an imaginary hat and said, "Good night."

He only made it to four steps before spinning around to ask. "Uh, I just had a quick question for you, if you don't mind."

She had not moved, as though waiting for his inquiry. "Yes?"

He tried to make it a casual thing, prefacing the question with a small chuckle. "I was just wondering, uh, just so I don't misunderstand anything; what your relationship is with Joe's 'Uncle Johnny.'"

"Oh?" There was a slight tilt of the head, again.

"Yeah. From what I gather so far, it looks like Father Tom and John Courtney and you are like a team, all involved in raising the boy. Am I right?"

"You're exactly right, Mister Chief of Police," she teased. "But what brought this up, just now?"

He forced another chuckle. "Well, if you must know, Della McBain saw him give you a peck on the cheek." He shrugged. "Don't want to butt in, Lenore. Just thought I should be aware. After all, you are my neighbor, and I... *we* try to take care of, you know, the neighborhood."

"I see. I guess that's part of the job, for you." She glanced at the brass pinned to his uniform's shirt. "Well, I want you to know I really do appreciate the way *my neighbors* are watching out for me and Joe."

"Yeah, sure." He shuffled his feet. "So, I'll see you later." He was stopped by her soft giggle. "What?"

"It was only a peck on the cheek, Robbie Allen." Her smile told him his secret was out there in the open: She knew he was jealous, and she knew that he knew that she knew it. So he did the only manly thing he could think of: He acted like the chief of police.

"You just get your pretty little self into that house, young lady, before I arrest you for loitering!"

She laughed as she backed up, then hurried toward her front door. Before she went in, she gave him a little wave.

He didn't move. *"What the heck just happened, here?"*

***

The same day the McBains' dog, Carmen, discovered the crime site, Jessie Wilson was having another counseling session. "I'm glad Jack isn't here for this meeting," he told the Collinses. "I've had a lot of things to think about, and I'm not happy with some of the conclusions I keep coming to."

"Like what?" Don wanted to know.

"Oh man, I hope I'm wrong, but I keep seeing how my boy — " He tried to swallow the lump in his throat. "I keep seeing how he could have lost it, and maybe, just maybe, he really *did* kill Blow."

"Alright. So take us step-by-step through this line of reasoning, Jessie." Don folded his arms and waited.

"Well, for one thing, he can't, at this point, forgive himself for not keeping that truck properly serviced. The fact is, we do a lot of our own maintenance on our farm machinery; no wonder the kid thought he was doing it right. Ay-yuh, I blame myself for that attitude. He was only being a farmer, and farmers fix their own mechanical problems, you know?"

Don acknowledged this with a short jerk of his head.

"And then, I can just imagine how he's so mad at himself for not even stopping to let the train pass, like he knew he was supposed to. The engineer was blasting a warning, and Jack still felt like there was a lot of time, which there would have been, if this dog or whatever it was, hadn't shown up." He clenched his teeth. "So, he has a lot of bad feelings about his actions, you know? And, if that's not enough, he wakes up at night, trying — and failing — to pull his mother to safety." The man covered his eyes. "I can't stop seeing it, myself. I can't imagine the huge load of such a nightmare." His hands dropped to reveal the grief in those eyes. "I have to tell you, I don't know what *I* would do, if I was in his place. I honestly don't know." He wiped a calloused hand across his tear-stained face.

"So, you figure the chances are pretty good that Jack killed Blow." Don's arms remained folded.

"Ay-yuh. I guess so." He wiped his cheeks again. "But I hope I'm wrong."

Connie tapped her pencil on her notebook, getting Don's attention. "May I just make an observation, here?" Her husband's blink gave permission, so she took a deep breath and went for it. "When we ended the last session, we were all in agreement, it was an accident. 'A perfect storm,' I think you said, Don. So whatever happened to that conclusion? Are we now back to the blame game?" She looked directly at Jessie. "I'm also hearing a lot of self-blaming from you, sir. So what happened when you got back home?" Her eyebrows lifted. "Been listening to mean voices in your head?"

"What? What does that mean?" He wiped the end of his nose.

"Where are you getting these ideas, these thoughts that disturb you so much?"

He was confused. "I, I don't know. I'm just thinking about things, I guess."

"So, where do you think these things, these ideas, these accusations are coming from, Jessie?" She let him take a moment to think about it.

"Uh, I guess it's just that I have a guilty conscience. I guess that's what's bothering me."

"But, if these things happened by accident, why are you, or even your son, being blamed for what happened?" She tapped the pencil again. "An accident is an accident. That's how it is, Jessie. That's how this world operates."

"So, there's no hope? The love of my life is gone, and for no good reason? We just get shafted, and that's how it is?"

"It's a fallen world. We really don't have complete control over our lives," she said.

Now he was getting irritated. "You guys talked about that in my first session. But I have to admit, it went over my head. What's a 'fallen world,' anyway?"

She nodded to Don, who took up the gauntlet. "This world was created by God, and it was perfect, until Adam and Eve ate that forbidden fruit. Remember me saying something like that?" Jessie acknowledged this with another small shake of the shoulders. "Well, it happens to be true." Don unfolded his arms. "Once they disobeyed God, all of creation changed. We went from the peaceful reign of a loving Father, to the evil whims of the devil, himself."

"But I don't believe a devil even exists," the man stated.

"Well, he sure believes *you* exist." Don leaned toward the dairy farmer. "As a matter of fact, he loves it that you don't believe he's real; that way, he gets to torment and mislead you in all kinds of ways, and you don't have a clue — *not even a clue* — what's being done to you and your son."

Jessie snorted his rejection of that statement.

"Whoa! Are you saying that you don't want to protect yourself from the bad things in this world?" the counselor asked.

Another snort came forth. "I'm not buying the idea that there's a real devil, Don. Get used to it."

"Sure. I see what you mean. It's too complicated, because, if you admit there's a real devil, you'll have to admit there's a real God. But, do you know what's really scary? That you could be wrong, and that's the difference between hope and hopelessness, and even whether or not you end up in Heaven, or in Hell, for eternity! You need to see the reality of not only this earthly world, but a spiritual world, as well."

Jessie shook his head in disbelief. "Sorry, but I don't buy that, either."

Don took a big breath. "No. Look, we have to deal with the fact that we know there is good and there is evil — direct opposites. C'mon, Jessie, even a little kid knows there's bad behavior and good behavior, right?" There was another shrugging acknowledgment. "So, we need to talk about making choices, here." He buckled down to the real facts. "I recall telling you before, God doesn't want puppets. He wants folks who will choose to love Him, or not. It's something called 'free will,' and every human being on this planet has that — the choice to love God, or not."

"Okay, I know there is good and bad, but I don't believe

there is a God, or a devil, for that matter. People just... well, like you said, they just choose to do what they do." His head wobbled for emphasis. "But that doesn't mean there's a God, or a devil, not for one minute. I just don't believe that stuff."

"So there you go: At this very moment, you have used your free will to reject those facts." Don waited for him to absorb that. "You choose to ignore the *sources* of all good and bad, the reality of all hope and hopelessness." He threw his hands up. "So, where does that leave guys like you and Jack, after losing Laura?"

The dairyman then lifted his hands. "He made a couple of bad choices, and maybe one of them was to kill that dumb dog. Maybe." He drew a noisy breath through his clenched teeth. "I just can't stop thinking about the gun, you know?"

"But," Connie noted, "*you* also feel guilty about the accident and the dead dog." She scrunched her mouth, then went on: "Just why do you even think such thoughts? Wake up, my friend. Those are evil spirits telling you all those lies, about who's to blame. Don is right: You don't realize all that because you don't know the devil and his lying demons are real!" She tapped a little drumbeat on the tablet. "You sure you don't want to get a little reality, here, and maybe a little of the peace that comes with it?"

The conversation continued until, forty-five minutes later, when Don finished the session with a closing prayer. Afterwards, he looked up at Jessie. "I don't want you to leave here without any hope, Jessie. I want to reassure you that God is real, and He has a plan for your life, and your son's life, as well. You just can't see it, yet." His voice grew softer. "Are you sure you don't want to recognize the reality of God?"

"Hey, I don't want to hurt your feelings, you two, but... no, thank you."

***

The next morning, Bernie attempted to start his second day of investigating at the Wilson Dairy Farm, but Jessie met him at the back door, and told him to "Please leave us alone." The Scotchman took a quick glance around as he turned to leave, noting the large barn, the carriage house, the woodshed, and of course, the rusty water pump a few yards from where he now stood, at the back door. He proceeded down Old Colchester Road on foot, finally turning left onto a dirt road used by the Wilsons to reach their southern cornfields. He crouched down amongst the stubble long enough to be sure he had not been seen, then slinked farther along, to the very end of this work trail, where he came upon the family burial plots. The gate in the white picket fence was not locked, so he slipped inside to have a look. He counted five plots, including the one where Laura's body now lay. "Not much room left inside this fence," he whispered to himself. "Oh, I see. They must be doing the cremation thing, for that very reason. Her grave is much smaller."

He saw the movement before he heard the flutter of the crow gliding down out of the pale morning sky. It perched atop one of the pickets, then turned one yellow eye to observe him. The man felt a strange foreboding, a need to get away. "Yeh won't find any corncobs in here, yeh rascal," he snarled, as he hastened to exit the graveyard. Once outside, he chose to follow a path between the two rows right in front of him. A few feet along, however, he realized he was treading in the same path that the sheriff's department had chosen. Immediately, he began a crisscrossed pattern on that last cornfield, before the property ended at Indian Brook. It was past noon, and a lot warmer, when he finally heard the trickle of the little stream.

"Del will be waiting for me over at the creamery," he thought. He paused before heading in that direction. As he wiped his brow with a dusty hand, he took in the view of the quaint Spofford house just across the drizzle of water. "So, that's where they found the dog's body," he mused. Turning to the

right, he made a quick assessment of how all those body parts had been transported from behind the creamery, all the way over to that sloping location near the brook. "Had to be in a bag, I think. All at once. No tire tracks, but maybe dragging marks?" He made a mental note to ask the sheriff's team about that. Meantime, somewhere there had to be the rest of the evidence: bloody clothes, and probably a big, plastic bag of some sort. There had to be.

A shadow flickered across his eyes.

It was the crow again, circling and then landing on the other side of the brook, just a little to Bernie's left. Immediately, it was down near the water, strutting around, pecking at something. The man squinted. "Oh-oh," he muttered, "something dead over there. Maybe I should take a look."

He navigated the rocks above the rippling rivulets, moving more to his left as he crossed over, and coming at last to where the dead animal lay, half out of the water. The annoyed bird cawed loudly at him, then flapped away.

If he hadn't been in the doggy contest with his Carmen, he would not have recognized the shaggy body. A broken chain was wedged tightly between rocks, pulling the little head tightly into position for the death blow.

It was Mop.

CHAPTER NINE

Nightcrawlers

"The evidence seems to point heavily to May Spofford," Douglas Courtney pointed out. "She could have killed Blow at the creamery and hauled the body parts over in the gardening wagon, to make it look like she was being framed."

"But there were no wheel marks in the grass," Chief Rob reminded him, as he put a cup of coffee down on the conference table. The lawyer nodded his thanks. Sheriff Max Duncan did likewise as the chief served him a cup. Taking a seat at the table, which was located in one corner of his office, the Essex Junction chief of police continued: "And that load was too heavy *not* to leave tracks. But I do think it looks like somebody is trying to frame her, what with Mop's remains being placed on the Spofford property, even though the corpse was all the way back at the edge of the old dump site."

"Ay-yuh, it's not likely she would kill two dogs on her property," the sheriff said. But then he scratched his head. "'Course, we have to think twice, after the way she made all those threats and got the boy fired. Almost too coincidental, you know?"

The lawyer agreed the woman had an abrasive personality, making more enemies than friends. "But it all seems too pat — too planned — and she isn't that dumb."

"No, but she is capable of putting it all together, purposely making it look like she is being framed," Robbie conjectured. "Again, she's no dummy."

"Right," Douglas concurred, "but we should take a closer look at the facts. The evidence shows clearly it wasn't a blow to the head that killed the smaller dog. Because there have been two gruesome incidents in only a few weeks, the report got priority treatment. It came back this morning and it shows that Mop died by drowning. There was brook water in his lungs. Not sure where that actually happened, though."

"Could have been right there on that spot, because the animal was underwater and couldn't yelp," Max noted. "Nobody would have heard him, not even up in the house." He twisted the cup clockwise, just once. "What did they say the phony death blow was from?"

"No definite answer — just that it was a heavy, blunt instrument. This could be a mallet, or back side of an axe head," Courtney postulated.

"Or a heavy rock, right there in the water," Max suggested. "Let's not forget this crime scene is accessible by stepping stones from the cornfield side. Remember, also, this area is part of old dump site now buried under truckloads of dirt, so that the house might be built there. It was not nice grassy area, like the rest of the slope to the right. Whoever swung the instrument for the fake death blow must have been standing up there, just above the little mutt, and the blow was so violent, the person shook loose the hidden pot, slipping downward for several inches. All the team has to work with, is that tip of the toe imprint. Oh, and the pot, of course."

"I think we've all decided the pot is incidental to this case. It just made it easier for the attacker to slip as they delivered the blow to the dog's head."

The chief spoke up: "Regardless, it stands to reason the killer got splattered with blood, again. But probably only the shoes got blood on them, judging how the person was standing so high above the victim. And again, those had to be disposed of somehow," Rob added. "If we find those, we'll probably solve the case."

"No doubt about it," the lawyer said.

"Speaking of the search for those clothes, I understand our

amateur detective is staying over for yet another day at Mrs. Curtis's place, so he can do one more search." Max grumbled. "I think the McBains have been there almost four days now."

"I heard that," the chief stated. "By the way, did you ever come up with anything on that guy? You were going to do a background check."

"Nothing much, Chief. Just a reputation of being a dingbat who'll do just about anything to make a buck." He emitted his usual snort. "Trouble is, they're the ones who get away with stuff. Everybody thinks those folks are stupid."

"Speaking of getting away with stuff," Douglas said, "what about alibis for any of these suspects?"

"Well, Douglas, we can go down that list, if you like," Rob offered.

"Please, call me Doug. Douglas makes me feel like an old man," the fellow laughed. "But yes, let's give that list a quick look."

"May Spofford: We need to know that she was in bed with her husband all night on the date that Blow died. We haven't asked Hank about that. Also don't know where she was when Mop died. So, technically, no alibi for her." Rob looked up from the list to see if the other two agreed, before he moved on.

"Then we have the Wilson boy, Jack. Uh, a young man, really. He tried to shoot Blow, and Mop was there at the time, also. Then of course, he believes it was Blow who caused the death of his mother, Laura Wilson."

The lawyer held up a wait-a-minute pointer finger. "Sure. But what did he have against the smaller dog?"

Max huffed it out. "Nothing. Maybe he just wants to make sure May gets fingered as Blow's killer, to save his own skin." He took off his hat, placing it on the table. "What do you two think about that?"

Both men got a "maybe" look on their faces, then Robbie checked the list for the next name. "Oh yes. The Thompsons. But why would they want to kill their own dog?"

Sheriff Duncan sat up straight in his chair. "We might want

to take a closer look at those two, gentlemen." He turned to the lawyer. "Doug, I'm not sure you are familiar with what happened up there, a few years ago." He took a couple of minutes to relate the murder of a high school girl in the Thompson barn and then the disappearance of a farm hand into Canada. "He was later reported as being killed up there, but we've never had any evidence of that. And, it just so happens, he was Winnie Thompson's uncle." He twisted the cup clockwise, once more. "And when Mr. Thompson decided to investigate Blow's death, he aroused the ire of — guess who? — May Spofford." One more twist of the cup. "Those Thompsons sure are involved in a lot of crap."

This time, it was Rob who held up a staying hand. "But wasn't that all about Blow getting her show dog pregnant? My understanding was that she wanted them to pay her for loss of income." He turned to Doug. "She breeds the dog once a year, and this 'bastard' litter, as she calls it, is costing her a bundle."

Doug Courtney pursed his lips, thoughtfully. "Okay, so do the Thompsons even have motives to hurt these dogs?" Rob looked to Max for the answer, but there was none forthcoming. "And has anyone asked what these two were doing on the dates of these killings?" He observed the two men. "So I guess that would be the next step in this investigation, and we had better get on with it, gentlemen." He rose from the table and stretched. "Well, I'd better get over to Lenore's and pick up Johnny. He and Father Tom are attending to Joe's situation. He's so shocked, he's barely even talking."

A few minutes later, Robbie sat down at his desk. "Whoa... that was quite a meeting," he murmured. "Doug is really pulling this thing together." But the encouragement was suddenly overshadowed. At first, he thought it was because he wasn't happy about Johnny Courtney being over there at Lenore's again. But she had assured him that it was "only a peck on the cheek," so he dug a little deeper into this uneasiness. And then he put his finger on it: the list of suspects had not been fully checked out.

"I can't shake the idea that Sheriff Max Duncan has a couple of motives, too," he thought, *"but I'll just keep that to myself, for now."*

***

"Oh, no you don't, Bernie McBain! Your investigation is over. We need to get out of here. Somebody's killing dogs, and our Carmen could be next." She was near tears. "I just want to forget the whole thing and go home."

"Way-yell, of course yeh do, Del, and I can't say I blame yeh. Don't yeh think the same thought crossed *my* mind?" He wrapped his arms around her. "I don't want anything to happen to our little lass, either." He stroked his wife's back as he observed the chihuahua curled up on their guest bed. "But all I need is one more try. Surely, yeh can keep our Carmen close by yer side for another twenty-four hours or so. Yeh can do that, now, can't yeh?"

She sighed. "Well, maybe for just one more day." They slipped apart to let her find her tissue. "So, you going out right now?" She blew her nose. "You'd better, because it will be dark in a couple of hours."

"Nah, I'll be needing you to drive me up a little ways on the Old Colchester Road, as soon as it gets dark."

"What? You're going out snooping around at night?" She stuffed the paper hankie back into the pocket. "Are you crazy, or just plain stupid?"

"Take yer pick, Del; I just have a feelin' I'll find those bloody clothes, right up there on the Wilson farm." He grinned. "All yeh have to do, is keep checkin' the drop-off point once every hour. And no headlights."

She dropped him off at the farm road leading to the Wilson

cemetery, somewhere around eight in the evening, being careful to turn around and head back to the village. He went north through the upper cornfield, as far right from the road as possible, arriving at the dairy barn a few minutes later. There, he paused to make sure no one was around. A lone light bulb illuminated the wide farmyard between the barn and the old carriage house, where his sharp eye spotted a barn cat padding silently across toward the woodshed behind the house. The farmhouse, itself, displayed faint rims of light around the edges of dark shades on the upstairs windows. *"No lights coming from the downstairs, so they must be going to bed."*

He waited, sitting back on his haunches. Car lights flickered from the new Colchester Road, just past the slumbering Thompson household, backlighting the smooth line of the railroad tracks, then everything went dark again. *"Pretty damned cloudy,"* he thought. *"But then, it is November."* He glanced back to the Wilsons' upper windows, just as one of them blinked out. *"One down, one to g —"*

It must have been a commercial truck, because the flickering light behind the metal rail's horizon lasted much longer this time, exposing movement across the train track — as quick and effortless as it was — of a mysterious figure. "What the hell was that?" he whispered, keeping his keen eyes in the vicinity. And sure enough, in the cornfield below the track, betrayed by brief glimpses of movement in the shadows, this crouching form wove a serpentine dance toward the home of Cecil and Winnie Thompson. For a little while, Bernie contemplated what just happened there, until he noticed there were no more slits of light from the other upstairs window of the Wilson house. It was time to get to work.

He had four targets: the two barns, the woodshed, and the old water pump. Moving outside the globe of light in the barnyard, Bernie crept slowly behind the dairy barn, then around the back of the carriage house, checking carefully for any disturbed soil where bloody clothing might be buried.

Finally, he circled to the dark side of several cords of firewood, stacked within inches of a shingled roof. He stopped at this back entrance to the woodshed to plot his next move, and that's when, somewhere in the inky interior, there rose a low, raspy howl. He froze, trying to identify the animal that had him in its sights. Again, the howl warned of an attack.

"Aw, hell, it's that damned barn cat. Must be a tom, out to claim his territory." He grabbed the nearest piece of wood. Another growl revealed the direction of his challenger. Slowly, he lifted the wooden weapon, waving it in the air. Another low rumbling howl pinpointed the location. It took Bernie's loud hiss and the clack of wood hitting wood, to drive the tomcat away. But there had been a noise — one which might wake the Wilson men.

And so, he waited for another five minutes, watching for lights to come on, listening for steps descending stairs, for a back door to open. But it turned out that this little pause in his activities was a blessing in disguise, because he was squatted down against a stack of wood-chopping implements, right there inside the back entrance to the woodshed. He endured the discomfort of the instruments against his backside, as he waited to be safe, until it was apparent he had not, after all, awakened the Wilsons. At that point, he pulled a flashlight from his backpack, to inspect this stash of woodshed equipment. A couple of axes and a heavy stump-splitter maul leaned against the wall, towering over a couple of camper's hatchets, and, of all things, a collapsible, metal spade, lying flat on the ground. "What do we have here?" he whispered in delight. Careful not to leave fingerprints, he wrapped his wadded handkerchief around the handle and lifted it up into the glow of the flashlight. The square digging edge was shiny, showing recent usage. "So, I'll just have a little look-see across some of these chips under foot." He moved slowly, careful not to disturb the packed chip-and-sawdust floor. "*I prefer nobody suspects somebody's been snooping in their woodshed. Especially, not an animal killer,*" he thought. But at the end of the search,

Bernie had found not one single spot where the pressed floor appeared to be loosened in order to bury something. It then occurred to him that he'd probably not only found the shovel used to bury evidence, but — whoa! — the chopping weapon, itself. So he decided to confiscate the darned thing, and it folded down to fit nicely inside his generously sized backpack.

Still, he did not consider his investigation finished; there was yet the matter of the rusty hand pump out there in the yard. "Just in case the shovel doesn't work out," he muttered. "I need to check whether the metal watering tank has been moved recently." He stood at the front entrance of the woodshed, surveying the space between Old Colchester Road and the pump. When nothing seemed to be moving, he moved stealthily toward his goal, staying low in the shadows, where he could. He crawled the last six feet, where the outside light bulb at the house's back door shown upon the dry, cool dirt. Putting the pump between him and the road, he flicked the flashlight to peer at the edges of the old tank along the ground, first one side, then the other. They were deeply embedded into the dirt. Nobody had lifted that tank, probably in a very long time. He wouldn't find bloody evidence under that thing, for sure.

He lay there, not so much disappointed as he was relieved to eliminate one more piece of the puzzle. As he did this, the outline of the large silo attached to the dairy barn caught his eye. "Oh, hell, I forgot about that." For a moment, he considered checking it out as a possible hiding place for the blood-stained clothing, but then he remembered that the silage inside that storage area gave off a deadly gas. There was no way he would risk such a thing. The most he would do about the silo, is to alert the ASPCA's team. "Besides," he murmured again, "the killer would probably have choked to death, trying to hide stuff in that place."

Probably because he had one ear on the ground, he heard the crackling approach of a car coming toward the bend in the road that separated the two homesteads. "Oh no, Del! Yeh've come too far north! I told yeh to wait at the farm road between the cornfields." He rose to a crouch and waddled to the ditch at the side of the road. As he hovered to a stop behind the tall, brittle grasses, the tire noise increased, until it got so near, he positioned himself to make a dash for the door, as soon as she got close enough. One foot on the road side of the ditch, he leaned forward to judge the distance, and sure enough, there she came, with no headlights on, creeping slowly toward him. Bernie figured he had about ten seconds before Della was alongside. His body tightened up for the leap. Licking his lips, he glanced once more through the weeds, as the white vehicle approached.

"White?" He looked again. "White!"

The drop to his knees was painful. Still, he managed to peek through the veil of grass, just long enough to make out the lettering on the side of the passing vehicle: Chittenden County Sheriff's Department.

"What the hell is *that* all about?" he hissed. But he did not move until it disappeared over the railroad track. Then he made his way south, staying in the ditch, to meet Della at the farm road.

Meanwhile, someone had been watching all this, from the Thompsons' front parlor window.

CHAPTER TEN

Postulations

It was a Saturday morning stroll around St. Michaels College's empty football field, not far from their back yard. Don and Connie tugged their coats snuggly against the November breeze as they discussed the counseling session with the two Wilson men, conducted the evening before.

"Well, we've been through this many times," he reassured his wife. "It's pretty clear that neither one of them have the spiritual mindset to deal with Laura's death."

"I agree. Neither one wants to bring a real, compassionate God into the situation. No, this is more than just a spiritual battle. It's like there's a barrier, deliberately thrown up to stop us from making progress."

"Like what?"

She was almost apologetic. "It makes me wonder if, just possibly, one of *them* took revenge on Blow. I can't seem to forget what Jessie inferred." She shoved her ungloved hands deeply into her jacket pockets, and sought to make eye contact with her spouse. "Remember what he said at his last solo session, the one when Jack wasn't there?" She stopped him with a slight pull on his sleeve before attempting to quote the statement. "He said something like, 'I know we've been over the fact this was an accident, but I'm worried my boy has gone off the deep end. I can't stop thinking about the gun, you know?'"

"Ay-yuh. I did notice that." The impish mouth drew back

into a grimace. "Pretty condemning, for a loving father."

"That's right. Or maybe *Jessie* actually killed those dogs, and he's blaming..." It no sooner left her lips, when she regretted the accusation. "Oh no. I don't really believe that, and neither do you."

They resumed their walk in silence, turning back at the far end of the field. Overhead, gray clouds gathered, harbingers of the first snowfall of the season. The couple linked arms for the return stretch toward home.

"So, what do you think?" she asked, as they passed the fifty-yard mark.

"If we *did* follow that line of thought, that Jessie could have done all that," he said, "we'd have to wonder if maybe Jack figured out it was his dad who did away with Blow, and then he (Jack) killed Mop, to cover Jessie's tracks, and make Mrs. Spofford the chief suspect."

"But why May Spofford? What did she ever do to the Wilsons?" she wondered.

"Nothing that I know of," Don replied. "So, maybe it was just a way to hide what his father did. *Or* maybe one of them did the double slaughter, and the other one found out and is trying to cover for the guilty one. Either way, I'm thinking May was just a convenient, ornery scapegoat, or something."

They came to a standstill.

"Oh my," she murmured. "Maybe we're taking this too far. We don't have any proof that either one of them did any such thing, now, do we?"

"No, no," he said softly, as he guided her toward their sheltered patio, "but we can't dismiss Jack's fierce denials, again, last night! He made it very clear that he had not, mind you, *had not*, killed any dogs, even though he's never been actually charged with such a thing." He led her into the enclosure of their patio, where the wind could not reach her.

"Yes, I remember. He's been adamant all along. Maybe too much so." She frowned as she stepped inside to the warmth of the kitchen. "Not only is he mad that he's a suspect, but when we talked about God — *again* — he kept dismissing the reality of spiritual warfare — *again*. Remember?"

He helped her off with the jacket, hanging it on a hook there by the back door.

"And did you take note of how the two of them are still resisting the concept of 'free will'?" she went on, as she pushed the silvery bangs back off her forehead, "and then Jack started talking about some whole, new stuff, like not being a dairyman anymore, joining the Navy and traveling the world."

The man hung his coat beside hers before following her slowly into the living room.

She slipped into her favorite chair as she reminded him of something else. "There was another new and interesting thing he said last night: 'I avoid that railroad crossing like the plague. I take the new Colchester Road when I come into town.'" Her frown was still there. "That shows condemnation, so I'm thinking he's still carrying the guilt — "

"And that's why he's so bent on running away," he interrupted her.

"Only, he can't really run away," she concluded. "This thing will follow him for the rest of his life, unless he gives it all to Jesus."

"But he doesn't know that," the man pointed out.

"No, he doesn't," she agreed. "But let's remember that Laura prayed for them, and God the Father, has absolutely heard that petition, and He will honor it."

He smiled. "And that's how we know there is spiritual warfare over those two — Jack and Jessie — even as we speak." Suddenly, he checked his watch. "Our next client will be here any minute. Are we ready?"

She rose to visit the restroom before the arrival. When she came back out, she crept slowly down the stairs to where Don was already seated at the desk.

"So, Don, I just had another thought: What if it's an involved scheme cooked up by the two of them — I'm assuming one of them is guilty — where they build up a case showing Jack was mentally disturbed? After all, it was Jack who shot at the dog, which is a kind of proof he was unstable."

"And then?" He was listening carefully.

"What if they plan to have Jack confess, then throw himself on the mercy of the court, with the high possibility of getting off with a temporary insanity plea?"

He was disappointed. "I doubt it, babe. Does that sound like something Jessie Wilson would do?"

"Okay, you're right. Jessie has already lost his wife; does he want to lose his son, too?" She tilted her head. "*But*, what if he really knows Jack has actually — you know — gone off the deep end? Wouldn't he want to help his son?"

"Even so, confessing involves a high risk. Jack's life could be ruined, either way, crazy or not."

"Mmm, you're right about that, too."

"Besides, it sounds like the young man wants to run, not go to trial."

"It does. So, maybe we should stop making wild guesses. At this point, it's just too confusing." She blinked slowly. "I'm backing off for now, but, I do have to say, it's too bad they're coming at this whole thing from a worldly point of view. I mean, more spiritually minded folks are usually brought to their knees by such a mess, and then God takes care of it all — both their messes and their souls."

"Well, we sure want to see them both saved, babe, although — hopefully — not by such horrendous circumstances."

The front door's buzzer signaled the end of the discussion, but it would come up again, very soon.

***

That same Saturday morning, Bernie was convincing Della

to stay one more day.

"Are you out of your ever-loving mind?!" She drew her flannel bathrobe closed, reaching for the cord which would tie it tightly in place. "You shouldn't even be on that property, you old fool. And I have no desire to be the wife of a jailbird."

"I won't be doing that, Del. I'm real, real careful."

"Hmph! Like I believe that. You're not so spry as you think, slinking around in the cornfields. Somebody will catch you, sooner or later."

"Nah-nah-nah." He grinned. "Besides that, Mr. Thompson thinks it's okay. Now what d'yeh think of that?"

"I think it's not Mr. Thompson who has the gun; it's the Wilsons who could shoot your butt off."

He howled with laughter. "Way-yell," he finally said, "then yeh'll have two thousand in insurance money and the Canadian stout all to yerself!"

As usual, the lordly Scot got his way, hastening to lay out his plan for the upcoming night. "I've got this feeling, Del, those bloody clothes are hidden on that dairy property — not necessarily buried, but could be just hidden somewhere. And," he added, "there's that whole north cornfield I haven't checked out. So, we need to change our drop-off and pick-up place."

"Where's this north cornfield, anyway?" she asked nervously. "I don't know much about anything north of their house."

"It's really not north of the house; it's the field right in front of the house, between it and the railroad tracks." She still looked worried. "In fact, it's the one right across the road from the Thompsons' driveway," he reassured her. "It's the road that goes over the railroad tracks. Yeh remember it, don't yeh, lass?"

"Oh, yes. Now I know what you're talking about." She had a thought. "Okay, if you're just checking out that one field, it shouldn't take too long." There was one more thing. "So, where is our meeting place, then?"

"Yeh'll be right across the main road, on the other side of

the train tracks. Don't worry, I'll be showing yeh when yeh drop me off."

And he did. As their car approached the steep ramp to the rail crossing off the new Colchester Road, he drove partly onto it, then backed out to pull the car toward the village, parking it a few feet north of a row of dilapidated housing. She looked around while he adjusted the car as far off the road as possible. "What are those shacks?" she asked, as she drew Carmen closer.

"Doesn't matter. We're not botherin' anybody." He handed her the keys before he got out and reached into the back seat for his backpack. "Yeh just need to sit tight. Don't move. If the cops come by just say yeh got sleepy and pulled over for a quick nap, then go into the village and come back out. By that time I should be done, and waiting for yeh." She nodded in obedience. "Lock yer doors!" he cautioned over his shoulder.

Very shortly, Bernie was squatting down in the corner of the field near the crossing. He had not counted on it being so cloudy, or cold, for that matter. His eyes adjusted to the velvet as he drew gloves from his pocket. He was tucking the fingers snuggly when he finally got a clearer picture of the cornstalk stubbles. "Too bad I don't have more cover," he whispered to himself.

"Ay-yuh," a soft voice said behind him.

He turned so quickly, he couldn't defend himself, landing awkwardly on his behind.

The man, barely visible in the dark, held up two fists. "Don't get excited, you," he warned sternly, "if you want to keep living." He shook his long hair. "I got battle fatigue. You know what that is?" Bernie nodded instantly. "Good. Just sit still and tell me what goddim hail you think you're doing, you. This is private land."

Bernie's heart sank. "Oh, don't tell me, yer after the reward money, too."

The stranger dropped his fists. "You that Scotchman?"

"I... am." He was surprised.

"That's different." He motioned toward the field. "You

checkin' out this frickin cornfield?"

"Maybe."

"You should be, if you know what the hail you're doing." He snickered at Bernie's suspicious glance. "Aw, hail, I don't want no reward money, me. In fact, I'm going to tell where the frickin' hail you should be looking for evidence — that is, if there really *is* any." He went from his squat to bend on one knee, pointing to the north boundary line of the Wilson property. "Over there's where the original house was built. Most folks don't remember it. The goddim foundation is still there, and a goddim outhouse hole is somewhere outside of it. I guess if I was to check out a hiding place, those two would be my first choices." He shrugged. "Only thing is, you have to work in the daylight, right out in the open, otherwise those Wilsons would spot your flashlight moving in the dark, and those bastards shoot people." He went back to a squat. "Anyways, that's about all the goddim advice I can give you."

Bernie turned his full attention to the old homestead site, surveying it in his creative mind. "I bet yer right, mister. If somebody wanted to bury bloody clothes or whatever, in a place where everybody's forgotten about, why, that would be exactly where they would choose." He rubbed his chin. "So now, all I have to do, is find a legitimate reason to go diggin' around the place, and, of course, I'll have to start workin' from home." Another little rub of the chin. "I don't suppose yeh might have a little hint on what kind of excuse I could use for diggin' that place up, now, would yeh?" he asked, as he turned back to his advisor.

There was nobody there.

***

Just about a mile down the road from where Bernie had this mysterious encounter, May Spofford was working in her flower garden, thinning out daffodil bulbs. Aided by the glow of a yard light and a nearby streetlight, she dug her garden spade methodically along the edge of the dirt bed. Occasionally, the lady pulled a tool from a small wagon, in order to tackle something more precisely. Only yards away, a very pregnant Suzie, the black lab, lay gnawing on a fresh bone, oblivious to the chain that kept her from wandering. May's husband, Hank, sat grading papers on the screened porch across the yard from where the petite gardener was quietly working.

Suddenly, the dog's head jerked up, on high alert, eyes piercing the backyard shrubbery behind her. The low growl made May look up from the digging. Curious, but cautious because of the darkened bushes, the woman froze in place and waited. Still, she wasn't prepared for the ferocity of the attack that exploded from the hedge. The coyote was after the bone so quickly that Suzie hardly had time to wiggle her bulky body just enough to latch onto the thing and twist it away from the drooling snap of the wild animal's jaws. In an instant, the hunter clamped down on the top of Suzie's head, tearing at her ears with a snarling determination, setting May into action. She was across the yard on a dead run, pointed little shovel held high. Without pausing, she took one huge, arcing swing, smashing the weapon squarely on the middle of the attacker's matted back. The animal let loose, howling and writhing in pain, its back broken. For a few seconds, May let it suffer, but the agony was too much, even for a deadly enemy. The woman lifted the spade and brought the blade down, again and again, even when the noise stopped, and only her own dog was whining softly.

By this time, Hank had made it to the scene. He pulled her trembling body away from the bloody mess. "Stop! Stop it, May!"

She dropped the shovel, sobbing. "Suzie! Suzie's hurt." He could see the woman was dazed. Quickly removing the tether, he spoke sternly. "Take her inside and tend to her. I'll be in, in a minute."

As soon as May entered the house, he turned back to

survey the situation. And then it hit him: "Oh my gosh. So, that's how she did it…"

CHAPTER ELEVEN

Bereavement

Thanksgiving break brought the college kids back home to the village; Diana Bixby was one of them. She immediately linked up with her old high school buddies, Scottie and Penny, for a ski trip to Stowe. There had been a dusting of snow the night before the three pulled into the parking lot of the feed store, just a few blocks off the five corners. The Park Street parking area was nearly empty as they sloshed through the white slush toward the front entrance.

"So, what are we looking for?" she asked Penny.

"Chicken feed," the girl replied. "We need to drop it off at my aunt's place on the way to the mountain."

"She's an old lady," Scottie explained, "with no car. We do this all the time for her."

"Nice," Diana commented as she slipped past him into the old store.

A fragrant mixture of grains and leather welcomed the trio. Merchandise lined the long aisles in a comfortably haphazard display — bulging feed sacks stacked next to shiny metal pails and glistening five- and ten-gallon milk cans, while big aluminum funnels stood in a wobbly tower between an assortment of large, white containers of teat balm. Other rows featured more gadgets, stacks of drawers with smaller items, equine brushes, and some colorful horse blankets. Above all of that, powered by the overhead fan, harness parts, and other tack items dangled in happy freestyle twirls. Scottie spotted the chicken feed on the third aisle over and hefted it up onto one shoulder before teetering up toward the cash register's counter. It was there that the three of them ran into May Spofford. She was quick to make conversation. "You kids buying feed for your aunt, again?" When they confirmed this, she complimented them. "Nice to see young people helping out."

Penny, ever the pleasant, forthright young lady, smiled brightly. "Oh, Mrs. Spofford, have the puppies been born yet?"

May clutched her paper-bagged purchase to her chest. "Uh, yes, Penny, they have."

"Oh, I would love to see them. Puppies are so cute. Has anybody asked for one yet?"

"Not really. I'll just take them to the pound as soon as they're weaned." The friends hummed approval. "Well, yeah, I'm not happy, but even *I* wouldn't kill little ones, bastards or not." There was a triumphant glint in her eye. "Just remember this: Actions speak louder than words. I'm not the killer some people have made me out to be." Then, as she spun around to leave the store she called out, "But they're ugly as hell, kiddo!"

Scottie laughed, digging out the money to pay for the chicken feed. "Let's hit the slopes!" he said, as they headed out the door.

A tall young man was standing just outside the entrance, his back turned toward them. It appeared he was watching May Spofford hurrying to her car. The nervous lady glanced back at the fellow as she sped out of the parking lot. When he turned around to step aside for the three friends, Jack Wilson's face slowly paled.

"Oh, my goodness," Penny declared. "Jack! Hey, Jack, how nice to see you." She reached out for a quick hug.

"Hey, Penny..." He whispered, but he wasn't looking at her; his attention was on Diana's wide, blue eyes. Eyes filled with emotion. Eyes he had not seen for a long time.

"Nice to see you, man," Scottie called out from behind the sack of grain.

Jack's gaze did not move, but he answered politely. "Yeah. It's been a while."

To escape the awkward moment, Scottie wobbled theatrically under the feed sack. "Um, Penny, I need to get this thing into the trunk before I drop it." The two of them hurried off to their vehicle.

There was a short time of silence, while the connection moved from shock to heartache. Nevertheless, unspoken words passed between them, until the blue gaze began to shimmer.

"I've missed you," she finally murmured.

He blinked before looking down at his snowy boots. "Yeah. Well, it's been hard for all of us. My dad is still a mess."

Her eyes did not move, waiting for him to reconnect. "I could have stayed, I could have helped — somehow."

He shook his head, keeping it bowed low. "No, you needed to move on. It would have been stupid to stay."

"I would've liked to have made that decision, myself, Jack." His head was still lowered. "You sent me away, in no uncertain terms." She blinked the tears out onto her cheeks. "Told me to get out of your life."

Suddenly, his head jerked up and he was sneering. "And I meant it. I meant every damned word of it." When she sobbed, he dropped his attention back to his boots. "You might as well get used to it, Diana. We're done. Really done."

"But I don't understand what I did. What did I do to make you stop loving me?" The tears were flowing freely.

He seemed to summon strength by sucking in the cold air. "Damn it, can't you understand this? The Jack Wilson you knew is not here anymore. He's gone. He's dead, or might as well be." He bent closer, without looking into her eyes. "Get it together, will ya?" She could feel the heat of his breath. "Everything's changed. I'm not the same guy. I'm not staying on the farm. I'm joining the Navy, and I'll be gone before next spring." He pushed her aside, clearing his way into the store.

"Get over it, will ya?" he yelled. Then he was gone.

Scottie's small sedan hummed along toward the ski slopes of Stowe, Vermont. Their destination was just a few miles ahead when Diana spoke up. "I guess it's really over between Jack and me." The other two did not answer. "He's right, of course. The Jack I knew and loved, well, he no longer exits." Still no reaction from the couple in the front seat. "It makes me wonder, though, about those dog killings."

"Oh?" Scottie asked, "You knew about those?"

"Oh yes, my mom kept me up-to-date on that whole thing. She said they suspected Jack was involved." Her head rested back against the seat's top. "I have to wonder, you know, if maybe he *was* the one who did it — twice. I mean, that would be enough to change your whole life, doing something like that." She saw the look between the two of them. "So, what do you two think?" There were two shrugs, in unison. Diana Bixby finally faced the real question, all by herself, and she actually spoke it out loud: "Do you *really* think Jack could have done that to those two dogs?"

Silence engulfed the passengers as the little car powered through the snow. Stowe was just ahead.

***

A lot of people were asking questions after May Spofford killed the coyote, but none were as zeroed in on that, as Chief Rob Allen. *"She used a shovel to break its back, and then finished it off with chops to the throat. Who would have really believed someone so small could do something that horrific?"* He turned over in his bed. *"And yet, Hank says she was in 'fight or flight' mode — not at all like her usual assertive personality. That was what the sheriff's office and the ASPCA seemed to have accepted about the whole situation. Her husband said she was shaking and disoriented. Said he had to get her attention on taking care of the injured Suzie, before she could function again."* He sighed. *"Not like a vicious killer; more like a mother protecting her baby."* He punched his pillow before adjusting his head into its crevice. *"Still, she could have been in that mode when she killed Blow, and then Mop."* He lifted the covers and sat up. "She certainly had motives to kill both those dogs," he whispered to himself. Suddenly, his reasoning settled down to the bottom line. "Revenge. That's it. Revenge on Blow for impregnating her show dog, and revenge toward a stupid newspaper boy and his yapping dog, for waking up her household every single morning." He rose and visited the bathroom. When he finally settled back into bed, he was sure Mrs. Spofford was still on the list of suspects. Furthermore, if she was, indeed, guilty, May had done a lot more damage to a whole lot of people, than she would ever really know.

The next morning, Rob got a call before he even got in to work. Young Joe Turner had been taken to the Fanny Allen's emergency room, for treatment of severe cuttings on his arms. Rob got there before anybody else, to find Lenore quietly weeping. He was embracing her before he realized it, his face buried in the flaxen hair, holding her without talking. Finally finding his tongue, he whispered, "Hold on. Hold on, Lenore." He drew back, guiding her to a nearby chair, just before the nurse came out to ask the usual questions. The lawman stood aside, listening carefully as the shocked woman answered.

"Has this boy ever done this before?"

"I think maybe. In the Children's Home. But that was a long time ago."

"Do you have any records of these incidents?" The nurse poised her pen.

"No, I don't, but maybe Father Thomas, or maybe Johnny Courtney. They might have something about all that."

"And just who are they?" the nurse asked.

"They... they're in charge of his estate," she mumbled.

"What estate? Aren't you this boy's foster mother?"

"Yes, but not really. It's not really under the Social Services, but we are answerable to them. It's complicated."

"I don't understand," the nurse quipped, "either you are responsible for this child, or you are not."

Robbie stepped in. "Excuse me, but these are questions which Mrs. Curtis needs to have legal advice about answering." He flashed his badge. "I'm Rob Allen, Chief of Police in Essex Junction, and I'm notifying you that this lady has a right to legal representation before she answers any more questions." He tilted his head in a friendly manner. "I'm sure you understand the situation."

The nurse tucked her pen into a pocket. "Of course, Chief. I'm just doing my job."

"Of course," he echoed as he slipped his hands to his hips. "I think what needs to happen here, is that we get a report on the status of the patient." His brows raised. "How is he?"

The nurse rose to leave. "The doctor will be with you shortly," she said.

The waiting room door swung open for Gracie Allen's entrance. She went straight to Lenore, wrapping her arms around her. "Oh, honey," she whispered, "I'm so sorry, I'm so sorry." She moved away just enough to brush the hair from Lenore's brow. "What's the doctor saying?" The blonde head barely moved above the shrug. "Okay, nothing yet," Gracie concluded, handing the young woman a Kleenex.

"Thanks for coming, Mom." Rob gave her a quick hug, then motioned the women to be seated. "So. Right. Nothing yet." He tugged at the uniform's collar. "It may be a while." He took a seat next to Lenore. "Ed, the officer on duty, responded to your call, and he's got a report for me when I get back. Right now, my job is to fill in whatever details I can, from the doctor." He leaned forward to catch her eye. "So, Lenore, is there anything *you* need to tell me?"

She twisted the soft tissue in her hands as she answered. "Let's see, I went to see why he wasn't coming to breakfast, and when I knocked on the door, there was no answer, and so I opened it a little, and that's when I saw him lying in all that blood."

She dabbed at her eyes. "I guess he'd done all the cutting sometime in the night." Gracie gave her a comforting pat on the forearm. Lenore took a deep breath and went on. "I just freaked out. There was so much blood. I thought he had to be dead. I just started screaming at him, 'Get up! Get up! Joe, you have to get up!' But he didn't move and I thought he was dead, and I ran to the phone."

"You got our dispatcher, Lily, right?" he asked.

"Right. She said the ambulance was on the way, and so I dropped the phone and went back to Joe, thinking maybe I could fix a tourniquet or something. But," she wiped her nose as she spoke, "it was such a mess, I didn't know where to begin." Her voice was barely audible. "So, I just sat there and prayed and prayed, until I heard the pounding on the front door."

The doctor entered the room, eyes searching for the right person. "Are you folks with the patient, Joe Turner?"

All three acknowledged the question, but it was Robbie who spoke up, glancing at Lenore. "Mrs. Curtis is who you need to talk to."

The doctor noted the chief's uniform, then turned to Lenore. "You the woman who he calls 'Ma'am'?"

"Yes, sir." The full lips suddenly pinched into a thin line.

"Okay," he continued, as he collapsed into a chair just across from her. "Well, that's one lucky kid, ma'am, I can tell you that. He's lost so much blood, he should be dead." He shook the front of his white jacket, letting in air. "You must have been feeding him superfood, or something." There was a faint smile. "We need to finish giving him plasma for a couple of hours, but, if there's no infection of the wounds, and he doesn't pull out any plugs, we can probably get him back home in a couple of days." He leaned toward her. "But the kid needs some serious counseling. Do you hear me, ma'am? *Serious* help." He stood up slowly, weary from the struggle. "We'll be keeping a close watch on him for the next few hours. You might get to see him by this evening, okay?"

Lenore rose to face him squarely. "Should… should I stay here, just in case?"

"No. He's not going to die, ma'am. You can thank God for that."

"Yes, I can," she replied. "Yes, I certainly can."

Gracie followed Lenore home, where the two of them cleaned up Joe's bedroom. "Oh, look," she said to the older woman, "there are used flashbulbs on the dresser. Was somebody taking pictures?"

"Part of the police report; just a normal investigation, honey," Gracie assured her. "It will clear you of any accusations that might come up later… you know… like, from Social Services or whoever."

"Really?" Lenore was suddenly frightened.

"Oh, don't worry about it. It's just standard procedure, honey."

That evening, Gracie and Lenore got to see Joe. He was sitting up, talking quietly with his counselors, Don and Connie Collins. They moved back to let the two women give the boy a gentle hug. The visit was short, but important, for Joe saw clearly he had a place in Lenore's heart. His dark eyelashes flickered over the deep brown eyes as he spoke. "I'm sorry, Ma'am. I'm really sorry." She blinked back the tears and whispered, "Okay. We'll get through this, Joe."

On the way toward the front entrance, however, Lenore turned to the Collinses. "Did he tell you why he did this to himself, by any chance?"

Don caught Connie's quick glance, indicating caution, so he answered carefully. "That's probably something we need to talk about as soon as we can set up a session with him." He cleared his throat. "But, I'm curious, Lenore. Do you know anything about a 'blood brother'?"

She stood still. "Uh-huh, I remember something about — oh, my gosh! That's what he called his little buddy who got kidnapped and murdered. That put an end to that childhood vow."

"Do you remember who that little 'blood brother' was?"

Don inquired.

"Oh yes, I'll never forget it. His name was Dicky. Yeah. Dicky Dupree."

"Lenore," Gracie asked quickly, "was he related to the hired hand up the road at the Wilson Dairy Farm?" Her face clouded over. "Hmm, what's his name, again? Oh yeah, it's 'Roy,' or something like that."

Connie promptly came to the question. "You think there may be some connection to the killings, there?"

Don blinked slowly. "Oh brother, not another suspect. If we don't stop adding to that list, the authorities will end up questioning half the population of Chittenden County."

CHAPTER TWELVE

Hints

Robbie Allen did not visit the hospital that night. His day was consumed with unusually busy police work, in addition to filing his report on the cutting incident with young Joe Turner. He retired early to his bed, hoping to forget that most disturbing event of the day, but found himself re-living the feelings which had overwhelmed him in the waiting room, as he held Lenore Curtis in his arms.

"I really need to draw back from any personal involvement," he reminded himself.

But he couldn't get over the soft warmth of her body pressing against his, for support, for strength. Most alarming of all, he couldn't shake how fiercely he wanted to do just that. "Have to keep my cool. Keep things in perspective. Be the professional I've been all along." But the gentle churning down deep in his gut just would not go away.

He was staring from his bedroom window, strangely enchanted by the frosty gleam of Lenore's yard, when she and Gracie came home from the hospital. His mother's voice bid a cheery goodnight, right there in their driveway, and Lenore headed up the sidewalk toward her home. He watched her graceful walk all the way to the door, where she inserted the key, and then disappeared inside. "Oh, my god," he whispered. "I'm a goner, for sure, if I don't keep my distance." He sat down on the edge of the bed. Downstairs,

Gracie was rattling the tea kettle in the kitchen. It seemed the logical thing to do, since he couldn't sleep, so he ambled downstairs for a cup of chamomile tea with her.

She spoke across the kitchen table about the visit, especially about the "blood brother," Dicky Dupree. "Lenore says you can get more details from Father Tom and Johnny Courtney, but the gist of the story is that the boy was kidnapped and murdered by Joe's uncle, a man with the same name: Joe Turner. The Dupree boy's body was discovered on the Turner property." She blew on the steaming cup. "I can just imagine what that did to that poor youngster."

"So, that's the motive for cutting himself — the memory catching up with him, the loss of a 'blood brother,' or something along that line?"

"Don't know, son. Maybe." She took a sip. "Guess that's something you should talk over with the priest and the lawyer."

He sampled the hot beverage, and then the question just came out, surprising even himself. "I'm worried about Lenore; how is she holding up?"

"You know what, Robbie? She's a smart cookie, that one." Another sip. "And tougher than you might think."

"Really ? Why do you say that, Mom?"

"You should have seen how she tackled that mess in the kid's room. She was all business. You know, she could probably be a nurse." A longer sip. "When we finally got it all cleaned up, she stood in the doorway and I saw the tears finally come, and then she said, 'This will never happen again. I won't let it. Joe needs to have a chance for a normal, happy life.'"

He sat there for a moment, then drained the cup. "Ay-yuh, she would probably make a good nurse." He rose and moved toward the stairs.

"She's also compassionate; want to know how I know *that*?"

He waited, indulging her.

"On the way home tonight, she was asking how *you* were

doing."

"Oh yeah?" He hoped he sounded nonchalant.

"Oh yeah. But then, she asks about you *a lot.*"

"Oh yeah?"

"Ay-yuh." She lifted her cup. "I think she kinda likes you."

He pretended to scold her. "Aw, Mom... really?!"

But when he climbed into bed, it was as though someone had placed a warm blanket over his cold feet. He fell into a deep, sweet sleep.

***

Another conversation was taking place at that very same moment, about a mile up from the Allen home, on the Old Colchester Road. Sheriff Max Duncan caught up with Bernie McBain, who was squirming along on his stomach toward the old, abandoned Wilson homestead near the edge of that northernmost stubbly cornfield. Bernie and Della had driven up from South Burlington, to make a quick survey of the original home's location, and the Scotchman had neglected to allow for the light snow covering. His footprints led the sheriff to where this self-appointed investigator had just dropped down — right there at the edge of the deserted property — to become a belly-flopping snoop. For a few seconds, the lawman viewed the comical rotation of Bernie's behind, weaving its way high in the frosty air, as the old fellow grunted along. He took it as long as he could, then called out, "McBain, you old bastard, get up off that ground before you freeze something important."

The man hunched to a stop, then collapsed onto the frozen dirt. "Aw, crap," he muttered.

The sheriff approached slowly, since he had left Deputy Smith in the vehicle. "You armed, mister?"

Bernie flopped over onto his side. "'Course not. I don't work that way."

"I'd say you don't work, period — at least, not very well."

"How'd yeh find me?" Bernie wiggled into an awkward sit.

"Okay, in the first place, your wife said she was taking a nap back there in the car. She doesn't realize I know your car, your wife, and your business." Max motioned toward the old homestead. "You need to stay away from that property. Do you hear me, mister?" Seeing the doubt about the authority of that directive, the sheriff bore down. "Oh, I know about you contacting a surveyor at the town office."

"Oh, yeh do, do yeh?"

"I do. You forget this is a small town operation, Mr. McBain. That guy is my cousin."

"Aw, crap."

"Ay-yuh, it's 'Aw, crap,' for sure. But it gets a little more interesting. Seems you offered to hire him for a private job, checking out a deserted property line. Said you wanted to make sure it was still legal. Said you had a condition for him getting the job, though." He grinned. "Whatever made you think he would be willing to pass you off as his assistant?" The older man shrugged. "Ay-yuh. Bad move, Mr. McBain, asking a government employee to compromise his integrity, like that." He stepped a little closer. "I could arrest you for something like that, you know."

Della came crunching into sight, holding Carmen under one arm, with Deputy Smith right behind her. "Oh no! No-no-no," she panted. The sheriff's palm signaled her to stop. She did so, with an impatient stomp. "Don't you dare arrest that old coot. He's not bad; he's just stupid. I *told* him not to do this."

Bernie raised his hands to push away her presence. "Nah, Dell, don't…"

She turned to the deputy coming to a screeching halt behind her. "And I told *you* to stay in the car 'cause I could handle this myself." Whirling back around to address Max, she let loose on him, again. "This man is not mean. He's not a crook. He comes from good stock, from the Fart-quhar family — "

"*Farquhar*," Bernie whined.

"Don't interrupt — and I suppose you don't have any idea what that name means, now, do you, Sheriff? Well, it means 'nice guy.' That's right. And Bernie is a nice guy. Just stupid. Sometimes." She ended her speech with an emphatic bob of the head.

The two lawmen were momentarily baffled. Bernie covered his face with one hand and muttered "Aw, crap," once again.

Since the two officers seemed speechless, she took the opportunity to make yet another point: "I suppose you know that Bernie is working for Mr. Thompson, as a private investigator, no less. I doubt that he would be happy about you two getting in the way of his hired help." She moved the wriggling dog over under her other arm. "He happens to be very pleased with Bernie's work. I'll have you know that Bernie has actually found the murder weapon, and Mr. Thompson is turning it over to the lab people, to check for blood or something. *So*, I would be careful, if I was you."

Suddenly, she had their attention. Max glanced at Smith, then cleared his throat. "Oh really, Mr. McBain?" Both hands clasped the sloped gun belt. "You found the weapon that killed those dogs?"

"Aah, *crap*, Della. Yeh need to shut yer trap."

Max bent to help the old "nice guy" up. "Alright, get up off the ground before you catch pneumonia or something. We're going over to talk to Cecil Thompson."

Bernie rose, knees shaking from the cold. "Um, nope, Sheriff, we probably shouldn't do that."

"Why not, sir?"

"Um." There was a nervous chuckle. "Way-yell, it's like this: I haven't turned it over to him, yet."

"I see. So, where is it right now?" Max was all ears, but the Scot just pointed to the backpack resting against his own shoulders. "I see," the sheriff said again, "so I need for you to open that pack and show this thing you think is the weapon."

Bernie slowly slipped the thing off his back and dropped it to the ground, where he pulled a couple of straps loose and slipped the folded shovel out.

"Well, at least you were careful enough to wrap it. You didn't leave any of your own prints on it, did you?" Max didn't look up from the package to ask the question, so he didn't see the man shake his head no. "Huh? Did you?"

"Nope. It's clean as a whistle." He folded his arms and glared at Della, who didn't notice, because she had been proven right, and she was proud of it.

"My Bernie found that," she bragged. "Just you remember that, Sheriff."

Max finally looked up. "So, where did you find this, Mr. McBain?"

"Aw, yeh probably don't want to know that."

"Or maybe I really do. So," the sheriff tucked the bundled weapon under one arm, "where *did* you find this thing?"

"I, uh, *requisitioned* it, Sheriff." He winked at Max. "Like we used to do in the armed forces. It just showed up before I got the paperwork in."

"You stole the damned thing," Sheriff Duncan concluded.

"I wouldn't say that," came the reply.

Max Duncan looked down at his own boots. "Tell you what, Mr. McBain, you tell me what I need to know, or I'm going to have to arrest you for possession of stolen property, right here and now." He looked up at the old investigator. "You'll spend the night in jail, for sure."

"What?!" Della bristled at the notion. "Oh, for Pete's sake, Bernie, tell him." She had a second thought. "No. Never mind. *I'll* tell him" She turned to Max. "He found it in the Wilson's woodshed."

"Ach, nah-nah-nah!" He punched the backpack. "Yeh need to back off, woman!"

"Me? *I* should back off, you old goat? I'll tell you what, you should never have listened to that guy in the bushes. *That's* how we ended up here, tonight."

Another look was exchanged between the lawmen. Then Max moved in closer as he spoke to the Scotchman. "There was a man in the bushes?"

"Aw, hell." The fellow was cold and tired, and he just wanted to go home. "Some guy just appeared — like a ghost — right behind me."

"Where?" The sheriff motioned for his deputy to move closer, to hear the answer.

"Back there, near the train crossing, last time I was up here."

"When was that?" Max's face was like a stone statue in the pale moonlight.

"I don't know, for sure." He looked to Della. "Last week?" She hunched her shoulders and turned her nose up. After all, he had just told her to shut up, and so she was happy to accommodate him. He turned back to Max. "He told me the old homestead would probably be a good place to hide the bloody clothes."

"Of the dog-killer. I see." The two officers exchanged another look, and then Max shifted his weight to a more friendly, nonchalant posture. "So, could you tell me what this guy looked like?"

The old Scot sighed. "It was dark, but I could tell he was about my size, with long hair. Knew the property. Talked like a Frenchman." He paused, rubbing the chill off his arms. "Oh, yeah, he liked that I was working for Mr. Thompson." Then it hit him: "But it was like he just disappeared, yeh ken tha'? Yeh understand that?"

The sheriff stared at Bernie McBain for what seemed a long time, before he finally asked the last question: "Did he swear a lot?"

"*Sheriff!*" Deputy Smith dropped to his knees as he spoke. "Walker on the road."

"Get down," Max grunted, as he dropped to a squat. Bernie followed suit, signaling for Della to comply.

She panicked. "You *know* I can't squat!"

Bernie put a hushing finger to his mouth. "Just bend down behind me," he whispered.

The whole group — including the little dog — froze in

127

place, all eyes watching the lone, manly figure striding steadily toward the tracks. As he passed over the crossing and descended from sight, Max murmured the obvious: "It's just that hired hand at the dairy. What's his name, Smith?"

The small group rose to their feet as the man answered.

"I'm thinking it's Dupree. LeRoy Dupree, Sheriff. Lives in one of those shacks on the other side of the highway."

Max looked at Bernie. "He'll spot your car." He needed to make sure of the situation. "You *are* parked in the same spot as last week, right?"

Mr. McBain was surprised to know Sherriff Duncan had been aware of this fact, but he answered with an affirmative grunt. "You better have a good reason for parking there, folks, if the man starts asking questions," the sheriff threatened, as he glowered at the McBains. "Otherwise, I'll have to cite you for casing out the neighborhood for possible theft or vandalism, or whatever else I need to do, to keep my own nose clean." He zeroed in on Bernie. "You get my drift, mister?"

The self-styled snoop suddenly had his wits about him. This high-falutin' cop didn't want people to know he was on the Wilson property tonight, for whatever reason. Then it flashed before him — a picture of the Chittenden County Sheriff's Department vehicle, traveling with headlights off, past the Thompson house. The guy was on a clandestine hunt. "Oh, no problem, Sheriff. The takin' of a nap happens a lot, with older women. We've got yeh covered." He rose to the moment. "And don't bother yerself about being spotted here, tonight. Yeh're official presence will not be noticed by that poor, bedraggled walker, since yeh're parked too far up the highway, judgin' the direction Della came in from." He grinned underneath the little mustache. "Nah, as far as the rest of the world is concerned, the two of you were out on patrol over the last hour or so. As for the shovel, sir, you can have all the credit." He turned to Della. "Wouldn't you agree with that, lass?"

"My legs are like rubber. You guys do what you have to do," the beleaguered woman replied. They all move quietly out of the moonlight, into the safety of the shadows.

Meanwhile, across from the cornfield, Cecil and Winnie Thompson had been watching the whole drama from their darkened back porch. The part where the group froze into a *tableau vivant* — a "living picture" — was especially entertaining. After the cast of four actors and a dog scurried out of sight, he slipped his arm around her. "Looks like the first part of his plan is working, Win."

CHAPTER THIRTEEN

Secrets

It was not a happy Thanksgiving for Lenore Curtis. While she was relieved to get Joe home from the hospital, there would be no celebration, no dinner. The youngster went into his bed, bandaged and medicated, to begin the healing process. By the grace of God, he could be back in school in a couple of weeks. Meantime, Connie Collins would bring his homework, and the two women would help the boy keep up with his classmates. But Gracie showed up early that evening, with Rob toting a piping-hot meal for the weary "Ma'am."

"There's enough for two," Rob's mother noted, "but you can put Joe's portion in the fridge for a day or so, I guess."

"Oh, he's out for the next couple of days, I think," the grateful foster mom estimated.

"Okay, that's probably the reality," Gracie agreed, "but at least he'll know we were thinking about him." She glanced around. "Are you two okay, honey? Anything you need?"

"You know, Gracie, I'm really missing my mom right now. I mean, even Father Tom and Johnny are with family. I wish you could stay and have a bite with me, but of course, I realize you have a houseful over there." She smiled faintly. "Did Scottie join you, or go over to Penny's folks?"

Rob laughed. "Would you believe, he had *two* Thanksgiving dinners?"

She was suddenly aware of the heavy tray in his hands. "Oh my goodness, Rob." She motioned toward the kitchen.

"Let's put that thing down. Here," she said, "right under the clock."

Gracie did not follow them, heading instead for the front door. "Hey! You two figure it out. I have Scottie and Penny and my sister and her husband, and their two grown kids, to attend to." She opened the door. "Happy Thanksgiving, Lenore!"

He slid the dinner tray onto the tiled shelf, noting that the clock was in the belly of a white, plastic cat, whose tail moved back and forth to tick off the seconds. *"Cute, just like her,"* he thought, before turning to ask, "So, do you *even feel* like tasting all this?"

"Not really." The attractive "Ma'am" did that little head tilt, again, this time as an apology. Rob looked away, afraid she would see how much he liked the way she did that.

"Right. So, we can just put it in the refrigerator," he suggested, pretending to study the tray's contents in front of him. "Do you have Tupperware stuff like Mom, or do you just want to keep it wrapped in the foil?" He watched the cat's tail ticking, ticking, ticking, as it marked off Lenore's hesitant pause. Still, the hypnotic movement of the swinging pendulum helped very little, to keep his attention off the lovely blonde lady beside him.

"It *does* smell good," she said. Out of the corner of his eye, Rob saw her move closer to savor the aroma.

He glanced over to where she was standing near the shelf. "It does," he agreed, before quickly looking away. The clock ticked on for a few more seconds, as the silence in the room, in the whole house, turned electric. Here he was, alone with Lenore. It was probably not a good idea. "So," he said, in his police voice, "how do you want to handle this?" He lifted the end of the top foil wrapping, then spotted the refrigerator. In an instant, he was over there, checking the inside. "Yup, looks like you can fit it all in, just fine." In a one swift move, he was back, fiddling with the now-loosened top foil, as though he needed to find something. But that charade only worked for five swings of the plastic tail, before it was, once again, painfully quiet in the kitchen, except for the persistent "tick... tick... tick." Still, he kept his eyes on the dinner tray.

She finally broke the awkward silence. "Uh, Rob, you aren't looking at me, for some reason. Are you mad at me or something?"

"What? No, I'm not mad at you; it's just the opposite." He turned to answer her question and there were those lovely eyes, gazing right into his. "Oh my gosh, I just don't want to make you uncomfortable."

"Should I be?"

"I don't know. Maybe. Probably. You're so... pretty." He gulped, wishing he hadn't said that. But then, he saw something so vulnerable, so tender, coming from the very soul of Lenore Curtis, that his *own* inner being crumbled, removing all defenses.

Suddenly, there were no more secrets.

She didn't blink, didn't break that contact, speaking as though addressing someone else in the room. "I'll let all that food cool down just a tad, and then I'll wrap it up and get it refrigerated."

He heard himself say it: "Okay. Sounds like a plan. So, I'll just be on my way." But he couldn't ignore the message coming from those gorgeous green eyes. The clock's rhythmic beat now filled his head, pounding all the way down into his chest. "I'm so sorry. I didn't mean to —" When he saw the tears brimming, he whispered, "Are you crying?" He moved closer. "Why are you crying, Lenore?"

"Robert Ethan Allen, don't you know?" The velvet lashes flickered, releasing little, shiny streams over those glowing, pink cheeks. "You must know by now, Robbie, you're the only man I know who can make me blush, right down to my toes."

It took a couple of seconds before he realized this was the permission he'd been waiting for. Heat flashed through his whole body. "Oh... my... gawd," he murmured, as he reached for her.

There was a piercing cry, then a gurgling and hacking from

Joe's bedroom. They found him hanging over the side of the bed, throwing up onto the small area rug below. It took half an hour to clean up the mess, and longer to confer with the doctor.

"It's the damned medicine," Robbie concluded. "They're saying just no more pain meds until morning. By then, they'll have a new prescription at the drug store." He wiped the vomit from his shirtsleeves, then checked his watch. "I should get back to the house."

"Yes, you need to do that." She brushed a blonde curl back from her face. "Listen, Robbie, thanks so much for your help, and everything." He felt the tug down deep in his belly, as she continued: "I want to give you a hug, but I smell like puke."

"That makes two of us." There was a quick bow of the head; when he looked up at her, his smile was almost shy. "But tell me this, Lenore Tanner Curtis: Even though I stink to high heaven, do I still make you blush right down to your toes?"

"Ab-so-lute-ly," she purred, "that's never going to change."

He stood there, enjoying the moment, before he took his leave. Halfway down the sidewalk, he took a quick look back, over his shoulder.

Sure enough, she was watching him from the front window. He stopped. Everything in his being longed to go back to be with her.

But there was this other matter: They both stank.

When he entered the house, everybody held their noses. "That poor guy is upchucking his guts out," he informed them, as he headed for the shower. It wasn't until everybody had left, and he was crawling into bed, that he got the full impact of what had taken place at Lenore's house. "Nothing indecent, nothing immoral," he whispered. He pulled the blanket up under his chin, knowing that his reputation was intact, and Lenore's, as well. They were both still persons of integrity and respectability, and he had his whole family to prove it.

He was sure glad that kid had puked.

***

At nine o'clock the next morning, the Collinses arrived at Lenore's place, bringing the new prescription with them.

"Thanks for picking that up," she said, ushering the couple into the living room. "I'll give him a dose right now. It will be a few minutes before you can start your session, though, so I fixed coffee and homemade coffee cake. Please help yourselves." A few minutes later, Don hefted a couple of kitchen chairs into Joe's bedroom, since the new medicine would make the boy drowsy. "Better safe than sorry," Connie remarked. "The last thing we need is for you to fall on those arms."

Joe leaned back onto his plumped pillows, bandaged limbs carefully placed on his lap.

"The pain will slack off in a few minutes," Ma'am told him. She moved toward the door, but Don waved her back.

"We're needing you to stick with us, this time, Lenore." He motioned toward a chair in front of the boy's desk. "Have a seat." As she did that, the man uttered a prayer, then turned to the lad. "So. What do you have to say about all this, mister?"

Joe looked up in surprise. "What?"

"What do you have to say for yourself? You just almost *killed* yourself, upset a whole *bunch* of people, and racked up *who-knows-how-much* in hospital bills that *somebody* has to find the money to *pay*." He folded his arms. "You'd better have one heck of an excuse for all this." Lenore started to object, but was stilled by a stern look from Connie. "Well?" Don demanded.

The boy dropped his chin to his chest. "I... I don't know," he murmured.

"What do you mean, you don't know? Was this just some kind of a whim? Like, a fun thing to do on a Monday night?"

Joe Turner shrugged, keeping his chin low.

"Oh no, we're not playing *that* game, young man. You don't get to do the 'slouch and pout' with *me* — I won't stand for it. You need to give us some answers, or you will pay the consequences for this whole mess, do you hear me loud and clear?"

The chin began to quiver, as he raised his eyes to plead with Lenore. The foster mom glanced at Connie, who gave her that same hard look, so she bowed her blonde head in obedience.

"We're waiting," Don droned.

The nostrils flared as he looked sideways at his inquisitor. "I don't have to tell you anything. You can't make me."

Don leaned forward, switching to his teaching voice. "You know, Mr. Turner, I don't think you understand the situation, here. What you have done is stuff that crazy people do. Right. That's what I said." He nodded toward Connie. "Now, my wife and I are your counselors, and we have the authority to declare you mentally unstable, to turn you over to the authorities for further evaluation in — guess where? In a *mental institution*. Now," he continued to explain, as he leaned back and folded his hands over his tummy, "these evaluations take weeks and sometimes months, to complete. In the meantime, you are under lock and key. You don't have pizza and pop for lunch, you don't get to ride your bike, you don't get to choose your own TV program. Why, you don't even get to go to the bathroom by yourself." He paused before emphasizing it. "They stand right there and wait 'til you're done and then they'll help you wipe your butt, if they have to."

"You aren't going to do that. You're supposed to be godly. You're supposed to be kind," came the smug reply.

Don laughed softly. "And so I am. I am going to stop you from hurting yourself and all those other people, because that is the kind, godly thing to do." He squared his shoulders.

"What I am *not* going to do, is let you drag this thing out through umpteen counseling sessions, while you enjoy the limelight, and then, when you get bored, or *we* give up on you, you do the same 'attempted suicide' thing, all over again." He shook his head. "Nope, not gonna happen, Joe. You get this thing out in the open right now, or you'll be in the Waterbury facility by the end of this week." He crossed his arms, again. "Your choice: Tell us what's going on, right now, or its toilets with no doors and a paid audience, day after day, week after week."

It only took an hour. It turned out that the boy had been labeled as a "Wild Indian" by one of the housemothers at the Children's Home. When he made the pact to belong to a real, live person, Dicky Dupree, he realized his first feelings of fitting in. Further, Dicky loved pretending to be one of those hooting, dancing characters portrayed in various western comic books and movies, right along with him. It was like having a fellow warrior — fun and affirming, at the same time. But when his blood brother was murdered, there was no longer an intimate link with anybody or anything. He was a floater, looking for some place or someone to belong to.

"Is that why you call me 'Ma'am,' instead of 'Mom'?"

"Do I have yellow hair, Ma'am?"

"Did I ever make fun of that, Joe?"

"No, Ma'am. I just didn't have yellow hair."

"But, what about Father Tom?" she asked. "He loves you so much."

"I don't have red hair and freckles, either. And I don't look anything like Uncle Johnny, that's for sure." Suddenly, there was a tear at the end of his tan nose.

When the session was over, Connie could hardly get her husband out to the car, fast enough. "Okay!" she was saying, before he even turned the key in the ignition, "So now we know!"

"What do we know?"

"The first cutting incident was after Dicky Dupree got kidnapped, and Joe felt abandoned. Am I right?"

"Ay-yuh."

"So, this second incident is a repeat: Joe's attachment to the Wilsons was cut short when Laura was killed. It just took him a little longer to act out."

"Uh, well, maybe." He started the engine.

"So, I don't know how we just kind of skipped over that fact, in that one session where I asked him if he was mad because he had lost his new family. Remember that?"

He checked for traffic and pulled out onto the street. "I do remember that, and he just blew it off."

"Well, we shouldn't let him do that, again. He's Abenaki, and he needs to get reconnected to that identity, Don."

"What, with all that Indian totem pole worship?"

She laughed heartily. "Oh my goodness, I can't believe you *said* that."

"Sorry. I'm just not up-to-snuff on those particular details, I guess."

"You can say that, again. But never mind, the real point I'm trying to make is that boy is Abenaki, and he needs to have an Abenaki family."

"And just how do you think you're going to bring that little miracle into reality?"

"Oh, I might know of one possibility." She smiled. "But I'm not going to tell you just yet. Let's wait and see what God will do."

***

"I can't believe you're still thinking of going back up there," Della McBain told her husband.

Bernie was on his third Canadian stout. "Way-yell, yeh just don't ken yer husband, lass!"

"Don't use your sexy Scottish brogue on *me*, mister. I'm not 'ken-ing' anything about my husband that's going to land him in the clinker." She wiped the foam off the top of his bottle.

"Besides, the sheriff knows what you're up to, and he'll be three steps ahead of you."

He wiggled his mustache with glee. "Nah-nah-nah, Del. Thank God, the man's got no clue..."

CHAPTER FOURTEEN

Suspects

Hank Spofford looked across the living room at his wife, who was on the sofa, reading the newspaper. Once again, he found himself dealing with the incredible notion that she was a killer. But he knew what he had witnessed; the desperate effort to save her show dog, Suzie, went far beyond anything he thought this little woman could ever do. *"She turned into someone I didn't know,"* he thought.

May rattled the paper, peeking over the top. "Whoa! That's interesting. Looks like Sheriff Duncan is running for a third term."

"Oh yeah? What's so surprising about that?" he wondered.

"That's not the part that's interesting. It's the fact that Deputy Smith is running against him."

"No kidding? But they're still working as a team. That's odd."

"Not really. It's Duncan's way of keeping the reins, even if he loses the election. So, it's all for show. Got to have an opponent, or it's not a real democracy. That deputy is Max Duncan's biggest bootlicker." She looked up at the clock, and yelled, "You girls get down here! It's time to be off to school." When she got no response, she rose to check on what was going on upstairs, but as she left the room, she gave her husband a bit of a shove, also. "I know you don't have to go in until later, Hank, but you need to shower and shave pretty soon."

"Got it under control," he replied. For a few minutes more, however, he returned to the matter of her killing that coyote. He had seen what she could do, and that brought a terrible dread that she could have done the same to Blow, and certainly to the little mutt, Mop. And, although the idea was completely repugnant, he knew he could not swear that May had been in bed, asleep by his side, during either one of those killings. Now, worry churned his gut, day after day. But he still didn't know what to do about it, didn't know how to answer the questions from the investigating team — and that was most certainly coming up, any day now.

Suddenly, the older daughter, Bella May, came bounding into the room. She turned her blue eyes toward the father she resembled. "Daddy, I don't know what to do."

"About what, princess?"

"About what Sylvia keeps saying about Mama."

"Who's Sylvia? One of your classmates?"

"Yes. She's a snot."

"Don't say 'snot'; it's very unbecoming for a young lady to use that kind of language."

"Okay, but she still is."

"Why do you say that?"

"She says her mom and dad told her that Mama is a dog-killer." Her face clouded over. "Is she, Daddy?" May was honking the car horn, but Bella wanted an answer. "Is she, Daddy?"

He coughed. "Of course not, and anybody who says that is asking for trouble." He reached over to pat her on the head. "You just tell Sylvia that if her folks don't stop spreading rumors, I'm going to sue the hell out of them."

Her eyes widened. "I'm not supposed to say 'hell,' Daddy."

"Right. But you have my permission to say it, loud and clear, to Sylvia. But only once. You got that?"

There was an unladylike smirk. "Yes, sir," she called out, as she headed for the car.

He leaned back in his chair, stomach churning. "Aw, hell... aw, hell... aw, hell..."

***

The clock over the intake desk at the Essex Junction police department's office indicated, at eleven o'clock, that lunch hour was coming up for Rob. It had been a busy morning, though not the usual hang-dog atmosphere that came with angry ticketed citizens and domestic disturbances. Life had taken on a new meaning for this thirty-something fellow, and her name was Lenore. He decided to call her before his left for his eleven-thirty barber shop appointment. The phone booth outside the post office provided more privacy, but he still glanced around before stepping in and drawing the door closed.

"Hello?"

He smiled at the sound of her voice. "Hey! Just checking in with you. How's our young patient this morning?"

She laughed softly. "The Collinses just left. It was an eventful session, which I got to be part of, this time."

"Oh, really? What happened?"

"It's kind of a long story. Maybe you could find some time for a cup of coffee."

"I would be happy to do that." He grinned. "I have to go get a haircut, so this call has to be short and sweet." The grin got wider. "Or maybe I should say, 'abbreviated.' I sure don't want to make you uncomfortable." He heard the chuckle. "So," he murmured, "are you blushing?"

"Oh, my goodness! How could you tell?" A quick breath. "I think I need to hang up now."

He was surprised to see Father Joseph Levi, the Jew who was a Catholic priest, occupying the one chair in the shop. Charlie, the barber, looked up. "Almost finished," he reassured the policeman.

Father Joe spotted the chief out of the corner of his eye. "Hey there, young fella! How's it going?"

"Going well, thanks. And you?"

"I'm covered, thank God." He looked at Rob's reflection in the mirror that filled the wall in front of the chair. "I've been wondering how you fellows have been doing with the investigation of those dog deaths. Got anything new, yet?"

"It's moving along," Rob replied, hanging his hat on the rack near the door.

"I suppose you can't really comment on an ongoing case," the priest ventured, "but this village is mighty upset by the whole thing. People are suspicious of each other, you know?" Charlie brushed the man's ears and neck. "I feel sorry for that teacher and his wife, over there by the railroad tracks." He sat still, letting the barber slip the cape off. "They seem to be bearing the brunt of all the speculation."

"It seems like it," Rob agreed.

"Of course," Father Joe continued as he moved out of the chair, "you fellows can't talk about it, but if you ask me, there are some individuals I would be checking out, if I were you." He handed Charlie a five-dollar bill. "But you're probably already doing that." He reached out to shake the chief's hand. "Just want you to know we still appreciate all your work."

Rob had time to think about that, while Charlie combed and clipped and buzzed through light conversation about the weather and the cost of gasoline over there in Burlington. "Outrageous," the man concluded, as he shook Rob's hair off the cape.

Outside, the lawman made a couple of decisions: First, he would determine whether Hank could confirm May's whereabouts on the days the two dogs were killed. That would be followed by checking alibis for both the Thompsons and the Wilsons. Then second, he would ask for a private meeting with Douglas Courtney, the ASPCA legal advisor. This thing had gone on too long, and if the Chittenden County sheriff wasn't getting this investigation on track, the police chief of the village of Essex Junction *would*.

He got lucky, spotting Hank Spofford just getting into his car, right there at his house. May's car was nowhere in sight.

It was the perfect opportunity. Hank's face paled when the squad car blocked his exit from the driveway. He swallowed hard as Robbie approached the car window. "What's up, Chief?"

"Got a quick question for you, Hank. Just need a 'yes' or 'no' answer, okay?" He purposefully folded his hands behind his back, careful not to appear aggressive. "I hate to ask it, but I have to know — or, I should say, the investigating team needs to know — does May have an alibi for the hours those dogs died?" He glanced at his own boots, then back toward the man. "Can you, yourself, vouch for her?" When he saw the former submariner's face turn red, he realized he had his answer. Still, he waited. The man deserved some respect.

"I wish to hell I could, Robbie." Hank could not look the chief in the eye. "I've gone over this again and again, and I just can't be sure — and I'm sure as hell not going to lie."

Robbie drew his arms back around, placing his hands on the car roof directly over Hank's window. "I appreciate your honesty, my friend." He gave the roof a gentle tap. "And it doesn't mean she's guilty. Keep that in mind."

He drove immediately up Old Colchester Road to the Wilson Dairy Farm, finding both men in the barnyard, working on a tractor. They also knew why the chief was there, and seemed to be prepared. "We were both at home asleep when Blow was killed, milking when the other one got it," Jessie answered for both of them.

"Any witnesses to confirm all this, gentlemen?"

"Just each other," Jessie answered, again. "So, I guess it doesn't look too good for us, right, Chief?"

"I wouldn't assume that," Rob urged them. "In this country, you're considered innocent, until proven guilty." He tipped his hat politely before leaving.

Across the road, he found Cecil Thompson cleaning out stalls in the milk house.

This time, the questions were mostly directed at Rob. "Well, it's about time you got up here to talk to me, Chief. I've been waiting for some kind of word on this so-called investigation, and if you hadn't showed up today, you would've seen me in your office tomorrow."

"Is that right?" He stood back, letting the slop from the shovel splash something other than his pant legs. "Well, here I am, and I have a couple of questions for you, Ceese, if you have the time."

"Oh, if you've got updates, I've got the time," he quipped, leaning the shovel against the whitewashed wall. He seemed amused. "Guess we should step outside, where you won't be so distracted by the manure." He motioned the chief out the door, then pointed to the back porch of the house. "Let's go sit for a spell."

Faded cotton cushions covered the bedraggled cane seats of twin rockers positioned at the north end of the covered structure. Cecil grabbed the arms of one, lowering himself heavily onto the pillowed surface, then lit up a cigarette. "So, I'm listening," he said, dropping the book of matches onto the small folding table between them.

"Sure. But let me get my questions out of the way first, okay?"

The farmer blew smoke toward the railing. "So, what did you want to know?"

"Just need to verify your whereabouts on the dates both dogs were killed."

"Oh, right. Well, when we lost Blow, we were in bed." He winked. "Don't ask me why I remember that." There was a small puff. "As for the other one, well, I would have been milking, and Win would have been just getting up." He scratched his temple. "Wasn't that on a weekend?"

"Yes. It was the last day of Joe Turner's paper route. They let him finish out the week."

"So, that's it, to the best of my knowledge, Robbie." He looked worried. "Not a very good answer, I guess, but as accurate as I can get."

"Any witnesses?" He quickly corrected himself. "I mean, uh, on the weekend thing."

"Can't think of anybody."

"Any phone calls or people dropping by?"

"Maybe. Winnie would know that, I guess, but she's not here."

Rob nodded, then addressed Cecil's inquiries. "So, what did you want to ask *me*?"

"How come that damned search party didn't spot the place where Blow got killed? It wasn't that hard to find."

"Good question. I guess you'd have to ask Sheriff Duncan about that — he and his deputy were working with that search party."

Cecil blew smoke from between his teeth. "That useless S.O.B. Why would I trust anything he told me?"

This was new to the chief. "I don't follow you, Ceese. Why don't you trust him?"

"If there ever was a no-good cop, he would be it." He flicked ashes into the wind.

The lawman was careful to phrase the question. "That sounds pretty serious, Ceese. Care to explain?"

"It started when that cheerleader was killed here in our barn. You remember that?"

"Very well, sir."

"Mister high-and-mighty sheriff was sure Winnie's uncle had something to do with it, so he started doing drive-bys late at night." He tilted his head toward Robbie. "You remember that Uncle took off that night." Rob slowly bowed in agreement. "So, we didn't know why that happened, Winnie and me, but we figured he knew something we didn't, so we decided to just wait and see. But then we heard Uncle had been killed by a bear, somewhere in Canada." He took a long draw on the cigarette. "That was a tough time. But then, Sheriff Duncan stopped creeping along this road, with the headlights off. That was a relief, 'cause Winnie was going through hell." He flicked ashes again. "But now, he's at it again — sneaking around the property, to add insult to injury."

"Hmm," the officer voiced his curiosity, "why would he suddenly start doing that again, do you suppose?"

"He has to think Uncle is still alive, that's why. It's the only logical answer."

"And do *you* think Uncle is still alive, Ceese?"

"Let me put it this way: If I did, I would never say so."

It was late into the afternoon when the chief got back to his office in Lincoln Hall. Lily White was busy at the switchboard when he came in, so he didn't bother to ask how things were going. Instead, he went directly to his desk, drew out a large tablet, and started making notes. Once he did that, he put each page into its own envelope, marking them with the suspect's name. Then he tacked them on a bulletin board behind his desk. For a few minutes, he studied the three items, until it became obvious something, or someone was missing.

"Okay," he asked himself, "who else did we talk about this afternoon?" And there it was: Sheriff Max Duncan.

Robbie went back to the tablet and began to scribble notes: *Why did Max miss crucial evidence concerning the location of Blow's killing?* Rob had no answer to that one. *Why did he accuse May Spofford of having a history of harassing the Thompsons, when all she did was threaten to sue them, once? Was she simply a handy target to distract attention from the fact that Max has a long record of tracking activities at that farm?*

Rob made a guess: "He thinks Uncle is still alive, and is out to get him, but why is he so adamant?"

The answer was a shot in the dark, but he made it his next point: "Max Duncan hates Abenakis. Both Winnie and Uncle are full-blooded Abenakis, and dedicated to each other's welfare. In order to get Uncle to surface, there would have to be serious reason — like coming to Winnie's rescue at her time of grief. Everybody knows he would be there for the dear niece, who he calls, "Winnie, the Pooh.""

He put it down on paper: *What if Blow's death really was a ploy by Sheriff Duncan to lure Uncle into coming back to comfort Pooh?* Once more, there was the same question: *Why is Max being so aggressive about it?*

The light finally went on.

"He's running for re-election." An ironic chuckle rose from his throat. "He wants to go out swinging, solving this so-called cold case. That would be quite a feather in his cap. Oh yeah, like killing two birds with one stone," he murmured, getting it all down on paper.

Chief Rob Allen pulled out another envelope and slipped the notes into it. *"Douglas Courtney needs to look this over,"* he thought. Then he scribbled a code name on the thing, and pinned it up on the bulletin board.

It read, "S.O.B."

CHAPTER FIFTEEN

Moves

"Oh my goodness, that happened so quickly," Gracie declared to her beautiful neighbor. "We figured it might come to that, what with his wife being gone, and all those memories, but not so soon."

"When is he moving out?" Lenore asked, as she poured hot cider into the two mugs.

"By the end of November, and I believe that's next week," Rob's mother replied.

The patio was cool, despite the bright sunshine, so the ladies tucked their lap robes under their thighs, and warmed their fingers around the steaming vessels.

"How long have the Wilsons run that dairy, anyway?" Lenore was still the new kid in town.

"It seems like forever. But I guess it's like fourth generation, or so." The silvery head moved slowly to one side. "I remember most of them. Very nice people, but not really religious, if you know what I mean." She blew on the spicy brew. "That's probably the basic problem for Jessie. No faith. Nothing to fall back on, when the going gets rough."

"Umm, that certainly can be true." The steam was making her nose run, so she pulled it away, sniffing gently like the well-mannered young woman she was. "So, what will happen to Jack, do you think?"

"He was supposed to join the Navy in the spring, but now he's decided to just go do it, and just before Christmas, if you can imagine *that*."

"Ay-yuh. That means he'll still be in basic training during the holidays." Lenore's brows moved. "Although, it might be okay. You know, that first Christmas without his mother would have been tough there at the farm."

"I'm thinking it's one of the reasons *Jessie* is moving right now," Gracie guessed.

"Sure."

The back door opened. "Could I come outside with you?" Joe Turner inquired.

Delighted, the women invited him to join them. A light coat was draped over his shoulders, the bandages being too bulky to slip into the sleeves, but he had been careful to drape a wide scarf from his neck, down over his chest. He drew a chair into the sunlight, leaving just enough room to protect his teenage autonomy from any adult contamination, and sat down. He wiggled, then shivered. "Cold chair," he noted, shyly. When "Ma'am" offered him a blanket, he chose a manly decline. "It'll be okay in a minute."

Gracie smiled. "How are you doing, Joe?"

"Pretty good. It doesn't hurt so much today."

"I'm proud of him. He's taking it like a man, I can tell you." He sent a grateful look to his foster mother, for the compliment. "Are you in the mood for some hot cider? If you grab a mug from the kitchen — " He was already declining that one, too. Instead, he had a question.

"Ma'am, did I hear you say on the phone, the Wilsons are closing down the farm?"

Gracie answered first. "Oh, that was me, just a few minutes ago. I wanted to call and let you folks know." She held up one hand. "But they're not actually closing it down, just moving out."

Joe was suddenly upset. "But, what about Jack? Is he moving out, too?"

"Oh no. Joe, I'm so sorry. I thought you knew he was joining the Navy," Ma'am declared.

"What?" His chin quivered. "No, he wouldn't just leave the farm. He wouldn't."

"I'm afraid he is, Joe," came her quiet reply. "He leaves for basic training next week."

Slowly, the hurt morphed into confusion. "But what's going to happen to the farm?"

Gracie turned to Lenore. "I was just getting to that." She paused, collecting her thoughts. "So, yes, the farm is going to be run by that hired hand, Mr. Dupree." This time a finger touched her temple as she remembered. "I believe his name is LeRoy, but most folks call him 'Roy.'"

"But, he can't run that farm all by hisself," the boy objected. "It takes two or three guys, at least, and at harvest time, it takes a lot more."

"You're right about that, Joe," the older woman assured him, "but Roy has run a big farm before this, and besides, he'll have the help of his oldest son, Sonny."

"But... but," the lad's tone was increasingly anxious, "you can't just leave a job like that, every night. Somebody has to be there all the time. Otherwise, the place could burn down, or something."

"Oh, that's no problem, Joe," Gracie reassured him, "the whole Dupree family is moving into the farmhouse. It will be fine."

Suddenly he was on his feet. "Oh no it won't," he shouted. "It won't be fine. I don't trust those people!"

"Why?" the ladies whispered together.

"I was in The Home with those brats. Their mom and dad threw *them* away, too. No wonder they turned out like me. No wonder they lie and turn their backs on the ones who trust them." He started toward the kitchen door, but Lenore was blocking it before he got there.

"Hold it right there," she said in a Don Collins' voice. "You don't go stomping off without explaining yourself." She twirled a hand in the air. "Back to the chair, and tell us what you're all ticked off about." She looked like she meant it, so the kid turned around. But he refused to sit down.

"So, what do you mean, 'They lied and abandoned people who trusted them?'" Her arms were folded, as she stood between him and the house.

He lowered his head and muttered something.

"We can't hear you, mister," the Don Collins' voice declared.

"She lied."

"Who lied?" Her blonde hair glistened with the determined jerk of her head.

"Lisa Marie. Lisa Marie Dupree."

"And just how did she do that, sir?" Ma'am was out to get solid answers.

He shuffled his feet and stroked the scarf, working up the words: "She said me and Dicky would be 'blood brothers' forever." His nostrils moved defiantly when he looked her in the eye. "But he got kidnapped, and then they left me at The Home, and she never helped me again," — the voice was trembling — "not even when they found him dead." He wiped the end of his nose with the back of his fist. "No such thing as 'blood brothers,' and no such thing as taking care of the ones who trust you with their whole hearts, like you was worth it, or something."

Lenore allowed a few seconds to pass before she answered. "Okay, Joe, thank you for making the situation clear." She stood aside, waving him back into the house.

The two women sat deep in silence, sipping the lukewarm beverage. It was a comfortable companionship, but a disturbing situation, for both ladies had quick minds and powers of deduction. It was all adding up, and it was not pretty. Gracie broke the quiet. "I think we should talk with Robbie."

"Ay-yuh. I agree." There was a short sigh. "A lot of betrayal in that kid's life."

"In all of those kids' lives," Gracie corrected her.

"Kind of lucky, how LeRoy Dupree got to take over that farm, wouldn't you say, Gracie?"

"It couldn't have worked out better, even if it had been

planned."

***

"Okay, I'm ready to talk about it now," Connie said to her husband.

He was spreading strawberry jam on his breakfast toast. "About what?"

"The plan to restore Joe Turner's ethnic roots. He needs to get a little more foundation in his life."

"And Jesus isn't enough?"

"Oh, Jesus is absolutely enough, once you open the door and let Him in, but *this* kid doesn't even know where the door is, let alone that he's even able to open it." She waved her coffee spoon in the air. "He doesn't know whether he's coming or going."

"Mmm, I'm not sure I'm following you." He bit off one corner of the glistening slice.

"Oh. Sorry. Let me reword the statement." She blinked and put the spoon down on the edge of the saucer. "Okay, what I'm saying is that Joe Turner needs to experience a little bit of who he was born to be. He needs to know what it's like to be Abenaki."

He licked the sweetness off his fingers. "A little late for that, don't you think? Over half of his childhood is gone, already."

"No, it's not too late, Don. The boy is still very impressionable. I really feel he would respond to this, if we could get him into an Abenaki household." The grim look on Don's face sparked her to present the whole, healthy picture. "Can you just imagine how inclusive that would be for him, surrounded by folks who had that same gorgeous tan skin, and the shiny, black hair and those deep, dark eyes? Can you imagine it, hon?"

"Ay-yuh, if you get the right family, Connie. Just because

152

you're Indian, doesn't mean you're perfect." He took another sloppy bite.

"So, we're not looking for perfection, here; we're looking for identity, right?" She sipped the coffee. "I guess I really mean, 'affirmation' — knowing who you are and where you came from — because nobody wants to feel like a mongrel." She winced at her own words. "Sorry, I didn't mean it like that."

He finished chewing and washed it all down with the coffee. "Okay, babe. You have a point there, but I recommend a lot of caution. You can't just move the boy in with some Indian family, because you 'think it would be good for him.' You could end up looking like an obnoxious white lady, interfering with ethnic matters. A lot of people could take real offense at this, you know."

"Which is exactly why I'm going to talk with Winnie Thompson. I believe she can help in this situation. She'll certainly know how to do it, without stepping on anybody's toes."

"Just remember, this is one very damaged youngster. He could turn out to be a handful. Still," the man suddenly looked hopeful, "if you get the right household, well, this might just work, after all." He blew a strawberry-flavored kiss across the table. "Go for it."

***

He was pleased, very pleased, that Lenore had invited him to lunch. Before he left the office, he handed the phone number to Lily White. "This is where I can be reached during my lunch hour."

"Sure thing, Chief," she replied, turning her head so he couldn't see the amusement on her face.

Lenore greeted him at the door. "Hi." Her eyes were twinkling, but she did not hug him.

"Hi." His hat was held against his chest, like the proper suitor, which he was.

"I promised you a hamburger," she said, but he could see that wasn't what she was thinking.

"Yes, ma'am, you did." He wasn't thinking about a hamburger, either.

She turned to lead him into the kitchen. "It's all ready. You just need to put the fixings on it."

He saw that there were only two settings on the table. "So, where's Joe today?"

She reached for his hat. "Your mom asked him over for pie." There was that twinkle, again.

He grinned as he sat down. "Good old Mom."

She laughed and set out two hot hamburgers, each on its own plate. "Oh boy, those look great, Lenore." She motioned to the tomatoes and toppings already in front of them, and he dug in. As he assembled the feast, he kept glancing up. "I know you wanted to share what happened during Joe's session with the Collinses, but before we get into that, I just want to tell you, you look super-gorgeous today." He stopped tapping the catsup bottle. "I just wanted to tell you that."

She opened her mouth to thank him for the compliment, but when their eyes met this time, she lost her voice. Still, the conversation went on, without words, lasting for what seemed like an eternity. Then she blinked, striving to keep the flush of color from coming. He was kind enough not to tease her, but once again, he was pleased to see the roses in her cheeks, very pleased.

"So anyway," she chirped a little too lightly, "the session with the Collinses was very enlightening. Don came on like a drill sergeant. I was so surprised."

"A drill sergeant? Really?"

"I'm not kidding. He held Joe responsible for what he did to himself, and what he did to a whole lot of other people, and he even reminded him that there were hospital bills to be paid — all because he cut himself." She shook her head in awe. "That boy was blown away! He couldn't believe he was getting scolded, instead of being coddled." She licked the beef drippings off the tips of her fingers. "Don even demanded that the boy explain himself, and when Joe got pouty and didn't want to do that, Don threatened to send him to Waterbury, where, he told him, 'You don't even get to go to the bathroom, without an audience.'"

Robbie laughed, and took a long drink of his glass of milk. "I have to hand it to that so-called Christian counselor; he went for the throat." He wiped his hands on the paper napkin. "So, it worked, huh?" She nodded. "Okay, so what did he offer as an excuse for his behavior?"

"Being Abenaki, without being Abenaki."

"Like what?"

"I guess he got teased about it, in The Home. Said he didn't fit in, anywhere." She was suddenly very serious. "You know, Robbie, all that time he has lived with me, I never even thought about that. He was just a kid who was hurting, uncertain, kind of drifting from one crisis to another. Father Tom, and Johnny and I, just couldn't get through to him. But now, I see. At least, I see *some* things."

"Mom said she had hot cider with you, and there were some other things, about the Dupree family."

"Ay-yuh." She leaned back, not interested in the food any longer. "He yelled about kids being abandoned. Hates the whole family."

The phone rang. She answered it quickly. "It's Lily. Says she hates to interrupt, but your one o'clock appointment has arrived early."

He rose immediately. "This is important. I'm sorry."

"That's alright, you ate most of it." She handed him his hat and led the way to the front door, but before she could open it, he closed his hand over hers.

"Wait," he whispered, not letting go. "I don't want to leave without saying thanks for lunch. Mind if I give you a little family-style peck on the cheek?"

"I wouldn't mind at all," she murmured.

He gave her a gentlemanly sideways hug and bent to

lightly kiss the near side of her face. The surface of her cheek was like warm velvet against his lips. "Thanks again," he whispered, moving slowly down to kiss the tip of her nose.

As he drove back to the office, he struggled to get it together. He should not have kissed her that second time. It was too forward. And besides that, he knew he would not soon forget the flutter of her breath against his mouth.

But Douglas Courtney was waiting.

CHAPTER SIXTEEN

Plans

It was Parent-Teachers Friday at Summit Street Grade School. Hank Spofford got a surprise when he picked the two girls up at one o'clock: Eight-year-old Ina May had a bruised lip. "What in the world happened to *you*?" her father asked.

"Sylvia slugged her," Bella May reported.

"What? You talking about the girl with the gossiping parents?"

"Yup, the same one," the ten-year-old declared. "She would've slugged me, but I'm bigger than her, so she stuck her tongue out and ran."

Somebody honked behind him. He nodded and waved, then pulled the car out to the street. "So what were you fighting about, this time?"

"Same thing. I told her if her mom and dad don't shut up, you were gonna sue the hell out of them, and she said, 'What does *that* mean?' I didn't know the answer, so I said, 'Why don't you ask your big-mouthed father?' She said, 'Take that back,' and I said, 'No, I won't, 'cause he's a big, fat liar, and so are you!'" The proud daughter took a breath. "That's when she stuck her tongue out at me, and that made me mad, so I made believe I was gonna deck her, right there on the spot."

"Aw, Bella, Bella, Bella. You didn't have to go that far." He glanced at Ina May, who was gazing back at him in the rearview mirror. "So why did she hit *you*? Were you close by, or what?"

"Nope. I was in the lunch room, Daddy," she reminded him.

Bella Mae amended that statement: " — where Sylvia ran, to get away from me."

"So, what happened, Ina May?" He wanted to wrap this up before they got home.

"I don't know. I was eating at the lunch table, and all of a sudden, she was on the bench beside me, all sweaty and mad."

"Tell him the rest of it," her big sister insisted.

"She called Mama a dog-killer." The bruised lip quivered. "I told her, 'You shut up, 'cause you're a liar. My dad told me. And so are your mother and father, and prolly your little brother, too.'"

"Oh, for Pete's sake..." They were crossing the railroad tracks in front of the house. "So she slapped you on the mouth?"

"N-no," the quivering increased. "She pushed my face into my food tray."

He pulled the car into the driveway, noticing May's was not yet there. "Alright, I'm assuming the teacher monitoring the lunch room took over from there. What did *she* do?"

"It was Mr. Charbonneau. It was a *man* teacher," Ina corrected him.

He turned off the engine. "Wait. Before you jump out and get busy, just tell me what Mr. Charbonneau did about all that ruckus."

The little daughter, who was the spitting image of her mother, rolled her dark eyes. "He just said, 'Shame on you two, that's not how young ladies should behave,' and then he said we should be careful about what we say about other people, because we could do a lot of bad things to those other people, if we don't be nice, instead."

"And he's exactly right, so don't you forget it. Meanwhile, you need to pay *no more attention* to kids saying things about your mama. She's a wonderful person, and we love her a whole bunch, right?"

They spoke as one: "Right!"

He waved them out of the car, but took a minute to settle his own feelings. "Damn. We may have to do something about this mess," he told himself.

***

Douglas Courtney apologized for being in such a hurry. "I thought I would have more time, Chief, but I need to be back in Montpelier by two thirty."

"Actually," Rob Allen said, as he motioned toward the conference table in his office, "this won't take too long." He went to the bulletin board and brought back the white envelopes. "Let me just say, I found no alibis for either the Thompsons or the Wilsons, and Hank Spofford can't swear as to his wife's whereabouts on the night of the first killing. So, we're no closer to those answers than before. I hope to have something more definite by the time we have the official investigation team meeting, but, in the meantime, we maybe need to include LeRoy Dupree and Joe Turner on the list of suspects."

"I see. So the list has actually grown," the lawyer mused.

"Yes, sir. But there's more: I have come across some disturbing info on Sheriff Max Duncan."

"Oh boy," Jack moaned. "He's on the team."

"Right," Rob said. He handed the contents of the S.O.B. envelope to the man. It took a few minutes for Doug to go through the notes. "This looks pretty serious." He stroked his chin, eyeing the list again. "Some allegations, others eye-witnessed." He leaned back in his chair. "You know, you might just do a quiet check on the folks who had animals in that dog contest. I would be interested in knowing if there are any irregularities, any motives, for the first killing — " He glanced at the ceiling. "That was the Thompsons' pet, uh, 'Blow' was his name, right?" Rob agreed. "So, if these allegations against Max Duncan have any substance, there might be proof of motive to also use the fiasco at this contest, to incriminate Mrs. Spofford in that first killing." He looked grim. "Also, I can't help but wonder if an Indian-hating lawman wanted to flush out a so-called fugitive, killing Blow might just work. My understanding is that Mr. Smart and his niece were very close."

"So, you smell a rat, too?"

"Something like that." He handed the notes back to the chief before rising to leave. "Let me know what you come up with, and please do it before the official meeting."

"Sure. Next week, right?"

Mr. Courtney held up a cautionary finger. "*Quietly*, Chief."

Robbie laughed softly. "Ay-yuh. It's a small village. Nobody sneezes without somebody handing them a tissue."

The lawyer smiled broadly as he reached to shake Rob's hand. "Alright! You're right on top of it, Chief. See you next week."

He decided to start by tackling the possibility of the dog contest being a cover for the killing of the older dog. A half-hour later, Rob was talking with Hank and May Spofford. She poured coffee as he sat at their kitchen table, explaining the plan. "Listen," he said to her reluctant husband, "May is so involved with the 4-H Clubs and that contest, nobody would ever suspect what she's doing." He turned to her. "So, you're the logical one to contact all these contestants. You convince them that it was a great success, despite a few glitches, and now you're doing a survey, to see how you might improve the upcoming event in August."

"Are you crazy?" Her eyes were wide. "Too many of those people hate me. I threw a fit at that contest. Why would they even talk to me?"

"But don't you see, May? This is your opportunity to prove you're not the, uh, horrible — "

"Dog killer," she muttered.

"But, I happen to believe you're no such thing." He was fudging, hoping it didn't show. "I think you could clear your name, if you come up with some solid evidence that the contest was tampered with, or whatever. Who knows what you could find, May? And that very thing could restore your reputation in this village, once and for all." He paused to let them think about that.

The couple exchanged a wistful look, before her words came forth as a rhythmic sigh. "If only you could be right."

Outside, the winter sky was darkening, signaling the snowfall ahead. By morning, the area would most certainly be wrapped in a heavy coat of white, disturbed only by crunching footsteps and the scrape of snow shovels. It would be the beginning of another long, albeit mostly beautiful, Vermont winter.

Rob saw the gray sky and decided to use a different tactic. "Looks like winter is finally coming to stay." He smiled. "But that's okay. I love the change of seasons in Vermont. Life changes a bit for us in Chittenden County when winter comes, with snow plows, and ski trips, and ice fishing, and sledding with the children." He smiled even broader. "Now, that's who makes winter so much fun — the children."

This picture touched Mr. Spofford's fatherly heart. Innocent children needed to have time to enjoy that innocence. He sighed. "Damn," he said.

"What?" May's attention went from the scene outside the window, back to her husband.

"There were a couple of school incidents with the girls this week," Hank began.

"School incidents?" She was suddenly alert.

By the time he related the Sylvia stories, she was crying. "Damn it!" She sniffled. "Now they're after my kids!" When she rose to get a tissue from the phone table, Hank followed, to fold his arms around her.

She melted.

Chief Robbie Allen waited just long enough for the two of them to finally come around; then, carefully and slowly, he laid out the plan.

"I've seen you work on projects in this community, dozens of times, May. You can pull this off in just a few days. You could probably do this mostly by phone, but I would recommend you do as much of it as possible in person. These people need to see you as the person you really are: a caring, involved member of the village of Essex Junction." He drew out a sheet of typing paper. "Here's a list of questions. These folks will never know what we're really asking, but that's okay. It's all for the common good." He focused on her eyes. "Are you okay with this? Any questions?" Hank had his arm around her; they were a team. "Okay then," he said to May, "just be your normal perky, pleasant self. That will win them over, eventually." He noted her weak smile. "Hey, you'll do fine. I trust you, May. Go clear your name."

Hank followed him to the car. "Robbie, thanks for the second chance."

"Everybody deserves a second chance, Hank." He slipped into the driver's seat. "Just remember, the investigating team needs this information by next Friday, okay?"

"We'll get it done," the World War II veteran assured him.

He steered the official Essex Junction police car toward the office, hoping he had made the right moves. Involving the Spoffords was a risky choice, but the one which, he hoped, would raise the least amount of suspicion. If there were any clues found, it would be worth the gamble.

The rest of that day was filled with the usual November Friday night shenanigans: a fight at the pool hall over by the train depot; teens making too much noise at a house party; and traffic problems ushered in by the steady, heavy fall of snow. It was almost midnight when Robbie pulled into the unshoveled driveway. He thought to clear it out, but decided it would have to be done again in the morning, and besides, he was tired.

Inside, it was quiet. Gracie had gone to bed, and Scottie was away for the weekend. He paused to peer out the kitchen window, toward his blonde neighbor's place. There were no lights on. "Of course not," he reminded himself, "It's late." At the top of the stairs, he hesitated, surprised at how disappointed he was.

He had wanted to call her, just to say good night.

***

The next morning, there was a forecast for more snow, probably around early afternoon, but Gracie was undeterred, still hustling about, getting ready to hostess the Maple Leaf Sewing Circle meeting. It had been months since the group had convened, mostly out of respect for Laura's passing. It would have been too raw, with the ladies feeling her absence, so there had been a pause, but now it was time to get things moving again. December was at the front door, and there would be no time for a get-together during the busy holiday schedule.

Robbie, who had come down to shovel the driveway earlier, now descended into the kitchen, in uniform and ready to go to work. Gracie was putting together a pan of scalloped potatoes and ham. "Hey, that smells good," he commented, as he reached for his uniform jacket. Even though he was the chief of police, Essex Junction has only a few officers, and he shared responsibility for weekend duty.

She looked up. "I can fix you some toast," she offered.

"Nope. You keep doing your thing, Mom. I'll grab something at Muncy's." He pretended to fiddle with the zipper on the jacket. "So, how many were you able to pull together for this thing? It's been a while."

"All of them," she said with a smile.

"That's great, Mom." He bent closer to sniff the casserole. "Maybe I'll drop by for a quick bite. What time is lunch?"

She was busy, but not too preoccupied to figure that one out. "Now, Robbie, I know you've got a lot of work, so you don't need to *bust* a ladies' luncheon. Just go back to Muncy's and get a sandwich." He grinned and saluted. "Oh, and yes, she will be here." He pulled the back door open. "Try a little later — like maybe two thirty or three. We should be here in the kitchen, doing the cleanup." As he stepped out the door, she just let him know: "Johnny Courtney's taking Joe for the afternoon. Going to Burlington to buy the kid some new tennis shoes; they'll be back sometime around four or so." He was looking at his boots. "Close the door, Chief," she commanded.

Lily White was, as usual, the first one to arrive, a green salad in hand. "Let me set the table," she sang out. "My-oh-my! I'm so glad we're back to doing this, again!"

By noon, Anna Morgan, Connie Collins and Winnie Thompson were there, and five minutes later, Lenore arrived. Instead of the seven, there were now only six, but the atmosphere was like a high school class reunion. There were squeals and hugs and food and handiwork and mutual encouragement, until, at three o'clock, it was time to wrap up this fulfilling time of fellowship.

He showed up, loosely following his mother's advice, at ten minutes past three. Sure enough, Lenore was there, up to her elbows in suds, washing dishes. Lily and Grace left to help Anna, Winnie and Connie finish up in the living room.

"Hey," he chided her, "you getting overtime for this?" Something stirred down in his gut, as he watched the rosy flush appear on her cheeks. Green eyes sparkled a welcome, as she stood up, flicking the suds off her hands. There was something she wanted to say, but the words wouldn't come out.

"Hey..." was all she could whisper.

For some reason, he couldn't move, could not tear away from the glistening prisms in those eyes. "I, uh, wanted to call you last night." He licked his dry lips. "But it was so late." He ran his tongue across the tightness, once more. "I just wanted to check in with you."

Her gaze did not leave his, as she moved back from the sink. "I was hoping you would call."

"Yeah? You were?"

The intense eye contact continued, as she wiped her hands on the towel at her waist. She took one step toward him. "Robbie Allen, you have my permission to call me, at any time, to check in with me, or just to say good night, or just to say, 'I want to hear your voice,' or just for any other reason you can think of."

There was another one of their conversations without words.

"Oh, look at that," Gracie blurted as she came back into the kitchen, "it's already getting dark." She peered out the kitchen window, then turned to Lenore. "Okay, it's really coming down out there. You need to stop all this cleanup and get home, before the snow gets too much for you to get up that sidewalk."

"Oh no, Gracie. I'm not leaving you with all this mess." Her hands went back into the soapy sink. "It'll only take a few more minutes."

The woman went back to her son. "Look, either you talk some sense into her, or you pick up a dish towel and help her get done, and then walk her home." Her head cocked to one side. "You *are* done with your duty shift, right?"

"Ay-yuh. Done at three."

"That's what I thought." She handed him a dish towel. "Pitch in, then escort the young lady home, so she gets there without losing a boot, or something."

It was actually dark by the time the two of them headed for her house. He slipped her hand inside his elbow as the two of them stepped out through the thick layer of snow. They slowly made their way up the street, arm-in-arm, leaning into the comfort of their companionship, her head touching his shoulder now and then.

When she opened the door, the phone was ringing.

"Hello?" She was stepping out of her boots. "Oh yes, Johnny." She bent to toss the boots toward the rubber mat inside the front door. "Oh, really? Another hour?" Her voice showed her concern. "Are you sure? I mean, you don't really have to drive all the way back to Montpelier in this mess. Why don't you just stay here for the night?" He was saying something. "Oh no, you can stay in the guest room." He was saying something else. "No, no, the McBains are not here, right now. No, please don't try to go all the way back there, in this weather. Just keep coming — you're almost here, for Pete's sake. Just keep coming. It'll be fine." Another pause. "Just call Doug when you get here. It'll be fine." He was talking, again. "No problem," she said. "We'll see you in a little while."

Robbie was staring at the small puddle around his boots.

"It'll be a little while before they get here, Robbie. Can you stay for a few minutes?"

He gave it a couple of seconds more before he raised his head. "Yeah. Just for a few minutes."

She wondered why he wasn't moving. "Don't worry about the boots. I live with a teenager, remember?" But the look on his face told her this was not the source of his hesitancy. "Oh. So, you have something on your mind." She motioned to the sofa. "Come sit down. We'll talk about it."

"Nah, I don't think that would be a good idea." He pushed his police hat toward the back of his head. "You're right, though. I do have something on my mind."

She was almost afraid to ask. "What is it, Robbie?"

"You," he whispered. His hands went to his hips as he got his voice back. "You, Lenore. I think about you all the time, and it's damned scary." He laughed softly. "I can't get you out of my head." His hands stayed in place, despite the massive shrug. "I feel like a stupid schoolboy, for Pete's sake."

She smiled in relief. "Oh, good, 'cause you make *me* feel like a silly schoolgirl. I'm afraid everybody in the village sees me blush every time you look at me." Her hands went to *her* hips. "It's embarrassing, going all to pieces like that, right in front of half of Essex Junction."

The stand-off stopped when she opened her arms. "Robbie, if you feel that way about me, why are you so distant? Aren't you *ever* going to hug me?"

"Oh boy, you don't know how much I want to do that, but it could get us into a whole bunch of trouble." He pulled his hat back toward the front.

"You don't want to kiss me?"

His voice dropped to a whisper, again. "Lenore, if I kiss you, I might not be able to stop right there."

She dropped her arms. "Right. And I might not be able to stop, either." The reality hit her. "This is serious stuff we have going on, here."

"I sure wouldn't want to do anything that would harm your reputation, or mine. We could regret it for the rest of our lives."

The blonde head was nodding in agreement. "So, we're obviously in love, wouldn't you say?"

"*I* am, for sure."

"So am I. You make me so happy, just being in the same room." There was that tilt of the head, again. "So, what're we going to do about this, Robbie?"

"Keep our heads on straight, get to know each other better, enjoy each other's company, build a solid relationship."

"In other words, learn to be friends, so we can be in love — probably a lot longer, right?"

"Right."

Suddenly, she laughed out loud. "I can't believe we're having this kind of conversation."

"I can't, either," he replied through a chortle.

"On the other hand, I can. That's the kind of guy you are, Robbie; honorable to the core." She decided to take it a little farther. "And I have to admit, I love it, that you want to protect my reputation. I really do." He looked relieved, exonerated for all those secret thoughts he'd been entertaining. She caught that. "Ay-yuh, I guess that's why I love you so much. You're so honorable. And," she fluttered her eyelashes as she spoke, "you are so attractive, what with that nice, tight backside."

"Oh, hey! Nice to know — but no touching, okay?" He unzipped his jacket. "I really want to stay for a few more minutes." He stepped out of the boots and moved to the overstuffed chair at the end of the sofa. "I want to invite Uncle Johnny to stay with Mom and me tonight."

"Oh?"

"Of course." He was grinning. "Can't have some guy staying overnight in my girlfriend's house, for Pete's sake. What would the neighbors say?"

His girlfriend slipped onto the end of the sofa. "Robbie Allen, I am so in love with you."

The chief of the Essex Junction police department leaned forward, a happy man. "I'm gonna give you no more than sixty or seventy years to stop stirring me up like this."

"Oh yeah? Well, I'm only gonna give *you* seventy years to stop looking at me like that." She reached to playfully touch the end of his nose, but he caught her hand before she could draw it back. Once more, there was that eye contact, as he slowly turned her palm upward, to press it against his mouth.

A car door slammed. Joe and Uncle Johnny had arrived.

CHAPTER SEVENTEEN

Abenakis

By the time Connie Collins left Gracie's house, the Old Colchester Road was almost invisible. "I'll get you home, Winnie, but when we get there, I need to call Don and see what he says. He had today off, so I know he'll answer the phone."

"Of course." Winnie Thompson's voice reflected her concern. "If it's this bad all the way back to Winooski, you need to just plan on staying overnight. I wouldn't let you go any farther out into this weather, Connie." It was a slow trip, the car coming to a complete stop more than once, while they waited for the sheets of sleet to clear, and they could spot the lights from the houses along the sides of where they figured the road was. When they finally reached the Thompson farm, Connie turned the car into the driveway, partly cleared by Cecil's tractor. He was just parking it over near the barn door, when Connie's headlights swept across the yard. Both women were shaking as they left the car. Ceese held the door for them, then bent down to help remove the rubber overshoes. "Gawd, I was getting worried," he said. When he stood up, he addressed Connie, firmly. "You won't be able to continue on to Winooski. You need to call your husband, and stay here for the night."

It turned out that this storm was a God-send, for it opened the door to Connie's talk with the Thompsons, about Joe Turner. The three of them were settled in the sitting area, under the arch that separated them from the dining room table. "So, Winnie, tell me about being Abenaki."

"Why do you ask?" She was cautious, like most members of that group.

"Well, I think you know that Don and I are counseling young Joe Turner. I swear, that fellow is so lost. I'm guessing it has to do with his being out of touch with his ethnic background." She smiled. "I'm hoping you can give me a little insight, like, are there lots of Abenaki people in Vermont?"

"More than you might think," Winnie replied. "They're all over the place, but pretty well scattered."

Cecil got a sly smile on his face. "Got some right down there in the village. Bet you didn't know that."

"No, I didn't." She was curious. "Anybody I know?"

He got the nod from his wife. "How about May Spofford?" He waited for Connie to absorb that.

"Isn't she the chief suspect in — " She stopped short of mentioning Blow's name.

"That's right, and just for the record, she's full blooded, too. Comes from a band down there in the southern part of the state; can't remember the exact place. I'm told they're keeping a list of each band."

"Who, Cecil? The government?" She was wary of this information.

"Don't really know, myself. Just something I heard — more than once. There was a short puff on the Camel cigarette. "Anyway, those bands are all over, but most Abenakis seem to be up there in Swanton."

The conversation continued, slowly revealing what Connie had suspected: This woman could give the boy a sense of belonging, if nothing else. Still, the counselor was hoping for something more. As she listened to Winnie's stories of growing up in Swanton, and those years on the St. Francis Reserve in Quebec, Connie Collins' resolve deepened, until, she finally asked the question. "I'm especially impressed that you know the old language, Algonquin or whatever, and this gives me a great idea." She leaned in. "Winnie, do you suppose you might have time, say, once a week, to teach Joe this language? I mean, if the young ones don't learn it, your people will most certainly lose it, don't you agree?"

"Mmm, probably. I only use it with Tall Tree, my cousin, and of course, my father, Raven's Wing. Oh, and of course, Uncle." Her head bowed to hide her face. "But they aren't around anymore."

Connie looked to Ceese for support. "I think Winnie could do something very important, here: Not only keep the old language alive, but give that boy some sense of identity. What do you think?"

Cecil mashed the stub of the cigarette into a tall, pedestaled ash tray standing on the floor beside his chair. "Guess I'll have to agree with you on that one, although I don't know where she'd find the time." He clanged the metal trap doors to drop those ashes out of sight, then rose to get ready for bed. "But it's up to her."

Connie had helped clean up Uncle's apartment when the news of his death had come, so she was familiar with the surroundings. Winnie led her up the stairs from the front door hallway, unlocking the door into the small living room. She made a sharp turn to her left, to open another door. Winnie had not remembered there was another bedroom tucked under the slanted ceilings. "Oh," she exclaimed, "I get my own room!"

Winnie chuckled. "Well, of course. It's always ready for company. I came up and wiped some of the dust away, and opened the floor vent so's it would warm up. It should be fine." She turned to go downstairs. "Have a good sleep."

The room was, indeed, quite small, with one dresser and a single bed topped with a plump patch-worked quilt. Above the bed, winter light glowed from a window, down upon the neatly folded flannel nightgown and crocheted slippers Winnie had laid out. Connie peered out at the storm, which was swirling in the lights from the Wilson farm. "Thank you, Lord," she prayed, "for the shelter."

She washed and changed in the small bathroom down the

hallway from the kitchen, remembering that the creaking stairway down to the back door of the house was located just on the other side of that bathroom wall. When she heard water rushing from below, she realized that the downstairs bath was located directly below this one. "Of course," she reasoned, "they would have plumbed it like that, when they turned this attic into an apartment."

Once back into the little room, she pulled the covers back, electing to leave the window shade open for light, and slipped in between the chilly bed sheets. As was her habit, she spent a few minutes in prayer, then wished her Savior a sweet good night, and turned over to sleep on her left side. From there, she noted a faint glow coming up from the kitchen below. A little smile crossed her lips, as she realized the vent was not only a source of heat, but also a cozy night light. A comfortable sigh settled her for the night. All was well.

It seemed like she had just closed her eyes, but suddenly, she was dreaming:

She could hear the crackling beat of footsteps running through the woods, budding tree branches flashing past in the moonlight, and the heavy, frantic breathing that increased and subsided with each rising ridge or downward gulley. Someone was running, not her. She was witnessing without actually seeing, feeling without touching, frantic, without knowing why, but she knew the running needed to continue, to get to something, or away from something, or maybe even to keep up with something — whatever it was, and it was absolutely urgent to keep running, running, running.

"Hey! Hey!" she called out. "What are you doing? Why are you running?" But there came no answer, only faster running. She was sure she couldn't keep up with the sprinter. "Wait!" she called out. "Wait a minute!" But the speed of those footsteps only increased.

"Stop! Stop, for God's sake! I can't keep up with you!" The rapid tread increased, moving away — farther and farther ahead, until she could hardly hear them. "No, wait." She was weeping now. "Wait. Just please wait. Wait for me, will ya?"

Suddenly, there was silence, there in the spring forest. It was so quiet; she could not hear the night wind in the trees. She could only hear herself sobbing.

Then, it was morning. Winnie was tapping on her door. "Hey there, sleeping beauty! Breakfast is served."

Connie bolted upright. "Oh my goodness. I'll be right down." She swung her legs around to stand beside the bed. "Do I have time to get dressed?"

"By all means." There was a shuffle. "By the way, take a look out of that window."

"Really?" She opened the door for Winnie to come in. "What's up?"

"Up to about eighteen inches," the little lady replied. "Take a look."

A moment later, they were kneeling on the bed, together. "Omigosh, Win. I can't believe my eyes."

"I know. Worst storm we've had in years." She slipped back to stand near the dresser. "Ceese has been out there for a half-hour, already. The driveway is clear, but he's still trying to get an open road over the tracks." She put her hands together, to emphasize the point. "By noon, the county will have the main roads plowed, and you should be able to get back home." Her lips pinched together for a second. "In the meantime, very few folks will be able to make it in for church." Another little pinch of the lips. "Sorry, but we'll just have to do what we have to do."

"And what's that, Win?"

"Stay home, and pray the rosary," she said.

Cecil made it in for breakfast, forty minutes later. His face was red from the icy spray blowing back from the plow on the front of his John Deere tractor. He rubbed his hands together in anticipation as he sat down to eat. Winnie served up sausage and eggs and pancakes with real Vermont maple syrup. Steaming coffee topped it off. By nine thirty, the three of them pushed their chairs back from the table. It was time to make plans for the rest of the day.

"By the way," Winnie said to her guest, "Don called at eight thirty this morning. I reassured him you were fine, and he asked if you would please call him. I guess the buses are on reduced service schedule over there in Burlington. You know, cities do worse than us countrified folks, in these big storms. We get out there and clean up our own backyards; they yell and point fingers."

Connie joined Cecil's laughter. "I hate to admit it, Win, but you just hit that nail on the head." She took the opportunity to make a point. "It's sort of like the Abenaki thing, you know? They may not have a part of the complicated state system, but, they still have that sense of community, that's for sure."

The salt-and-pepper hairdo bobbed in appreciation. "Thank you, Connie, and you just hit *that* nail on the head."

Cecil had gone back out to continue the snowplowing, and the two ladies were finishing up the dishwashing, when Winnie suddenly stopped. "Ceese and I both had dreams last night," she said.

Connie paid attention. "Oh?"

"Ay-yuh. Kind of unusual. I dream all the time, but he hardly ever does." She rinsed a plate and set in the dish rack. "But this was really unusual, because he told me his dream first and my mouth must have dropped open," she laughed as she spoke, "and he says, 'What's so shocking? I was just chasing somebody through the woods.'"

Connie picked up the plate. "*That* was his dream?" She started to dry the Melamine saucer.

"Not only was that *his* dream, it was *mine!*"

Connie put the saucer down next to the stacks of dried dishes, and slowly shook out her blue-and-white checkered dish towel. "Are you saying you both had the very same dream, Winnie?"

"Well, pretty close. Both trying to catch somebody or something, both upset 'cause we couldn't catch up." She wiped the empty shelf where the dirty dishes had been, stopping mid-swipe to emphasize a point. "Only difference was, I knew those woods. I recognized them as part of the St. Francis Reserve." She turned to look at Connie. "Whatever, or whoever, I was chasing, was running right there, in those woods." She caught the look in the Christian counselor's large, gray eyes. "What?"

"Last night?" Connie pointed to herself. "Same dream, kiddo."

"No."

"Oh yes. I can even give you details."

Winnie dropped the dishcloth into the water. "Okay, let's just see about that." She folded her arms to show she meant business.

"Well, for one thing, I could hear it breathing." She saw Winnie nod to confirm that one. "Then, it ran up and down, through gullies, or whatever they were, and the breathing got easier when it went down, and then heavier when it climbed back up." The little hostess rolled her eyes to the right, then the left, before she acknowledged this, as well. "And I remembered that there were buds on the tree branches, and it was night, because there was moonlight."

Winnie was stunned. "This is hard to believe, but you just called it. That's the dream, alright." She turned to carefully empty the dishpan. Neither one of them spoke as the sudsy water flowed from the tilted vessel. Winnie was wiping its enamel surface when she finally said it. "Maybe somebody is trying to tell us something."

"Sure looks like it." Connie folded the checkered dish towel. "It surely does."

"Maybe we need to have another cup of coffee, and figure this out," the petite lady suggested. "Here. Take a cup, and tell me about dreams. After all, you're the counselor, not me."

By the time Cecil came back in, the two ladies had hit another nail on the head. Winnie brought him a steaming cup of coffee before she let him in on it. Then Connie called Don.

"I'm fine. It's been a wonderful visit, in fact. And Don, I have some great news: Winnie is going to teach Joe Turner the old language!" She paused, letting him proclaim his approval. "Yeah, she doesn't want that part of the Abenaki heritage to die. Time is running out, and those who know how to, need to speak up, otherwise, they may never catch up. That would be a crying shame, you know?"

By Tuesday morning, snow cleanup in the village was nearly complete. The police department had worked alongside the road crews for almost thirty-six hours, and everybody was tired. Robbie came home for a short nap, before heading back out that afternoon. Paperwork was piling up, and there was still the matter of the ASPCA's investigation team's meeting coming up on Friday. He made a quick call to May Spofford, who let him know she had contacted almost half of those who took part in the dog contest — they were all snowbound, so she had a captive audience, so to speak — and only three people had been nasty, which, she figured, was a pretty good sign. He was laughing when he hung up the phone.

Lily White poked her head around the half-closed office door. "Uh, Chief, you got a minute for Connie Collins?" He really didn't, but waved her in, anyway. She was clearly in a hurry, also, ignoring his invitation to have a seat.

"I know you're busy. By the way, great job with the snow removal." She pulled a manila envelope from under one arm. "This is the information on Joe. Douglas Courtney said to just drop it off here, for you to keep in the safe. I guess you have a meeting this week, or something."

"Information on Joe?" He noted the thing was sealed shut. "What's this all about, do you know?"

"All I know is that it's for Mr. Courtney's eyes only. Mind you all of *our* counseling records are private, but these lawyers know how to circumvent that little detail." The gray eyes fixed steadily on the chief. "I hope all is well for the boy. You know, Winnie Thompson has agreed to teach him the old Abenaki language. Don and I are hoping this will help Joe to get some identity issues resolved."

"Winnie Thompson, huh? I'm surprised."

"Oh, she surprised me, too, but not about the language lessons. About what a sense of community these Abenakis have." She started toward the door. "Did you know we have some of them living right here in the village? That's right," she said, opening the door a little wider, "and I bet you didn't even know, but May Spofford is one of them."

"What?" He wanted to hear that again. "Where did you hear that? From Winnie Thompson?"

She laughed. "Heard it from *both* Thompsons." She was pulling the door closed behind her, but stopped to make it clear. "They've known it all along, and it wouldn't surprise me if some of your law buddies might know it, as well. Cecil seems to think there are lists being kept."

CHAPTER EIGHTEEN

Trust

"Ach, it's the damned snow, lass," Bernie complained to his wife. "It'll be a good two months before we can get back up there."

"Well, if you ask me, you've already covered just about every nook and cranny on that whole area. Just where else were you going to look, anyway?"

"No, but I mean, we never got to really look at the *old place*. I bet there were lots of clues there. Look at the location: A couple hundred feet from where I found the shovel — "

"Which we no longer have," she interrupted him. "I almost wish it wasn't the murder weapon. It would serve him right, taking all the credit." She pooched out her lower lip and blew upward to dislodge the drop of water off the end of her nose. "Darn! It's too hot in here."

"Yer own fault. Yeh do it every time, Del." He turned the newspaper page, with much rattling and shaking. "I see they really got it up there, too. Paper says they got about eighteen inches." He shook his head. "Oh aye, it'll be a couple of months, for sure."

"Why can't you just use snowshoes?" Della was pleased with her suggestion.

He shook the paper, again. "Won't matter. Footprints are footprints, and snow shows all of them."

"So then, get your thinking cap on, mister. There must be something you can do. We need that money."

He peeked over the top of the paper. "Oh, I'll have yeh to know, yer royal highness, that I have been thinkin' and I've got some ideers."

"Well then, that's more like it, your royal highness over there on the throne." She wiped the moisture from her forehead. "So let's hear it."

"Nah-nah-nah. I'll tell yeh when I'm good and ready."

There was that pout, again. "Okay then, be like that, you old goat."

"Ah, those words of endearment," he crooned as he rose and drew up his britches.

"Don't try to be funny," she scolded. "We really need the cash."

"We'll get it," he assured her over the noisy royal flush.

Princess Della pouted through the steamy bath bubbles. "Well, alright then. So, are you gonna just stand there, or are you gonna do my back?"

***

Wednesday was Don's day off from Burlington Transit, and the snow was still worrisome to Lenore, especially since it got dark at four o'clock these days, so the Christian counselor picked up his wife from Essex Junction High School and the two of them headed over to make the three thirty session with Joe Turner. The meeting was held, once again, in the privacy of the boy's bedroom. This time, however, Lenore was not asked to join the three of them. Joe waited while Don opened with prayer, which seemed a little longer than usual. At last, the man addressed the thirteen-year-old.

"So, how's it going, young man?" He watched the nervous twitch of Joe's cheek as the noncommittal answer came forth. "Okay, so let's begin with something obvious: You've got new tennis shoes." The boy had been swinging his feet as he sat far back on the edge of the bed. "How do you like them?"

"Fine."

"Get them in Burlington?" The boy grunted an affirmation, and slid slowly into the conversation. It seemed his Uncle Johnny had taken him last Saturday, then stayed overnight with Chief Allen, next door. "Yes, well, that was quite a storm," Don said.

Joe snickered. "Kind of funny, though."

"Oh? In what way?" The two exchanged male smirks.

"Uncle Johnny usually just stays with us, whenever the weather gets bad." The polite couple waited for him to explain. "But he had to stay next door that night." The youngster's head bobbed like this was a big announcement. "Those two got the hots for each other."

Connie decided to make it funny. "Who? The chief and Uncle Johnny?"

"Aw, jeez, of course not." The wind was definitely knocked out of his sails. "Ma'am and Chief Allen."

"You sure about that, Joe?" He tried to keep the youngster from seeing Connie make a quick note.

"Yup."

Don pushed it, just a little. "So, how does that make *you* feel?" Joe's shoulder hardly moved. The man drew his left ankle up to rest on his right knee, as he addressed her. "Hey, babe, does that sound familiar?" She responded with a faint, knowing smile. He turned back to the boy. "My dad passed away when I was twelve. For a couple of years, it was just Mom and me, and then, Harold showed up. He was a nice enough guy, but it made me kind of nervous." He laughed. "Man, I didn't know what would become of me, if those two got hitched." He adjusted the sock on the raised ankle. "Spent a lot of time, secretly planning how to get rid of him. You know — blamed him for breaking a lamp, pretending to be sick so she had to stay home to take care of me." He laughed at himself. "Stuff like that."

Joe was amused. "You really did that?"

"Yup."

"And how did that work out for you, mister?" Connie

chided him.

"They figured it out, sat me down, and had a long talk with me." The left foot went solidly back to the floor. "You know, they never punished me, really. And in a few months, they actually did get married." He looked to Connie for confirmation. "He turned out to be a really good father, right, babe?"

"He really was," she remembered fondly.

"And from what I know about Robbie Allen, he's a really nice guy, too." He leaned closer. "I hope you will give him a chance."

This time, there was a definite heave of the young shoulders. "Doesn't matter to me, one way or the other; I don't belong here, anyways."

She glanced at Don, who backed off to let her say it: "So, if you don't belong here, where *do* you belong, Joe?"

His head bowed. "I dunno," he spoke weakly. The two adults waited politely, again.

There was a moment or so, before the boy tried to make it more precise. "I don't know where the heck I belong, but I'm pretty sure, it's not with white people."

"And that's because...?" Don led him along.

"Um, because I'm not white."

"So if you're not white," — Connie encouraged the logical conclusion — "then, *what are you*, Joe?"

The beautiful tan face twisted in revulsion. "I told you, I don't know what I am. I only know what I'm supposed to be — a goddim Indian, that's what."

"Oh, don't call yourself 'God damned,' son." Don winced at the thought. "You were born Abenaki, and, like any other group of humans, there are good people and there are bad people, so don't call your people 'God damned.'"

The black eyes flickered with fury. "What difference does it make? I don't even know how to be a good one or a rotten one." He looked helpless. "I don't know how to be Abenaki. Don't you get that?"

"Of course you don't know how to relate to your own

people; nobody ever gave you the chance to find out." Connie reassured him. She stood up, clutching the notebook in her arms. "Thank you, Joe. We've been waiting for this." Bewilderment washed across the teenager's countenance, as she moved close to her husband's chair.

"So, Mr. Joe Turner," Don said, "how would you like to learn how to be Abenaki?"

The quick breath registered the depth of the thought. "Yeah?" There was a glimpse of hope. "I could do that? Really?"

"Really," Connie replied. "And we have arranged for you to start, by learning the old, traditional language of your people."

"What? What does that mean?" He slipped closer to the edge of the bed, letting his feet touch the floor. "Learn a whole language, huh? That sounds hard. Maybe I can't do that."

"Oh," Connie almost sang it out, "not only will you do it, but it will preserve a vital part of your people's history."

"*My* people? Are you sure?"

"Let me tell you how sure we are, Joe: We know an Abenaki chief's daughter, who is anxious to teach you that precious language."

"A chief's daughter?" He was standing up. "Are you sure? Why would she do that? Why did she choose me?" He wiped his hands across his face, nose-to-cheek.

"Uh, I don't expect you will believe this, right away, son, but she was specially selected to teach you."

"Yeah? Really?"

"Really, Joe." Connie stepped closer. "So, do you want to start learning how to be Abenaki, or not?"

The kid was frozen in place for a full seven seconds, while he weighed the pluses and minuses, then he exploded. His "Yes!!!" resounded all the way out into the living room, where Lenore hastened to throw open that bedroom door. The Collinses were standing arm-in-arm, watching the young Abenaki beating the floor with some kind of wild Indian dance he had seen somewhere in a movie. Having cleared the language lessons with Lenore, days before, they turned to smile broadly.

"He said, 'Yes!'" Connie announced.

***

May Spofford seemed to have actually enjoyed getting back into the swing of things in the 4-H circles. Her report to the chief was delivered with bright, snappy little remarks. "So, no big bad dog-owners on the whole damned list, unless you want to count the Thompsons, who obviously didn't know how to control that mutt. But, in my humble opinion, they have paid the price, which is too bad, but 'a lesson earned is a lesson learned,' right?"

He switched the phone to the other hand. "Uh-huh, that's what they say. But, are you sure about this? Not even one person who'd want to kill that old dog?"

"Only that lady who threw a fit in front of the whole grandstand; yours truly." She laughed. "If I learned one thing while doing this research, it's to never do *that* again." There was a quick "tsk" of her tongue. "Talk about getting caught with your pants down!"

He erased that picture from his mind, immediately. "Well, okay then, May. I'll take your conclusion to the team this afternoon, and I want you to know how much I appreciate all your work."

"Hey, you're very welcome. I just ask one favor, Chief. When you tell them I'm the only suspect, tell them the truth: I didn't kill that dog, or the little one, either. In fact, I'm very anxious to find out who did. *Very.*"

He was careful to quote her statement, as he closed his report to the search team at the four thirty meeting in his office.

"Okay, so no new suspects — at least, from the

183

contestants," Douglas Courtney concluded. He looked at the men seated around the conference table. They were the same group as last time, with the exception of Hank Spofford, who had moved from witness/crime scene status, to the position of spouse of a suspect. His chair was filled, mostly by happenstance, by Deputy Smith, whom Sheriff Duncan invited at the last minute. "You don't need to listen for dispatch. We're officially off duty. Might as well come in and see if you can add anything to the investigation," he had suggested. The deputy had accepted the offer eagerly, taking a seat right beside the private investigator hired by Cecil Thompson, Mr. Bernie McBain. "So, anything else new?" the lawyer asked.

"We may have found the weapon used in the first incident," Max Duncan announced, rather nonchalantly. He reached for the bag, opening it to carefully draw out the wrapped shovel. "It's a fold-down shovel, like what folks carry in their cars for emergencies," he explained as he slowly unwrapped it. "As you can see, it fits the size and shape blade that could have been used in the dismemberment of the animal, and you'll notice how shiny the tip of the thing is, which could mean it was probably used to also bury, um, probably bloody clothing or such, and then," he proposed, "the killer probably scrubbed the shovel clean and put it back in the woodshed."

Doug's eyes never left the shovel as he asked, "What woodshed, Sheriff?"

Max ignored the stares from Bernie and Deputy Smith. "That would be on the Wilson property, sir."

Chief Allen cleared his throat. "Has this been sent in to the lab, yet?"

"No. I thought I should run that by you guys, first."

Doug Courtney rubbed his chin. "Looks pretty clean, but yes, by all means, send it in." He looked up for approval. "Unless any of you have some objections?" There were none, so he motioned for the sheriff to re-wrap the thing. "Anything else?"

The chief tapped a finger on the tabletop. "Maybe." He shifted his body in the chair. "I received a piece of information this week that I feel we need to pay attention to." He paused, to recall just how he had planned to say it. "I'm not sure how accurate this is, but I was told there is some speculation about certain bands of Abenakis being surveilled, to the point that there were actual lists of the members of these bands." He looked politely concerned. "I just wondered if any of you law enforcement guys had heard anything about such a thing?" He turned to Douglas Courtney. "Have you been aware of these so-called lists, Doug?"

"Ay-yuh, I have. I've heard it a lot, but that's all I can say about it."

"Ever defended a client who had been, uh, fingered by that kind of list, sir?" Robbie saw the answer before it came.

"I'm not at liberty to answer that," Doug replied, as he relaxed into the chair to watch the chief of police perform a little slight-of-hand.

"So, Mr. McBain, have *you* ever heard anything about such lists?"

"Nah, but it wouldn't surprise me. It's the sort-a thing that we — uh, that happens when yeh start gettin' information on yer enemy. It's done all the time, in certain military circles, if yeh get my meanin'."

"So, it wouldn't surprise you?" The chief made sure the point was made, before focusing on Max Duncan. "And what do *you* think, Sheriff? A real possibility, or just paranoid claptrap?"

The man was dismissive. "I think we've all heard this one, Chief. Myself? I choose to call it exactly what you just did: 'Claptrap.'"

Robbie made eye contact with Deputy Smith. "How about you, Smitty? Have you any insight on this matter? Do *you* think there really are lists of these people?"

The twenty-something officer didn't see the question coming. He suddenly focused on his own hands, folded in place on the table. "Well, Chief," he replied quietly, "I wish I could help you on this one, but I'm afraid I can't."

"You don't know about this, or what?" Robbie wasn't letting it go.

There was a quick glance toward his boss, before the deputy replied. "I guess I need more proof, myself. I don't want to think anybody is ever set up, or whatever. I just want to enforce the law, for the good of the county." He swallowed and smiled, for this, he felt, was a *really good* answer.

Chief Allen let that very telling non-reply hang in mid-air. These men would all draw their own conclusions, for sure.

Doug flipped a page on his notebook, ran a finger halfway down the page, then sat up straight. "Oh yeah. Do we have any further developments on the toe mark at the second crime scene?"

Sheriff Duncan held up a hand. "Oh, *that's* what I wanted to ask you, Doug. Do you have an extra photo of that imprint?"

Doug quickly pulled one from his briefcase. "Anybody else need one?"

"I'll take one," Robbie said.

Max was looking it over. "So, that's what I thought; there's a tear on the rubber wrap-around. We just need to find a match."

Bernie stood up and moved to look over the sheriff's shoulder. "Way-yell, it's a tennis shoe, for sure."

"Not necessarily," Max corrected him. "It's more likely an overshoe. Remember, it was raining for several days."

"So, it could even be a lady's overshoe, like the kind that snap over the top of the foot," the deputy suggested.

Max jumped on that theory. "And it may be no coincidence that our chief suspect is none other than May Spofford." He slid the photo into his shirt pocket. "You know, if she isn't careful, that woman could end up like Laura Wilson, six feet under, in a pretty pine coffin."

Doug and Robbie were careful not to exchange that knowing look.

"Except," the clueless Mr. McBain blurted out, "Laura

Wilson isn't in a coffin." He looked directly at the sheriff. "She's in a little mahogany box, instead, like other folks who get cremated."

The others were surprised.

"Who told you she was cremated?" the deputy asked.

"Nobody in particular. I just took a peek at the gravesite." Bernie suddenly wanted to be vague.

"Well, she most certainly was not cremated," the deputy asserted. "I worked the escort on that funeral, and I can tell you, that was a full-sized coffin that went into that grave. I saw it."

"Oh, yeh did, did yeh?" The Scotchman backed off. "Way-yell, I guess I got the wrong information. Sorry about that." He was relieved to see a mutual acceptance of the apology amongst the group.

Doug's eyes surveyed the team members. "I'm pretty much through here, gentlemen, unless someone has something else." When nobody responded, he thanked them and rose to use the restroom down the hall, before heading back to Montpelier. Rob said goodbyes and returned to his desk to wait for Doug. He had something in the safe for the busy lawyer.

At the take-in desk near the switchboard, Sheriff Duncan paused to chat with Lily White, but Deputy Smith exited, hot on the heels of Bernie McBain. He caught up with the investigator at the other end of the parking lot.

"Say, Mr. McBain," he called out, "a word with you, please?" The slender fellow stopped to listen, letting the lawman approach close enough to murmur a word of warning. "Mister, I don't care if you were hired by the President of the United States, if you go poking around that gravesite, you'll be in big trouble. It's against the law, do you understand?" Bernie nodded in agreement. "Okay, so if you go digging in that plot, we're gonna know it; you're not that good, mister. You're just an amateur private eye, that's all. We'll end up throwing the book at you."

A defiant smirk spread slowly under his little mustache as

Bernie watched the deputy walk back to the other end of the parking lot.

He loved that kind of challenge — snow or no snow.

CHAPTER NINETEEN

Traditions

"My name is Tall Tree," said Michael Smart. "I'm Abenaki, and I go the University of Vermont over there in Burlington. My distant cousin is your language teacher, Winona. She wants me to talk to you about the Abenaki way of life, before you get started on the language."

Joe Turner stood in the doorway, taking in the presence of this tan-skinned fellow with the bright red scarf around his neck. He didn't look like a tree, and he certainly wasn't tall.

Lenore spoke from behind the boy. "Oh yes, Mr. Smart. Come on in." She beckoned for him to hang his wool jacket on the peg by the front door, but he just stood there politely. "Would you like to come in, Mr. Smart?"

"I will walk with the boy," Tall Tree stated. "If you are uncomfortable with that, you may follow along."

"Oh!" She remembered this was Winnie's well-respected cousin. "I think you two will do just fine without me." She drew Joe's warmest coat from the front closet, adding a wool hat and a pair of mittens. "How long before you will be back, sir?"

"When we have had the proper introductions," the man replied. "Today we learn to trust each other." There was a twinge of apprehension, as she watched the two of them start down the front sidewalk. The instructor turned to the left on Main Street, toward the Drury Brick Yard.

At that point, Joe was ready to speak up. "Why are Indians

called names like, 'Tall Tree'?"

His companion did not break stride as he answered. "Tradition has it, that when a woman gives birth, she opens her eyes, and the first thing she sees, is the name for the baby." He chuckled. "I'm not sure that one is accurate, but it sounds so... Indian, you know?" Another chuckle. "Now, in my case, my mother saw a great ash tree — you know, the ones we used for so many years, in basket-making — and so she named me something like, 'Great Ash Tree.'" This time he turned with a smile. "Can you imagine me being called such a thing, in this day and age?" He stomped a little snow off one boot, then kept going. "Nope. The white folks would have made fun of that, so, the name got anglicized, into 'Tall Tree.'"

"What's 'anglicized'?"

"Made more like the English language."

"Oh." He was curious. "Did you like that? Or did it make you mad?"

"I never had a choice. But, when you stop to think about it, it's a pretty respectable name, don't you think?"

"I guess so." They walked a little farther before he asked the expected question: "Can I have an Indian name like that?"

"That is not for me to talk about. I am here to teach you the history of your people. What you are called, well, that remains to be seen." The college student shoved his hands into his pockets. "So, let me begin by telling you how the Abenakis believe Lake Champlain came about."

It was almost two hours before the teacher delivered the young student at the front door. Lenore was relieved to open it as they came back up the walk. She tried to seem unconcerned. "Hey, you two! How did it go?"

The boy looked to his teacher for the answer. "It went well, Mrs. Curtis," Tall Tree replied. "We will continue next Saturday morning. Meanwhile, Winona is waiting to start language lessons this afternoon."

"Of course. Thanks so much. This is so much appreciated." She closed the door and turned to enjoy the glow on Joe Turner's face.

***

That same Saturday, a group of five left the Curtis residence at noon, to find a Christmas tree for Lenore and Joe. The McBains made a special trip up there to join them, and Robbie had the day off — barring any emergencies — so he brought the axe and Joe carried the saw, and they set out for a friend's wooded field, which just happened to be located a little east of the Wilsons' lower cornfield — the one just north of the Spofford house. It was a happy trek, with Bernie in the lead, drawing a sled for transporting the tree back to Lenore's. Della followed, making conversation between labored breathing, much to the fascination of her young walking partner with the saw bouncing on his shoulder. Lenore and Robbie brought up the rear, pretty much oblivious to the rest of the crew.

"How much time do we have, sunshine?" he asked, as they crossed the bridge onto Old Colchester Road.

Lenore could feel the flush rise in her face, revealing her pleasure at this new, affectionate nickname. She saw him smiling at the way she was blushing, enjoying the moment as much as she was. "Joe has to be at Winnie's at two-thirty," she whispered loudly. "But Bernie has already located the tree, so this shouldn't take too long." She took a skip to keep up with him. "And you *will* help decorate it tonight, right?"

"Let's see," he teased, "does that offer include hot chocolate and a sprig of mistletoe at the front door?"

"Oh my goodness! I don't know about that." Her green eyes sparkled as she bent close to whisper, again. "Can you just picture the McBains kissing?"

They laughed softly, then walked along together until reaching the farm road that led to the Wilson family plot.

"Here," he said, as he moved the axe to the other shoulder and took her hand, "watch your step." They moved off the plowed road, treading through the thick snow, where the whole party slowed down to a steady, rocking trudge. Robbie held onto her hand, lest she should fall. Ahead of them, the other three seemed to be maneuvering just fine, but that was beside the point; Rob Allen wasn't passing up an opportunity to make a few points with this beautiful blonde.

Before long, the team had progressed all the way to the end of the unplowed road, to the Wilsons' small cemetery. "It's just a few feet past here," Robbie called out. "See that barbed-wire fence up ahead? That's it. There's a gate to the right, if we can get it open."

It took a little digging and dragging with boots, but the gateway was made available. Just a few hundred feet down the slope, they stopped to view the targeted tree. "My dad's best friend owns the property," the chief commented. "Dad's not here anymore, but the friendship still extends to the family." He took a few steps toward the small spruce. "Ay-yuh, I've been waiting a long time to get this one, and wouldn't you just know it... Mom decides she doesn't want pine needles anymore."

Della spoke up. "Don't tell me: She bought one of those new-fangled tinsel things, right?"

"Right," Robbie replied, as he moved a little to his left, sizing up the situation. Joe came up beside him. "Well, what do you think, Joe? Think this one will do?"

"Oh boy! I think it's swell!" He looked up at the tall lawman with the axe. "We can have this one, for sure?"

Rob laughed. "For sure."

The actual harvesting of the tree took a full half-hour, and then everybody yelled "Timber!" as it hit the snow-packed ground with a soft thud. "Okay, let's get it onto the sled," Rob shouted to Bernie.

But Bernie was nowhere to be seen. The sled was there, His footprints were there. But the fellow had disappeared, without one of them even noticing. Or maybe not.

"I think he had to, you know, *go*," Della suggested. "He's around here, someplace."

All four of them called to the man, and he answered immediately, trudging back through the open gate. "Sorry about that," he called. "Yeh didn't seem to be needin' me, so I took a little tour of the cemetery back there." He approached them and smiled. "Way-yell, would yeh look at tha', now?" He bent down to grasp the opposite side from the chief. "It's a fine-lookin' tree, it is." Robbie nodded for Joe to take a careful grip near the top of the evergreen, and on the count of three, the six-footer was lifted onto the sled. Bernie grunted in satisfaction. "So, yeh can all see why I put such a long pull-rope on the sled." He looked around to see that they all got it. "We have to keep the bottom up off the ground, without letting too much of the tip trail off behind. That means we have only the center of the tree actually on the sled." He nodded at Joe. "So, yeh stay back there, lad, and see that the top is movin' along smoothly."

Lenore helped Rob close the gate, and the two hurried to follow the others, but at the picket fence of the Wilson family plot, the chief of police came to a sudden stop.

"Bernie!" he yelled, "what the heck did you do, here?"

The man paused, letting the rope droop. "Hold it, Joe!" He moved his shoulder nonchalantly. "Just curious, Chief. No harm done."

"Still, that's trespassing, mister. You could be arrested for that."

Bernie stepped carefully back there to reason with the lawman. "Of course, I was on the property, but," he invited Robbie to make a more detailed inspection, "take a closer look, sir." He voice became quite gentle. "Why, if I didn't know better, I might just think some good person came to pay respects, say, on the way to gettin' a Christmas tree."

Chief Allen stepped closer, checking out the tracks that seemed to encircle one grave in particular. "Looks like you've been looking at Laura Wilson's gravesite, Bernie. Is that accurate?"

The Scotchman bowed his head. "It is. And, yeh might say, I prayed a little prayer right there on the spot, sir."

The chief's eyes rolled. "*And* I might say, 'Don't be doing that again.' Understand?"

"Ma'am? Ma'am? *Please*, could we just leave?"

All eyes focused on the boy's twisted face. It was time to get off the subject. By the time the little band reached the plowed country road again, the McBains were at their bantering best. "Okay, I should have known it. My boots are full of snow," Del complained.

"What? There's no snow out here — it's been plowed," he corrected her.

"Well, there was snow back there before, and my boots are *full of it*," she pouted.

"Aw, *yeh're* full of it," he laughed as he tugged the sled over a bare spot on the road.

***

At twenty minutes past two, Don and Connie picked up Joe for his first language lesson. The boy was excited. "Must not be too far, if we're starting out this late," he commented as he buttoned his coat.

Don used his favorite Vermont farmer colloquialism: "It's just up the road a piece."

But when they pulled away from the curb, he got serious. "So, I guess you didn't know that Mrs. Thompson is Abenaki."

"Who?" Joe couldn't believe it.

"Mrs. Thompson," Connie called out over her shoulder. "She's actually the daughter of Chief Raven's Wing." She twisted to speak toward the boy's backseat position. "That's pretty cool, huh?" When Joe seemed speechless, she stared at him. "Didn't Tall Tree tell you all this, this morning?"

He nodded. "But he said she was named Winony, or something like that." He was definitely unhappy. "He didn't tell me my teacher was Mrs. Thompson. Shoot, she doesn't even like me. In fact, she hates me, because she thinks I chopped up her stupid dog."

Don checked the rearview mirror. No one was behind them, so he drew the car to a slow stop right there in the middle of Old Colchester Road. This time, it was he who turned to speak to the troubled youngster. "Listen, Joe, we," he motioned to himself and Connie, "have worked on getting you this opportunity to explore your heritage, and it has not been easy, what with all the contacts we've had to make. Some of your own people didn't even want to bother, but that wasn't the case with Winona. If she hated your guts, she wouldn't be waiting for you to come to her, right now." He paused to let that sink in, then went on. "I'm not sure whether I should show you this, Joe, but I'm going to take a chance, because I think it will tell you how this chief's daughter *really* sees you." The boy's dark eyes reflected the intensity of the moment. "Winona sees you as someone who could help preserve the Abenaki tradition, the rich history of that nation, and she sees you as part of a great number of Abenakis who have suffered so much neglect and damage. She sees you as one of them, who has lived through the heartbreak and the loss of identity, and who better to help others? Who better to bring them back into their own noble heritage, than a kid who was dropped off at a white man's children's home, never to learn about his own people until he was thirteen years old?" He saw the boy's head slowly bow. "So, you have a decision to make, mister, and you're going to make it, right now: You either tell the Thompsons to take a hike, and go your own grumpy way, or you gladly go to visit and learn from Winona Thompson just who you really are, and what you are meant to do... for your people." He turned back around and shifted into gear. The car crept slowly along until it nearly reached the Thompson farm.

A sob broke the silence.

Once more, Don brought the car to a slow stop. "You okay, son?" Don asked.

It was Connie who turned around to face him. "So, Joe, what's your decision?" she inquired softly. "Do we turn around and leave, or do we go in for your first lesson?"

There was a horrendous snuffle. "Go in," the kid said, wiping his nose on his coat sleeve.

An hour later, the Collinses picked up a happy student. Before they got him home, he was demonstrating how to say *hello*, and the word for *friend*, and another word for something else that the couple failed to recognize, until he stopped to take a breath.

"So, you think this whole thing is going to be okay, Joe? You want to keep coming?" The boy looked at Connie. "Yeah, for sure! It was fun!" He fairly jiggled on that back seat. "Firstborn said I could come and visit her any time. I just have to call first, because that's the polite way to do it."

"Firstborn?" the couple said, together.

"Yeah, yeah, that's what her name means. 'Winona' means 'Firstborn Daughter,' but they just call her Firstborn." He ignored the smile between the two counselors. "And she wants *me* to call her that: 'Firstborn.'" He nodded confidently. "Yup, I think learning Abenaki from Firstborn is gonna actually be *fun!*"

***

The Spoffords were sitting down to a late supper that same Saturday night. "I guess you've probably heard about Jessie Wilson," May said to her husband. When he didn't answer, she plopped mashed potatoes onto his plate and filled him in. "He's moving off the farm."

Hank cut into the moist pork chop. "That so?" He fixed a disapproving look on his younger daughter. "Ina May, do *not* stir your chocolate milk with your finger; it's bad manners. You have a spoon, young lady. *Use it.*"

"Ay-yuh, and I don't know why we all didn't see that

coming, what with Laura being gone, and now Jack gone off to the Navy." She spooned applesauce onto one corner of his plate. "Of course, it seems like the end of an era — know what I mean?" He was savoring the chop, chewing slowly, but managed a hummed confirmation. "So, I guess he's renting a house over there in Indian Acres." She watched him nod an acknowledgment. "I didn't know they could do that over there, did you?"

"Guess there's no law against it," he said, between the chewing.

She slipped into her place at the table, straightening the woven placemat under her plate. "So, I'm thinking he'll be alone in that little house, for the holidays."

"Pretty soon it'll be Christmas," Bella May piped up.

"Yup," Ina May agreed. "I want a new bike." Her fork stopped in mid-air, applesauce dribbling through the tines. "I *am* getting a new bike, aren't I, Dad?"

Hank stopped eating. "You know, I'm getting just a little bit ticked at your attitude. What makes you think you can just demand something for Christmas?" He put down his own fork. "In my day, we were just glad to have a new pair of slippers and some candy or something. We didn't go around demanding stuff. Where the heck did you get that idea, anyway?" The two girls waggled their heads in bewilderment. "Exactly. Exactly. It's like things just changed overnight, or at least, in one generation."

"Well, Hank," the mother hastened to point out, "things really do change. In the past, your folks spent hard-earned money on stuff the kids didn't really want. Today, well, the money goes to items that will be enjoyed, instead of only being utilitarian."

"What does that mean, Mom?" the two chorused.

"It's the difference between getting a jar of homemade pickles, and getting a genuine silver pickle tray. One is practical, but the other is both practical and worth money." The little Abenaki lady made a final point: "Of course, if you don't ask, you probably won't get that nice silver tray." She leaned toward her husband to make the point really stick. "He who hesitates, is lost, right, Hank?"

The WWII veteran leaned back in his chair, slowly surveying his bevy of little hens. "Or," he announced, "we could settle for whatever folks choose to put in our Christmas stockings." The brows rose as he continued: "Now, wouldn't that be a novelty? Just being happy and grateful for all we have."

"That's a lovely attitude, honey. Take Jessie Wilson, for instance. He doesn't even have a family to be with for Christmas. We do need to just be grateful."

"I'm grateful, Dad," Bella May lovingly reassured her father.

"I want a bike," Ina May said.

"I think we should have Jessie come for Christmas dinner," May declared.

"No," the littlest daughter whined.

"I agree with your mother. We should at least invite him." He turned to the one with her finger in the chocolate milk. "Don't you want to do something nice for somebody?"

"I want a bike," Ina May replied.

But the next morning in Sunday School, the little brown-eyed girl heard the story of the Good Samaritan, who took care of the wounded traveler, and she changed her mind about Mr. Wilson coming for Christmas dinner. So, that afternoon, May made a call to Jessie. After the usual greetings and comments on how the weather was warming up and there might not be a white Christmas this year, she spoke out in her usual boldness. "Jessie, do you remember my younger daughter, Ina May?"

"I do. She looks like her mother, I believe."

"Right, that's the one. Well, sir, she has a question she'd like to ask you. Would you mind if I hand her the phone?"

He was obviously amused. "Not at all. Go right ahead."

The girl nervously leaned forward beside her mother's face. "H-Hello?"

"Hello, Ina May. How are you today?"

Her eyes rolled toward her mother, who mouthed the word, *Fine*. "F-fine." She was still locking eyes with May, who nodded encouragement. "Um, Mr. Jessie, could you come and have Christmas dinner with us? You don't have to, if you don't want to, but if you do, we're having mincemeat pie with whipping cream on top." She took a quick breath. "Or you can have ice cream, instead."

There was a soft laugh from his end of the line. "Well, how nice, Ina May. Are you sure this is okay with your mom?"

"Absolutely," May spoke up. "Ina May just wanted to be the one to invite you. So, what do you think, there, Mr. Jessie?"

There was a slight pause, with what sounded like a shaky clearing of the throat. "I would be delighted, ladies."

May slipped quickly into the bed, looking for warmth under the covers. "So, Ina May invited Jessie Wilson for Christmas dinner."

"Oh yeah?" Hank said, as he drew her close. "How did he take it?"

"Sounded like maybe he was crying."

CHAPTER TWENTY

Holidaze

The weather forecast proved to be correct, with temperatures reaching above the freezing mark for four whole days before Christmas. Skiers headed for the higher schussing grounds, while ice fishing came to a crawl due to inches of melted ice water across the lake's surface. For most families, Christmas vacation was filled with muddy walks along thawed paths, bike riding on bare sidewalks and streets, movies and Christmas shopping, and of course, gathering goodies for the big day and the big dinner. And that was how Bernie managed to get the two of them invited to Lenore's for a Christmas Eve get-together. "I'll buy the sliced meats and cheese, and whatever else we need, and yeh'll make it purty," he told his hostess. "We'll leave right after breakfast Christmas morning, so's we don't interfere with yer big dinner invitation over at Gracie's." Della volunteered to bring Nova Scotia eggs and a bottle of champagne, and they showed up at two in the afternoon. After all, the ladies needed to prepare the snacks before Robbie and the Collinses showed up at six, and Bernie didn't mind, since he was wanting to take a little walk before it got dark.

He did that.

Wearing the new backpack Del had given him for an early Christmas present, he slogged through the mud until he reached the Wilson family cemetery. There, he took a visual measurement of where Laura's coffin would most likely be buried. Spotting the soggy slice in the sod at the middle mark, he finally figured it out. "So, somebody made a cut and rolled the grassy blanket toward the foot of the grave. No wonder I thought it was a cremation site. I mistook that cut at the middle mark for the foot of the grave." He slipped the knapsack off, hanging it on the picket fence to keep it up off the wet ground. "So, that slice was made sometime *after* the burial." He leaned closer. "Yeh'd think they would've tried to disguise it a little better."

Minutes later, he pulled a smashed-flat plastic bag out from under the rolled-back sod. "And there yeh are." A faint smile stretched under the little mustache as he carefully wrapped his precious treasure inside another plastic bag, then slipped it inside the backpack. Before he left, Bernie carefully rolled the rooted carpet back into place, stomping the jagged edges closed. There was some shuffling of the footprints, but he wasn't worried about them so much. After all, the chief of police could testify that this private investigator had walked all over that area, while helping to cut a tree. And besides, it was forecast that winter would be returning with a vengeance in the next day and a half. "Eight inches of snow predicted," he muttered, "that should take care of it."

He would have gotten away with it, if it hadn't been for the man crouching in the dusky field, just a few yards away. Bernie froze, squinting through the mist. It took a few more seconds before he recognized that crouch, that long hair. "Way-yell," he joked, "look at yeh, all squatted down in a front row seat."

The man laughed. "And enjoying the whole goddim show." He stood up. "I guess you found what you wanted, mister. Now, what're you gonna do with it, you?"

The Scotchman ignored the question, having one of his own. "Just a minute. Are yeh that 'Uncle' person the sheriff is tryin' to catch?" The long-haired man laughed, again. "I thought maybe." He moved toward him, making sure the guy didn't just melt away into the woods, again. "Yeh're Mrs. Thompson's uncle, right? So what's the big to-do about him catchin' yeh? Yeh supposed to be dead, or somethin'?"

"Something like that," Uncle replied.

Bernie looked around. "Aren't yeh scared he'll catch yeh, right out in the field like this?"

"Nah, he's tied up with an accident over there in Colchester. I'll be home before he gets his goddim butt anywheres near here."

"Yeh're headed for the Thompson place? What're yeh doin' away down in *this* field?"

"Came from the south, this time." The Abenaki uncle moved casually toward him. "So what's in the goddim bag, anyways?"

"Don't know, yet. I'm just goin' to take it to Mr. Thompson, and we'll open it together."

"Well then, let's go."

Bernie got back for the evening's festivities shortly before six o'clock, explaining how he had lost track of the time. Robbie noted the late arrival and the excuse, but said nothing. After all, it was Christmas Eve. The company was good, and when the Collinses had left, the McBains retired to the guest room, leaving Lenore and Robbie alone for kitchen clean-up.

"Did you find anything?" Della asked from her side of the bed.

"I did, indeed. Took it right over to Mr. Thompson."

She turned on her side to face him. "So, you gonna tell me, or do I have to hit you over the head?"

He grunted happily as he pulled the bright-colored quilt up under his chin. "Way-yell, I found a pair of pants with blood stains, and something that looks like a big tomahawk."

***

Robbie and Lenore were saying goodnight under the mistletoe that dangled over the front doorway, when the phone rang. It was their first real kiss, deeply intoxicating, and the ringing interruption seemed so far in the distance, it had nothing to do with them. The boy had to yell from his bedroom down the hall. "Hey! The phone is ringing!"

She reached to pick it up. "Got it, Joe!" There was a little lick of the lips before she spoke into the mouthpiece. "Hello?" It was Gracie, and they were looking for the chief. Lenore hung up the phone. "There's been a shooting over in front of Robinson Fuels. Two people dead."

***

As soon as the McBains left, Lenore began preparations for her part of Christmas dinner, to be held at one o'clock at Gracie's. Joe was looking for a notebook, to keep a record of new words and all the traditions he was starting to learn. *"Wish he would do that with all of his studies,"* she thought. But it was a beginning, and she wasn't going to make little of that. By noon, the two of them had packed up the fragrant offerings and headed down the sidewalk toward the Allen household. It was starting to snow, and snow heavily. "Good thing we're wearing boots, Joe. There could be a few inches on the ground by the time we head home this evening."

Inside the house, more delightful aromas greeted them. Gracie's face was pink from leaning over the oven and steaming pots that crowded the stovetop, but she was smiling and gave them both a warm hug. "Just set those down right over there," she motioned. "My goodness, we should have sent someone to help you. But Robbie never got home from that call last night, until somewhere around three in the morning. I thought we should let him sleep."

"Of course," Lenore agreed. "Let him sleep."

"Oh, he's up now, but just barely." His mother rattled the cover on one of the sizzling pans. "I guess he had his hands full, most of the night." Suddenly, she stood still and looked directly at Lenore. "That's how it is, being a cop, never mind being the chief of police. That's his life." Her mouth pinched into a thin line. "You ready for that, missy?"

"Missy" was surprised that Gracie knew how far the relationship had come, but she slowly blinked and replied, "I'd rather have him and his lifestyle, than not have him at all." She did that little tilt of the head, again. "I'm very proud of that guy."

With that, Lenore pulled her snow boots off, placing them beside Joe's near the back door. Then she slipped the winter white high heels from the paper sack and slipped them on, brushing her matching pleated skirt a couple of times before tugging the bright red sweater back down where it belonged. She was fingering the single strand of pearls around her neck, as she entered the living room.

A wolf whistle cut through the cozy atmosphere, followed by Penny's musical laugh.

"He does that to all the girls," she reassured Lenore. "That's Scottie Allen!" Beside her, Rob's younger brother flashed a square-toothed grin.

"Okay then, I won't let it go to my head," Gracie's "missy" humbly replied. She watched them both turn their attention to the stairs, then followed their gaze. Robbie took the first two steps down before he saw her. He stopped for a second, then descended slowly. "Hi," he whispered loudly. "Wow! You look great."

She checked out the mostly tan ski sweater and corduroy slacks before she returned the compliment. But what she really noticed was hair, still damp from the shower, and the shiny smooth, freshly shaved jaw line. He slipped his hand around the back of her arm, gently guiding her to the nearest Early American chair. She sat, then watched him draw a hassock over beside her, where he assumed a manly elbows-on-the-knees position. "So, what's up with my little brother?" he teased.

Across the room, Don and Connie Collins listened to an excited Joe Turner's latest report on things with both Tall Tree and Firstborn. They sat quietly, nodding and enjoying all of what the young fellow related. It was like they knew something that he didn't. And indeed they did, but all that would come after the novelty wore off, and the rubber hit the road. But for the time being, they entered into the joy and fellowship of Christmas Day.

By the time the Collinses left for Winooski, the sun had set, and there were four inches of snow on the sidewalk. Robbie insisted on walking his two neighbors home. "Looks like it's really going to snow a full eight inches," he told Joe. "Are you ready for that, mister?"

The boy, who had enjoyed telling everybody about his new Abenaki lessons, was still flying high. "Aw, this is nothing. My people have been handling this stuff for a long time. Watch this!" he said as he picked the pace up to a solid run. The lawman turned to grin at his girlfriend. "It'll be a while before he settles down for a long winter's nap, I think."

She smiled. "I think we can blame all that energy, half on the Abenaki studies, and half on all that sugar."

They were almost to the Curtis house, when Gracie called from her own back door. "Robbie! It's Cecil Thompson on the phone. I think you'd better take it."

***

It took three days before they located the dry cleaner's location. When Robbie was notified, he headed for Cecil Thompson's place. "So, they're uniform pants and they belong to Max Duncan. Are you sure?"

"Here are the receipts," Ceese declared. "Now, Doug Courtney's connections got us these. Of course, they're only copies, but Doug says they'll work."

"And Max doesn't know we have these, right?"

"Right, Chief. And nobody's touched anythin', I saw to it, myself," Bernie bragged.

Rob leaned back in the chrome and white plastic kitchen chair. "That son-of-a — " he stopped short, out of respect for Winnie, who was pouring coffee. "He killed the dog in order to flush out Mr. Smart."

"Uncle always comes to Winnie's rescue, if he can," Ceese agreed. "Sheriff Duncan knew that. So, ay-yuh, I think you're right. It was planned."

"And it frickin' worked," a voice stated from the shadows of the dining room.

Rob twisted around in surprise. Sure enough, Mr. Raymond René Smart was leaning against the corner of the front hallway's wall. "Except that goddim fool don't know how to catch an Abenaki, and he never frickin' will." He moved to join them at the table. "So what the hail are you going to do about that jackass? I'm frickin' tired of his harassing and tracking and gossiping... and what the hail about?" He tossed the long hair. "Something I never did, that's what the hail it is."

"I'm thinking it had something to do with the murder of that cheerleader." Rob frowned. "In fact, it had to do with the shoving of a pitchfork into her dead body." He looked the man in the eye. "So, did you *do* that?"

Uncle looked right back at him. "No, sir, I did *not*."

"Well, if you didn't do that, who did?" The cop wasn't ready to drop it.

"If I knew that," the Indian said in a steady voice, "I sure as hail wouldn't tell."

"Why not, for Pete's sake? That was a brutal thing to do."

"I agree." The man called Shining Waters shifted his weight. "Something somebody out of their frickin' mind would do, right? I mean, what the hail good is trying to kill somebody who's already very dead?" His hands went palms up to emphasize the question. "Jeez, it's all so damned beside the frickin' point."

"He's got a purty good argument there, Chief," Bernie commented. "If the body was already dead, nobody really got hurt, wouldn't yeh say?" Robbie emitted an irritated gasp.

"Besides," the Scotchman continued, "there's no proof of anything against Mr. Uncle; it's all guesswork, and for what? Because the sheriff doesn't like Abenakis? Both me and Della heard what he said, and that Deputy Smith heard him, too. And somethin' else yeh should know, Chief: He admitted he was after Mr. Uncle, and he wasn't foolin' about it. Me and Della heard it, and so did the deputy." He wiped two fingers across his mustache. "I think yeh're right; I think he killed the dog so's he could flush out this Abenaki. That's it, right on the nose."

Suddenly, Winnie spoke up, from the kitchen sink. "You know what makes it all come together about Sheriff Duncan?" She turned around to look at the men, wiping her hands on the flowered apron. "That he used a *tomahawk*." Her hand went up, to allow her to make her point. "He could have used a hatchet or a big axe, or something else. But no, he was careful to use something that would point to us Indians — Abenaki, or otherwise."

"Never mind the 'otherwise,'" Cecil admonished his wife. "That was deliberate." He turned to Robbie. "I don't know if you're aware, but there are lists."

"And we're on those goddim lists, and we're frickin' tired of it." Uncle's fist hit the table like he was pounding on a drum. "I'm frickin' *tired* of being *harassed* and *prevented* from coming *back home!*" His eyes pleaded with the chief of police. "Can't you do something, you?"

Robbie looked from face to face. "Well, there's one more piece of evidence, if we stop to think about it: Sheriff Max Duncan is running for re-election next fall. Capturing a rogue Indian might prove to be quite a feather in his cap." Only Bernie laughed at the "Indian feather" thing; the other three waited expectantly to see whether the chief would step up to the plate. After all, the Thompsons knew what was *really* going on: Uncle was taking advantage of the tragic killings. It was not how he wanted to do it, but it was the perfect opportunity to execute a carefully constructed plan to get back home, for good.

Robbie actually went for it.

There were two more days of phone calls and meetings, in between his regular duties at the village's police department, but at the end of that second day, a strategy was in place, and, if Doug Courtney approved, it would all happen on New Year's Eve.

***

There had been more than eight inches of snow, but Joe had shoveled the sidewalk between the two houses, so Robbie hastened to touch base with Lenore, before it all broke loose about the sheriff.

If it did.

He drew her outside the front door, into the dusk of an early winter sunset, where they could have a little privacy. "Hey," he said, touching the hairline across her left temple, "I know tomorrow night is New Year's Eve."

"Yes, I know, Robbie," she whispered into the shelter of his embrace.

"That's one of the busiest times for law enforcement guys." He kissed the top of her head. "And it's going to be especially busy for me, this year." He pulled inside his open jacket to keep her warm. "I need a hug from you, sunshine. I need to know you won't feel like I don't want to be with you, when that shiny ball falls at midnight in Times Square." He spoke gently into her ear. "I need a hug from you, Lenore, I really, really do."

"Hey, " She moved her hands around to the warmth of his back. "All I really want, is for you to come back to me." She turned her face up for the early New Year's kiss.

It was the move that sealed the deal. This was the woman for him.

CHAPTER TWENTY-ONE

Ceasefires

There was some doubt in Douglas Courtney's voice. "I don't know, Chief, this is a pretty complicated plan. Are you sure you need all those people?"

Robbie leaned across the conference table to push the S.O.B. envelope toward the lawyer. "It's all in there, but we can't prove it, unless we do this." He turned to answer the knock on his office door. "Yes?" It was Lily, notifying him that the two rookies on the hiring list were there for their interviews. "Have them take a seat; I have to finish this meeting, but I'll get to them shortly, for sure. Don't let them get away, whatever you do." He turned his attention back to Mr. Courtney. "I've cleared everything with all those concerned, Doug. I believe we can do this, because Max will be trying to catch Mr. Smart on a holiday. It just makes sense."

"You do realize, that if this thing goes south, he might sue the hell out of everybody, including the ASPCA?" He looked reluctant, to say the least.

Robbie had anticipated that one. "Even if we don't get a conviction, he won't sue, because we all know about his racial bias against a particular Indian nation. Look at how he targeted May Spofford, throwing those body parts on her lawn. He knows she's full-blooded Abenaki." He went for the throat. "Your nephew, Johnny, told me that Sheriff Max Duncan was a man who manipulated the newspapers to 'snow' the public, in order to look good for the next election. This mess, right now, could kill his chances for getting re-elected, and the Max Duncan I know, would never take that gamble."

"You have some valid points there, Chief." He pushed the envelope containing Rob's notes on Max Duncan back toward the village's chief police officer. "Tell you what — I'm not going to authorize this plan, because it could put my client in jeopardy. In fact, I never even heard about it; I just had a short update on your investigation, and that's all that took place over the last fifteen minutes." He rose to button his heavy overcoat. "But," he whispered with a wink, "let me know how it goes."

The chief followed Mr. Courtney to the door for a courteous goodbye, then invited the first interviewee into the office. An hour later, he watched two new temporary Essex Junction police officers leave the building. Ed was standing nearby, grinning.

Rob shook his head. "You better watch them close, Ed. They're still wet behind the ears."

Likewise, the Chittenden County Sheriff's Department deputized a couple of extra guys, but it was because Sheriff Duncan was cock-sure that Uncle would want to be home for the holidays, and Max wanted to be freed up to do his own thing. He had been busy at an accident site on Christmas, and probably missed the fugitive then. But now, New Year's Eve was coming up, and the lawman was sure he could catch the little savage and put him away, once and for all. Somebody else would have to take care of all those New Year's drunks.

***

The teacher, Hank Spofford, looked up from the pile of papers he was correcting. There was no hurry about this vacation-interrupting task, the living room was warm and cozy, the Christmas tree still sparkling, and the girls had long since wobbled up the stairs to bed. But May was sitting on the Early American couch, staring out the window into the dark winter night. "What-cha doing over there, shortstuff?" She moved her gaze toward him. "Something on your mind?"

The little Abenaki woman drew her short, shapely legs up under her, pulling her robe down to cover them. "You know, I was just thinking about our Christmas dinner guest."

He laid down his red pencil. "Jessie? Like, what about him?"

She waggled her head. "Can't quite figure out that guy."

"He's lonely. He doesn't usually drink. He stayed overnight. What's to figure out?"

"I don't know... unless it's how he talked about the dog being killed on my lawn."

"Hey, he said he didn't think you could've done it. What's wrong with that?"

"Well, nothing, because I didn't. But he must have thought about it, before."

"So?" He stretched back to listen.

"You know, I never really knew him and Laura. I guess I'm surprised by what a gentleman he is." She huffed out the little confession. "I just thought they were a couple of country hicks, you know?" There was another little huff. "He's really very well-spoken, it turns out, so shame on me for judging the guy. Of all people, I should know that you can't judge a book by its cover." Her eyes went back to the black window. "He's going through a rough time. I hope he's not embarrassed about having too much wine."

"Hey, these things happen, May. I honestly thought he'd had so much food, it would come out even. But I was wrong." He carefully folded a page to mark his place in the homework. "But I made it very clear before he left in the morning, that he had our utmost respect, and well-wishes."

"I hope you had the presence of mind to not say anything about what he told you about his son." Her deep brown eyes were fixed on her husband.

"I never said a word, May. And I doubt that he'll even recall accusing the boy of chopping up the dog that killed his mother."

"Good. Because I don't think it was a dog."

Suddenly, Hank remembered how she had killed the coyote. He stood up and stretched, again. "So, is there any of that wine left?"

***

Old Man Winter was making up for the barren landscape over Christmas. Not only did the forecasted eight inches of snow show up, but scattered blizzards swept across the Essex Township on New Year's Eve. On that festive evening, snow plows pushed through one highway after another, trying to keep ahead of the onslaught. Somewhere around eleven o'clock, however, the call went out for all trucks to pull back; it was a losing battle. But the participants in the plan to catch Max Duncan were well ahead of the snow. All vehicles were parked far back from the road in the Wilson farmyard, slowly being covered by the fat, feathery flakes. There was one final warning for the Duprees to keep away from their windows and stay inside until Chief Robbie gave the all clear. The only thing left to do, was wait.

"Just pull over," the sheriff instructed Deputy Smith. "We're close enough." The lights of the Thompson house were barely visible from where they were parked, just over the rise of the railroad crossing. The two of them exited the vehicle, careful to close the doors quietly. He tried to see through the swirling blizzard. "Okay, he's probably already inside the house. I doubt he's left, yet." There was a quick wave. "Just do what I told you: approach the back door and stay put. I'll come in from the front porch. It's a hook-and-eye lock — no problem, I can bust through that." The two wiped the wet cold from their eyes as they maneuvered through shifting drifts toward their respective goals.

A flash of light from the railroad crossing behind stopped them in their tracks. The sheriff crouched down, peering back over his shoulder. "Freeze!" he whispered. The two of them did not move for several minutes, as the storm converted their vehicle and their bodies into part of the dizzying, pale blue landscape.

They could see him before they could hear him, trudging along over there near what they knew was the Thompson barn. Max waited until Uncle turned the faint light off that marked the milking parlor door.

"Got him!" he whispered to his partner. "Let's go for it." He pointed the deputy toward the milk house door, while he headed for the wide open main entrance at the front of the barn. A few feet along, he spotted the rear end of Winnie's '47 Dodge, just inside the large opening. He paused. He was sure he saw a small movement on the far side of the vehicle, just under the hay mow.

There it was, again.

"Somebody's head," he whispered to himself. Slowly, he unbuckled the gun on his belt, but he did not take it off safety. Oh no, he wanted this guy alive and well. The sheriff took a deep breath, and let it out slowly. The next move was executed swiftly.

"Hands up! Hands up! Hands up!"

Uncle jumped forward from where he'd been leaning against the driver's door.

"Get your goddim hands up, mister! I won't tell you again!" Max moved closer, and a somewhat amused Mr. Smart lifted his hands just a bit higher than his shoulders.

"What took you so long?" he called out.

"Chittenden County Sheriff's Department! Put your hands on top of your head. Do it right *now!*"

Uncle rolled his eyes, but complied. Max moved in fast. "Turn around." He looked up at Deputy Smith, coming quickly from the back door. "Cuff him," he told the young lawman.

"Wait a minute," the prisoner objected. "What the frickin' hail are you arresting me for?"

"I'll give it to you in plain English," the sheriff replied, as he watched the handcuffs click into place. "...suspicion of aggravated assault and unlawful flight across the border. I could add a few more; take your pick."

Mr. Smart turned back around to confront his captor. "So, you finally did it, huh? Well, don't be bragging about it, Sheriff, 'cause it took you long enough. How many goddim years you been harassing me and Winnie and Ceese, huh? Four years of your frickin' patrolling this road, night after goddim night?"

"More like *five* years, buster, so, as you can imagine, I'm most happy to finally put your little Abenaki as — "

"That's all I needed to hear," Robbie shouted from a dark corner. "Put the gun down, Max." The sheriff whirled around to see the chief of police emerge from behind the other side of the car. He slowly moved the gun toward its holster, but suddenly stopped. "Hold it, Chief. You have no jurisdiction here; this is sheriff territory."

"He's here because we asked him to be." Sheriff Duncan twisted toward the voice. Cecil and Winnie Thompson emerged from the storage area under the hay loft. "As far as we're concerned," Ceese continued, "this is the end of the trail for you, you son-of-a-gun. No more harassment. You need to leave our family alone."

"What the" — a string of expletives filled the air — "is going on, here?" He slid the gun into place. "Are you people out of your mind? You can't push a lawman around like this. I have a duty to keep things in order in this county. You should be grateful I'm right on the job."

"So, what's yer job, Sheriff?" Bernie McBain yelled down from the hayloft. "Gettin' rid of those — let's see, what did yeh call them? Oh yes, 'wild savages,' I think yeh said." He moved to the ladder which led down to the astonished officer. "And yeh said it more than once, along with a few other words of deaf-ee-may-shun." He snorted. "By the way, my wife, Della, heard yeh say that stuff, and so did yer very own deputy."

Robbie motioned for the Scotchman to come down, but Bernie stopped on a rung which put him just a little higher than the sheriff, where the two men met eye-to-eye. "And, it's also my understandin' that yeh made the same remarks to a couple of gentlemen, let's see, in front of the library." He smiled. "I believe those two fellows are named John Courtney — who's a lawyer, by the way — and Father Tom Ladue, who's a *priest*."

"That's hearsay," Max objected.

"Not if yeh hear it from the horse's mouth. And, I might add, those same horses also told the ASPAC's lawyer, Douglas Courtney." He dropped to the decaying wooden floor.

"Sure wouldn't do your re-election campaign any good, to have all that information floating around," Cecil suggested. "Could really put a crimp in your style, Sheriff."

"What? Are you people blackmailing me? That's against the law." He took a step backward. "I advise you to think twice about what you're doing, folks. This could backfire, big-time."

"Don't think so," Ceese corrected him. "There's the matter of you taking credit for finding the assault weapon used in those killings. Hinted you found that folding shovel in the Wilson woodshed." He watched the sheriff's face go pale. "Never happened. Bernie found it, and you confiscated it. Della and your deputy were also witness to that little move."

"As part of the investigating team, I have the right to bring in evidence, Mr. Thompson. "I don't recall taking credit for its discovery."

"Well, you certainly let us *think* it was *you* who found it," Winnie remarked.

"I never claimed credit for that," the man replied, "you just made an assumption."

"Even so, Sheriff, you could have corrected us, but you

didn't." Her nose twitched. "That's the same as lying, if you ask me. Why should the committee even trust you, after that?"

"That's not for you to judge, ma'am." He was shifting into defensive mode.

Chief Allen leaned back against the hood of the Dodge. "Okay, so you took credit where you shouldn't have, Max — and that certainly doesn't make you look like the ethical lawman you'd like us to think you are — but it turns out to be a moot point, since the latest development in our investigation of the two dog killings, seems to indicate that the shovel, itself, is not the weapon used, after all." He looked at Bernie. "I think Mr. McBain can fill you in on the details."

"Ah, yes. That I would be happy to do." Bernie assumed the position of a prosecutor stating his case before an imaginary jury, pacing slowly back and forth, hands behind his back and eyes on the hayloft. "On Christmas Eve, I made a little discovery, over there in the Wilsons' family plot. I found the evidence we've all been seekin'. It was buried right over Laura Wilson's grave. It was surprising how easy it was to spot, but that's beside the point. The point is, I found a smashed-flat plastic bag, just a few inches under the sod, and," his eyes went directly to the sheriff's, "it contained a pair of Chittenden County sheriff's uniform pants with blood stains all over the lower part of the pant legs." He paused, for emphasis. "In that same bag, was what looked like a replica of an Indian-style tomahawk."

Max seemed stunned. "My gawd, man, why didn't you tell me?"

Robbie stood up. "I can answer that." His hands went to his hips. "There is a dry cleaner's tag on those pants, and we traced it." He shook his head. "Those pants belong to you."

"The hell they do!" The sheriff's face turned red. "The hell they do, I'm telling ya!" He scanned the faces around him. "I never killed any dogs. I never had a motive to do such a thing."

"Not even to frame May Spofford, who happens to be on

the Abenaki 'list'?" Winnie cried. "You knew that; you *had* to know that."

He took another step backward. "Hey, even if I knew such a thing, I don't go around killing dogs."

"The evidence shows that yeh *did*," Bernie insisted.

Cecil stepped up to speak directly to the accused. "So, here's the deal, Sheriff: We have the evidence, all of it, and we can do you some real harm. But we have a proposal where you can be protected — not that you deserve it — and things can work out for *everybody*." The farmer shoved his hands deep into his heavy denim jacket pockets. "I have the authority to call off this whole ASPCA investigation. I started it, and I can end it." He leaned in to insure the sheriff could hear clearly. "So, all it would take for me to do that, is for you to back off and let Uncle come home again." He smiled softly. "That's all we want. You can take it or leave it."

Five minutes later, an agreement was reached, and all was well. Sheriff Duncan was going to have a scandal-free campaign, and Uncle was finally back home. When Max got back into his vehicle, he turned to his partner. "Would you have testified against me, Deputy?"

"Well, sir," Smith replied, "I sure wouldn't want to perjure myself."

"Aw, crap," his boss grumbled, "I can't even trust you, you bastard."

But Deputy Smith didn't seem to be bothered by that.

CHAPTER TWENTY-TWO

Identification

Lenore always had a project set up, right after New Year's. "For me, January is probably the longest, most boring month of the year," she told Robbie, who had dropped by on that Saturday afternoon.

"So, you're painting the guest room," he concluded.

"Uh-huh" She flashed a bright smile from under the pink bandana covering most of her curls.

"Did you actually move all this furniture by yourself?"

"Oh good heavens, no. Joe helped me before he left for his language lesson." She tucked the loose cotton shirt into the waistline of her snug-fitting slacks.

"I like your pants," he grinned.

She laughed through the sudden blush. "Yup, they're old. Don't fit me anymore, but perfect for a sloppy painter like me."

"Makes me wish I could stay and watch, but I have to be out on patrol in twenty minutes." Still, he reached for her arm. "Come and sit for a minute, if you can do that without splitting a seam." She laughed through another flush of color, taking a seat on the sturdy nightstand snuggled into the center of the room, with the rest of the furniture. He drew a chair around to sit right in front of her. "Did you want to talk to me about something?" she asked, doing that little tilt of the blonde curls.

"Nah, just want to sit here and look at you, in your pink

thing on your head, and the sloppy shirt and the tight pants, and, oh will you look at that? Where did you get the beat-up tennis shoes?"

She laughed again, crossing her legs and swinging the top foot. "Found them in the trash last fall. Knew I could use them for this painting project, so hid them in the garage. Don't tell Joe, okay?" She leaned forward to wrinkle her nose. "These were his."

"Those were Joe's?"

"Yes. Can you believe it? We wear the same size!" Her swinging foot came to a stop so she could put her feet together on the floor. "Pretty convenient, wouldn't you say?"

He seemed to be enjoying how she wiggled the worn-out high-toppers. "It's pretty amazing, sunshine, how you can make even a torn pair of dirty tennis shoes look so good."

She was pleased, but changed the subject, since he was leaving shortly. "Hey, are you coming for dessert tonight? We're having hot apple pie."

"Sure, if I can. It's Saturday night, so who knows?" Their eyes met, and the room got quiet. Somewhere under all that furniture, an alarm clock gently ticked away the next few minutes, while they talked without speaking. Then he glanced at his watch. "Got to get a move on." He rose, pulling her up into his arms for a tender kiss. "I'll call, if I can't get away," he said as he went out the front door.

He was patrolling all the way out to the end of Maple Street, before he realized what he'd been looking at when Lenore was wiggling her feet and laughing about the high-toppers: One of those tennis shoes had a tear on the tip of the toe.

He found a phone, rather than sending a message through the dispatcher. It took her a little while to answer the call, since she was right in the middle of rolling out paint on the first wall. "Hey there, Mister Chief of Police," she cooed. "What's up?"

"You need to take off those tennis shoes. Don't get any paint on them, and put them away until I can pick them up."

"What? What's happening, Rob?"

"You're just going to have to trust me on this, Lenore."

"But why? I don't understand…"

"Listen to me, sunshine. Put those shoes someplace safe. I'll get back to you in a couple of hours, okay?" She didn't respond. "Lenore, you need to do this. I'll explain tonight. I'll be coming over, for sure. But don't say anything to anybody, and especially not to Joe."

"Well, okay…"

At eleven o'clock, he tapped lightly on the front door. She answered it quickly.

"Do you have them?" he asked. She reached into the top shelf of the front door closet, pulling out a shoebox with string tied tightly around it.

"Oh, Robbie, what's happening, here?"

When he told her how the tear on the toe of the one shoe matched the photo of the imprint at Mop's killing, her eyes filled with tears. "Oh, Lenore," he said, drawing her close. "Oh, I'm so sorry."

***

Sheriff Max Duncan was beside himself. He threw the newspaper so hard against the office wall, the venetian blinds on the window let loose, crashing to the wooden sill below. "That goddim bunch of lying bastards!" Another long string of foul language preceded the kicking of his metal wastepaper basket across the room. "They lied! They got me to agree, and then they stabbed me in the back."

"Sir?" the newest deputy on the Chittenden County Sheriff's Department ventured to inquire. "You all right, sir?"

"Mind your own damned business, Deputy. You've got dispatch duty; get your sorry butt in there, and don't say another word, you hear me?" The young man was hurrying to obey, but didn't make it to the doorway before Max yelled again. "Get me the editor of the *Burlington Free Press*, and do it *now*."

It was a full ten minutes before he got the editor on the line. "What the hell are you guys doing to me?" the sheriff shouted. "I've bent over backwards to accommodate you, to give you good stories, to back your op-eds, and this is how you repay me — by printing hearsay like this, just before my re-election campaign? Where the hell is your head, huh? I thought we were working together, for the common good." He took a breath. "You better have a damned good answer, that's all I can say."

The editor's reply was calm and professional. "Now, Max, it is our policy to always keep the public informed on the state of our law enforcement agencies, all over the state of Vermont — "

"Including whatever crap you can report, to draw readership?" He growled out the accusation. "You have no right to print gossip and speculation about *any* individuals, let alone, law enforcement personnel, that could lead to unwarranted public distrust, in any shape or form, whatsoever." He slammed his fist on the desk. "I want to know who told you lies about my opinion of the Abenaki nation. This is simply not true, and I want a retraction, do you hear me?"

"Our information came from a very reliable source, Max. We double-checked with members of that tribe, who verified the presence of a list. I'm sure you can appreciate our diligence when it comes to matters like this." The sheriff was beside himself; it was all he could do to let the newspaper man continue. "Now, if you would like to issue a formal statement of denial, we'd be happy to print it. For instance, are you aware of such a list?"

"Let me just say this, sir: If there *is* such a thing as these lists, I'm not involved in it. That would be in conflict with my duties as sheriff of Chittenden County. I hope you understand that."

"Uh-huh, Well, I do find it interesting that you're talking about more than one list, Max. I only mentioned *one*. Our source stated that there were *lists*, that is to say, more than one — a lot more than one."

"Aw crap," he howled, dodging the point, "this is nothing but political shenanigans. No, it's worse than that. It's somebody trying to take me out." He gritted his teeth. "If you allow this stuff, the public will get wise to it, real fast. I'm not kidding, mister, I want a retraction, and I want it in the next issue."

There was a brief pause, with some shuffling in the background. "Tell you what, I'll review the story again, and if there is any element that should be reinvestigated, I'll make the public aware of it. But," the editor's mind was made up, "if there is nothing, then I will retract nothing — understood?"

Max swore and hung up.

He had been fingered, cornered, and exposed.

***

Jessie Wilson was getting tired of fried eggs and peanut butter sandwiches. Being on his own was, at once, terrifying and an immense relief. Starting over was not easy for the man who had lost his wife and son in less than six months. At the same time, new surroundings held a promise of some sort of future. He spent the first few weeks getting things organized in the two-bedroom house located in the Indian Acres housing project. By the end of that first month, he realized he needed to buy some real groceries, so he headed for the IGA located down the footpath behind his rented house. At the store, he moved slowly through the aisles, realizing he had no clue as to what he was doing. The bewildered fellow was standing in front of the cereal display, when he heard a friendly voice: "You look like you could use a little help,"

Lenore Curtis whispered.

He grinned sheepishly. "Oh well, is it that obvious?"

She smiled. "I don't know if you remember me, but I'm Joe Turner's foster mother."

He was relieved that she had renewed his memory. "Of course. Sure. You came to the sewing group at the farm."

"The Maple Leaf Sewing Circle, that's right." Her eyes went to his empty basket. "So, I take it, this is something new for you?" He nodded. "That's okay, Mr. Wilson, you'll get the hang of it before too long."

"I hope so. I have my folks coming to help me do all this stuff, but not until a few days. I think my mom will help me get it all in order."

"Right." She thought he could use a little encouragement. "So, what do you need for the next few days? Breakfast food?" She motioned toward the collection of cereal boxes. "Take your pick. What do you like?"

He picked the corn flakes, and so she led him to the milk and sugar. "Nothing you have to cook, until your mom gets here," she reassured him, as the cold cuts, mayonnaise, and bread piled into the basket. "And you can always go get a steak and baked potato at the Lincoln Inn. Then, before you know it, your folks will be here, and you'll get a whole new education in the kitchen." The two of them launched into the rest of the shopping project, oblivious of the customers around them, including a certain one who spotted them, then maintained a careful distance, until the couple had checked out at the cash register.

The happy shoppers ended up in the parking lot, loading bags of groceries into Lenore's car, because he had come by the path, and there was no way he could get all that home. Just before he closed the trunk, a grateful Jessie Wilson made an observation, which caused her face to turn a bright pink.

Through the wide front window of the grocery store, Robbie watched the exchange. His gut turned, as he witnessed that blush — something, she had told him, only *he* could make happen.

He stood there for a long time, staring out at the parking lot. Then he went home. There would be no visit, no phone call to her that night. He needed to get real about Lenore Curtis.

***

Yesterday's grocery store incident bothered him, but his police training kept Rob focused on a more pressing matter. It was time to get some unbiased opinions from the experts on the investigative committee. The Courtney brothers filled the bill, neither one of them being emotionally involved in the dog killings — at least, not yet. He met them in Burlington's County Court House, the three of them huddling in the corner of a conference room. The two lawyers melted into the padded chairs; the morning hearings had been especially rigorous. Robbie hoped to get right to the point and to arrive quickly at a reasonable conclusion.

"Brought you a couple of iced teas," he said. The men reached for them, grateful for the wetting of the whistle before they returned to the courtroom for another battle. "I'll make this quick," he spoke apologetically. Rob explained what happened at the confrontation with Sheriff Duncan, including the agreement between Max and the group. Doug noted that this is highly unusual, but agreed that Cecil can call off the whole thing. "Remember, this may not be acceptable to the ASPCA. But I'll see what I can do."

"Okay, and there's one more thing: I've found the shoe that fits the imprint we photographed at the crime scene for the second killing — the drowning of the smaller dog, Mop, who, you'll remember, belonged to Joe Turner." His eyes looked up to verify the agreement on the others' faces, before he let the bomb drop. "Unhappily, the shoe belongs to Joe."

"Oh, hell," Douglas muttered. Johnny wiped his mouth with the back of his hand, stunned into silence. "Are you sure?" Johnny's uncle asked.

"Ninety-nine percent, but the results won't be back for a few days." He apologized again. "Sorry, Doug, but I felt we needed to get right on this, and you were so busy."

The head of the law firm waved it away. "You did the right thing. We have another ASPCA meeting coming up in few days; we'll need those results." He tugged at his collar, wiggled his shoulders, and took another sip. "How'd you find the shoe?"

"Lenore was wearing it. That is, wearing the shoes, to paint the guest room."

"How'd *she* get a-hold of them?"

Robbie went on to explain the rest of the story. Johnny sat silently sipping, while his uncle grunted and hummed punctuations to the lawman's recitation. "So, Chief," he finally said, when Robbie stopped, "tell me this: How did Lenore manage to get into a thirteen-year-old's tennis shoes?"

Rob chuckled. "They wear the same size, believe it or not."

Douglas Courtney's eyes closed for a couple of seconds, then opened to fix on Rob Allen's curious gaze. "I trust you see the implications, here, my friend."

"What?"

"It could have been *her* who was down at the edge of Indian Brook, wearing those shoes."

CHAPTER TWENTY-THREE

Sifting

Bernie McBain was crouched over his yellow writing tablet, down at his workbench in the cellar of the rental home he and his wife, Della, inhabited. At the creak of the cellar door that led down from the kitchen, he slammed the tablet closed and shoved it, along with the ballpoint pen, into a secret drawer beneath the shelf. By the time Della had navigated the plunging stairway, he was carving a bit of wood. He looked up. "What's up, Del?"

"Don't be cute with me, you old goat." She paused to catch her breath. "You've been down here every night for the last week." She looked around. "So, what've you been up to, huh?"

"Ach! I knew you'd find me out, lass!" He waggled the knife in the air. "And so, yeh've caught me, red-handed." He went for the "little white lie" tactic. "I swear, I can't surprise yeh with a birthday present, no matter how hard I try."

"You're working on my birthday present?" She checked out the stub of wood in his hands. "What is it, a wooden nickel?" He laughed and winked mischievously, but it didn't work; she was already noticing the lack of wood shavings on the floor. "I don't believe you," she said, with a squint. "What're you up to, Ber-nard?"

It was time to *really* lie. "Way-yell, I suppose yeh'll find out, sooner or later." He put the wood down. "I'm plannin' how to spend the reward money."

That took her off the trail, very quickly. "So," she asked, leaning against a nearby post, "how much *do* you get for solving the case?"

"Nah-nah-nah, lass. I can't say I really solved the case. That's not what the offer was, at all. It was one hundred dollars to anybody who could bring about the conviction of the person or persons who killed their dog, Blow." He waited for her to get that straight. "So far, it looks like I have helped, but there's been no conviction, yet."

"Oh, that's just a matter of time, Bernie. You got the goods on him, for sure." Della looked around. "So, what're we spending the money on? If I know you, there's notes somewhere."

"Aw crap, Della, couldn't yeh just let me lay it all out on paper?" He recognized a way out of the lie. "I've been makin' notes, okay?" He pulled the notebook drawer open. "Here they are." When she moved forward to have a look, he lifted both hands. "Nah-nah-nah, woman! I'll keep it to myself until I'm ready. That's my final word on the matter."

"Hmph," she grunted. "I'll just read it when you're not looking, and if you're thinking of hiding it right in plain sight, forget it; believe me, I'll know it, when I see it."

"Nah-nah-nah," he repeated. "I'll be about findin' a new hidin' place, for sure."

"We'll just see about that, you mean old man," she quipped. It was difficult, because the stairs were so steep, but she managed to slip in a couple of Mae West moves on the way up.

"Yeh'll not vamp me with yer words of endearment, lass, not this time," he murmured.

And he meant that. After all, there might not *be* a conviction. Sheriff Duncan had agreed to let Mr. Uncle come home for good, in exchange for the end of the investigation, as directed by Mr. Thompson. No, there was no guarantee of any reward money, unless the Thompsons were so grateful to have their family circle physically restored.

And there was something else bothering the Scotchman —

something half-hidden in the depths of his Canadian Forces memories. The old family line of the Farquhars had a long history of military service, and he had learned a lot from that source, as well. The old warrior leaned forward, elbows on the work shelf, to once again ponder this troubling hunch. When he finally figured it out, he heaved a heavy sigh. The solving of this case just didn't feel right. It had almost been too easy. "Way-yell," he told himself, "I'll just sleep on it. By mornin' I'll shake it all out."

He reached over to grab one of Della's canning jars, making sure it had a tight lid on it. She usually did that, to keep the dirt and dust of the cellar from getting inside those glass containers. Quickly, he tore the thick layer of pages out of his notebook and rolled them into a heavy, solid cylinder, just enough to fit inside. One forceful twist ensured no air or whatever else could get into the jar. Then he snuck upstairs to the bathroom, where he flushed the toilet, then placed the sealed information inside the tank. He waited until the water had brought the float valve ball up to where it needed to be. The heavy jar was still settled firmly on the bottom. All was well.

"Let's see yeh find *that*, woman," he whispered.

***

"I can't remember any counseling sessions being as enjoyable as these with Joe and Winnie," Connie remarked. She and Don had just dropped the boy off and were now on their way back to their Winooski home. In the waning sunlight, the tires of the Studebaker Champion were throwing clods of muddy snow behind them, irritating drivers, and slowing the movement of those trailing vehicles.

"Well, it's such an inviting atmosphere because they don't seem like counseling sessions, that's why, and that's exactly what we want to do. Joe feels like we're all in class together, and this is the reason he's so relaxed." Back behind, unhappy commuters honked their horns.

"True, true," she agreed. "and in these sessions, we're establishing an atmosphere of trust and fellowship, which is laying the groundwork for our ultimate goal: revealing Joe's actual family history."

Don finally made a hard right onto Florida Avenue, letting the roiling traffic push onward.

"He needs to do that," Connie stated. "He needs to come into the reality of that family history."

"Ay-yuh, his *real* family history," Don emphasized, "which is the *family of God*."

"It could take a while," she said. "He needs to work it through."

"Just like the rest of us," Don mused. "Just like the rest of us."

***

Inside the house, Joe was telling Lenore about his latest lesson. "Today, Uncle was there," he was happy to inform her. "His Indian name is 'Shining Waters.' He wants to show me how to fish, and how to disappear into the woods." He looked around the kitchen. "I'm hungry. Okay if I fix a peanut butter sandwich?"

She left him doing that, wandering out into the living room where the phone sat quietly on an end table. It had not rung in two days. "Where are you?" she murmured under her breath. Once more, she checked the Allen driveway, hoping to spot the squad car. This time, it was there. Her face flushed. He was home. Surely, he would be calling soon, wanting to come over.

A half-hour later, Joe was ready for some television. She busied herself cleaning up the sandwich mess on the kitchen shelf. By the time she was wringing out the woven dishcloth, another whole fifteen minutes had passed. Again, she went to a window, where she saw that vehicle still there. "I should spruce up a little," she told herself.

She chose the red sweater she'd worn at Christmas, then brushed the unruly blonde curls into shape. "Only a touch of lipstick; we don't need to have it all over our faces," she whispered, happily. It was another half-hour before she lightly tapped her favorite rose water under both earlobes.

Still no phone call.

A little tug of concern drove her back to the living room window, where she saw the police car gleaming under the glow of the bright porch light. "Maybe he's sick. I should check." Relieved to have an excuse, she quickly made the call. It was Gracie who answered. "Oh, hi, Gracie. It's Lenore."

"Yes, Lenore. How are you this evening?"

"I'm good. But I am concerned. I haven't heard from Robbie for a while. Is he okay? He's not sick, is he?"

"Um, not exactly."

She waited for Gracie to finish the sentence. When it didn't come, the girlfriend spoke hesitantly. "What does that mean, Gracie? Is there something wrong?"

Rob's mother seemed sympathetic. "I don't know how to answer that, dear."

Lenore's grasp tightened on the phone. "Well, can I at least talk to him?"

There was a pause, as though she was listening to someone in the room. "That might not be a good idea, Lenore. He's exhausted, and headed for bed. I'm sorry." The conversation ended with the soft click.

"What the heck...?" She felt a rush of anger, but was careful to gently replace the phone into its cradle. There was time for a long, dry swallow, before she made her move. Joe was watching Snooky Lanson crooning something about love in the park, on *Your Hit Parade*. She was pulling on her coat, when he looked up.

"We going somewhere, Ma'am?"

"No-no, I just have to run over to Gracie's for a few

minutes. Are you okay with that, Joe?"

He shifted his bottom to a more comfortable position. "Sure."

"You have homework this weekend, mister?"

"Yeah. Two things. I'll work on it tomorrow."

"You sure that's enough time?"

"Yes, Ma'am. No big deal. Don't worry."

"Alrighty then," she tried to sound unconcerned. "I'll be back in a few minutes. If you need me, you know where to call."

It was risky, but once she made up her mind, there was no turning back. Her rap on Gracie's back door was loud and rapid. She repeated it only once, before it opened. Gracie was standing there in her coat. "Oh, thank God," the woman whispered. "I was on my way up to *your* place."

"Well, alright then, can we talk privately, Gracie?"

"I doubt it; I'm sure he heard your loud knocking."

"Yes, I did!" Robbie appeared just behind his mother. The silvery-haired lady pulled her coat tighter as she moved to leave the house. "I need to go to the IGA," she said, gently skirting around Lenore.

The blonde lady stood her ground, halfway inside the doorway. "Don't you slam that door on me, Robbie. We have to talk."

"I… wouldn't slam… I wouldn't do that."

"Good, because I'm coming in," she announced. She slid out of her coat in the dark kitchen, as he closed the door. "Are you sick, or what?" The headlights of Gracie's departing car moved slowly across Lenore's face, then disappeared.

"I don't know how to answer that," he softly replied.

"I can wait," she said. "No, don't turn on that light."

He stopped and turned back toward her. "Why not?"

"Because you owe me at least ten minutes of phone calls, where I can hear your voice, and love every minute of it, even if I can't see your face."

"What?"

She gave him a disciplinary shove. "How could you *do*

that? You *know* how crazy I am about you! How could you just *shut me out* like that?" The frustration came forth in tears. "I thought we had something. I thought you really..." The sobs could no longer be contained.

He grabbed her upper arms, to keep her from pounding on his chest. "So, okay, let's get it out there on the table, young lady." He shook her gently. "Stop the pounding," he demanded as he reached for the light switch. The bright dome illuminated her flaxen hair, now leaning toward his chest. He stepped back. "I guess I should tell you, I saw you with that Jessie Wilson, flirting around in the aisles of the IGA store. I couldn't believe my eyes."

She stood erect. "What? Flirting around?" She folded her arms to make the statement: "I'll have you know, Mister Chief of Police, that I was helping that clueless man stock up on food, until his folks come in a few days." She sniffed the wet stuff glistening under her nose. "And I was glad to do it. I was glad to do it for Laura's sad, lost husband." There was a defiant jerk of her head. "And if you'd had your wits about you, you cop, you would have come over and joined us, and seen for yourself what was really going on!"

"Oh no you don't, missy. I left you alone, giving you the benefit of a doubt, until I saw what happened out in the parking lot." It was his turn to fold the arms. "I saw you. I saw you, blushing like that."

"Oh." She was beginning to understand. "You're right, I did blush. In fact, I blushed big time." The arms slipped out of the fold, as she shyly lifted her eyes.

That look made him loosen his own locked arms. "So, let me get something straight," he said, slowly dropping the defensive stance. "Did I hear you wrong, or did you mean it, when you told me — right there in your own kitchen, that I was the only man in the whole world, who could make you blush like that?" He couldn't let go of their visual, passionate connection. "Didn't you tell me that?" She blinked slowly and nodded the affirmative answer. "Lenore, I... just don't get it; why did *he* make you blush?"

Lenore smiled through the slobber. "Because he was talking about *you*, my Robbie." She leaned into his arms. "He said I was a really nice person, and he was glad to know that I was linked up with a real stud, like the chief of police." She was laughing softly against Robbie's chest. "Mind you, he's a farmer, and talks like that, but," she looked up into his eyes, "the notion of you being my *stud*, still made me blush right down to my toes."

Robbie, the cop, resisted the urge to kiss that woman. "I really want to believe you, but there's still something else that's raised a big red flag."

She pulled back. "Oh my goodness! No wonder you haven't called me." There was that erect posture, again. "So, what else is going on?"

He didn't let go of her, caressing the backs of her upper arms. "There's the matter of the tennis shoes," he started.

"Oh yes," she interrupted. "Joe could have, probably *did* have something to do with the demise of his own dog." There was a short pinch of the lips. "I've been dealing with that, too."

"So, okay, I've taken this tennis shoe thing to your lawyer friends, the Courtneys, because we're getting ready to close this whole ASPCA investigation, and they brought up the fact that you and Joe wear the same size shoe." He waited for her to realize what that meant. "So," he hemmed and hawed for a few seconds, "that kind of makes *you* a suspect, too."

It was almost too much for her to absorb. "Oh, my gosh, Robbie."

She paced back and forth in the kitchen, her boots slapping smartly against the linoleum floor, then stopped in front of him. "I think it's time for the two of us to have a little talk with my foster son," she said. "We need to get to the bottom of all this."

CHAPTER TWENTY-FOUR

Jousting

Meanwhile, Sheriff Max Duncan was on the prowl. There was at least one more ASPCA committee meeting in just one day, and he was scrambling to clear his name. There would be no prosecution, of course, because the Thompsons had already withdrawn the complaint, but somebody was out to ruin him, and he wasn't going to stand still for it. "There's no missing trousers in my closet. Every uniform item is there, so where did those pants come from?" He brought the county vehicle to a stop, right in front of the dry cleaning establishment that had identified the incriminating clothing item. Inside, he spoke privately to the owner. "I'm sure you remember me, sir, since I'm the only sheriff in this county, but when I moved from Colchester last spring, I changed cleaners because it was just too far to come all the way back here."

"I remember that you thanked us, the last time you picked up your uniforms. How have you been, Sheriff?"

"Well, things have certainly not gotten any better. I figure you know what's going on." The proprietor acknowledged this with a sad look. "Well, I'm trying to figure out how those pants got there, and all I can remember is that I stopped coming here last spring." He leaned back against the office wall. "I was hoping you might have something you could help me remember, like maybe somebody else might have come in here and put my name on the order. You sure would remember that, because I had already thanked you guys, and left for good." He looked hopeful. "Anything like that happened?"

The man's eyes squinted for a second. "I don't think so, because the date on that pair of pants was on the same day you said goodbye to us — June twenty-ninth, I believe."

"It was? Nobody told me that." He needed to be reassured. "You sure about that?"

"I am, because I was a little worried about how that uniform looked. I mean, it was pretty worn out. I remember thinking it was time for you to get a new one."

Max paused to think. "Okay, now that's something to consider." Then it hit him like a brick between the eyes. "*I buy one new uniform every year, rotating it with two that were bought the two previous years.*" He shook the man's hand and returned to the driver's seat, where he sat still, trying to see how it all fit together. "*That had to be the last pick up made at this cleaner, because I now have three sets, all of which are tagged by the* new dry cleaner." He pondered what that all meant, slowly tapping his fingers on the shiny steering wheel. "It's one of my old uniform pants, and it hasn't been cleaned since last June." The tapping grew louder. "But they were fresh and clean, so I probably wore them at least a couple of weeks, before I got rid of them, and got me a new set." He counted the weeks, and was surprised to see that he'd made that new purchase sometime around the end of July.

"That would be the date, give a few days or so, that I would have tossed out the old uniform, and that would include the worn-out pants, as well." The fingers suddenly lay quietly at the top of the wheel. "If I killed the dog while wearing those pants, it would mean I never threw them out, because that killing occurred — what? Almost three months later?" A glimmer of hope appeared in his eyes. "No way. I always throw the old uniform out. I wad it up and throw it in the burn barrel." There was a check in his reasoning. "But wait, I had just moved to the apartment in Burlington, where there was *and still is, no burn barrel.*" His fingers moved to grip the curved top of the wheel. "So what did I do with that old uniform?"

He was halfway back to Burlington before he remembered: "I bagged it up, to throw into the garbage at the office. Sure, that's what I did. And then Smith and I went on patrol." The relief came like a cool breeze. "Okay, Smith is my witness. He'll remember."

***

"I agree," Robbie said to Lenore. "We need to confront the boy, and do it right now, because tomorrow will probably be the last meeting for the ASPCA committee."

He was pulling on his shirt jacket. "Nobody has actually filed any complaint about Mop's death, do you realize that?" He escorted her out the door, the photo of the tennis shoe's toe tucked safely into an inside pocket.

Joe was still watching his program when the two of them came through the front doorway. "Hey," he greeted them.

She signaled Rob to remove his jacket, as she did the same. Once those were in the closet, the couple moved to sit on either side of the boy's laid-back position in the center of the couch. "What-cha watching?" Rob asked.

"Aw, nothing much," the kid replied, sitting up straighter.

"That's good, then," Lenore said, "because we had something to talk to you about."

Joe grinned. "Aw, I knew this was coming."

"Oh?" Rob glanced at Lenore.

"Yup." The boy was confident. "Knew it would happen, sooner or later."

"You knew *what* would happen, sooner or later?" she asked cautiously.

"You guys gettin' hitched." His approval was somewhat tentative. "So, that's a good thing, I guess, but I don't know what you want to do with *me*, that's all."

Her face was pink, but her voice was level. "Uh, no, Joe,

that's not what we wanted to talk about." He was surprised. "We actually have something we need to show you."

"Oh. Sorry. I just thought, you know…" He watched Robbie draw the photograph from his shirt pocket. "Oh! You got a picture, or something?"

"Ay-yuh, Joe. Thought maybe you could help us solve a case." The eyebrows raised. "Think you can do that?"

"Wow! Really?" He leaned forward. "So what's it all about?"

"It's about an imprint. You know what that is?" the man asked. Joe looked lost. "So, an imprint is what happens when somebody steps into, say, a muddy path, and leaves a footprint of their foot, or their shoe." The youngster got that. "And that's what I have here: a picture of an imprint, and it's of a shoe, but only the toe of the shoe. Here, take a look."

The thirteen-year-old held the photo in his hands, peering closely. "Whoa, that's really something."

Rob drew a pen from another pocket, using the top end to trace the outline. "Do you see how it's just the toe of the shoe?"

"Oh! Yup, yup, I see it."

"And do you see how there's just a little, ragged tear in the wrap-around?"

"What's a wrap-around, Chief?"

"So, let's look at your own tennis shoes, right now." He bent to point the pen at the strip of rubber that covered the seam between the sole and the upper part of the shoe's toe area. "That's the wrap-around, right there." The boy got that, too. "So now, look at the picture, again." He touched the area of the tear on the imprint. "Now, we can look at this torn part, and if we can match it to somebody's shoe, we know who made that muddy imprint." He smiled softly. "That's how we know who the shoe belongs to. He leaned back, taking the photo with him. "Pretty good detective work, wouldn't you say?" The boy agreed. "Well, in this case, in this particular picture, we have found who was wearing that shoe." He tilted the photo under the lamplight before getting to the point. "So, in this particular case, well, this imprint was found right where the authorities found your little dog, Mop." He watched the boy's face go somber. "Well, we found the shoe that made that imprint, and, I'm sorry to say, that shoe belongs to *you*."

The terror on his face moved Lenore so deeply, she reached to hug him. The boy moaned and collapsed in her arms, wailing loudly. Rob watched her hold the broken kid, tears streaming from her own eyes. He waited until, at length, she murmured, "Okay, son, okay. Just tell us what happened."

He could not lift his face from her shoulder, but the words were clear. "It was a accident! He went for a dip in the brook, like always." His shoulder shuddered. "Damned, stupid dog!" he moaned. "The chain got caught. He must-a pulled on it, and it got more caught. By the time I pulled him up, he was dead, his tongue all hanging out." He pushed his face into the hollow of her shoulder. "Damned, stupid dog!"

She looked at Rob. "It's true, we couldn't keep him tethered. He kept breaking the chain. The dog shouldn't have even been down there, following Joe on that paper route."

Joe raised his head and wiped his nose on his sleeve. "I... I should-a put him in the bike basket and took him home." He sniffed. "But I didn't. I didn't."

The chief of police, who had witnessed many confessions, stepped in. "So, what did you do about that mess?" Joe sniffed again, but didn't seem to have an answer. Rob pursued it. "Why didn't you just bring Mop's body home? I mean, Lenore would have helped you deal with all that, right?"

There was a shaky breath before he answered. "Probably. I guess so. But it was what all the other people would think, like maybe I chopped up that other dog, or whatever."

"So, what did you do, son?" She let go of him, and he leaned back, his eyes on the ceiling.

"I just thought, I'll make it look like that mean woman, Mrs. Spofford, did this one, too."

"She was a mean woman?" Rob asked.

He sniffed and wiped his nose, again. "She swore at Mop for barking and running on her lawn… said she was going to get me fired, and she did. She got me fired from my paper route." The mouth went hard. "She's a mean woman."

"And so," the chief emphasized, "you wanted her punished."

The young chin shot upward with certainty. "Well, she killed the Thompsons' dog. She should be punished!"

Rob looked at the floor, then back up at the young judge. "As a matter of fact, Joe, we think we have found that attacker, and it is *not* May Spofford."

"What?" He could not believe it. "She didn't kill Blow?"

"We're ninety-nine percent sure it was this other suspect."

"No. No. No, she's the one who did it. She's a mean dog-killer."

Lenore reached out to touch his hand. "Actually, Joe, she's nothing of the kind."

"Oh yeah?" he challenged her, "then who killed Blow?"

"That question will be answered before too much longer," Rob replied. "Right now, we want to end the mystery of how Mop died… and I think we have."

"Am I, you know, going to jail, or anything?"

"Well, you certainly did not kill your own dog, and there have been no charges on that death, but, if you would attend a meeting with me tomorrow, I think we can finally put an end to this very sad, sad, situation."

The boy agreed to cooperate.

Lenore drew a hot bath for the boy, and laid out a fresh pair of flannel pajamas, before coming back to the living room, where Rob was still sitting on the sofa. He beckoned for her to join him, pulling her into a sideways embrace. "You are something, do you know that, sunshine?" He kissed her temple. "You handled these two situations like a pro. Well, except for the part where you pounded on my chest."

"I wasn't pounding, I was *pleading*."

"Okay, I'll give you that one," he said with a squeeze. "I'm sorry for thinking you were a flirt and a phony."

"You should be."

"And you were so good with the kid. I'm impressed." There was another warm touch of his mouth against her temple. "Joe is lucky to have you as a foster mom, and as for me, I probably can't go on one more day without you."

"Aw, thank you, Robbie," she replied, cuddling in.

"So, do you want to?"

"Do I want to what?"

"You know... get hitched?"

"*What?!*"

"Well," he moved his mouth over to the closest blonde eyebrow, "Joe seems to think it's a good idea."

"Oh yeah? Well, he's just a kid. What does he know?"

"Aw, c'mon, honey. It's like your farmer friend said: I'm such a stud!"

Her hands covered the blush. "Oh my gosh, Robbie Allen. You *have* to stop talking like that!"

"Only if you marry me, and then only if we get bored, like, in maybe fifty years or so."

***

Bernie McBain woke up the day of the meeting, with the question nicely answered; the only problem was, just when and how to present it. Most importantly, it needed to be put out there in such a manner that some*one* or some*thing* would confirm the accuracy of that answer. "*Maybe if I just bring it up, sort-a casual, like, 'Anybody else been wondering why it was so easy for me to find that stuff on Laura Wilson's grave?'*" He turned over in the bed, rethinking that one. "*Or maybe I should just tell them right out, 'I'm bothered by how easy it was for me to find those bloody pants hidden on top of that grave.'*" Once again, he flopped to his other side. This time, he noticed Della wasn't in bed. A quick glance at the clock showed it wasn't quite the five o'clock hour. That was unusual for her, up so early. He sat erect, thinking maybe there was something wrong.

"I'd better take a wee look around," he muttered, shoving his boney feet into a pair of worn slippers. A sweep of his arm brought a faded robe around his body as he headed out into the upstairs hallway. All was quiet, so he decided to go on down the stairs, but as he passed the bathroom's open door, he stopped dead in his tracks.

Della looked up from her seat on the toilet. The tank cover was placed across the top of the sink, and the glass canning jar was on the floor beside her feet. She grinned. "So, you're writing a book, Bernie?" she cooed, shaking the yellow stack of notes toward him. "Well, I think you should include some stuff about the Fart-quhars. You know, something about your old family history."

"Aw crap, woman. I swear, yeh have a nose like a bloodhound!"

"Oh, I don't know… it took me two days to find it." She held up the notes, again. "But I still think you should tell about your old family ties with the Fart-quharhs."

"Gimme that," he demanded. "An author has a right to his privacy, Del!" Then he stomped out of the room.

"Don't bother to hide it," she called after him. "Although, I do enjoy the challenge."

He thought about concealing the manuscript in the trunk of the car, but decided it would be too hard for him to access it for a quick session. The workshop in the old cow barn was too obvious — she'd be on that track in five minutes. But the would-be author was determined this was to be *his* own private project. "Even if I have to hide it, chapter-by-chapter, in a hundred different places," he muttered, "it's my own stuff and that's how I intend to keep it." Then he realized he had just solved the problem. All he had to do, was to write one or two chapters at a time, put them into their own sealed canning jars, and hide them all over the place. Even if she found one or two, it wouldn't matter all that much, because she would think she'd been successful, and would stop searching, maybe for a day or so, but the complete manuscript would not be found, until he was ready. He was jubilant.

Bernie's thoughts went back to the idea of the workshop in the old cow barn. He knew exactly where he would hide the next few chapters of the book: Old Joe Turner had cleaned the one stall for his milking cow every morning, and now there was an old, dried-out manure pile, just thirty feet from the back of the building, overgrown with weeds, and long forgotten.

***

That same morning, Lenore was on the phone with Don Collins. "Joe is off to school," she prefaced the message, "and I know Connie is already there in her first classroom, but I was counting on you being home, and thank God, you are." She went on to tell about Joe's confession concerning Mop's demise, ending with an encouraging note. "Chief Allen and I thanked him for his honesty, and he seems to be *so relieved* to have it all out in the open. It truly was an accident, but the boy was afraid nobody would believe him, so he tried to put the blame on May Spofford." She paused, not sure what to say next.

"Thank God I am home this morning. I have swing shift at the bus company this afternoon. So," he seemed to be collecting his thoughts, "I'm glad you called."

"Well, you also need to know that Joe is attending the ASPCA investigation's meeting this afternoon, to clear up that part of the mystery." There was a little click of her tongue. "I hope that goes well. You know, if they come down hard on him, it could set back everything being accomplished up there at the Thompsons." The worry turned into impatience. "You know, I just don't understand how so much bad stuff could happen to one small boy. First, dumped in a home for destitute and disturbed kids, then his little 'blood brother' is killed by a predator uncle — you remember little Joe was named after the uncle, Joe Turner. Then he goes to live with that uncle and gets molested, and who knows the extent of that? And then he goes into foster care, where he has never really bonded with me. He still calls me, 'Ma'am' to this very day."

"Right," Don confirmed all of it.

"But he *does* start to bond with Laura Wilson and that family, only to have her taken away, and the whole family disintegrates right before his very eyes." Her voice rose to a higher pitch. "And now *this*! His dog dies, for Pete's sake." There was a small sniffle. "I just don't *get it*, you know?"

"I hear you, loud and clear. It's a rough world out there, for sure." He moved the phone to his other ear. "And, the reality is, Lenore, that nobody goes through this life without taking some serious, if not deadly blows." He made a little humming noise through his nose. "I guess you could say, we're all damaged, in one way or another, at one time or another, and for some of us, the damage is far greater than what we can take." He drew a long breath. "And that's where the rubber meets the road, so to speak."

"What does that mean?"

His reply came slowly. "So, maybe this meeting will actually help the kid to get a more balanced perspective on how to handle life, in general, Lenore. It may just drive the boy more firmly to depend on God, instead of man — Abenaki, or otherwise. I think we adults really need to let God work in this situation." She could hear the tsk of his tongue. "Tell you what, let's agree in prayer, that there will be tremendous good coming out of this confession."

"I'm not sure what you mean, about agreeing, or whatever."

"Well, do you believe in prayer?"

"Uh, yes, I guess I really *do*." She was surprised at how comfortable that felt.

"Good. So let's pray, right now."

"Now?"

"Yes, Lenore. Just bow your head in the presence of God

Almighty, and agree with His own Word."

"Oh, wow, Don, I'm not sure I should be doing that. I mean, I go to church and all that, but I haven't been all that close to God, to tell the truth."

"But you do believe that Jesus died for your sins, and you're going to Heaven, right?"

"Oh! Of course. I do believe that. I know that's true."

"Good. Now, just bow your head."

In the next few minutes, something happened to Lenore Tanning Curtis. When she finally hung up the phone, the words blurted out: "Okay, Jesus, I'm back."

CHAPTER TWENTY-FIVE

Investigations

Chief Robbie Allen just could not go to the meeting later that day, without making sure Joe Turner had not — in one way or another — been involved in the killing of the Thompsons' dog, Blow. The chief recalled the conversation between himself and Lenore, a few days after Joe had cut himself. The boy had told her he hated the whole Dupree family. Had he done something, just to get even with the Dupree girl, Lisa Marie, for urging him and Dicky Dupree to become "blood brothers"?

And then, there was the matter of that family now living in the farmhouse, instead of the worn-out shack on the other side of the tracks. "What was it my mom said, the same day I talked with Lenore? Oh yeah, her very words were, "It couldn't have worked out better for the Duprees, even if they tried."

"*So, what about Roy Dupree?*" Robbie wondered. If the Wilsons left him in charge of the farm, what would he have to gain? A nicer home for his family, for sure. A place of authority for somebody who was never respected for his skills? Maybe. "Well, I've heard from the boy; I guess those other folks need to be heard, as well."

It was time for a visit to the Wilson Dairy Farm.

Sonny and Lisa Marie were just leaving for school when Chief Robbie Allen pulled into the yard. Dory was at the back doorstep, calling out final instructions for staying warm and not catching cold. She stopped and stared at the police car, before turning to say something through the open doorway behind her. By the time Robbie reached the back step, Roy had appeared just over her shoulder.

"'Morning, folks!" Rob said, with a smile. "It's a cold one!" He pointed a thumb over his shoulder. "Those kids walk to school every day?"

"Ay-yuh," Roy answered, then asked if he'd like a hot coffee. He gratefully accepted. Inside, a toddler wiggled in a beat-up wooden high chair, trying to reach something on the littered breakfast table in front of him. Ceecee wandered in from the living room, holding her abdomen. As Dory poured, Roy took a seat beside the policeman. "So, what can I do you for?" he said, in his best Vermont farmer jargon.

"Well, sir," Rob tried to echo the lingo, "I was sort-a hoping you could help me find a needle in a haystack."

"Hey," came the slow, melodious reply, "what's your problem, Chief?"

He pushed the police hat toward the back of his head. "Oh, it's this thing with the dogs. I assume you folks have heard about it?" They acknowledged this. "So, I'm getting out there in the neighborhood, asking questions, hoping somebody knows something." They nodded courteously. "So, I was sure hoping you folks could help me out." Realizing they needed a reference point, he put one out there: "Like, for instance, what do you know about the Thompsons? Any enemies that you know of?" The parents looked at each other, clueless. Ceecee just sat there, holding her gut. "No? Okay, so how about the other dog, the little one, that belonged to Joe Turner. Got any ideas about that?" He knew they didn't know about the boy's confession, but it was a good way to get where he was taking this conversation. They didn't seem to have an answer, so he went for the heart of the matter. "Uh, Ceecee," he asked casually, "maybe you can help me out, here. Didn't you kids know Joe when you were in The Home?"

"Yeah, sure. He was the little Indian kid. Him and Dicky were friends."

"Somebody told me that, now that I think of it. Matter of fact, Ceecee, those two boys were supposed to be 'blood brothers' or something. You know about that?"

The large brown eyes moved left, then right. "Um, yup something like that. I don't remember too much about it, though."

"I was told that Lisa Marie came up with that idea. Do you remember if she did?"

The eyes moved again. "I guess she did, because Sonny was sick and he was gone and Dicky was missing him. I think that's why she did it." She rubbed the unhappy belly. "But that's how Lisa Marie is. She tries to be everybody's mother."

Dory laughed. "It's true."

"So, she did it, to be kind, would you say?"

LeRoy smiled softly. "Ay-yuh, that's our Lisa Marie. If you lose a button, she'll sew another one on." Dory patted her husband on the shoulder, then rose to take their youngest son away for a bath.

"So," Rob asked the father and daughter, "you folks ever hear from Joe, after The Home?"

LeRoy shrugged and looked to her for the answer. "Not that I know about," she said, carefully. "We never tried, because it made us think of Dicky." She sat up a little straighter in the chair. "I guess that's why he never talked to us, either. It probably made him too sad."

"But he did work here for a while, right?" He looked at Roy, who acknowledged that fact. "What did you think of him... um, just off the top of your head?"

"A nice kid. A little confused, upset about Laura, and her family falling apart. I guess when you have a life with no real family, well, it gets to be more than you can handle. But he's a good kid, and he'll probably do alright."

Robbie stood up. "One more thing, Roy; you people feel safe up here? Any worries?"

"Aw hell, no," came the answer. "We're good, and we have the sheriff rolling by pretty darned often." He grinned. "We must be pretty special, getting all that attention."

The Essex Junction chief of police pulled out onto Old Colchester Road, careful to keep his tires in the pressed-down tracks. Moving slowly along, he came to some conclusions: Joe Turner might be a troubled kid, but he was no killer. Nobody was even afraid of him. "Just because he tried to blame the accident on May, doesn't mean he was capable of chopping up a dog a few weeks before — not even if he believed the animal had caused Laura's death. No," he told himself, "the emotional turmoil in that kid is probably more about abandonment and grief, than it is about an intense hatred toward the Duprees." He corrected the path of the police car. "He probably doesn't even realize he's blaming one family for his lost childhood." It was pretty clear, now. "And I can't get around the fact that everybody (except May Spofford) either likes the kid, or considers him a non-threatening, casual acquaintance."

That left the questions about LeRoy Dupree. "Okay, definitely not cosmopolitan, in fact, I would guess he's had limited formal education. I doubt he has the skills to run a business, which is what the dairy thing is, in the case of the Wilsons. No, Jessie is still the owner and manager, and LeRoy seems comfortable with that. He really has no motive to kill that dog."

The center mound of snow was getting lower, letting him speed up a bit. Before he got back to the office, he was satisfied. If anybody brought these issues up, he felt pretty much ready to handle them.

There were no more qualms about reporting to the ASPCA's special investigation team.

***

The meeting took place, as usual, in Rob's office. Gathered around the table were Douglas Courtney, Bernie McBain, Sheriff Duncan and his deputy, and Joe Turner. Seated beside the boy was his estate lawyer, Johnny Courtney and one of his counselors, Connie Collins. At five thirty, Douglas took charge. "Well folks, it looks like this could be our last meeting. As most of you know, the Thompsons have elected to drop any charges concerning the death of their dog. It took some doing, but the ASPCA has reluctantly stepped aside from any further actions, other than to keep a permanent record of this case. It still is, after all, animal abuse." He looked around. "Any questions?"

Max Duncan spoke up. "I don't have a question, but I would like to make a brief statement." He gritted his teeth, then let a slow breath hiss through. "I realize that the charges have been dropped by the Thompsons, but the fact remains that somebody is responsible for killing that dog. I just want you all to know, I intend to find the killer." The left fist smacked into the right palm. "And I won't stop until I get that bastard."

Everyone in the room, except for Joe Turner and Connie Collins, knew what the man was really saying — that he was not guilty, and was out to prove it, come hell or high water.

"Okay, I guess that's up to you, Sheriff," Douglas replied. He turned to the chief of police. "I believe you have a couple of things to tell us, Rob."

"I do, but we need to hear from Joe's attorney, first."

"Thanks, Chief." Johnny leaned in to speak. "I'm here today, to advise and protect my client, who has come, *voluntarily*, to tell us how his own pet died. I would remind you all that this is a statement, not a confession of animal abuse. He will merely inform you of the circumstances, so that this part of your investigation may also come to an end." The lawyer spoke to Connie. "Mrs. Collins, you are part of the counseling team working with Joe, is that correct?" She nodded. "And Joe has explained to you what happened?"

"Yes, just a few minutes ago."

"You've heard the whole story, and believe him?"

"Yes, sir, I absolutely believe him."

Johnny nodded to the boy. "So, it's all good, Joe. Go ahead

and tell the committee what happened."

Young Joe Turner swallowed hard before he started. By the time he had finished, he was weeping, and tears were streaming down Connie's face. Douglas Courtney took over. "Alright," he said slowly, "then that's what happened. I will report that to the authorities, with the recommendation that you continue with your counseling," his eyes signaled that to Connie, "and we report back to them on a monthly basis, to reassure that therapy is being carried out, and this will never happen again." He looked the youngster in the eye. "I believe you're a good person, Joe. You just made a really bad decision." He tapped a finger on the table, for emphasis. "You're a good kid, but you're not God. Remember that."

"Yes, sir," Joe whispered.

"Meantime, Chief, you can let the Spoffords know what happened to the little dog found down by their bank of the brook."

Douglas nodded to Johnny, who rose as a signal for Connie and the boy to leave.

The door had hardly closed behind them, when Bernie called on Rob to talk about the evidence.

"So," the chief of police replied, "that's the other thing I wanted to mention." He set his chin in defense mode. "It's pretty much beside the point, Mr. McBain, since the charges have been dropped. Therefore, I don't feel the issue needs to be addressed."

"The hell, it doesn't! We've got some real issues, here, man."

Douglas raised a cautionary finger. "Oh, but I tend to disagree with you, sir. If there are no charges, any evidence is meaningless."

"Meaningless or not, it's still damned funny how easy it was for me to find, I can tell yeh!" His head bobbed in unbelief. "I'm tellin' yeh, it was just too damned easy, and I think I know why."

The sheriff's face was red with rage. "Why in hell do you even have to bring it up, in the first place? You heard the lawyer; are you deaf, man?"

"Nah-nah-nah, just listen, will yeh?"

"I don't have to listen, and neither do the rest of these guys. Just drop it, you old fool!" He jumped up from the chair, nearly tipping it over. "Just shut your stupid trap, and leave it be!" In a flash, Bernie was on his feet.

"*Whoa!*" Douglas yelled. "Both of you! Sit down and shut up. This meeting is not over, yet." The two men noted Rob's hand on phone, ready to summon help from the front office, then stepped back and slowly settled into their seats. "Now, Chief, do you have anything else to bring before this committee?"

"No. I think we're done."

"And indeed we are. I want to thank you all for your work in this investigation, and then we are officially ending the inquiry." It was a gentlemanly bow of the head. "Thank you, and this meeting is dismissed."

Outside, Sheriff Duncan couldn't let go. "I bet you're the son-of-bitch who leaked that drivel to the newspaper. I should beat the crap out of you, you little frickin' liar."

"I never did any such thing, you loud-mouthed jackass!" Bernie opened the car door. "Where I come from, a man keeps his word. I was just tryin' to tell yeh why it was so damned easy for me to find your britches." He slid into the driver's seat and reached for the door handle.

The sheriff's hand stopped the door from moving. "What did you say?"

"I told yeh, I know why it was so damned easy for me to find the evidence."

Max Duncan's attitude was suddenly under control. "It was too easy? What're you talking about?"

"I probably would never have gone back to that cemetery and dug up that grave, if he hadn't goaded me into it."

"Who goaded you into it?"

Bernie glanced around to be sure he wouldn't be heard by the wrong people, then whispered the answer: "Yer goddim deputy, that's who."

CHAPTER TWENTY-SIX

Doubts

"So, are you going to marry me, or not?" He wasn't sure whether she had even answered him, two days ago. There had been a long kiss, and then the phone interrupted, once again, with another police emergency. After that, the ASPCA meeting had taken all of his attention. Now it was the start of another day, and he was catching up on an important matter.

"Oh yes, yes, yes! I thought you got that."

"When?"

She laughed. "I've always wanted a June wedding. How does that sound?"

"Uh, it's only January."

"Yes, and that means we have to get busy with invitations and a wedding gown, and all the trimmings."

He sounded disappointed. "Oh. A wedding gown, of course." He had an idea. "We could go buy one of those, like maybe tomorrow."

"Tomorrow? Really?"

"Sure. Why not?" Another idea. "So, what else do we need?"

"We'll need flowers and candles and a Best Man and a Maid of Honor, and food and music and a hall where we can do all that." He wasn't responding, so she asked it: "Are you overwhelmed, Robbie?"

"A little. I guess I just didn't think about all those things. But you're right. The first thing we need is a marriage license, for Pete's sake. I forgot about that, too."

Over breakfast, he talked to his mother. She was delighted that he was finally getting married. "And you'll probably just move into Lenore's, so you'll still be right next door." He hadn't thought about that, either. It took him a good five minutes to decide that would be alright... even convenient, if they had kids. Kids: something else that probably hovered in the near future. That one took a little longer to feel comfortable about. *"Maybe we should take our time about this,"* he thought. *"A June wedding would be just fine. In the meantime, we get to make out on the sofa."* He smiled, and went up the street to give his sweetheart a morning hug. She was moving around in the kitchen in that fuzzy, pink housecoat, the blonde curls bouncing on her shoulders. He watched her get Joe off to school, blowing the boy a kiss as he went out the door. *"Oh Lord,"* he thought, *"it's still only January. I really don't want to wait that long."*

"More coffee?"

He checked his watch. "Nope, I'm good."

"So," she said, slipping into the chair opposite from him at the table. "Something else we need to talk about, honey." He was listening. "What about Joe? Is that going to be a problem, having an almost fourteen-year-old boy in the house?"

"Oh. I didn't think about that." He rose to leave, bending down for a warm kiss.

"We'll get to that discussion later. After all, it's only January; we have lots of time." He was suddenly relieved about that. "Lots of time; no hurry," he whispered to himself.

The office was buzzing with activity when Robbie showed up. "Got two things for you, Chief," Lily called out from her perch at the dispatcher's call board. "You're to be at the mayor's office at ten this morning. Something about the budget. Did we hire those rookies at full time, by mistake?"

"Tell Ed to look into that, and get back to me before nine thirty," the chief commanded. "What else ya got?"

She turned around to make sure he was ready for it. "We got an arrest warrant for an AWOL sailor. The Navy thinks he's headed here. They have a couple of Marines flying in sometime tomorrow, so I guess they figure we'll have him in custody by then."

"Got a name on that warrant?"

"Yes, sir. It's Seaman Apprentice Jack Wilson."

***

"She did what?" May Spofford asked the principal of Summit Grade School.

"She cut off one of Sylvia's braids, that's what!"

"I don't understand. What happened?" the mother inquired.

"There was an altercation, and I feel we need to get the parents together, see if we can't put an end to this ongoing bickering. I'm available between four and eight this evening."

"My husband gets home at five."

"Fine. Let's make it six thirty. That gives us all time for supper. I'll be in my office."

When she picked the girls up from school, they slid into the back seat, heads down. May did not speak until they were back home. "You two go in and wash up and then I want you at the kitchen table, and you'd better have a good excuse for what happened today."

It turned out that Sylvia had yelled across the schoolyard, in front of all those kids, "Your mother chops up dogs, Bella May, and everybody in the village knows it!" Since she was pumping higher on a metal swing, the Spofford girls could not reach her, so they waited in the girls' restroom, pulled her into a stall and then, while Bella May sat on her, Ina May grabbed the pigtail and cut it off with a pair of blunt-nosed scissors from the third grade art closet.

Upon hearing this, May held up her bossy finger, murmuring, "Don't move!" before she dashed up the stairs and covered her mouth with a bed pillow while she snickered with unbridled glee. After a few minutes, she yelled down the stairs: "Your father is going to hear about this. In the meantime, you sit right there in those chairs, until it's time for supper."

Mrs. Clark looked at the four parents, before settling her gaze on Mrs. Spofford. "The problem seems to be that Sylvia takes great delight in embarrassing the Spofford girls by calling you a dog-killer. Have you addressed that issue with your daughters?"

"Yes, I have. I've told them, in no uncertain terms, that I did not, and never would, do such a thing." May turned her attention to Sylvia's parents. "Your daughter told my girls that she heard I was a dog-killer, from you two." She stared hard at the mother. "Is that true?"

The mother looked to the father for the answer. "I don't know." The fellow squirmed as he answered. "It might have come up. You know, there's a lot of gossip in this little town. People say stuff all the time."

"Stuff?" Mrs. Clark echoed. "I would think we could categorize this kind of talk as something more than just 'stuff.' How do you think this makes Mrs. Spofford feel? And worse, how do you think it makes those two little girls feel?"

The couple looked down at the floor. "I suppose it must feel awful," the mother murmured. She looked up at the principal. "But we didn't know what Sylvia was doing at school; we only just learned about these fights, when you called this afternoon."

"That's right," the husband agreed. "So, I guess we need to put a stop to it," He rose to the occasion, by making a manly observation. "Meantime, Sylvia has learned her lesson, getting her hair chopped off like tha — " He corrected himself immediately. "I mean, getting her braid cut off. I think she's learned her lesson."

"I hope we have all learned something, here. I sure don't want to have to call you folks, again."

On the way out the door, Hank pulled the guy aside. "Just so you know, buddy, if there is any more of this crap going on, I'll contact my lawyer. My wife would never do such a thing, and you'd better make sure your sweet little girl understands that, loud and clear." He forced an evil grin, while tapping the guy on the shoulder. "Just so we understand each other."

But at the end of the day, after the fatherly lecture to his children, and a connubial snuggle with his wife, Hank Spofford lay awake in the dark. He was glad to know that *Mop's* death was accidental, but he still didn't know for sure, whether or not May had killed *Blow*.

***

Earlier that same day, Father Joseph Levi, the Roman Catholic priest who was a Jew, was walking his dog, Abe. He followed the long-haired dachshund through the stragglers in front of Summit School, all the way to the corner of Summit and Pearl Streets, before crossing over to a familiar route through Indian Acres. The sidewalks were still covered with snow, and there were frozen puddles where the sidewalks ended, so the pair moved along slowly. Nevertheless, it was a clear, beautiful winter afternoon. The sky was actually blue behind the shimmering housetops. Children were still making their way home from school, stopping to throw the occasional snowball. A pair of noisy fourth graders were especially enjoying that little activity, picking off targets, then dodging out of sight. The priest stopped to watch, not wanting to get too close, lest he and Abe become a tempting bullseye. It was a wise move. Across the street from the two marauders, a slim adult figure came hurrying to within throwing distance. The boys checked for a place to duck out of sight, then pretended to just be patting snow between their mittens, until the young man was close enough. Suddenly, the two let loose with their white cannonballs, striking the fellow solidly in the midriff. He turned quickly, spotting the kids ducking behind a snow-covered shrub. With a loud curse, he took off after them. Knowing they were spotted, the youngster scrambled. The target came to a stop only a few feet from Father Joe and his barking hound. Father Joe blinked in recognition. "Hey!" he called out, "Jack? Jack Wilson?"

The young man froze, then without looking up, took off on a dead run, disappearing behind a house.

"Well, I'll be," the priest exclaimed. "I was sure that was him." He turned around to head back to the church. "Well, never mind. I guess my eyes aren't so good anymore," he told the dog.

Back on Pearl Street, he crossed over where the bus stops were, one on each side, and where traffic was more likely to watch for pedestrians. This put him on the Lincoln Hall side of the road, and when he was passing by its parking lot, he was glad. "Hey, Chief!" He waved at the man, who was just getting into the police car.

"Hey, Father Joe!" Rob smiled. "Taking Abe for a walk?" When the older man did not answer or move, Rob sensed there was more the fellow wanted to talk about, so he ambled over, pretending to pet the dog. "Hey, Abraham, you little rascal, how you doin'?" He looked up at the priest, who still had not moved. "You got something on your mind, Father?"

"Well, Chief, it was kind of weird. I just ran into somebody up in the Indian Acres housing, and I thought I knew him." He chuckled. "I could've sworn it was Jack Wilson."

***

Sheriff Max Duncan didn't get the call on his radio, because he'd made this trip solo. There were still unanswered questions, and he needed to find them on his own. He stood at the back side of the abandoned creamery, studying the crime scene where Blow had been bludgeoned to death, then dismembered. The photos had shown the dog had been distracted, trying to tear the nailed meat off the wooden panel beneath. Now that Max knew it was that tomahawk, he figured the flat side of the hatchet's head had done the job. "Probably stunned him the first time, killed him the second or third time." The weapon had been small, light enough for even May Spofford to handle. But the chopping off of the head was another matter. That had to have been a lot harder. Somebody bigger had to have done that part of the job. For a second, he wondered if there could have been two people involved in this killing. "Worth thinking about," he noted out loud.

He looked up, surveying the field, now covered with large patches of snow. "Let's see," he instructed himself, "we came from the railroad track and walked straight across to the new Colchester Road. It was the last portion of our search territory." He turned toward that road, picturing how the search had been conducted. "By then, there were only five of us. That's all that were needed, because we had six feet between us. So, the three ASPCA guys were to my right, and Smith was on my left." He stopped, looking first to his right, then back to his left. "Okay, six feet between me and my deputy." He began to pace it off, ending where Deputy Smith would have been walking slowly along, scanning the long grass around him.

Suddenly, Max came to a stop.

The sun was almost down on this January afternoon, but he could see enough in that gray-blue dusk, to send a chill down his spine. Off to his left, in the six feet between the building and where he now stood, was the spot where Blow was killed. It was in plain view.

***

"Thanks for stopping by on your way home from work, Winnie." Connie took her coat, hanging it on a hook near the small kitchen's back door. She reached for the coffee pot. "I had hoped Don would be here, but he had to fill in for a sick driver." She laughed. "Don't want to celebrate anybody else's bout with the flu, but we sure could use the money."

"No problem." She watched Connie pour the deliciously aromatic brew. "I don't get to visit with my sewing circle friends very often, except at the meetings, of course." She moved the cup up to where she could blow on the steam. "Which reminds me, we have a meeting pretty soon. At Lily's, right?"

"Right." The counselor looked fondly at her friend. "I can't thank you enough for taking Joe under your wing, like this. My-oh-my, what a change in that boy, Win!"

"I know. I can see it, too."

"So, that brings up the thing Don and I wanted to ask about." There was a polite little clearing of the throat. "What do think of Joe moving in with a real Abenaki family? Not permanently. Or maybe permanently, I don't know." There was a small sip. "Don and I were actually thinking maybe Joe could write a letter of apology to May Spofford, and get some sort of healing going in that relationship."

"Oh," Winnie seemed pleased. "Yes, yes, that's a pretty good idea, Connie. They're a young family, and May is absolutely Abenaki, right to the core. Did you know she has an Abenaki name?"

"Oh my gosh! Really? What is it?"

"Her name," Firstborn Daughter announced ceremoniously, "is 'Snow Falling.'"

Connie inhaled with delight. "Oh my, that's so beautiful." Her eyes sparkled. "And that's Abenaki?"

Firstborn got a mischievous look on her face. "I won't swear to that. Sometimes I wonder where these names come from. I had a cousin named Horsetail, so there you go." The two ladies laughed out loud. "So, you can just imagine what kind of teasing he got, poor guy." Her fingernails tapped lightly on the coffee cup. "But I think the idea of a letter to her, apologizing — and he should start it by saying 'Dear

Snow Falling,' because I know these folks, they like to be recognized and respected."

"Okay," Connie replied softly. "Of course; who doesn't? And that's probably a good place to start building a relationship, don't you think?" Winnie nodded in agreement. "So, Don wanted me to be sure and point out, Joe will still need to keep up the language lessons. Oh, and by the way, thanks for letting us sit in on those. We get to counsel without looking like that's what we're really doing." There was another fond look. "Winnie, you're really something. I want you to know, Don and I see you as one of God's great treasures."

"Oh, I'm just doing what I can."

"You really are. And now, we have Uncle stepping up, offering to teach Joe to fish and all those other Indian skills." She shook her head appreciatively. "That man is something else, you know that?"

The conversation continued until Winnie noticed the clock on the kitchen wall. "Oh my goodness. I need to get home. Ceese will think I've gone back to Canada, or something."

Connie helped her into the warm winter coat. "So maybe you could run the idea of Joe getting closer to May Spofford — to her family. Just run it by Cecil and see what he thinks."

"Oh, I already know what he thinks." She was headed for the front door.

"Oh?"

"He thinks she has a bad temper." She was buttoning the last button. "So, I don't think he'll like the idea, but who knows? He could surprise me."

He would do just exactly that.

***

It was Gracie, pounding on the front door. Lenore looked up from the supper table at the clock with the wagging tail. It was almost five thirty. The knocking grew louder before she finally opened the door. Gracie's face was ashen. "Get your coat," she commanded.

"Why? Where am I going?" Lenore asked.

Gracie looked past her and called out to Joe. "You wait here. Mr. Thompson is on his way. You'll be spending the night with him. Get your stuff ready."

"Gracie, what's the matter?"

The older woman was still concentrating on the boy. "Make sure the stove is turned off, you hear?"

"Yes, Ma'am."

The two women were halfway down the sidewalk when Lenore grabbed Gracie's arm. "You tell me, right now. What's wrong?"

The mother made it brief. "They were making an arrest, but the guy had a gun." She yanked her arm loose and ran around the front of the car. Lenore pulled the passenger door open and pressed on. "What happened? Is Robbie...?"

"All they told me, was to get to the Fanny Allen Hospital." She pulled out onto the half-plowed street. "If you're going to marry a cop, you'll have to get used to these calls, and believe me, you do get these calls, sometimes two or three times a year."

Lenore's head bowed under the load of that information. "That often?"

"You'd better hope they come, however often. Unless your cop husband is retired, you just be glad they keep coming."

"What? Why would I want these calls to keep coming like that?"

"Because, if those calls ever stop coming, it will be because your husband is on permanent disability, or," Gracie tried to put it gently, "he gave his life, protecting the people he served."

CHAPTER TWENTY-SEVEN

Blood

Someone had had the wisdom to call Robbie's younger brother, Scott. He met his mother at the front door of the Fanny Allen. "Now, Mom, you know how this works." He glanced over at Lenore, then went back to Gracie. "You know that head wounds always bleed really bad."

"Head wounds?" Lenore choked out the words.

"Scottie," his mother cautioned him, "you need to know — Robbie and Lenore got engaged last night."

The young man froze. "Oh... okay. Um, okay." Now he was including the fiancé. "So, we all know that head wounds bleed. A lot. So," he slid between the two women, steering them toward the emergency room, "just be prepared for that, okay?"

Gracie slowed down as they approached the end of the hall. Before the three of them turned the corner into the bustle of the emergency room, she pulled the other two aside. "Lenore," she spoke sternly," whatever you do, don't make him feel guilty." Her words were sharp. "You tell him how proud you are of him, no matter what shape he's in. You tell him how proud you are of him, young lady. Act like it's all part of the job."

"What are you talking about, Gracie? I'm terrified!"

"Of course you are. You love that man." She pulled a tissue from her pocket. "Here, wipe your nose."

"What?"

"Just do it, missy. You have to go in there, so proud of your hero, *regardless of what you see*! And you will not be crying and moaning." She pushed Lenore's blonde curls back from her face. "Alrighty then, here we go."

It was worse than Lenore had imagined. Robbie was seated on a chair, waiting his turn for medical attention, holding a large, blood-soaked wad of gauze against his left temple. It wasn't doing much good. The bright red, sanguine fluid was literally flowing down the side of his face and neck, soaking the whole shoulder of his shirt.

She sucked in a big breath. "Hey!" she called out to him. When he saw her, he nodded and waited for her reaction. "Wow!" Lenore quipped, as she slid onto the chair next to him, "that's quite a mess you have there, Mister Chief of Police!"

It was almost a corny thing to say, but it made him laugh, so she went on. "I should have brought my first-aid kit."

A nurse appeared from nowhere with a fresh pad. "It should stop bleeding in a few minutes," she reassured everybody. Then she disappeared.

"Oh boy, would you look at that shirt? I guess you're going to have to buy a new one." There was that little tilt of the head, again. "But, I guess we can manage that little problem okay, don't you think?"

He reached for her hand. "Yes, we can, sunshine, yes we can."

The next morning, Robbie awoke with a throbbing headache. Jack Wilson's bullet had scraped a chunk out of his forehead, just above the left eye. There were stitches and swelling and cold packs on a schedule. This was not going to be fun. He sat up on the edge of his bed, fighting the nausea. "Must have been the shot they gave me," he concluded. There was, however, a necessity to use the bathroom, so he rose slowly and made his way out to the hall. When he returned, he glanced out the bedroom window. Tall Tree and Joe were just leaving Lenore's place. "Must be Saturday," he told himself. He saw the front door open, again. Lenore moved carefully around the small drifts lining the sidewalk. "She's coming to see me," he whispered. "I should shave or something." But it was too much. Instead, he pulled on a robe to hide his underwear, and lay back down on the bed. "It is what it is," he muttered.

Sure enough, there was a knock, then the door slowly swung open. "Hey! Are you up?" Seeing him in the robe, she entered. "I have a cold pack for you, and some kind of pain pills." She brought it all to the bed stand beside where he lay. "Will it hurt your head if I give you a little kiss?"

"Tell you what, lady, let's have a *big* one, instead. I'll let you know, if you have to back off."

"Oh, you stop it, Robbie Allen. Just a little one." He tried to pull her closer, but jerked back in pain. "Oh crap. That *does* hurt."

"Told ya!" She gently lowered the icy pack onto the bandaged wound. "You need to keep this on for twenty minutes, your mom says. And then take these two pills and go to sleep."

"Fine."

The fiancé sat down on the edge of the bed. "You had a pretty close call, Mister Chief of Police; the doctor said if it had been one or two inches to the right, that bullet would have killed you." There was another tilt of the curls. "So we need to take real good care of you."

"Umm," he hummed, closing his eyes.

She reached over, straightening the folds of the robe over his chest. Suddenly, his eyes opened and he clasped his hand over hers. "One or two inches, huh?"

"That's what he said."

Their eyes met.

"We need to get married. Right away." He pulled her hand to his mouth.

"What do you mean, 'right away'?"

"Just as soon as I can kiss you without my head exploding."

"Tall Tree talked about the Gypsies and the River Rats, this morning," Joe told Firstborn.

She smiled. "And did he tell you that Uncle and I grew up as River Rats?"

"Yup. Said Uncle wants to teach me to fish, when the weather gets better."

"What in the world is this about Gypsies and River Rats?" Connie Collins wanted to know.

"Well see," the boy eagerly took up the story, "after Ira Allen wouldn't let us Abenakis be an official nation, we just faded into the woods. Some of us took up basket weaving and some of us became fisherman people."

"You know," Connie recalled, "those must be the native women who sell baskets and trinkets at the side of the road. I see them, every once in a while."

"Anyways, Tall Tree says maybe they took away the government reckoning, but we're still a nation. He says no matter *how* we make a living, we are still the Abenaki nation, and we're still like a great, big family."

"He's right," Winnie agreed. "There's an old saying: 'Blood is thicker than water.' We are still a people, no matter what."

Don and Connie sensed the quiet, desperation concerning that identity, as the conversation continued. Shortly, it evolved into the next language lesson. Halfway through the hour-long session, Uncle came in from the barn. Suddenly, the three of them were engaging in an old language discussion. The two counselors sat in awe, for the boy seemed to be hanging in there, holding his own. But most of all, they marveled at the glow on young Joe Turner's face.

On the drive back to the village, Don could not resist taking up the subject of blood ties between families. "Those ties are real, Joe, not like the 'blood brother' thing you and Dicky Dupree did. That was more like play-acting."

"I guess so. But it sure was real to *me*. I guess it was pretty stupid, now that I think of it."

"Oh now, don't be so hard on yourself," Connie urged him. "What were you, five years old or so?" She turned to look at him. "You need to let that memory go."

"Yeah," the reply came slowly, "I guess so." There was a short pause. "Lisa Marie probably didn't know any better, either."

"You're absolutely right, son," Don said. "So, does that mean you forgive her?"

There was a boyish laugh. "Aw, I guess so."

"Good for you, Joe Turner." He caught the youngster's eye in the rearview mirror. "I'm real proud of you." Joe responded with a happy grin.

"But, that doesn't mean there are no *real* blood ties, right?" Connie reminded him, with a cautionary wave of her hand toward the back seat. "I mean, there are still blood ties in the Abenaki nation, right?"

"Yeah, that's right," Joe happily agreed.

"Just like there are blood ties in the family of God." She looked at her husband. "Am I right about that, too?"

Don picked up the cue. "Absolutely. All believers are covered by the blood of His son, Jesus. In fact, they can't get into Heaven without that blood covering, because it washes them clean from all the bad stuff they've done in their lives." There was silence in the seat behind them. Don tossed the ball to his wife, with a twitch of his eyebrows.

"Oh, honey," she seemed to address her husband, "Joe already knows about that, I'm sure." She turned once again, to look the boy in the eye. "You already know that Jesus shed His precious blood on the cross, so that anybody who follows Him could have life — *real* life, *forever*. You do already know that those people then become part of the family of God, don't you?"

"I guess so. I heard about it, anyway."

"Well, that's good," she said, turning back around to the front, "because I sure wouldn't want a great Abenaki kid like you to miss out on Heaven."

"Abenakis don't go to Heaven?"

"Only if they choose *not* to be part of the family of God." Then she was quick to show the whole picture. "If you want to go to Heaven, you have to be part of the family of God, and that goes for *everybody* — not just Abenakis."

***

The next day, Don and Connie took a detour on the way home from church. They had an appointment to talk to Ceese and Winnie about approaching the Spoffords with the idea of either providing a foster home, or possibly adopting Joe Turner.

"We were entertaining the thought that this would provide at least a modicum of Abenaki relations. After all, May is a full-blooded member of this disinherited tribe. She would at least understand the boy's feelings of abandonment."

Cecil leaned back in his navy blue recliner. "You have to be kidding me," he snorted. "That woman is carrying enough personal baggage to warp half the Abenaki bands in the state of Vermont!" He puffed lightly on the cigarette in his hand. "You shouldn't even *think* about doing this."

The counseling couple sat quietly, absorbing the ferocity of his words. Uncle's shuffling slippers directed their attention to the back hallway, as he entered the kitchen. The man spotted the four of them. "Thought I heard voices down here."

"You did. We're talking about Joe having a closer relationship with a real Abenaki family, maybe even being adopted by one." Winnie nodded toward her husband. "Ceese doesn't think May Spofford and her family is a good choice."

"I have to agree," Uncle said. "You folks have had your goddim differences with her. I think it would be a frickin' mistake, myself."

"But how do you feel about Joe having a real Abenaki home?" Don moved over on the window seat to make room for Uncle.

"Aw, I don't know, Don." He took the offered seating space. "Not all Abenakis are what you call, good frickin' parents, you know?" He looked around. "Maybe he's better off right the hail where he is."

Connie sighed. "So, it was just something I thought would be good for him. I'm probably way off base."

"You know what?" Winnie asked. "I think it would be really good for him, if we could find the right place."

Don took another stab at it. "Got any ideas about that, Cecil?" The farmer shrugged his shoulders and took another draw on the cigarette. "How about you, Mr. Smart?"

Uncle concentrated on a hangnail. "Not for me to say, but I'd be happy to show him some fishing and hunting skills. I'm pretty damned good at that, me."

"Well, that's a very generous offer, Uncle," Winnie noted. "Too bad you swear so much, you."

"She's got that right, mister," Ceese said. "If it wasn't for that, the kid could probably stay right here."

Winnie's mouth dropped open. "What did you say, Ceese?"

"Why not?" He crushed the cigarette butt into the ash tray. "We could use a little more help around here. I'm not getting any younger." He looked at Uncle. You've got that extra room upstairs, you know."

"Yes, sir, I do."

"So if Joe wants to come and live with us, you think you could watch that mouth of yours?"

Uncle rose to his feet, eager to please. "Well, sir, I could sure give it one helluva try!"

Cecil Thompson addressed the Collinses. "You might want to bring it up with Lenore Curtis, first. Then you can ask the boy, himself. It's his life." He turned to his wife for approval of this plan.

Winnie's mouth was still wide open.

***

Sheriff Maxwell Duncan rubbed his chin. "I didn't get the alert about Jack Wilson, because I was out at the crime site behind the creamery," he told Deputy Smith.

"Oh?" Smitty took a right at the traffic circle in the middle of the village, heading north. "Well, at least nobody got killed. It could have been a lot worse, 'cause that dumb kid is really off his rocker. I don't know how he made it through basic without a major incident." The vehicle passed the Roman Catholic Church. "So, he got a Marine guard escort out of here, three o'clock this morning. What do you think will happen to him?"

"Don't know, don't care. I've got other things to take care of, right now." He motioned for the deputy to pull over, right beside the field behind the creamery. "Follow me," he instructed the man.

They went around to the descending ramp at the front of the abandoned building, avoiding the fence separating the field from the highway. Leading the way through a couple of low snowdrifts, Max brought his patrol partner to a spot, just six feet away from where Blow had been killed. There, he put his hands behind his back and faced the man. "I have a little story to tell you," he said.

Over the next few minutes, he told the young man what he knew: "Last July, I bought a whole new uniform, like I do every year. But I no longer had a burn barrel to get rid of the old one, so I bagged it up and brought it to work, where I asked you to dispose of it in the sheriff department's trash. You did that, before we went out on patrol, but *you kept the pants.* You kept the pants, Smitty. It took me a while to figure that one out."

The deputy seemed to be studying his boss for a couple of

seconds, then turned his back and took a few steps away. Max hastened to follow him, taking a stand directly in the man's path.

"Don't be turning your back on me when I'm talking to you, Deputy." His hands went behind his back, again. "So, you set me up, you sneaky bastard. Killed the dog while wearing my old pants, got them all bloody, then hid them, along with the tomahawk, in Mrs. Wilson's grave."

The deputy turned his back and walked away, again. Sheriff Duncan swore. "I told you not to turn your back on me. Are you deaf?" He was standing in front of Smitty before the fellow could take another step. "And what was it with the tomahawk, anyway? Supposed to make it look like an Indian did it? I guess you thought maybe folks would think that's what *I* would try to do. And then, putting those body parts on May Spofford's lawn — well, that was pretty clever, since we all know she's pure Abenaki."

The deputy turned and moved away once more. Max's face turned red with fury as he lunged toward the defiant underling. "Get back here, you — " But the arm he tried to grab was suddenly reversing direction, coming right back to the raging sheriff, with a shiny police whistle in its hand. One shrill blast set the sheriff's own hand automatically up to protect the hidden microphone under his jacket collar.

Deputy Smith grinned. "Gotcha!"

The sheriff's jaw went hard, the muscles so tight, he could not speak. It got worse when Smitty started waving a "Get rid of it" hand message. Max glared, then slowly reached up and pulled the whole thing loose. That hateful stare continued even as he carefully stuffed the tangled wires into his coat pocket.

"Now, Sheriff, I believe you had a story to tell me?"

The fuming lawman could hardly get the words out. "You set me up. I want to know why."

"I think maybe nobody set you up, sir. I think maybe you've been setting *yourself* up, for a long time now." He ignored the surprise on the man's face. "I watched you hound-dogging the Thompsons, all that time. That wasn't right. I finally got fed up. So, last spring, I told my dad about it." He stopped to make sure Max knew the man. "As you know, Sheriff, my dad has served on the detective division of the Burlington Police Department for a long time. When I started working with you, he was careful to warn me that you've always been one shifty move away from being a 'bad cop,' for years. Like the way you manipulate the public through phony newspaper stories or whatever."

Max made a hissing noise and shoved his hands into his jacket pockets.

"Anyway, my dad warned me not to run against you in this election. Said you just needed it to look like you had competition. Said it was all a sham, as usual, because that's the way you work." There was a low grunt from the listener. "So, I just sat back and waited. The pants?" He shrugged. "You told me to throw them in the trash. I think you should assume I did that. It would be a lot easier than making accusations you can't prove." He held up a finger to make the last point. "Let's not forget, this case is pretty much closed. The Thompsons saw to that. Why would you want to make a stink about it, draw all that attention to yourself?"

"You lying jackass," Max finally said, "you should lose your badge for all this." The veins at his temples were pulsating. "You killed that poor old dog. *You did that!*"

"Be careful, Sheriff; you have no proof."

"Oh, you did it, alright, and it was cruel, just cruel, what you did to him."

The deputy suddenly seemed indignant. "You are wrong about that. I would never be cruel to an old dog."

"Well, you were, this time."

"No, sir. No, sir, that did not happen." He gathered his thoughts, then spoke carefully. "I'm not saying that I killed any dogs. I'm just saying that I would have been merciful about it, if I had been forced to do it. I would have made sure the poor old mutt was out cold with the first blow, and then I would have finished the job. Nobody wants to make an animal suffer. I sure don't. But we shoot deer and squirrels and rabbits all the time, and we try to do that, in the most humane way we can, and *then* we skin them and cut them up and cook them and eat them. Right?" The sheriff squinted, trying to follow the reasoning. "Well, none of that happened to that dog. So, I'm not saying that I killed Blow, but if I had, it would have been in the most humane way possible."

"But you chopped him up!"

"No, I'm not saying I did any such thing. But, whoever did that, was trying to make it looked like one of your 'savages' did it, for sure. And when those body parts showed up on May Spofford's yard, that pretty much sealed the deal."

"Listen, you pontificating little jackass, I know you set me up, and I'm going to clear my name, if it's the last thing I do."

"Oh, you're not going to do a darned thing about it, Sheriff, because I've got the goods on you. The *Burlington Free Press* is my best friend, right now. I can pull your pants down in front of the whole county, if you so much as look sideways at me, or my family, or even my pet canary. You aren't going to charge me with anything, because you can't afford to — it would cost you the election, for certain. Now, on the other hand, if you just campaign like a good little soldier, you just might have a chance to beat me. But it will be a fair and honest race, sir, and that's all I'm after. That's it. No more 'snowing the public.'"

Knowing he finally had the sheriff of Chittenden County nicely boxed in, Deputy Smith turned his back on his boss, one more time, as he headed back to the vehicle.

A bullet caught him in the back, sending the man rolling along the loading ramp. He cried out in pain, as he reached for his own gun.

The second shot did not come near him, but he kept his head low, crawling to where he could get a good aim at his attacker. Reaching the edge of the loading ramp, he paused. No sound came from the field behind. He waited, then he had a thought: "Oh, God."

He put pressure on the wound that pierced the edge of his

right side, and rose carefully. Back in the field, the sheriff lay in a heap.

"Oh, God," Smitty said again, as he limped toward the man. When he saw the blood spurting from Max's right temple, he dropped down, hoping to do something. But it was over.

Max was dead.

CHAPTER TWENTY-EIGHT

Title

"No, you are *not* getting out of that bed!" Gracie fretted. It's too soon."

"I'm the chief of police, Mom. I need to be there." He was tucking in his shirt, his back to her. "It looks like attempted murder and a suicide, and in the sheriff's department, of all things." He pulled up the zipper and slid his belt into place.

"Don't go anywhere. I'll need help with my shoes. I can't bend over yet. Hurts my head."

"There, you see? You can't even bend over."

"So that's why Ed is driving me, and he'll bend if somebody needs to bend."

Suddenly Lenore was at the bedroom door. "I knocked, but nobody answered, so I let myself in." She saw he was in uniform. "Okay, Mister Chief of Police, I see you're back on the job."

"Ed's going to help me; it'll be fine."

"Yes, it will," she said, checking the bandage. "It looks good." She glanced at Gracie. "You must have put a new one on this morning."

In a few minutes, Ed was at the back door, and the pair was on the way to the creamery.

The two women stood in the kitchen, looking at each other. "Lord, I hope he'll be alright." Lenore's statement was a dead giveaway. She was worried.

"Was that a prayer? It sounded like one." Gracie was

hopeful.

"Well, if wasn't when it came out, I'm making it one, right now."

"Okay, so now we get busy. Cops' wives have to learn to keep a positive outlook. So do their mothers." She slipped on an apron. "Think I'll make some bread."

Lenore didn't have to go looking for something to do, because Connie Collins was coming by during her lunch break at Essex Junction High School. "This won't take long," she had promised. Sure enough, she was at the door at five minutes to noon.

"Are you sure you don't want a sandwich or something? It'll just take a few minutes."

"No-no, I ate one on my way over here. Now, that's an experience." She checked the front of her coat. "Do I have egg salad on the front of me?"

There was a shared laugh. Then Connie got serious.

"So, Don and I had a visit on Sunday, with the Thompsons. Those language lessons have been a blessing in more ways than one."

"Oh, I agree. I've never seen that boy so happy."

"And that's exactly what I came to talk to you about. That boy is so happy when he's up there with Winnie, and now her uncle is there all the time. Don and I watched them speaking the old language, the three of them just going at it. I tell you, it is amazing how quickly Joe has picked it up." She smoothed out the front of her coat. "Um, so, Don and I have been watching this for a few weeks, and we are so pleased. Um, Joe doesn't even realize he's getting counseling, you know? And he is *genuinely* happy." She crossed her ankles, trying to find the right way to put it. "So Don and I had this idea. We thought maybe, just maybe what Joe needs is to be with an Abenaki family."

"What? What does that mean?" Lenore was alarmed. "Do you think he doesn't like living here with me?"

"Oh no, Lenore. That boy actually loves you; he just doesn't know how to relate to you,"

"That doesn't make sense."

"Okay, at first, it doesn't add up. But when you consider that he's never really known where he fits in this world, it begins to make some sense." She got a little more to the point. "Think about it; the boy is Abenaki, but, until Tall Tree and Firstborn and Shining Waters, Joe has never known *how* to be part of the culture he actually comes from — Abenaki!" She leaned forward. "But now, he's finding a profound sense of belonging. And he's found it with the Thompsons."

"Ay-yuh," the foster mom answered slowly. "That does make sense. When I think about it, I can see how the poor kid has never felt like he really belonged *anywhere*." It was as though a light clicked on. "But he's happy when he's with the Thompsons."

"Yes. And that's probably where he should be, Lenore."

"What?"

"Cecil and Winnie want to adopt Joe."

***

The two priests were having coffee in the rectory's pleasant kitchen.

"I think it's a shame, so many shootings in just a few days," Father Tom was saying.

"I guess that young deputy — Smith. Yes, his name is Smith — is going to recover, although I hear that bullet went right through his liver or something." The older priest peered over the tops of his glasses. "I trust you've prayed for that fellow?"

Tom smiled. "Got it covered, Father."

"Well, that's good." Father Joe sipped the coffee. "Of course, we should be praying for all of those guys. There's an awful lot of cops out there who don't know Jesus, and they're literally playing with fire." He took another sip. "A lot of them are going to Hell, my friend, because they don't even know they're damned."

"I agree. It's very sad."

"Ay-yuh," the older priest said, "we have to get busy and get all those damned cops saved."

Father Tom was amused. "Did you just swear, Father Joe?"

"Oh no. If I was going to swear, I'd do a better job of it than that." He looked up. "Sorry, Jesus." Then he crossed himself.

"Well, Deputy Smith will recover, I'm sure," Father Tom mused. "He'll probably be our next Chittenden County Sheriff. After all, he's now officially one of our wounded law officers. He's a hero, and everybody loves a hero." He shook his head. "Remember how a broken tooth got Delwood elected to the school board?" He laughed. "I guess we don't always get to choose our heroes. I mean, he fell on the ice, for Pete's sake." He put it to the older man. "It's not like the guy had a huge injury."

"Oh, I don't know. Maybe there are *no small injuries*, when it comes right down to the nitty gritty. Little lies become huge deceptions. Little slaps become body blows. Look at Max Duncan. I don't think he realized that small attacks on a certain people group can lead to the eradication of that whole culture. I know about these things; I'm a Jew." He shifted his weight. "But nobody wins, because the Hitlers or the Max Duncans end up dead, as well."

***

"If Laura knew this, it would break her heart," Jessie stated. "I can hardly believe it, myself. Jack will be in the brig for a long time." He leaned back into the easy chair in the Collinses' living room. Connie was still at school this Wednesday afternoon, but Don had a day off from driving bus. He listened quietly, as his client continued. "He just showed up. I had no idea he was coming. Well, he was AWOL, so of course I didn't." There was a deep sigh. "So there he was, standing at my front door. I don't know how he found the place, what with all the little circles and side streets, but he did." Don understood that one; he'd been in that housing development a few times. "And he says, 'Don't slam the door in my face; just listen." Jessie looked up at Don. "'*Just listen*'?" Don responded with a sympathetic hum. "Then he says, 'What's the big idea, handing the farm over to some hired hand?' So I said, 'What do you care? You said you were done with the place, never wanted to see it again. Whatever.' So he says, 'You don't give away my inheritance. I need that money, and I need it now. I'm done with the Navy.' Well, I just got mad. I told him he had no business coming here and demanding anything, not after he stormed out like he did. Then *he* started yelling back, and he pulls out this *gun*!" Jessie touched his forehead. "The kid was out of it, and I do mean *out* of it. But I see the squad car coming down the street, and I think quick. I told him to come inside and we would talk about it. But he wouldn't budge. He says to me, 'Get your coat; we're going to the bank.' I tried to argue, but he aimed that damned thing right at my face, so I held up my hands, like this —" The two hands went up in front. "'Wait a minute. There's no need to shoot your own father, Jack.' And I'm seeing the two cops out of the corner of my eye, getting out of the car, one heading around the back, and the chief coming slowly toward Jack. But Chief Allen didn't see the gun, and there was no way I could warn him." He wiped his hand across his brow. "I tell you, it was right out of a movie, only it was really happening."

"But Robbie, the chief, was able to tackle him, right?"

"Oh, he tackled him, but the gun went off and the chief went down, and Jack tried to run for it, but that other cop came around the corner of the house and took him down. Jack hit the ground, and the gun went sliding across the snow. And there was blood all over the place." Jessie shook his head in disbelief. "I don't know if I'll ever get over it." His voice choked up. "I'm just so damned glad Laura can't see what's happened to our boy."

"Laura was a great lady, for sure. What's happened to Jack is something called 'battle fatigue.'"

"I thought that only happened to soldiers. They go through hell on the battlefield, and they take that stuff home with them. I guess they have nightmares and hurt people without thinking about it. My dad told me about his brother who had that." His eyes teared up. "You think that's what happened to my son?"

"I really do. Think about it, Jessie. Jack not only saw his mother die horribly, but he was driving the truck. How do you get over something like that, short of a miracle from God?"

"I... don't know what to do. I just don't know."

"Well, as I just said, it'll take a miracle from God." He leaned forward. "Maybe it's time for you to head in that direction." He saw the man wince, so he leaned back. "No pressure, Jessie, but I'm prescribing treatment, here; you need to start going to church, just for your own peace of mind. And," he gently added, "it would the perfect way to honor your late wife. She prayed for you so many times, sir, and I think that's the least you can do. Just go to church."

"Aw, I wouldn't have a clue where to go."

"You are certainly welcome to go with Connie and me. These people loved Laura, and I know they would welcome you, and accept you, just the way you are."

There was a moment of silence while the man thought about it. Finally, he lifted his eyes. "Okay, I'll do it for Laura," he whispered.

***

When Saturday afternoon's language lesson started, Firstborn and Shining Waters had a big surprise: Joe was to graduate into actually writing the language he now was speaking. It was true that he had a lot more to learn, but it was also true he would need to know how to write it, as well. "So, you will start that next Saturday morning, and Tall Tree will be showing you how to do that," Winnie proudly announced. "You are a very smart fellow," she added, "so we think you will do very well."

"Really? Is there a alphabet, like in English?"

"Yes, there is. It has letters like in English, but there's something that looks like the number eight, and, well, it won't be hard. It will be fun."

"I always have fun when I come up here," the boy commented.

"Yeah?" Uncle jumped right on that one. "You like coming up here, you?" Joe nodded enthusiastically. "Well, we like having you come up here. So that makes us even." He tousled the boy's hair. "I just wish you'd grow that hair out, like a real Abenaki," he joked.

"Hmm. I don't think Ma'am would want me to do that."

"Oh, I don't know," Winnie ventured, "Lenore wants you to be happy." Joe leaned over to watch Firstborn roll out a piecrust. "She's pretty nice, don't you think?"

"Sure." He picked up an extra sliver of dough. "Can you eat this stuff raw?"

"I guess you could, if you're hungry enough, but I don't recommend it." She rubbed more flour on the rolling pin. "So okay, no more English for a whole hour."

At the end of the hour, Don and Connie came to pick him up. They had missed this lesson so they could bring Lenore with them. She gave Joe a hug as she asked, "How did it go today?"

"Good," they all answered at once. She looked more closely at the boy. Sure enough, there was that contented demeanor. At Winnie's bidding, they all sat down at the kitchen table for mincemeat pie. Lenore took a seat beside Joe, trying to watch him, without staring. When he wiped his mouth and leaned back in the chair, she couldn't hold it back any longer. "Guess what, Joe? The Thompsons have asked me if you could come and live with them." His eyes went wide. "They didn't want to hurt my feelings, so they asked me first. Well, I see how happy you are up here, and, while I would miss you a lot, I think you need to have a chance to be a real Abenaki." His dark eyes blinked slowly. "So, I think it should be up to you." There was another blink, prompting Don to step in.

"You know, Joe, there's a verse in the Bible about this. It's in Psalm number sixty-eight: 'God sets the lonely in families, leads prisoners free.' And if there's one thing we've all learned from your situation, is the great value of a family. You might want to think about that."

"Just remember," Lenore emphasized, "you can decide, all by yourself. Would you like to stay with Winnie and Cecil, and Mr. Smart?"

Uncle jumped to his feet. "I have a room up in my godd — my apartment. It's small but nice and clean. You want to take a fr — a look at it?"

Joe looked for permission from Ma'am. "Go ahead!" The two of them headed for the front stairs, which were much nicer than the back stairs, because Uncle wanted to make a good impression.

At the end of the visit, Joe decided to stay with the Thompsons. But, to keep his official foster care agreement intact, he would sleep at least four nights every week at the Curtis residence. Nobody wanted to break the law, so the Courtney Law Firm went into alert mode. Further, the question of adoption needed to be addressed, because of Joe's finances. Johnny Courtney would eventually pull some legal strings, and by the very next Christmas, Joe Turner would be officially adopted. His Christmas present was the Abenaki name "Trail Walker." They decided to call him Walker, for short.

***

Two days after the visit to the Thompsons, Robbie and

Lenore went to apply for a marriage license. She drove, because any sudden movement still hurt his head, but nothing was going to stop the two of them. There was a three-day waiting period, before they could actually be married, time for buying a lovely white dress and hat, and all of the other small necessities. By Wednesday, Joe was living with the Thompsons, and on Thursday the bride and groom headed for a quick wedding with a Justice of the Peace. Gracie and Scottie stood up for them, while Lenore wept into her small bouquet of red roses. There were hugs and laughter, and then Mr. and Mrs. Robert Ethan Allen left for a honeymoon in Stowe, where they just held hands a lot, because his head kept hurting. But they were finally together, and that was what really mattered.

***

It was getting toward that Christmas of 1957, before Bernie finally had something to show Della. He came from the post office with a registered letter in his hand.

"What's that?" she asked from her dressing table in the bedroom. She was putting on makeup for no particular reason; it was cold outside, and she was bored.

"Way-yell," he crooned, "I've a wee bit of a surprise for yeh, lass."

She eyed him suspiciously. "That better not be somebody wanting money. I thought we were almost caught up on the bills."

"Nah-nah-nah. It's nothin' like that." He fluttered one end of the letter under her nose. "Yeh best be puttin' the powder puff down, and takin' a look at the mail!"

She did that, drawing forth a thick wad of typewritten pages. "What is all this?"

He fairly danced as he answered. "It's a contract, Del, that's what."

"Oh no, what have you done? Did you buy something?"

"Hah!" He did a little jig-step as he answered. "It's a contract to publish my book, Del." He couldn't believe she wasn't jumping up and down for joy.

"What does that mean, you old goat? Do we have to pay them, or do they have to pay us?"

"Both," he answered. "But we have what's called, 'an advance.' They only do that, if they think they have a winner." The stiff eyebrows and mustache bobbed together, in perfect rhythm. "We're goin' to be rich, woman, rich!"

Della peered at the paperwork. "Where does it say that, Bernie? Show me where it says we're going to be rich."

He gently removed the contract from her trembling hands. "Yeh need to sit back down, Del." Then he had a better idea. "Nah-nah-nah. Here's what yeh need to do: Go downstairs and have a Canadian stout, and then we'll talk about it."

Almost forty-five minutes later, she finally got it: A big publishing company wanted to put Bernie's book on the market, because it was a sure winner — an exposé of the dog killings that took place over the last year. And there was a check enclosed with the contract, for one thousand American dollars.

She finally got it. "Oh my gosh, Bernie. Oh my gosh." She took quick inventory. "So, are we going to be sued by the county?"

"Nah-nah-nah. The publisher is already takin' care of that, with, uh, somethin' like disclaimin', and it being a fictional story, but based on true facts, but not necessarily talkin' about real people." He took another swallow of his own bottle of stout. "So, it's all covered. These are professionals, Del. We're good."

"Well, that's a relief, but I have one more thing: I really wanted the world to know that you come from good stock. I'm talking about your old Scottish background." Her chin raised high. "I want you to be known for your rich cultural inheritance." There was a flip of the gray curls. "I won't sign anything that doesn't include that fact."

"Aw, Del," he reassured her, "it's already in the book. I mention the Farquhars right at the beginnin'. It's what's called 'establishin' the believability of the narrator,' or somethin' like that."

"Oh." She took a big breath, then let it escape over the top of a burp. "A thousand dollars, huh?"

"Yes, lass. A thousand dollars, right here on this check."

"Well then," she rose from her chair, and said, "I just want to tell you how proud of you I am." She bent down to kiss him on the top of his head.

"You did real good, Bernie. You finally claimed your family history; now you really are a genuine, old Fart-quhar!"

THE END

From L. E. Fleury's *Junctions Murder Mystery Series*:

Book One: LOST

Book Two: HAUNTED

Book Three: PORTALS

Book Four: CHAMELEONS

Book Five: DAMAGED

Stay tuned for more to come!

Made in the USA
Middletown, DE
28 July 2024

57978333R00177